"Kuzechkin's style sparkles with colorful dialogues, street talk and bon mots... A very good read... For many people this short novel may become a manual of survival..."

Novy Mir magazine

"Kuzechkin's book reads effortlessly... it is a fine contribution to the Nizhni Novgorod page in Russian literature."

Novaya Gazeta

"Kostin follows the best traditions of 20th century Russian literature. His characters are true heroes who are not averse to the currently unfashionable romantic aspirations. Their quest for the truth brings disillusionment but at the same time humility, a rare virtue nowadays... And they also come to realize that no matter what happens while there is life there is hope."

Novy Mir magazine

"Today an unusually gifted generation is entering Russian literature. Literature has not seen such an influx of energy in a long time. Perhaps this change is an anthropological response to the difficult position of culture and literature. This new generation writing in Russian – both the individual writers and the phenomenon as a whole – deserves great attention."

Olga Slavnikova
Russian Booker Prize winner
Director of the Debut Prize

GLAS NEW RUSSIAN WRITING

CONTEMPORARY RUSSIAN LITERATURE

IN ENGLISH TRANSLATION

VOLUME 49

This is the second volume in the Glas sub-series presenting young Russian authors, winners and finalists of the Debut Prize for writers under 25. The prize was founded by the Pokolenie Foundation for humanitarian projects in 2000 and celebrated its 10th anniversary with launching its international program of publishing young Russian literature in translation. Glas acknowledges the generous support of the Debut Prize Foundation in publishing this book.

Andrei Kuzechkin
Mendeleev Rock

Pavel Kostin
Rooftop Anesthesia

Translated by
Andrew Bromfield

glas
MOSCOW

GLAS PUBLISHERS
tel/fax: +7(495)441-9157
perova@glas.msk.su
www.glas.msk.su

DISTRIBUTION

USA and CANADA
Consortium Book Sales and Distribution
1094 Flex Drive
Jackson, TN 38301-5070
tel: 800-283-3572; fax: 800-351-5073
orderentry@perseusbooks.com

in the UK
CENTRAL BOOKS
orders@centralbooks.com
www.centralbooks.com

Direct orders: INPRESS
Tel: 0191 229 9555
customerservices@inpressbooks.co.uk
www.inpressbooks.co.uk

Within Russia
Jupiter-Impex
www.jupiterbooks.ru

Series' editors: Natasha Perova and Joanne Turnbull
Camera-ready copy: Tatiana Shaposhnikova
Front cover picture curtesy of Sever Publishing House

ISBN 978-5-7172-0089-9

Contents

Andrei Kuzechkin, born in 1982, grew up in a small town near Nizhni Novgorod on the Volga. Graduate of the Nizhny Novgorod University, majoring in philology, he worked as a village teacher, street cleaner, hospital security guard, librarian, and animator. He plays a harmonica and sings with the blues-punk band "2000 R". He is a winner of the annual prize of *October* magazine and a finalist in the Debut Prize for his novel *Mendeleev Rock*. His other published books include *Aborigine-digest, All The Ten Fingers*, and *Magma*.

Pavel Kostin was born in 1981 in Kaliningrad where upon graduation from the local university he worked in journalism. After several years in the press service of the State Drug Control he did a regular TV program on drug addiction. It was then that he wrote his first novel on the subject, *The Runner*, nominated for the Debut Prize, soon followed by *Rooftop Anesthesia*, which was a Debut finalist. Both novels are devoted to young people's tendency towards escapism and their feeling of loneliness in a big city. They were published under the same cover in 2007. Currently he is engaged in developing computer games and game design.

Andrei Kuzechkin

Mendeleev Rock

Prologue [infection]

I was riding home on the early suburban train, carrying a rucksack bulging with potatoes. An army of old women who had occupied half the carriage were amusing themselves with a choral rendition of folk songs, and I kept glancing at the individual sitting opposite me, trying to figure out why this lanky young guy with a swarthy complexion was ogling me with his slanty eyes and smiling as if he knew everything about me, even the things no one was supposed to know, and getting a kick out of it. I'd never seen him before in my life! A disturbing sort of feeling.

A leather coat and long, wet hair tied back with a ribbon made my chance travelling companion look like Brandon Lee in the film *The Crow* and Linda in the clip *The Crow* at the same time. The only thing missing was makeup on his derisive physiognomy.

"Why so miserable?" the long-haired guy suddenly asked out of the blue. Apparently, like me, he needed something to distract him from the strains of "Travushka-Muravushka" thundering through the carriage. Well, thanks for that, at least, stranger!

"Ah, you know," I told him. "I'm on a real bad downer."

"So what's the reason for the downer?"

"Well... I don't know what I'm going to do when I get back home. And just my luck, my girl's gone away for the weekend."

The stranger's friendly face was a positive picture of understanding:

"You'd like her to come back sooner?"

"Nah, for all I care she can stay away forever. It's just that I've got nothing to do without her."

"How would you like a charge of feel-good vibes?"

"Can you arrange that?"

"No problem," the young guy answered with a super-crafty smile. "Going to Petrochemist, aren't you?"

"Yeah. I, like, sort of live there."

"Drop in to the Star House of Culture this morning at ten. Only get changed first."

"What would I want with that place? This sectarian group has meetings there on Sundays – the Church of White Angels."

"So go take a look, just for the gas. They won't do anything bad to you, and you'll leave in a good mood. Only don't get the idea that I'm one of them too!"

"You don't look like them," I chuckled. "And that's a compliment, because they're all prudes and goody-goodies. I've talked to a couple of them! All so very right and proper! Holding forth about pre-marital relationships, Judgement Day, humility, patience, turning the other cheek, blah-blah-blah..."

"You know, I once had a chat on that subject with the pastor from the Church of White Angels. He said that maxim about the cheek shouldn't be taken too literally. 'Let's suppose I'm out walking with my wife,' he said, 'and some hooligan starts pestering her. I'm not going to put up with that, am I, I'm not going to 'turn the other cheek'? I'll just thump him so hard, he won't get up again.' Of course, he put it a bit differently, more politely, but that's what he meant."

"And you agree with him?"

"Possibly," the young black-haired guy said with a smile.

I realised he wasn't in the habit of baring his soul to everyone he met. But then it was him that started the conversation!

Meanwhile twenty-five old women's throats were still warbling away as loudly and raucously as ever. One by one all the other passengers who hadn't slept enough moved to adjacent carriages so they could at least grab a short nap.

"I'll tell you one thing. If you have to do someone harm, and there's absolutely nothing you can do about it, then ask that person's forgiveness before you do it," the stranger advised me.

"I'll do that," I assured him. "I've never really trusted the White Angels, though. Do you know how much money there is slopping around in that church? Have you seen the kind of wheels they ride? Do you think they bought those with donations from the believers? They're mobsters, the real thing! The Christian mafia."

"Sure they are," the long-haired guy agreed.

"And let me tell you, they almost scared me to death one time. It was two years ago, I was the singer in a rock band back then, and we used to rehearse in the Star House of Culture, they gave us a rehearsal spot with some pretty decent equipment..."

"For free?" my companion enquired.

"Payment in kind. That is, we used to play a bit in the occasional concert at the Star. And one time me and my friend Ilyukha were in our spot, flailing away, him on keyboards and me on guitar, then in come these four penguins in jackets and ties, and start wandering round the room, examining the speakers and studying the mixer board. We were slightly staggered by this. One of them says; 'We're from the Church of White Angels, we'd like to get to know you'. I say: 'We're kind of busy. Maybe a bit later?' He says: 'We've got a business proposition for you. You let us into your room occasionally to rehearse, and we'll pay you for it'. The point being that the White Angels have their own band and they rehearse in the

House of Culture too, but for serious money. So they decided we could help them economise a bit."

"So what did you say?"

"I explain to these guys: look, I say, they didn't give us this spot so we could use it for dodgy deals on the side. If we start letting you in here, the director will just sit us on our instruments and launch us down the stairs. They repeat their request, as if I hadn't just been talking to them, and I have to explain again that we can't help them. And then again. Then one of them says sadly: 'Ah, guys, we really wanted to come to a reasonable understanding with you, but look where it's got us'. And he turns towards the door. Suddenly I realised he was going to bolt the door shut, turn back and say in a completely different voice; 'And now let's talk seriously'. I size up the situation: two of us and four of them, and who knows what they've got hidden under those jackets. It only takes me a second to say goodbye to my family, my friends, my enemies... But they just open the door and walk out of the room, then one of them turns round and wishes us a pleasant day."

The long-haired guy realised that at this point, as a polite individual, he was supposed to laugh a bit, and he snorted into his hand a couple of times.

"I reckon you were shaking for a week afterwards, right?"

"Too right. We were afraid they'd ambush us in an entrance somewhere. But they did something smarter than that. They told the director we were swilling vodka and tumbling girls in our rehearsal spot. So we got thrown out. We had to set ourselves up in our bass-player's garage..."

I could have told the guy a lot of other interesting things too, but he shook my hand and headed for the exit. And I'd forgotten to ask what his name was. But what point was there, anyway? We weren't likely to see each other again.

On the wooden back of the bench, right where the other

guy had been sitting, there was a message written in thick red felt-tip: GET TREATMENT BEFORE IT'S TOO LATE! The inscription was surrounded by a chain of little red crosses.

The view outside changed. The sparse forest merged into a gloomy open plain. Scalped earth with not a single spot of green. Just columns of black smoke rising up over it everywhere.

We were approaching Petrochemist.

1. [incubation period]

I almost thought they wouldn't let me into the Star House of Culture. There were too many luxury cars standing outside the entrance and the guy on the door – a rustic-looking lad with a good-natured face – was far too expensively dressed. When he noticed my embarrassment, he opened the battered door wide and put on a well-practiced smile.

"Please, come in! Take your cap off, if you don't mind. You're entering a church."

It didn't look much like a church, though. A three-storey shack built in the times when Petrochemist was a workers' settlement. Back then it was an island of brick in a sea of rotting timber. Above the entrance there was a crumbling mosaic – "Lenin in October". Behind it was the fence of the local park, full of dead trees.

The lobby was empty, if you didn't happen to spot the table of merchandise right beside the cracked statue of Karl Marx, under the placard that read: TEN YEARS OF THE CHURCH OF WHITE ANGELS. Out of sheer curiosity, I ran my eye across the table. There were religious books by unrecognised prophets, naturally, and CDs with "Christian music", and stickers.

"How much?" I asked, choosing one of the stickers.

"Five roubles," a swarthy Central Asian guy with highlights in his hair said without any trace of an accent. I reached into my pocket for small change.

"Do you agree with what it says?"

"Absolutely." Actually I liked the picture – a skull inside a triangle, like on a transformer substation – much more than the text ("ALL SIN ENGENDERS DEATH"). The salesman followed up by rebuking me for being late.

The hall was full. As soon as I stepped inside, a girl with a shaved head and a badge that said "MARINA" took me by the elbow and led me down between the rows of seats.

"Sit there, with the brothers."

But as soon as I got a bit closer, I lost all desire to sit beside these "brothers". I'd seen more than enough junkies in my time. It looked like the White Angels were one of those sects that stood bail for drug addicts and then, instead of chemicals, pumped their veins full of a new narcotic – their faith.

I decided to sit in the back row. As I walked through the semi-darkness past the men, women, families with children and teenagers, I noticed how immaculate they all looked, as if the House of Culture was about to host a banquet with the president of the Russian Federation in attendance. Some of the parishioners, although not really all that many, were compatriots of the highlighted vendor of merchandise, with the same swarthy complexion and narrow eyes. But there was something that wasn't Russian about all the others too: impeccable grooming, a European air of respectability and efficiency. And not a trace of religious piety in their faces. The hall didn't have even a whiff of churchiness about it.

I was delighted when I spotted the vague white blur of Anya's head in the back row. I headed towards her and touched down on the next chair.

I was staggered to see how much she'd changed. I remembered her being as fluffy as a dandelion, covered all over in peace signs and little bells. But the present-day Anya had short hair and she was dressed in military camouflage trousers and an army shirt with the sleeves rolled up. She could easily have been taken for a fascist, but then who could tell what was lurking in the depths of this new image? John Lennon and Yoko Ono dressed up in military style a few times too. To promote the record *Power to the People*, for instance.

I first learned about that record from Anya, she's a fan of Lennon's solo work (at least, she was until we broke up). That's a clear example of how different Anya and I are: I get off on Ringo Starr's solo discs. Everything about Lennon the rebel is too harsh, from the words to the tone of his voice, but all Ringo's songs are as genial as he is, they're very calming.

"Hi there, Crybaby!" – the way Anya greeted me seemed to throw me back to the blessed old days. It was ages since she'd called me that.

We hugged each other tight.

"I didn't know you'd got back!"

"The day before yesterday. It's super that you've come!"

"Well, someone advised me to come to improve my mood. He said there was such an atmosphere of love and goodness here, I'd feel better straightaway. Only don't tell me you're one of these holy rollers!"

"Of course not, how could you ever think that? I just decided to drop in and listen to a few songs."

"Do you recommend it for me?"

"Sure, only I advise you not to get too carried away, or you'll be talking in quotations from the Gospels till the end of your days. How are things with you?"

I shrugged.

"No worse than usual."

"That's my Crybaby. How's the studying?"

"Okay."

"So where *are* you studying now?"

"Here, in Petro, at the College of Humanities."

"And what year are you in?"

"Third."

"Are you working anywhere?"

"Yes, the *Evening Petrochemist*, as a proof reader. A few days a week."

"Personal life?"

"Better than okay."

"Far out! So who's the girl?"

"She's in my group, her name's Christina."

"Been together long?"

"A year and a half already."

"Everything's super, then."

"Yeah, kind of..."

"So what are you so peeved about? Where did you get that sour face?"

"Well, what can I say..." I really didn't know how to describe it.

With anyone else I'd have launched into a long, detailed description of how wonderful my Christina was, how considerate and clever and serious, and how much she loved me. But I could have told Anya how my beloved kept me on a short leash, found fault with every little thing, and was always comparing me with herself, not to my advantage ("I love you more than you love me", "I'm more mature than you are" and so on in the same style)... Only I didn't like the idea of spoiling our meeting with a hysterical outburst.

"Everything seems just great, but something somewhere's not right... Something tastes sour. I feel sick... and bored," I said, just to put her off. "But how are you?"

From what my best friend told me, I learned she'd been flung out of Uni, where she was studying in the biology department (Anya didn't say exactly why) and had to come back to our town. Next year she was going to try to get back in as a paying student, and that meant she'd have to find work here.

Anya had never liked her hometown of Petrochemist, especially after the time in ninth grade when she went to a disco for the first time in her life and the girls beat her up – even though Anya hadn't done anything wrong, they scratched her face so badly that she was walking around covered in sticking plasters for two weeks afterwards. She wouldn't have come back of her own free will, not even to see me, sentimental old Romka.

"Listen, Crybaby, where's your army? Where's Adenoma?"

Don't ask about the sad stuff, toots.

"In the first place, it wasn't my army; it was mine and Ilyukha's. And in the second place, there isn't any Adenoma any more. Hasn't been for ages."

The "brothers" and "sisters" sitting all around were glaring at us with indignant looks on their well-groomed faces and wagging their fingers in front of their lips, begging us to shut up.

"We'll talk outside," I whispered. "Let's listen."

"All right, let's do that."

On the stage the pastor in his white collar had been yacking on for quite a while already, but I only started listening to what he was saying now.

"... And then Robinson Crusoe made his way into the broken ship!" The preacher declared in an inspired voice. "And there he found chests full of both gold and silver. But what good to you is money, if you're on an uninhabited island? How can you spend it? No, Robinson Crusoe found something far more valuable and useful to him!"

"A Bible," I suggested in a half-whisper.

Anya looked round at me, narrowed her eyes ironically and shook her head.

"He found grains of wheat!" The pastor started describing how wisely Robinson Crusoe acted by not eating the seed grains straight away, but planting them, then collecting the harvest and not eating a single grain, but planting them again, and so on until he had an abundance of grain.

"I want a song, I want a song!" Anya whined like a little girl.

The sermon was already nearing its conclusion. The moral of it was that man should be patient and diligent. The speaker rounded off his performance with a few lines from the Gospels, of course, and announced:

"And now our songs of praise group will come up onto the stage."

An entire big band appeared in an instant: drummer, guitarist, bass-guitarist, flautist, female key-board player with a synthesizer, vocalist (devilishly seductive) and about five backup singers. The pastor stayed on stage with his mike, he was a member of the band too.

After a minute to set up, the drummer started things off with a short roll and a seductive melody started creeping cautiously round the hall, like a snake creeping through the grass. At first only the flute could be heard over the rhythm section, then the synthesizer started dropping in lush, lingering sounds, like drops of nectar. Clear guitar chords with a metallic twang completed the atmosphere of flawless harmony and gentle sadness in the hall. And the vocalist's light voice, like cracked glass, added the perfect final touch:

> *On the fir tree's doleful branches,*
> *Sleep, my little darling,*
> *To the tender breeze's sigh*
> *And its gentle swaying.*
>
> *May the life that we two share*
> *Be ever sacred, ever bright,*
> *And the Lord's hand ever shield you*
> *From the evil of the night.*

The worshippers got up from their seats, walked out into the aisle between the rows and started making funny movements in time to the music. The drug addicts were the funniest dancers of all, they stamped on the spot with their arms spread wide, as if they were about to grope someone in the crowd around them.

"Come on!" said Anya, grabbing my arm and dragging me out into the throng of dancers.

2.   [incubation period]

"You know, Crybaby, I still have that article from the *Evening Petrochemist* about your gig at the Star. Did you ever read it, by the way?" Anya asked when we got outside. My mood really had improved – the stranger in the train was right. Thanks again, old buddy.

Did I read it? I wrote it. Under a pen name.

It turned out a fairly short little article, though – the editor cut it pretty heftily. So short in fact, that I could have quoted it from memory.

HOME TOWN STARS

What do all the numerous rock fans in our town have in common? If you ask any of them what their favourite band is, in addition to Aria, Kino, The King and the Jester, Nirvana and Zemfira, they're bound to mention our town's own popular youth ensemble, Adenoma.

The band became especially popular following a short concert at the Star House of Culture that provided the recording for their mini-album *Pentagram*. Radio presenter Konstantin Trepov made the recording for his programme and then edited it on his computer, and the resulting sound quality, if not entirely professional, was quite acceptable.

The name "Pentagram" refers not only to the five members of the band – Smurf (keyboards and vocals), Crybaby (guitar and vocals), Ferret (bass guitar), Angie (backup vocals) and Buddha (percussion), but also to the five interesting tracks.

Adenoma start their performance with an aggressive tooth-rattler called *Mendeleev Rock*, sung by Crybaby. The next number, sung by Smurf, continues at the same high energy level and is called *Coloured Balls*.

In the third composition, *I Want to Kill Your Love*, punk rock gives way to psychedelia. Crybaby's vocals switch from strident to melancholy and otherworldly, but this mood doesn't last for long, it breaks off suddenly when the third song segues into the fourth, which is called *The Last Day* and races along faster than an express train. The performance is rounded off by a smooth ballad called *Blondie*, a duet from Smurf and Angie.

The members of this young group are full of creative ideas. And there are more concerts ahead, so the fairytale of the five dreamers continues!

I didn't think up that moronic ending, by the way. But at least I managed to save the name of the group: they wanted to cut it out of the article because it was too shocking, or so the editor thought. I don't know what's shocking about it – it's just a disease, like any other. Maybe the phrase has unpleasant personal associations for Yegor Filippovich. It's no fun getting old!

"So where are all the others?"

"Ilya – that's Smurf – finished school and scooted off to Moscow to study. I envy him, breaking out of this shitty dive full of junkies and retards. He e-mails me sometimes. But Adenoma isn't Adenoma without him."

"And how's that charmer of yours, the backup vocalist?"

"Angie? She got out of music, for objective reasons. She met this pretty-faced young guy and got knocked up. Now she lives on her own, raising the child. And she manages to work as well, somehow. I've been round to see her a few times, just dropped in for half an hour; she doesn't have any time for anything, not even to tidy the place up. There are lumps of dried-up buckwheat the size of my fist on the stove... But true to form, she's absolutely happy. I even envy her..."

Just at that moment someone butted into our conversation.

"May the Lord send you a dress, you shameless hussy, and take away your trousers!" a priest with a collecting box for donations perched on his belly intoned staidly as we walked past the gates of the market.

"And may the Lord send you trousers instead of your frock!" Anya wished him in reply, without batting an eye.

Anya in a dress? In your dreams! Everyone knows dresses and skirts were invented by men to humiliate women.

The faded, unwashed priest blended into the background. How do you like the colour grey? There aren't any others in Petrochemist. In winter it's grungy snow, in spring and autumn it's puddles of liquid mud, in summer it's battered asphalt. And regardless of the season, it's acrid smoke from the factory chimneys, armour-plated clouds, high-rise fortresses, buses and trucks that are scabby with mud and jackets and coats that have faded under the heavy rain.

If anything with colour turns up here, whether it's advertisement hoardings, shop signs or posters, it soon turns pale and gets covered over with this grey coating. Not even spring can shake the dominance of the colour grey. The trees in the town were killed by the factory emissions ages ago, and grass can't break through the asphalt and hard-packed earth.

"And the bass-player?"

"Ferret's here, in Petro, studying at the Construction College. But you know, to be quite frank, I'm not on very good terms with him."

"Why?"

"Because he's a freak. Buddha's in Petro too, but he'll never come back to music. After our last concert they caught him and broke his arms. After that he avoided all of us, didn't even come to collect his drumsticks."

"They broke his arms?" Anya gasped. "Who dared do that?"

"The Doctors."

"Who?"

"One of the new youth gangs, lowlifes like skinheads. Only worse. No ideological hang-ups, they just cripple anyone who's different from them. Say they catch a guy wearing an earring, they'll tear it off, complete with the ear."

"And what if he's got long hair, will they tear his head off?"

"They won't tear it off, but they could smash it in. They reckon they're making our town a healthier place, that's why they call themselves the Doctors. They're still operating; they beat someone up every now and then. The pigs might pick a couple of them up sometimes, but there's another forty wandering the streets."

"But what did Buddha do to annoy them?"

"Our entire band annoyed them by the very fact of its existence. They're opposed to all manifestations of independent grassroots culture."

"Uhu, like as if there was any independent grassroots culture in Petrochemist," Anya said, waving her hand through the air. "All there is here is mud, there's isn't anything else."

"It's just that there are some people who simply have to beat other people up, no matter what."

The next person we met was Fast Foot – one of our town's three major attractions. Or, in simpler terms, one of our three famous local loonies.

This living embodiment of Chinese philosophy – "a man walking forwards, with his head turned backwards" (Fast Foot never looked where he was going) – went flying past us, waving his beanpole arms about with the air of a very busy man. When Anya and I turned into a short, narrow side street and came out at our stop on Marx Avenue, we saw the second of the three loonies, Mystery Man. The short old man with a dark complexion and an expression of fright in his huge eyes looked a bit like a scolded dog, and he was taking himself for a walk as he usually did at this time of day, tramping on the spot and gazing around with a hunted expression.

The crazies are all out today, I thought. *Does that mean it's going to rain?*

"Crybaby, you need to unwind," Anya told me. "Get out somewhere."

"Christina and me get out a lot..."

"You don't get what I mean," Anya interrupted offhandedly. "WITHOUT Christina. By the way, where is she now, why aren't you with her?"

"She went to her grandma and grandpa's place for the weekend."

"Excellent! Go out and have a good time."

"What makes you think I need to?"

"The fact that you're such a pitiful sight. You look as battered and downtrodden as a collective farm horse."

"And is that all?" I thought I smelled a trick.

"No, to be honest. A girl I know, my old neighbour Natasha, has invited me to her birthday today, and I don't know anyone there apart from her."

"No need to go on. I'm with you. Only if Christina finds out, she'll skin me alive."

Actually, Christina would skin me alive if she just saw me and Anya together now. I can just picture it. First she calls me aside and asks acidly: "Well, what kind of scene do you call that?" I start explaining to her that Anya's my friend and Christina declares: "I'm your girlfriend!" I try to object and Christina interrupts me with a loud shriek: "Oh, so you don't agree! Well, go to her then!" After which she swings round haughtily and sets off along the pavement, raising dust. I have to run after her and beg her forgiveness for half an hour.

That's what would have happened. And since Christina would probably have taken a fierce dislike to Anya, disfigured by her fascist gear and short-clipped haircut, my own personal dictator would have carried on mocking me for ages: "Well, didn't you find yourself a really ugly piece of work!"

But it wasn't the clothes or the haircut that made Anya look frightening to me. Her face had become sort of... worn, I suppose. As if she'd taken it off, like a rubber mask, then pulled it back on carelessly, and these faint, barely visible creases had appeared in it: under the eyes, in the corners of the lips, on the chin... What happened to you, Anya?

3.   [incubation period]

What wind had blown her in here? She didn't even know that herself, sitting there as if none of this had anything to do with her and pecking at her salad. Slightly plump, looking a bit like a stubborn little donkey because her round nose was raised far enough to make her nostrils seem too big. Somebody else might not have liked her – and I wasn't all that interested in her appearance myself, or in the festivities in general.

It turned out that apart from Anya. I knew absolutely nobody at the party – neither the birthday girl, nor her thirty-year-old boyfriend, nor their colleagues from work, little ladies (or little bitches, whichever you prefer) of widely different ages. Despite her misgivings, Anya had quickly got on talking terms with the other guests, who found her image slightly outrageous but intriguing. My companion had forgotten all about me and plunged into conversation on the eternal female subjects. As everyone knows, there are only two of those: 1) "All men are stupid jerks!" 2) "I've got absolutely nothing to wear!"

Time dragged on like an endless boa constrictor. Poor

old Romka here, dying from lack of attention, didn't feel like eating, or drinking, or singing. But even so he played his part as "a merrymaking unit" (as Ilf and Petrov once put it), sitting in the corner and glaring at the shaggy yellow dog lying motionless by the opposite wall.

"There's a story about that dog," said the girl I didn't know, breathing right in my ear. I hadn't noticed her creeping up on me. "I can tell you in secret, but make sure you don't blab it to anyone. It was a long time ago, when Natasha was still in school. She had a different boyfriend then, Alik. He came to see Natasha one time, sat on this divan for absolutely ages, and suddenly he needed to go to the toilet real bad for a number two..."

She switched to a loud, hoarse whisper and moved her face close to my cheek. Judging from the smell coming out of her mouth, she must have drunk a fair bit.

"But he was a very nervous type, he even blushed when he said hello to Natasha, and he was scared to death of asking where the toilet was. What could he do? Well this is what the booby came up with: when Natasha went out of the room to make them some tea, without thinking about it too long, he pulled his pants down and dumped on the carpet beside the dog." The girl snorted a few times, or rather, she honked like a young reindeer.

"Things like that don't happen," I declared.

"Oh yes they do. Well, Natasha comes back and she sees the carpet's ruined. Alik says: the dog did it. Natasha says: it couldn't have. Alik says: I tell you, the dog did it. Natasha says: it couldn't have! It's a STUFFED TOY!" My conversation partner stuck her nose down against her knees and started shaking. "That was the end of things for them," she went on when she stopped laughing. "She made him famous all over Petrochemist."

I laughed heartily at that story. Since then I've heard it

several times from various people living in different towns who didn't even know each other, and every time the characters were a boy and a girl with new names. I wasn't even surprised when the comedian Semyon Shaferman told the same yarn on TV, in some low-grade programme or other like *Full House*.

"And I've remembered another thing that happened too. Only it's vulgar, is that all right?"

"Sure, sure, just render it up quickly!"

"Then listen. A friend of mine was at a party, only not one like this. Everything here's very proper, but that was a total orgy. Everyone got plastered, then they paired off and scattered round the rooms. My friend met a girl there. She hints to him that it's time they found a quiet corner... But he can tell he won't be able to manage it: he's too tired after a hard day. Only he doesn't want to disappoint a lady, does he! And getting a reputation for being impotent is no fun either. Well, they went to another room, and he took a sausage off the table with him. They walked in, turned off the light and there was a bit of foreplay. And then in the darkness my friend sticks this sausage into his lady and starts pleasuring her. He gets carried away and forgets all about everything. Then suddenly she says: 'We didn't lock the door! Go and lock it before it's too late!' he gets up and goes to the door, but the sausage is still inside her. The girl thought for a moment, sizing things up... and then didn't she yell!"

My new acquaintance almost fell off her chair, writhing in drunken hysterics.

"You're classy!" the girl said when she'd finished laughing.

"I'm Roman," I said, introducing myself.

"Yeah, I know you!" the girl said, slapping me on the knee. "Roman, alias Crybaby. The guy from Adenoma!"

"E-er..." – I really didn't know what to say, it was so unexpected.

"Call me Priscilla. I was at your concerts, I really enjoyed them... Why don't you do gigs anymore?"

I recovered my wits.

"That's a long story. Listen, that pseudo-music's given me a splitting headache..." I said, nodding towards the tape deck.

"Yeah, me too," Priscilla agreed. "Let's split."

We moved from the room of communal merriment to the dark corridor. I immediately reached my lips out towards Priscilla's pretty face and kissed her hot cheek, and she literally fell on me and grabbed me with both arms. But at that moment it became clear to me that the girl hadn't done it on a sudden impulse of passion, but to keep herself on her feet.

"I feel bad," she complained. "Let's go out in the fresh air..."

We didn't hang about in the hallway – it had a foul smell of cleaning powder and cat shit. We walked straight through and out into the night. I held this young beauty against me with both hands, keeping her upright. It was excruciatingly pleasurable. Her hair smelled of something like pine needles, so it was like embracing a little Christmas tree. Near the end of the street (although it wasn't even a street, just a random accumulation of stunted skyscrapers) Priscilla puked up a dollop of something with a sickly-sweet smell.

"Spoiled all the romance, have I?" the girl asked sadly. "Sorry."

I asked:

"Shall we go back then?"

"No way! Let's walk all night long. We'll wander off to somewhere far, far away! Only... I could do with something to pep me up."

"You'll have it." I dashed to a kiosk and came back with a can of cola, a packet of instant coffee, a plastic spoon and two plastic cups. I divided the contents of the little packet evenly between the two cups and splashed in the cola: thick foam swirled up, filling three quarters of each cup and splashing over the side. I stirred the result with the little spoon to settle the foam slightly and poured in the rest of the cola.

"There. A thermonuclear cocktail by the name of 'Buster'. I warn you, your heart will yammer like a machine gun."

"Who cares, let it." Priscilla took one cup from me and downed it in a single gulp, together with the foam. I polished off the other cup.

"That's great, it's like ice cream!" she remarked.

Soon after that we moved on, although I was concerned about meeting one of the drugged-up "death brigades" you can run into in Petrochemist. And I really got the jitters when this group of guys loomed up ahead of us, sitting on a load of concrete slabs that had been dumped haphazardly.

"We have to go round them," I whispered.

We were slinking past the group like two spies, hiding behind the shells of the metal car shelters, when suddenly I heard the sound of a jangling guitar and a singer bleating off-key. "I don't believe it, do you hear that magical voice?" I said, and stepped out boldly from behind a garage, straight into the light of a street lamp.

"Romka!" roared the guitarist, a kid in glasses with a curved spine who looked like a dried-up crust of bread.

"Sanya!"

Yes, it really was my friend Sanya, better known in our town as Queazo. In his own circle Queazo was regarded as the greatest butthead and loser ever, and he would have been an outcast if not for his guitar. Queazo mostly played Soviet-style street songs.

"Guys, give him a warm welcome, this is Romka, a great mate of mine!"

"Hey, Romka's a regular guy!" a member of this nocturnal company of juveniles croaked gleefully and slapped me between the shoulder blades a couple of times. I hate being called that – somehow I feel like I've grown out of that age.

"So where are you now, Romka?"

"Meaning?"

"Well, you – Adenoma."

"Wake up, four eyes! Adenoma's been gone for two years already!"

"Yeah, I know about that... But aren't you going to get back together? That was the only rock group in all of Petro!"

"Well, you know, somehow..." I mumbled and hastily changed the subject. "Sanya, play something of your own for the lady, eh? Something cheerful," I asked him and whispered quickly to Priscilla: "Now you'll hear a song that's as stupid as he is."

Queazo was flattered by my request. He adjusted his glasses and gasped out:

"It hasn't got a title yet."

And he started singing in his high, thin, trembling voice:

> *I'm walking down the dusty road,*
> *When the rain begins to lash.*
> *I spot a bush across the way*
> *And set off for it at a dash.*
>
> *I was way down on my luck,*
> *But now I think I can relax,*
> *'Cause I'm well-rested and still dry,*
> *And I've just found myself an axe.*

I'd heard this brilliant work several times before, so I stood there with a straight face, but my new girlfriend bit me on the shoulder to stop herself from laughing until she cried. And the strangest thing of all was that no one but us found it funny.

> *I was searching hard for love*
> *But couldn't find it anywhere*
> *But one day as spring arrived*
> *A real true miracle occurred.*

> *I fell hard for your blue eyes,*
> *I simply couldn't help it.*
> *I made you a proposal then,*
> *And you did not reject it.*

"It's already funny," Priscilla whispered when we heard the bridge that took the place of a refrain.

> *I'm walking down the dusty road,*
> *When the rain begins to lash.*
> *I spot a bush across the way*
> *And set off for it at a dash.*
>
> *I was way down on my luck,*
> *But now I think I can relax,*
> *'Cause I'm well-rested and still dry,*
> *And I've just found myself an axe.*

The number was over, and Priscilla and I moved on. At the last moment, the young guy who had slapped me on the shoulder asked for some small change, and I gladly gave him everything that was left in my pockets.

By the way, Sanya was called up for the army soon after that and they brought him back six months later, with signs of severe beating all over his body and an army doctor's certificate with the conclusion: "Death due to heart attack", although Sanya never had any problems with his heart. And then out of nowhere a recording of several of Queazo's songs surfaced – he'd recorded them on someone's computer. And those songs, as simple and sincere as he was, made the rounds of Petrochemist for a long time.

I don't recall the details of that night – all the places Priscilla and I got to, the yards and alleys that we wandered through, what we chatted about – but I do remember very clearly the waste plot on the edge of Petrochemist and the rusty carcass of the dead truck beside which I started kissing Priscilla avidly, pressing the girl up against the metal.

Well, Christina, do you see what I'm doing? I gloated to myself. There was good reason to gloat.

Priscilla reached in under my shirt and started stroking my stomach. In the darkness I could see she was biting her lips.

"Respectable young ladies don't behave like this," she gasped.

"Probably," I agreed, and suddenly Priscilla squealed.

"Turn round!"

Someone was walking towards us. By the light of the streetlamps standing along the edge of the highway that cut through the wasteland, I could see it wasn't a human being at all, but something more like a monkey wrapped in rags, with long arms and a head with absolutely no forehead. Limping heavily on one leg, the creature was approaching us rapidly, in absolute silence.

"Who is it? Crybaby, I'm afraid!" Priscilla whimpered.

"Quiet... Let him walk past. If we don't bother him, he won't bother us. I'm certain."

As I whispered these words, I kept my eyes fixed on the lame freak. *Go past*, I commanded it in my mind. *Walk past. Don't notice us.* I felt my stomach turn to ice. Who was this? Was it really human? A street bum? A crazy wacko? Or some sort of crazed brute dressed up in rags for a laugh? Or... something that didn't have any name?

The creature stopped about twenty steps away from us. *It's sensed prey*, I thought and immediately drove the thought out of my head. Whoever this scarecrow was, it couldn't do us any harm, it was too small... And suddenly the final drops of my self-possession evaporated: I imagined this dwarf running up to us, jumping on me and biting into my neck.

"A brick! Get a brick!" Priscilla hissed.

I didn't answer. It was like I'd been set in plaster from

head to foot. I didn't even have the strength to lean my head down and look at the ground by my feet, let alone move my arm. I looked at the freak's face, bandaged up like a leper's. What was under that mask of rags – rotten, half-ruined teeth or animal fangs, as sharp as nails?

The freak peered at us. *It's thinking, the bastard*, I thought. The important thing was not to let this creature get any closer than five steps away. I couldn't just stand there any longer. I forced myself to look down and my gaze immediately picked out vague white patches of broken brick here and there on the ground. A moment later Priscilla shrieked: the creature had suddenly darted forward, it was rushing towards us.

"Get away!" I yelled as loudly as I could. "Clear off."

The rag figure hobbled closer and closer to Priscilla and me. I thought I caught the smell of live flesh rotting. I picked up a lump of brick and flung it at the monkey. The lump hit the creature on the leg.

Without making a sound, it ran back a bit and then came dashing at us again. I immediately picked up another lump of brick.

"Throw harder!" Priscilla squealed. "Finish the fucker off."

I hurled my missile, aiming for the freak's head, and I didn't miss. The rag monster staggered and limped away quickly.

That was when my girlfriend and I realised we were both shaking in terror, and we set off at full speed in the opposite direction. When we couldn't run any more, we slowed to a fast walk, and we didn't stop until we got back to Natasha's flat, where the merrymaking was still smouldering on. We knocked on the door, went inside, sat down on the divan, put our arms round each other and fell asleep on the spot.

4.   [incubation period]

What I dreamed about had actually happened to me. That summer my parents sent me and my sister to the dacha and only came to join us at the weekends. For a whole month we were left to our own devices, a brother and sister with names fit for kings and queens: Roman and Regina.

I was in the garden when I heard squeaky little-girl laughter. It was coming from the long shed that separated our plot from the neighbours' instead of a fence.

I peeped into the shed through a crack in the wall and saw Regina and her local friend, Nastya. The two girls always walked around together, they wore identical swimsuits made of nothing but pieces of string and long plaits hanging down below their waists, and they were both petite, like twelve-year-old girls, although Nastya was somewhere about fifteen and Regina was all of eighteen.

It looked completely out of proportion beside my sister, that massive prick she was caressing with her tongue; her eyes squeezed shut in delight. Her two tiny little hands slid up and down the thick trunk of it. Nastya was helping her cautiously with one hand, as if she was slightly afraid of something. I couldn't make out the owner of the prick through the small opening in the wall, all I could see were his broad palms, stroking the girls on the head, and I could hear his wheezing breath.

Regina opened her little mouth wide, which looked very amusing, and grabbed hold of the phallus as greedily as if she wanted to bite it off. The two male hands immediately grabbed her tightly by the ears and started moving rapidly up and down. Regina's partner was simply using her head to masturbate. Then he tugged his prick out, pulled Nastya over and carried on doing the same thing with her. The girl tried to break free and her eyes stared wildly, but the strong hands wouldn't let her go. Nastya started whining. Regina comforted her, stroking the back of her head, not forgetting to stroke her tormentor's scrotum at the same time.

Nastya's cheek suddenly swelled out, foam poured out of her mouth and the girl bleated. The hands holding her head didn't release their grip until Nastya swallowed everything that had gone into her mouth. When he'd finished, her partner slid down and sat on the floor, catching his breath. He was middle-aged, with a severely receding hairline and coarse wrinkles.

Regina nestled against him and started licking his cheek.

When I woke up, I discovered I was lying on the divan with my arms round a bolster instead of Priscilla. The sitting room, where last night glasses had clinked and guests had clamoured, was empty. The table was a confusion of dirty dishes, leftovers, puddles of wine, banana skins and tangerine peel. The clock showed eleven.

"Slept it off?" Anya asked, screwing her eyes up sleepily as she suddenly appeared in the doorway.

"Where is everybody?"

"There isn't anybody apart from you. Natasha and her man went to his place. And Natasha left me to look after you. The others all went home. Hmm... I suppose it's not everybody you're interested in, just one particular person."

Precisely.

"Crybaby, I understand everything and I want to give you a piece of advice," Anya said strictly. "Just one thing. Drop it!"

"Why should I?"

"As I understand it, you had a good time yesterday. I won't even ask exactly how. You know I'm no champion of strict morals."

"Right, and?"

"And nothing," she snapped sternly. "You had a blast, and now stop. Go back to your Christina."

"And why?"

"Are you so sure your new flame even remembers you? And even if she does, do you think she really wants you? She was as drunk as I was. And anything can happen when people are drunk!"

I adjusted the posture of my body from lying to sitting, realising in the process that I hadn't had nearly enough sleep.

"If you'd been paying more attention to me yesterday, Anyuta, you'd have noticed that I didn't drink anything."

My best friend remembers since we were at school together that if I call her "Anyuta", it means things are getting touchy, so she said:

"All right, Crybaby, don't get uppity! I'm trying to be helpful."

"Well, in any case, try to find out something about her. Please. It's important to me."

"Okay." Anya nodded without any real enthusiasm. "I'll try."

I'd already slept through my classes, so from Natasha's flat I went back home to catch up on my sleep.

Whatever, but it was really good Anya had come back to Petrochemist and she was my friend. Women make great friends, up until it comes to something more than friendship. Once, a very long time ago, I'd tried to win Anya's love... unsuccessfully, for which I was glad now. Anya was one of the few people with whom I could talk about any subject and be certain of being understood one hundred per cent.

I really love talking to people, but I reckon I don't have any luck with the people I talk to. I can talk to them about anything at all – sport, politics, women – but it's easy to imagine what would happen if, for instance, I told one of my acquaintances:

"You know, I think I'm not entirely a man..." Of course, he'd reckon I was hinting that I'm a homosexual, and stop having anything to do with me. But all I'd be trying to say was that in my personality the female principle is much stronger than the male principle. That doesn't mean I'm gay, just that I have lots of female character traits and I see the world a little bit differently... That's a bit too complicated for everyone I know, even for Christina. ESPECIALLY for Christina.

When I talk to people I often have to be hypocritical. If they ask me: "When you meet a girl, what's the first thing that you notice?" I can't really answer "her smell" can I? I have to say something that's easier to understand, like "her figure", and then the other guy nods happily, as if that's exactly what he was expecting to hear.

How had I managed to keep up a relationship with Christina for a year and a half? I simply knew what she wanted to hear from me, and I said it. I knew what I had to do to keep her well-disposed, and I did it. I apologised, although I wasn't to blame. I forgave her things that would have made anyone else fling her out on her ear. And the result was that now she genuinely believed we couldn't live without each other. Even on the card for our anniversary she wrote: "If we could have separated before, now we'll never part."

Why did I do all that? Ask me something easier. Not out of love – I hadn't loved Christina for a long time, just tolerated her. And bed definitely wasn't the reason. Christina was a diligent but boring partner. In one and a half years she still hadn't realised that sex is a game in which you can think up new rules every time, and not a mechanical routine for giving each other pleasure. That was why I was happily unfaithful to Christina whenever a convenient opportunity turned up – which wasn't very often, in view of the fact that Christina was always right there beside me – but I'd never been able to bring myself to give her up for someone else. If only there was someone else!

At home I caught right up on my sleep, but it wasn't easy. I was woken twice by my dad's drunken howling.

"What do you think you're doing?... You're not people, you're animals! You ought to be ashamed of yourselves! How can you do things like that?"

My father's an intellectual who gradually took to drink. He looks good-natured, with his grey hair, as curly as a little lamb's wool. He has two different degrees, but he works at the stadium as a night watchman or, rather, night alcoholic, and he adores his work so much that he's always bringing it home. My dear old dad is perfectly harmless when he's drunk. He doesn't break anything, he doesn't attack people, he doesn't sell things from the house to buy drink... In short, as long as you're deaf, he won't cause you any bother, but a little bit of drink is enough to start him weeping and groaning so loud, you can hear him all over the flat. And that carries on until my old man gets tired and flakes out.

The reasons for all the groaning and woeful howling couldn't possibly be more varied: reminiscences of friends and relatives who have died, his failed life, the estrangement from his wife. My mum took care of this helpless little lamb for a long time until she got fed up of it and pushed off to her relatives in Nizhny Tagil. Letters and money orders in my name often arrive from mum, and once a month I go to visit – we can't afford to meet more often than that. The moment mum left, the flat went into decline. My weakling of a father started bringing his drinking buddies home, and they took full advantage of his good nature, broke lots of stuff and ransacked the place.

At about six in the evening my father slopped feebly up to my door and knocked. (It took me several years to cure my parents of the habit of barging into your humble servant's chambers without knocking; I had to fit a lock on the door to do it.)

"Roma, someone to see you."

"It's open," I replied. I was sitting on the bed in the lotus pose with no trousers on, holding an electric guitar that wasn't plugged in.

Christina walked in.

My treasure by the name of Christina belongs to the category of people that I like best of all. Anyone seeing her for the first time in his life will say: "What a fright!" but then, when he gets a closer look: "Ah no, she's not too bad at all!" But the catch is that he might just say these two phrases in the reverse order. Lots of people (Anya, for instance) think I get really hurt when girls reject me, and that's why I go around with the kind you couldn't really call models of beauty, to make sure I can't fail. All lies. I only love a girl if she has something special about her appearance, something that no one else has. With Christina it's her narrow little piggy eyes, which give her that permanent dull, sleepy expression, even when she's shouting at me.

Christina had dyed her hair again for some reason; this time it was flaming ginger.

"Hi there, light of my life," I said with a nod. "That really suits you."

Christina looked at me without saying anything, folded her hands across her stomach and then asked peevishly.

"What's all this? Have you got a day off, then?"

"I had a temperature," I lied brazenly.

"And couldn't you have called me this morning?"

"I've been asleep all day," I said, this time without any deception. "I'm feeling better now."

"And what's that for?" Christina asked, glancing disapprovingly at the guitar. That's an entire separate story, the way Christina hates everything to do with Adenoma. My romance with Christina started about six months after the band finally fell apart. Back then I was still hoping to cobble a new band together, but Christina put me straight on that: she mocked me every time I even mentioned the idea in her presence. I tried to tell her about our band – after all, say what you will, we were pretty good! – but she interrupted straight away: "Do I really have to listen to this?"

My beloved hates "heavy" music and thinks I don't even know how to play the guitar properly, let alone sing. Even supposing I know that myself, a man has a right to his hobby, doesn't he? What's so bad about me wanting to yell a bit up on stage? When I asked Christina these questions, she held up our classmate Oleg to me as an example. He collects gold rings (just like Ringo Starr) – now there's a hobby for you! But what could you expect from me, I was still a little boy. When I was twenty-five, she said, with a job and a car and a family, all these infantile disorders would disappear of their own accord. And it wouldn't do me any harm to serve some time in the army; they'd knock a bit of sense into me there. She offered herself as an example. Christina always tries to use every second of her life productively: she went to make-up classes ("So I'll always be in demand and won't have to count the kopecks, understand?"), she went to eurhythmics classes ("I'm as fat as a hippopotamus, no, don't try to reassure me, you don't understand anything about it").

Of course, I had to agree with her every time, otherwise I would have lost her, and I didn't want that. Basically, if she knew what I really dream about, she'd have run off and left me the very first day. For instance, if I told her that after college I was planning to hitch a ride out of Petrochemist and take nothing but my guitar and the clothes I had on. And earn money by singing in pedestrian underpasses. And by the way, my plans haven't changed since then, either.

"I was just strumming a bit for fun," I said. "Is that contraindicated?"

But what I thought was: *Come on, tell me I don't love you.*

"You don't love me," Christina said in a dull, dreary voice. Her set of trump phrases hadn't expanded with the years.

"I love you a lot, Christie," I objected, putting the instrument down and reaching out for my presumptive beloved.

Christina stepped back towards the wall without saying anything. She looked down at the floor.

I had to get up and take a step towards her.

"Don't touch me..." Christina sobbed. *Ouch*, I thought. If Christina had decided to start bawling, it would last forever.

"Why not?" I asked, touching her ear cautiously with my lips. "What have I done wrong?"

"Monster!" Christina tore herself free and went flying out of the room in tears, straight through the hallway cluttered with empty bottles of hawthorn berry tincture (the favourite tipple of all elderly alcoholics with heart problems), grabbed her jacket, stuffed her feet into her shoes and slammed the door.

She never listens to my explanations or apologies when she's crying. So I usually just leave her alone, and she sits down and does her imitation of the fountains at Peterhoff – sometimes for half an hour non-stop, I've actually timed it. You can imagine what it's like: for an entire half hour she doesn't hear anything or see anything, just bawls at the top of her voice! What have I done to deserve that kind of torment?

I stretched out on the bed, staring aimlessly at the posters on the walls: the Beatles, Super Deluxe, Blur, Alexander Laertsky, John Wu, Chow Yun Fat with pistols in both hands, screenshots from movies by Takashi Miike (my favourites are the cockfights from *The City of Lost Souls* and the transformer from *Dead or Alive 3*). I downloaded most of the posters off the net, because in our country any right-thinking person (and especially anyone who produces posters) doesn't know who Super Deluxe and Takashi Miike are.

Of course, it wasn't hysterical Christina that I was thinking about, it was Priscilla. Everything that had happened that night

– our walk, the kisses, the rag-wrapped freak – it all seemed like a half-forgotten dream that had disappeared forever, leaving behind some kind of residue in my heart, a vague, indefinite feeling. When someone remembers a dream, it's the sensation and feeling he recalls, but it takes an effort to remember the events. I wonder if Priscilla remembers anything. It will be a real pity if she doesn't! I can just imagine her waking up in the morning and looking in bewilderment at me sleeping there, freeing herself from my arms and then asking everybody if she behaved decently, and how decently – she didn't go running round somebody else's flat with no underwear on, for instance, did she?

Anyway, now I knew for certain what I had to do, since my little piggy would be blubbering at home all evening or ringing round her friends and telling them what a rotten worm I am. So I was free until tomorrow morning.

And I also remembered the cunning character with the long hair and narrow eyes, the one I rode with in the train yesterday morning. If I knew where to find him, I'd turn up at his place with a bucket of beer; I'd buy the most expensive kind, especially. After all, if it wasn't for him, I wouldn't have met Anya, and then Priscilla. Thanks, stranger, for that crazy night, it was exactly what I've been dreaming about for so long!

I rummaged about in the document box, where the remains of my last pay packet were lying along with everything else, and raked out all the cash that was left. I got dressed. I shouted: "Dad, I'm going out!"

I ran down the stairs.

I went to the old Star House of Culture again.

5. [initial developmental period]

I padded along, trying to keep to the unlighted side of the street. I'm not afraid of the dark; on the contrary, it's the light that frightens me – daylight and the electric kind. There's nothing safer than pitch darkness. It defends you like black armour plating. If some bad bastard decides to give me a good thrashing or roll me over, he'll do it even in broad daylight. But in the darkness you can't see people's faces, it's hard to recognise them. Who knows who I might turn out to be, maybe I've got a rod in every pocket? I could just pull them out and plug him with both hands! And it's easier to hide in the dark, I know that. What with all the different people I've had to run away from in my short life.

There weren't any White Angels left in the Star – they only rented the main hall for their services on Sundays, and only for two or three hours. Just recently the House of Culture had only been letting employees inside, but the female janitor recognised me and unlocked the door.

I was looking for a good acquaintance of mine by the name of Natasha. She could only be found in the Star after seven in the evening, because during the day she worked two shifts as a teacher. I knocked on the door of the office where there was a meeting of youth leaders going on and called her out into the corridor.

I had time for a quick glance round at everyone there: a funny old granddad, looking like a superannuated punk, two women well chewed-on by time, three a bit younger, one of whom was Natasha, and a juvenile with a good-natured smile on his face. Actually, they were all smiling. When so many youth leaders get together, they always have a good time, even if they're discussing something serious. They always find time for a laugh at stupid little childish games they make up themselves, or "humorous" verses like "Across the roof a sparrow walks, With snot and slobber in a box..."

I remembered a song from an old cartoon film: "We should really all give thanks for this world's delightful cranks, with hearts as innocent as children." Maybe it was good for us that they existed. For instance, I liked to drop in and spend a bit of time with them. But was it good for them, these sincere and good-hearted people, who had absolutely no idea that for the most part the children they loved so devotedly were crude blockheads who couldn't give a shit for their mentors?

Natasha – a plumpish, squat little lady with a face like a red apple – came out of the office.

"Well now, we are honoured!" – it was ages since I'd heard that pleasant, slightly husky voice. Natasha gave me a firm hug in her usual youth-leader style. I must confess that when I was at the school camp and I was in her troop, I had a crush on her, so I hugged her as more than just a friend, my thoughts weren't entirely pure. And as a matter of fact, she's still not married...

"Let's sit down," I said, flopping onto the windowsill. "There's something I want to talk to you about."

"Only make it quick, Roma dear, people are waiting for me!"

"All right, then, the gist of the matter is: do you have any kind of event coming up in the House of Culture?"

"What kind, for instance?"

"A concert or, I don't know, some kind of celebration?"

"The next one's this week, on Friday."

"What's it in honour of?"

"Friday the 13th. There'll be the Witch Show, the Harmony Dance Club, the choir from school number 3..."

"I get the idea." I couldn't give a damn for all these choirs and dance clubs. "Can you put Adenoma in the line-up?"

"Adenoma? I thought you weren't playing anymore!"

"We are, as you can see. How about it?"

"Well, I don't know," Natasha said hesitantly.

"Please, Natasha, it's important..." I said, putting my hand on her fat thigh, as if by accident; I started stroking it cautiously. "There must be enough time for it, surely?"

"The whole programme's already planned down to the last

minute, you crazy loon! And straight after the concert there's a disco! Why couldn't you have told me in advance, at least a week or two earlier?"

"Stop being so cunning, Natasha. I know you always leave fifteen minutes to cover anything that comes up!"

I moved as close as I could to her and put my arm round her waist. Natasha gently pushed my hand off, moved away a couple of centimetres and drawled with emphatic resentment:

"Will you stop mo-lest-ing me!" Her neck smelled of baby cream.

"Will you put Adenoma in? If you do, I'll stop."

"You know, Roma, in principle, we could let you have five minutes, if that's enough for you... Right at the very end..."

She probably said that so I'd understand how difficult the situation was and leave her alone, but I simply exploded in delight.

"Just what we need! We'll have time to sing two whole songs."

Of course, if not for Priscilla, I wouldn't have had anything to do with this idiotic school party! But it wasn't all that bad. Adenoma had gigged in worse places – for instance, in a night disco where all the instruments played off key, blurred by feedback, and half-drunk young thugs pelted us with bottles (plastic ones, fortunately) – it was a miracle we got out of there alive.

"All right..." Natasha agreed thoughtfully. "Only you'll have to keep the drum kit down to the minimum so we can get it out on stage and clear it away quickly..."

"Consider it done. Thanks a lot!" I surprised Natasha by kissing her on the lips.

"Hey now, stop that! Don't be so impertinent..." Natasha frowned, pretending to be furious, but behind her angry grimace there was a smile that stretched from ear to ear.

"All right, I've got to run."

"Cheers, Roma."

I started bounding down the stairs.

"Priscilla, Priscilla..." I murmured. "Everything's going to be just great."

Although when I thought about it, I didn't know anything about her – not her real name, or her surname, or where she studied or worked. I didn't even know for certain if we'd ever see each other again. A shadow-girl. The shadow of something long forgotten...

English has this fantastic word – "oblivion". It's not easy to translate into Russian; the best our translators can manage is "city of forgetfulness". But if you want an exhaustive and precise translation, try taking a stroll round Petrochemist at any time of the day. You can saunter along Marx Avenue, the main street that cuts right across the whole town, but I advise you to turn off it and keep on walking. Like me now. You'll walk round heaps of crushed stone, huge wooden spools for cables, garages, buildings with no doors or windows and huge puddles. You'll walk past endless wire fences and brick walls, thread your way through narrow little alleys, jump over trenches, run into dead-ends.

After about twenty minutes there'll be just one question nagging at you: this is a huge town, so where is everyone? Where are the people? Where are the people? All around you there are excavators roaring, cranes twisting their necks, cement mixers twirling, pile drivers hammering piles into the ground – if you take a close look, you'll realise there aren't any people in them. These machines don't really need people – they know their job perfectly well without any driver. In the evening, like now, they stop too, and after that the maze-city is completely dead. You don't even have to worry about the gangs of wild roughnecks, if you know the places where they usually hang out and give them a wide berth.

Let me tell you a secret: Petrochemist itself isn't really all that big. It's grabbed a pretty large area of land, but most of that territory isn't residential at all, it's various different plants, factories, mills, garbage tips, automobile graveyards, waste lots and – most importantly – construction sites. These make up at least half of the whole town. In all the time I've lived here, it has never stopped, that roaring, rumbling and hammering. What are they building, who can explain that? In fifteen years, what's sprung up out of all the foundation pits that make the town look like a testing ground for monstrous aerial bombs is beyond all comprehension. Maybe it's some new, original kind of housing, or new factories and mills – but they haven't finished building them yet, and no one knows when they will.

Some people think or, rather, surmise, that immediately after the collapse of the Soviet Union several major Japanese corporations secretly bought sites in Petrochemist for their new industrial complexes. As soon as the construction work is completed – that is, soon – they'll buy up the rest of the town. Petrochemist will be called Little Japan. The municipal authorities, the managements of the plants, all the leading engineers and specialists, as well as the policemen and security guards will all be Japanese, but the labour force – 90% of the town's inhabitants – will be entirely Russian. It will be a closed town or, rather, you'll be able to come here, but when you enter, you'll sign a paper saying you won't try to get back out again. People will bring their families to Little Japan – for the decent living conditions and the long yen. And they'll settle here forever.

The town will change: they'll clear it of rubbish and scrap metal, cover the roads with durable asphalt that you can sleep on in summer, throw up lots of new apartment blocks (so there'll be room for the huge numbers of workers who'll pour in from all over the country), and carry out Euro-standard repairs in all the old flats. They'll stick up heaps of neon and holographic signs all over the place. To replace the old House of Culture, they'll build a colossal amusement centre in the shape of an immense tortoise with a shell made of mirrors. Millions of different-coloured lights will be reflected in millions of panes of glass in a berserk rainbow...

I flew on through night-time Petrochemist for about fifteen minutes, until I came out onto waste ground. Further on the factories began. Broken machinery standing along a wall: trucks with no wheels, bulldozers with no caterpillar tracks, even combine harvesters. The locals have named this place the Kursk Bulge. An ideal place for shooting a film about the world after a nuclear war.

And you'll see, someday I'm going to shoot my own low-budget movie in our town! I can borrow the equipment from PetrochemTV, since I know people there. For props I can buy toy pistols that fire caps. (In his first film, *El Mariachi*, Robert Rodriguez actually used water pistols.) The storyline won't be any problem; we'll do a remake of some action movie like *Lunar Cop* with Michael Pare and Billy Drago. And then it will become a cult movie and do the rounds in movie-freak circles. Oblivion deserves to have a film made in it.

At one spot there was a huge cross in a circle daubed in red paint on a factory wall, with an inscription below it: THE DOCTORS SEE EVERYTHING! Immediately after the end of the wall was the Krivitsky Ravine with its stone bridge. I stopped on the bridge and glanced over the parapet.

Down below was a street of identical single-storey buildings dimly lit up by street lamps. How long it was since the last time I'd shown up here!

I ran along the edge of the ravine until I found the rickety wooden steps, ran down them and knocked at the door of a small house of battered and chipped grey brick.

"Hello, I've come to see Ivan!" I shouted when a woman's voice, dispirited by obesity and age, asked: "Who's there?"

A minute later Ivan himself appeared on the porch.

"Well, look who it is!" he said in an unfriendly voice.

"A prick on a dish," I replied. "Cheers, Ferret."

"Hi... Crybaby," the bass-player said cautiously: since Adenoma broke up, I'd always called him by his real name.

Ferret is a typical Petrochemist abortion. An altogether revolting specimen, which is immediately obvious from just his appearance. As skinny as death, with his mouth half-open in a contemptuous smirk, his head covered with short hair that always stands up on end. Green teeth full of cavities. Smokes like a chimney, and smokes any old garbage – the mere sight of an ashtray stuffed with butts sets him gasping and rubbing his hands in glee.

"Why don't we take a stagger?" I suggested. "We'll have a beer."

"You talk as if you wanted to buy me one?" Ferret said with a sour grin.

"I do." I knew how to bribe this ghoul.

Ferret disappeared and came back in a hoodie with the inscription: "Punk`s not dead".

"Let's travel, Crybaby."

We set out.

"Don't you think walking round Petro at night in a hoodie like that might not be a very good idea?" I enquired as we walked along.

"That's nothing, take a look here." The bass-player stopped and turned his flea-bitten head so I could see the weighty earring shaped like a double-bladed axe that was dangling from his left ear.

"Amusing," I agreed. "Do you wear a bra too?"

"Naff off..." Ferret retorted sluggishly.

"I'm telling you: with an earring and that hoodie, you're a dead cert kamikaze."

"Yeah, sure," the kamikaze chuckled. "Now I'll show you what else I've got."

He took a little pistol out of his back pocket – single-shot from the look of it.

"Is it real?"

"Sure it is!"

"Where'd you dig it up?"

"It was a present. The pistol and four rounds, I've got a friend who's a gunsmith. He's only your age, but he's a professional. When he was a kid, he used to make all sorts of knives, swords, darts, shurikens, nunchakus, sais and other Japanese knick-knacks. When he got a bit older, he moved on to bows, crossbows and nail guns, he learned how to alter gas pistols to take a live round. Now that's how he earns his living. And once he found an old revolver on a rubbish tip and made it into this 'cricket'."

"How do you come to know him?"

"You know... We got friendly on the way to a Dynamo-Rotor match. We were travelling on the same dogs."

In his ape language the last word meant a train. Apart from everything else, Ferret is a football fan.

"The scrapes that guy's got into!" he went on after he put the little pistol back in his pocket and the two of us were trudging up steps that were on the point of total collapse. "It's hard to believe moronic stuff like that happens in real life. There was this time when he was hitching from Peter to Kiev and he came across an abandoned factory. It was the back of beyond, the nearest village was about thirty kilometres away. He decided to make one of his oldest dreams come true and hold a paint ball tournament in the place. He got five of his friends together and another friend bankrolled them all, rented a minibus and the equipment. Well, you know, what kind of tournament can you have with six people? They rang round everyone they knew in different towns, and in the end a hundred guys showed up with their equipment. They divided up into two teams and had an almighty shootout."

Once we were out of the ravine, we made a halt at a kiosk, and I supplied us both with beer.

"Right then. They're on their way home along the backwoods roads. And they pass this village, not even a village, just a heap of shit: everyone's alcoholic and there are marriages between close relatives, so the kids are all total retards. A few kilometres from this village there's a military base. Soldiers bloated from hunger, guarding some huts or other. The oldest lads from the village had developed the cute habit of running over to the base and swapping food for the soldier's guns and ammunition. They kept on swapping until they were armed to the teeth. Just imagine it: fifteen retards with submachine guns! Terrifying! They opened fire on the minibus, because they wanted to rob the guys, or maybe they just wanted to have a bit of fun. They did for the driver and three other lads, and the other three, who survived, abandoned the bus and legged it. And then, when they'd gathered their wits a bit, they weighed up the odds and went back. "

"And killed all the retards," I concluded.

"Precisely."

I would have had doubts about this fairytale if not for that freak with the long arms I'd seen the day before on the waste lot. Buggering hell! The things that happen in this world!

"I see your future, brother – it is murder..." I sang sadly.

"What song's that?"

"It's from the film, *Natural Born Killers*. You haven't seen it, of course... I just wanted to ask: have you already tried your toy in action?"

"Not yet. I told you, I've only got four rounds. I don't want to waste them for nothing."

"So you're keeping them for special occasions? You mean you could drop someone if you had to?"

"No problem," the creep answered without even thinking for a second.

"Not some lousy freak, a normal person. Get the cricket out. Have you got it? Well done. Could you drop me, for instance?"

"What the fuck for?" Ferret enquired perfectly reasonably.

We were standing on the bridge. Not a living soul anywhere near us.

"Just imagine: I'm your enemy." I grabbed his hand with the gun in it and lifted it up, setting the barrel of the pistol against my forehead. "Can you press the trigger?"

Ferret tried to free his hand, but I wouldn't let him.

"Ferret, I'm your enemy. If you don't shoot, you're a goner. You'll die a crude and messy death."

"Crybaby... This is... Stop it!"

"Shoot, or you're done for!" I said, squeezing his hand as hard as I could.

"Stop it!"

"What, dumped in your pants, have you? Shoot, you crud! Coward! Chicken shit!" I almost shouted. "I'll press the thing for you myself!"

"That's enough!" my scrawny companion shouted hoarsely. I could feel his hand trembling.

I opened my hands. Ferret took a step back, away from me.

"Crybaby, you're off your trolley."

"So what are you, normal?"

He suddenly burst out laughing and gave me a slap on the shoulder:

"You'll drive me into the grave with these gags of yours."

I smiled – the smile probably came out a bit sour.

"If only my brother had had a little shooter like that, he'd still be alive now."

"What happened to your brother? I know he was killed ten years ago..."

"Twelve," I corrected him.

"You told me about it, but you never mentioned any details!"

I never had told Ferret about it, but now I really wanted to tell him a story like the one he'd just told me.

I sat on the parapet of the bridge.

"My brother Sanya was killed when he was fifteen. I've kept the notebooks Sanya used to write his diary in, I know them off by heart. So I can easily picture what the situation was like in those days. Even now in Petrochemist, the young thugs are like cockroaches. There are always fights, sometimes they shoot a bit, but it's kindergarten stuff compared with what it was like back them. You know Petrochemist used to be a workers' settlement. And there was an entire neighbourhood left over from the settlement, they used to call it the Quarter. And the Quarter was the last area to be demolished, about five years ago. You remember that, probably..."

At this point the Bus Driver – the third of our town's major attractions, went dashing past us. Filthy, tattered coat and cap, slobbery beard, wide-open mouth... The Bus Driver circled this way and that on the bridge for a long time, entirely focused on pretending that he was driving. This gent normally "rides" around near some school or other, delighting in the wild roars of laughter pouring out of all the windows.

"Well then," I continued. "There was a real war going on between the 'town boys' and the 'quarter lads'. Not just a few skirmishes or fights here and there, but genuine military operations. That is, every evening after school the quarter lads and the town boys gathered into two crowds, got drunk, armed themselves with clubs and knuckledusters and set off deliberately to smash each other's heads in. At least, that's the way it's all described in Sanya's diary. Both sides declared war and introduced universal conscription. It was just like in the black ghettoes: if you're not a member of the gang, you're no one. Although it's all voluntary, of course. You can stay out of all the gang battles, but if you're going home late one evening and suddenly there's a brigade of quarter lads coming towards you, no one's going to help you. So whether you like it or not, you have to stick with your own. Which makes it obvious why Sanya's diary is so dark – there are lots of gloomy poems in it, and one very gloomy story. It's clumsily written, of course – Sanya was only fifteen. But I like to reread it every now and then. It's about this boy who discovered a tribe of little gnomes in the garden, and moved them into an empty fish tank at home. He forced them to amuse him and put on all sorts of performances. And if any of them refused, he killed them. Twisted their heads off."

Even though I'd got right off the subject, Ferret didn't interrupt. He sat beside me on the parapet and listened closely, nodding. He didn't even take any swigs out of his bottle.

"Anyway, my brother Sanya decided to keep well out of the battles. And so did his friend Kostik. They stuck with each other, and only went out together. They were forced to carry metal bars with them, and then they even got the idea of knocking up some little bombs for themselves. So one day Kostik and Sanya were walking home together from their girlfriends' places, and they were taking a long detour, through the construction sites, and didn't they run into three slobs from the Quarter. Without a second thought, my brother took out a bomb, lit the fuse and got ready to throw it. Then that idiot Kostik went dashing at them with his rod. Sanya hesitated, and the bomb exploded in his hand. That's all."

Ferret carried on nodding for a long time, then swigged on his bottle and said, without looking at me:

"A terrible business."

"You're telling me. I remember the way he died, with his hand blown off, and his face all black... Ferret, it's... I came to see you on business."

"What business is that?"

"There's going to be a concert this Friday at the Star. Do you fancy singing a couple of songs?"

He looked into my face and nodded:

"I might. What kind of concert is it?"

"I dunno, some kind of garbage to mark Friday the Thirteenth. What difference does it make? I just wanted a bit of a blast from the past. Maybe you'd fancy that too?"

"Yes, sure, sure. Have you already booked us in?"

"Of course. We won't have time to suss out anything new. We can play *Mendeleev Rock* and *The Final Day*, for instance."

"What line-up have we got?"

"The minimum – you, me and someone on drums."

"Buddha won't agree, that's a dead cert."

"It's all right, we'll figure something out."

"So what name have you booked us under?"

W-e-e-e-ll now, I thought. *You disappoint me, Ferret. Where were you when God was handing out the brains?* But out loud I said just one word:

"Adenoma."

That got through to him. Ferret opened and closed the garbage tip that everyone mistakenly took for a mouth a couple of times, and finally came up with this:

"You mean you want to revive the band?"

"So far all I want to do is play a couple of numbers in a concert to mark Friday the Thirteenth. After that, we'll see."

"Okay, Rom, it'll all be just great." It felt like I'd found some secret switch in Ferret's squalid little soul, because my freak-ugly bass-man suddenly lit up like a light bulb.

"Anyway, you stomp off home and get everything ready. We're meeting tomorrow evening at eight in your garage. And listen, Ferret, one final question. I saw this monster over on the waste ground... Like a human being, only with long arms, like a macaque, and a little head, all wrapped in rags from head to foot."

"You know who that is? That's Guerukha!" Ferret exclaimed with an insane kind of excitement. "Fuck it, Crybaby, I thought it was nothing but a wild story!"

"What Guerukha do you mean?"

"Someone told me about him... Supposedly this perfectly normal family had a son who was a monster, morally and physically. They raised him until he was 11, and then he ran off and he lives on the dump. They tell all sorts of horrible stories about him: like, he snatches little kids off parents who don't keep a proper lookout."

"But why 'Guerukha'?"

"Well, they say mummy and daddy called him Guerman."

6.   [initial developmental period]

Next morning (Tuesday), as I was hurrying to get to my first two classes, Oleg stopped me right there in the doorway.

"Roman, I want to have a talk with you."

Our Oleg is a well-groomed, laid-back little chap with aristocratic manners. He wears a little goatee beard, smokes an ebony pipe and smacks his lips irritatingly with every phrase he speaks.

In male company he's very fond of spinning all sorts of stories. The main features of his programme have always been two unlikely tales. One about a visit to an American pub, where, as a minor under the laws of the United States, he had to resort to all sorts of tricks to convince the waitress that he was twenty-one. And the other was a heartrending story about how he went to visit his friends at their dacha, and the first thing they did was send him off to swelter in the bathhouse with a naked girl – that was the way they used to test rookies. And he, being a true gentleman, was obliged to think about the Great Patriotic War and dead kittens, instead of simply enjoying a good steam as usual. And all he got for his pains was a sneering remark from the girl: "My, aren't you the reserved one. A real aristocrat!"

My comment was: "If I ever see a naked girl in the bathhouse, I won't hold myself back. I'll say: 'Mmmm, right... THIS IS REAL HOSPITALITY!' And then I'll add: 'I'm sorry, I left my condoms in my jacket. I'll just run and get them.' And if she starts trying to explain that she's not going to pleasure me, I'll put on an idiotic face and ask: 'If we're not going to get intimate, what are you doing here?' After that I'll make myself comfortable and start masturbating."

Oleg, who couldn't stand coarseness, frowned and said: "You really don't understand. She was my host's daughter. If I'd given way to my feelings, it would have been the end of our friendship." "So what? That's his problem," I retorted.

"So what have you got to say to me, honourable colleague?" I asked Oleg when he stopped me.

"It concerns you and Christina."

Oh yes, exactly as I thought. Of course, the first thing Christina had done was call Oleg, complain about me and ask him to influence me, talk to me man-to-man. Honest to God, what a person to turn to! But then, there wasn't anyone else. Where I study, guys are a scarce commodity, most of the students are dolls. I think if a genuine feminist ever visited our college, she'd leave with tears of happiness in her eyes. Girls are first in everything, and the young guys are all modest, polite and pretty passive. That's the way the population of our planet will look in many years' time, when the ordinary Russian male degenerates and finally becomes extinct. If only I could live to see it!

The full title of my college is "The Private College of the Humanities for the Gifted". The title makes it clear that mediocrities like me have no right being here. Sure, I made it through the external written entrance exam, got a high place in the internal exam, but the programme here is designed for people who have already read all the Russian and foreign classics before they leave school, who know two or three foreign languages, and are on intimate terms with a computer... In other words, it's not enough to be a good student and to study, you have to *live* to study.

Of course, I fitted in as well as I could, but even now on the French and German days (that is, the days when all the students have to speak a foreign language), I shrink back into the corners, like a poor relative. It's entirely logical that I wound up in this institution after school – that repulsive snake pit, swarming with young thugs, druggies and little whores (in other words, it was Petrochemist in miniature).

Oleg prodded me in the chest with the stem of his pipe (another repulsive habit of his) and said severely:

"Christina is a very good girl."

"So who's arguing?" I agreed readily.

"You treat her like I don't know who. (*Do you really know what you're talking about?* I thought.) But, you know, she wants to make a man out of you."

"Yes, that's what she wants... But has she ever asked what I want?" The semantic emphasis in the final phrase was on "I".

"I is an insignificant little letter."

Well, you don't say! I chuckled to myself.

"You know, she forgives you for so much! And you take advantage of that. That's not right. If Christina was my girl, I'd treat her like a princess!"

If she was your girl, you'd be ashamed to leave the house with her! As if I don't know you and I've never seen your women!

"Oleg, stop throwing meaningless phrases around. Let's suppose I agree with you. What is it you want from me?"

Oleg sucked on his pipe and declared:

"You have to apologise to her."

"I have to? I don't have to do anything for anyone, especially for you, my dear sir."

Oleg smacked his lips in astonishment.

"What's it got to do with me?"

"Precisely, nothing. You're getting involved in something that's not exactly your business."

"Roman, I'm trying to help you solve your problems!" said Oleg, getting heated. Calmness, politeness and deadly sarcasm are impeccable devices for raising someone's temper to boiling point.

"I don't have any problems, where did you get that idea?

"It's just that I think you ought to apologise to Christina."

Our Oleg had obviously recalled the golden rule of all inquisitors and orthodox communists: if a man doesn't want to be happy, he has to be helped.

"I already tried. Yesterday. She wouldn't listen and she ran off."

"So you didn't apologise properly. Try again."

"And what's going to happen if I don't? Are you going to take me to court or challenge me to a duel?"

"Who gave you any right to treat Christina like this?"

"And who gave you any right to stick your nose in where it's not wanted?"

"No one! Roman, you're a disgusting brute!" Oleg declared in annoyance. "Christina's my best friend! I like her a lot, unlike you."

"You mean you want your good friend to date a disgusting brute?"

"Christina is very honest and decent, and she'll make you the same. You'll never find another girl like her anywhere."

"All right, dear colleague, I'll do everything in my power," I said, adding to myself: *Just get off my back.*

I swung open the heavy door and walked through the turnstile. I said hello to the security guard:

"Cheers, Artyom!"

He saluted me lazily with his truncheon. I give a special vote of thanks to the founder of the College for Artyom: no lowlife is ever going to creep inside without permission from this good-natured athlete, who looks a lot like Olivier Gruner. (And don't ask who Olivier Gruner is!)

I tiptoed through into the auditorium where the lecture on twentieth-century foreign literature was going on and sat down at a free desk. The girls started glancing round at me: I always sit with Christina – in the middle of the back row. We have a jolly time in class; we write notes to each other (Christina has even acquired a special notepad for that), we draw little hearts and flowers for each other in our notebooks, and sometimes we lick each other, when the lecturer turns away towards the blackboard – and we still manage to take notes on the lecture.

In a year and a half, the entire college has come to know about our touching relationship. Christina found it flattering (and so did I – why hide the fact!) that they talked about us, set us up as an example, envied us. Naturally, an outside observer couldn't even imagine the god-awful beastliness that went on when the curtain of this theatre for juveniles came down and the "ideal couple" were left alone together. That's probably the main reason why my affair with Christina has dragged on for so long: breaking up with a girl is one thing, but destroying a beautiful legend is something else again. Especially since the other girls in our group, who have been initiated into the secret of the "ideal relationship", do everything possible to preserve the legend.

After the lecture Christina, speaking in a low voice and staring down at the floor, suggested we go out into the corridor and talk.

I knew what was going to happen.

Christina has this special quirk: she thinks she's terribly

ugly. Because of her little eyes, her thick lips, her hips that are too broad (or so she thinks) and for all sorts of other reasons too. So when she spotted me, by no means the stupidest of guys and not even slightly ugly, she grabbed me and hung on like grim death. Christina's girlfriends and friends (that Oleg, for instance) think her appearance is pleasant enough, but absolutely ordinary in every way. And since, in their opinion, your humble servant is also in no way outstanding, Christina and I make an ideal couple. And so, no matter what happens, we have to stay together.

A particularly nice touch was the way Christina had called me a monster the day before. That meant that now she was going to repent loudly. She's terribly afraid of losing me – that's her best quality (and her worst failing).

We moved across to the window, which offered a marvellous view of a heating main that had been dug up.

"Roma... Don't you want to talk to me? I've offended you, have I?"

"Have you only just guessed?"

"Forgive me..."

Yes, yes, first she raises hell, then she tries creeping back and soft-soaping. The last time we quarrelled was last week. I suggested going to the Star on Friday, to a gig by a touring band, Interval, who sing cover versions of Beatles songs. But my treasure replied with a laugh: "As if I'd go anywhere with a scruffy lout like you!" After that it took her about an hour to persuade me that she was joking. A brilliant sense of humour! We didn't go to the concert anyway, in the end. And we were right not to – I found out later that it was cancelled. Because they hadn't sold many tickets. Interval had definitely picked the wrong town.

"I have something to say to you, Christie," I said harshly.

"No, no..." Christina started muttering, the way she usually does when she thinks I'm going to dump her. And every time for the last year and a half it's always come as a total surprise, as unexpectedly as Doomsday.

"Shut up and listen," I said.

Christina looked at me pitifully and sobbed, shaking all over.

"Monster, scruffy lout, idiot, oaf, oversexed stud with a stunted prick... Have I forgotten anything?" I asked acidly. "Do you think I really enjoy hearing all that every day?"

"I'm just stupid... " Christina sobbed. "Forgive me..."

Aha, she humiliates me at every opportunity, and now she's humiliating herself!

"How many times do I have to forgive you?"

"But I love you..." said Christina, deploying her main argument.

So that's it. Could you give a girl the crude brush-off if she's looking at you with tear-stained eyes and telling you she loves you? Say what you like, but it's nice to know at least someone cares for me!

"You're really good and quite lovely, Christie, but... I need to take a break from you. Let's talk in a week's time."

Christie hastily wiped away her tears and nodded with a smile on her face.

"Let everything stay just the same as ever," I suggested. "But we'll only see each other here, in the College."

You should have seen that happy face! As if it hadn't been streaming with tears only thirty seconds ago! Ah, women...

Christina touched my cheek with her finger. I didn't react at all. She repeated the gesture and stamped her heel. I had to kiss her on the cheek.

"That's enough for now," I said. "All in good time."

Christina nodded. We separated, feeling pleased with each other. She had convinced herself yet again that I wouldn't dare leave her, and I had gained a week to put my plan into action. If it didn't work out, Christina would still be there, in reserve.

In the evening I called round to see Anya before work. On the way I met Mystery Man and read a fresh inscription in red paint on an advertisement hoarding: IF YOU'RE AN "INDEPENDENT", SAVE US THE TROUBLE AND SHOOT YOURSELF.

She opened the door herself, in a pair of old patched trousers, house slippers and a sweater covered with pellets of fluff.

"Ah, here's our heroic lover! Come on in."

I took my shoes off. She showed me through into her little room, crammed with jars of pickled cucumbers, sauerkraut and oats. The desk was piled with small grey sacks, wrinkled pieces of dried apples sticking out through tears in the material. There were wooden boxes hiding under the bed, still bearing wax seals with pieces of string sticking out of them. Under the window, leaning against the radiator, was a bicycle. Standing upright in the corner were fishing rods and skis.

"My parents cleared the balcony, they want to make it into another room," Anya explained with a guilty laugh. "And they dragged all the junk in here. They didn't know I was going to come back suddenly, out of the blue!"

"I just dropped in for a moment, Anya."

"I understand. I found out a few things about your princess from Natasha. Her real name is Tanya, but she likes to be called..."

"Priscilla. I know."

"She's seventeen and she's an external student at the College of the Humanities. She works in the flower shop on Concord Street. So what do you intend to do, now that you have this information?"

"I have a little idea in mind. Can you get a note to her via Natasha?"

"Let's assume I can. Pardon my curiosity, but have you really got any idea what you're doing?" Anya asked with a frown.

"I reckon so."

"A half-assed Don Juan, that's what you are!"

"Why half-assed?"

"Because you're always on the hunt for girls, but your taste is nothing like Don Juan's. You know what, Crybaby... I tell you, quite sincerely, I don't understand what it is you see in her. She's no beauty by a long way. In fact, I'd say she's pretty average all round. You weren't drunk at all that evening, were you?"

"I don't go in for that nonsense, you know that."

"You're an original, Crybaby. I don't think any hunk in his right mind would go after her."

I can't bear to be called that! That word immediately makes me think of something coarse and bestial, soaked in drink.

"Anya! Do you see any hunk here? Let alone in his right mind?"

"Crybaby, don't play with words. So what did you write in the note?"

"That on Friday there's going to be a concert at the Star to mark Friday the Thirteenth and, apart from everything else, Adenoma will be there to knock out a couple of numbers. She's certain to come."

"What do you mean, Adenoma?"

You should have seen Anya's face!

"Just what I said."

"You mean, with the old line-up?"

"Pared down a bit. There's a crisis going on, inflation. I'm on guitar, Ferret's on bass, and there'll be someone else on drums."

"What about Ilya? What will it be like without keyboards? And Angie?"

"We'll play the songs that don't need a synthesiser. And Angie's function was always purely decorative."

"But who'll be on drums?"

"I don't know that just yet. It makes no difference. Anyone

who can hammer out a basic rhythm will do, it could be a trained monkey."

"Right, right, I get it. You thought up this whole crazy deal so you could get Tanya?"

"Not only. I want a blast from the past. Even if nothing comes of it, it'll still be a breath of the old times."

"Philanderer, adventurer and braggart." Anya shifted the sacks of dried apples aside, sat down on the desk, with her legs dangling and her arms crossed over her stomach, and looked me up and down sarcastically. "Well, let's suppose I could batter the drums a bit for you. Happy now, you repulsive individual?"

"Do you know how?"

"Me? At Uni we had our own girl's band, it was called Okay Yoko. I tried playing the guitar in it, and the drums, and even singing. I can do a bit of everything. I don't suppose I'll have to do a half-hour drum solo?"

"No, it'll just be the usual. Come to the bridge over the Krivitsky Ravine at eight this evening. I'll meet you there."

Anya shrugged:

"For my good buddy – even the ring out of my ear."

For some reason I recalled the composition she once wrote on Fadeev's novel *The Rout*. It was read out for analysis or, rather, abuse by the entire class. Anya tried to demonstrate that the coward and traitor Mechik was really the only positive character in the book, because he was the only one who wasn't afraid to challenge the collective, and the collective is always a crowd of thick-headed idiots, and by definition anyone who tries to survive outside the collective is a hero... Anyway, how could our literature teacher, an old communist, possibly have tolerated this outrageous mockery of her system of universal human values? On that day Anya fought back as hard as she could and earned a "D minus" for her disrespect of the teacher, but she still stuck to her own opinion. Supergirl!

I showed up for work in an excellent mood.

I only work four evenings a week. And the work I do only takes half an hour: I look through the typeset columns on the computer with a fresh eye, to find and correct any mistakes, hand on the copy to the shaggy-haired page-maker, who's hyped-up after drinking litres of coffee, read the newly typeset pages again, say goodbye and leave. I only got the job because Christina insisted on it, and all my meagre pay goes on her.

But, of course, that was never enough for my insatiable little beast... "Why are you afraid of earning money?" – she dripped that question into my brains day after day, like acid, and she always brought up one of the girls in our group, who once boasted about her admirer: "We went to such-and-such a restaurant, and such-and-such a bowling alley, and he paid for me and my girl friends... he spent fifteen thousand roubles on me in two days!" In Christina's opinion, I should have dashed off somewhere straightaway and started making a career for myself. As a journalist, for instance. "You like writing things..." Iron feminine logic, every bit as good as army logic. ("An artist? Go and paint that stool!"). Of course, I do write the occasional short article for our *Evening Petrochemist...* But Christina wants me to do it professionally and illuminate, for instance, the political events in our town. "Stay close to the local authorities, that's where all the news is! Build up experience, and then when you leave, you'll be able to get a job in some regional publication..."

Pardon me for asking, joy of my life, but exactly why would I want to do that? So that you, or some other painted doll can bat her eyelashes and announce: "He spent so many thousands of roubles on me"? Why earn money, if every last kopeck is going to be sucked out of you by greedy bints? Honestly, I'd rather die of malnutrition and abstinence than that!

But I wouldn't mind doing a bit of work in the library – only about one person an hour shows up there anyway! I'd sit there in the silence, leafing through the books, writing poems for myself, drinking tea and not thinking about what's going on outside the walls. Maybe I'd sleep there as well. Damn the miserable pay – that's not the point. If little Christina knew about my dreams, she'd strangle me with her own hands. Or drive me so crazy with her hysterical fits that I'd hang myself.

7. [initial developmental period]

I don't understand why some people are afraid of the stage. The only thing you can see from the stage is a huge black hole that you have to sing into, which throws out various sounds from time to time, like laughter or applause. If you strain your eyes hard, you can just make out the first row of the audience, but only vaguely. Everything else is concealed by darkness as impenetrable as a wall.

The three of us waited our turn backstage, among all the other participants in the concert entitled "An Evening of Horrors". This spectacle was taking place on the same stage where the pastor and the "songs of praise group" from the Church of the White Angels had performed. Basically, apart from the MC's costume (the MC was Natasha, she's the mainstay of the entire House of Culture) and a plywood stage set of the walls of a Gothic castle, the occasion had absolutely nothing at all to do with Friday the Thirteenth.

To judge from the rumble of applause after every act, the hall was packed full of young people: some had come to support their friends, others were just whiling the time away before the discotheque, which was due to start straight after the show.

Ferret was finishing off a slobbery cigarette butt, grinning repulsively. (Yesterday I'd told him: "You bastard, you get a skinful before the show, and you'll be picking up your smashed-out teeth with broken arms".) Anya was standing there with a blank expression, leaning against the wall.

I stared hard at myself in the mirror. I was wearing a brown, sleeveless T-shirt, two brown bracelets, one on each wrist, my hair was tied black with a black ribbon (my thanks to that sly guy with the narrow eyes for an excellent idea!) and on my left cheek I'd drawn a streak of black makeup like the one Liza "Left Eye" Lopez from the girls' band TLC had (God rest her soul). If Priscilla was there in the hall, nothing could save her.

After yet another number – it was an Irina Saltykova song performed by kids from eleventh grade ("An Evening of Horrors" was the right name for the show, all right) – Natasha, wearing a long black dress a la Ma Addams and long black artificial nails, announced:

"At our concert this evening we have as our guests a group with a highly... how can I put it... unusual, even unforgettable name – Adenoma!" (Peals of laughter ran round the hall.)

I flew out on stage with my guitar on a strap, holding the wah-wah pedal in my hands and the plectrum in my teeth, connected up the guitar, ran the plectrum over the strings and signed to the sound engineer to turn up the volume.

Silence fell in the black hole in front of where I was standing, everybody even stopped whispering to each other.

On my left Ferret jangled the strings of the bass guitar and nodded to me: everything's fine. I glanced round – behind me Anya was frozen over the drums with the sticks in her hands.

"Hi, everyone!" I shouted into the microphone and stepped on the wah-wah pedal. "All right, shall we get wild?"

Anya immediately lashed into the drums and I lashed into my strings. We played *The Final Day* – a pretty straightforward punk rock number, but with plenty of drive.

> *Your former cosy little life*
> *Has been forever shattered,*
> *And memories of happy times*
> *Are melting in the acid.*

Arise and dress, be on your way,
For this is your final day!
Your final battle has arrived,
You will not leave the field alive!

In the suffocating heat
The towns and cities choke and die
And human souls evaporate
And fade into the empty sky.

And then the refrain again:

Arise and dress, be on your way,
For this is your final day!
Your final battle has arrived,
You will not leave the field alive!

While I sang (although I was yelling out the words rather than singing), two or three cameras flashed in the hall. Every now and then I glanced round at Ferret – he was standing sideways on to the audience, fairly well back on the stage.

On your clothes the blood has dried
Your fists are bruised and aching
And still as ever, there outside,
Your deadly foe is waiting.

The refrain rang out for the third time and the song was over in less than two minutes. As soon as our instruments fell silent, the audience started roaring in ecstasy.

Our songs had always got that kind of response in Petrochemist, not because we were the best around, but because we were the only ones. Apart from us, no one in the entire town played anything that you could really get off on and cut loose.

"Thank you!" I roared. "That was the song *The Final Day*, and now – *Mendeleev Rock*!"

Another hammering song with incredibly dark words to it.

That's the only kind I write. It's my very first, it even mentions my age at the time.

> *At fifteen I can still be found*
> *Ignoring all the world around,*
> *Living my life in this stinking town,*
> *Russian salad instead of a brain,*
> *And my enemies always remain*
> *Alert, trying to break me down,*
> *Corroding my skin with invisible flame.*
> *Do you want me to tell you their names?*
> *Copper, cadmium and bromine,*
> *Mercury, caesium and chlorine,*
> *Rubidium and plutonium*
> *Magnesium and zirconium,*
> *And their faithful ally, lead,*
> *They all just want to see me dead.*

We got done inside the five minutes allocated to us and ran offstage. I just had time to shout: "Thank you! Adenoma loves you!", but I don't think anyone could have made out the words through the wild applause.

"Yes! Yes! Yes!" Ferret yelled in the changing room, jumping up and down, as if he was on springs. "Give me five, Romka!"

"Ten if you like!" I answered, and then I simply scooped him up with one arm and happy Anya with the other, and squeezed them up against me. It was as if I'd fallen through time back to two years earlier – the last time I'd felt so high.

"Anya, how you doing?" I asked?

"Just great, Crybaby!" said Anya, giving me a friendly punch to the stomach.

We got dressed and left the changing room. They were already waiting for us backstage. I'd never have expected to see Critter at an event like this.

Petrochemist's most famous punk had got his nickname two years earlier, thanks to me. I once called him "nibbler" – after this film about ugly aliens that was called *Critters* in English. Critter had small, pointed teeth, like nails.

In the two years that had passed since Adenoma's last concert, he hadn't changed at all – he was still wearing his leather jacket with hundreds of rivets on it, his "Iroquois" hairstyle, consisting of spikes of hair glued together with lacquer, and the same T-shirt with a picture of Yegor Letov. (He used to go to school every day looking like that and sometimes, to give his nerves a real thrill, he even went to discos like that, but even so he was still alive and relatively well.) And he hadn't grown. His nose was still on the same level as my solar plexus. According to my reckoning, he ought to be about fifteen now, and I'll be seriously surprised if this enfant terrible lives to be twenty. I know one thing: even at his age he's already tried every combustible liquid and pharmaceutical preparation that can possibly be obtained in our town. Critter and self-destruction aren't just on close terms, they're bosom buddies. One summer he carved this kind of pattern on the outside of his arms with an ordinary knife, ten identical lines from the wrist to the elbow. It made him look like a tiger. He has no complexes at all. Once during break-time one of his classmates said to him: "Dare you to take out your doodads and shake them about! For two bottles of beer." "Where's the beer?" Critter asked, seriously interested. "Here it is." Two seductive glass receptacles suddenly glittered in the bright light of day. "And here are the doodads," Critter answered, unfastening his tattered trousers and performing all the manipulations required.

"How come you're here, Critter?" I asked.

I had to repeat the question twice: Critter's been hard of hearing since someone smashed him over the head with a tyre spanner in a fight.

"I just wandered in..." he said, slowly forcing every word

out, with an odd hissing sound. "To pick up this doll... Are you performing again?"

"Aren't we just!" Ferret confirmed with eager delight. "And you tell everyone that!"

Critter nodded.

She appeared behind their backs at the end of the corridor.

My Christmas tree. Priscilla.

She was wearing a short green coat and grey jeans. She took a few steps towards me and stopped, inviting me to come to her.

I immediately left Ferret and Anya to be tormented by Critter and went rushing to the one for whose sake I'd set up today's performance.

"Hi, Priscilla."

"Hi, Crybaby," Priscilla replied. There was this touching vulnerability in her smile, as if she was slightly afraid of me and hoped that smile would disarm me.

"Thanks for coming."

"Thanks for inviting me. So you got back together again after all?"

"Yes, for the time being, but we'll see how it goes. It was your idea, by the way," I reminded her.

"Was it really?" Priscilla asked, smiling in surprise.

"Don't you remember, then?" I asked, moving a step closer to her.

"Vaguely," Priscilla admitted. "I hope I didn't get too lecherous altogether... Will you forgive me?"

"As many times as you like."

The doors of the hall opened. The concert was over and they were driving the audience out of the House of Culture, in order to let them back in again, but this time for cash.

"The disco's about to get started, there'll be all sorts of freaks crowding in. Let's go!" I took Priscilla by the hand and led her up the stairs. We walked through a metal door into the second floor, and latched the door shut from the inside. After that we went out onto the gallery that ran under the ceiling of the hall with columns where the discos were held.

The wall of the hall was decorated with a drawing that stretched from the floor to the ceiling, depicting a huge mutant party-animal, dressed in beach shorts and a T-shirt, with two heads that looked like they belonged to eels. Each head was wearing a cap. Long, forked snakes' tongues protruded from the monster's open mouths. In one paw it was clutching an ice-cream, and in the other a CD. An inscription crept round the mutant in the form of an arch: THIS PLACE ISN'T THE PLACE.

This freakish drawing was made by the Star's court graffito artist, who went by the name of Two Heads. Whoever he drew – people, animals or fantastic mutants, they turned out just beautiful, if only you ignored the strange fact that for some inexplicable reason, the artist gave each of them a second head, an exact copy of the first one. Two Head's drawings were phenomenally popular among his friends. And he occasionally got commissions to draw someone's portrait – everybody wanted to see themselves from an unusual point of view.

We glanced over the railing, looking down onto the empty dance floor.

"I've never had any friends who were rock stars before," she confessed. "We are going to be friends, aren't we?"

"We are the stars of our own swamp," I chuckled.

"Well, you know... On the scale of Petrochemist, it's as if the Beatles had got back together!"

"Do you like the Beatles?"

"Very much!"

"Who's your favourite?"

"The quiet Beatle. George."

"Do you like mysticism too?"

"I like all sorts of things. Are you going to play again?"

"Looks like we'll have to, doesn't it?"

"I remember you had a girl on backup vocals..." from the way she said that, it sounded like Priscilla was about to make a move on me.

"Yes, she had to leave."

"Well, do you need a new vocalist?"

And isn't it you I've been looking for all this time? I was thinking in the meantime. I could sense Priscilla was totally crazy about me. For the first time in my life I was standing beside a girl for whom I was the ideal. Before this, all they'd done was try to make me fit an ideal that existed apart from me, the way Christina was always doing. I actually believe that Christina wishes me well (although she wishes herself well first and foremost), but has she ever once asked what I want myself?

"So you only vaguely remember what happened then?" I pulled Priscilla towards me and kissed her passionately. "Shall I remind you?" The next kiss was longer. Priscilla wound her arms round my neck and we kissed until our lips got tired. I don't know how many hours went by: we fell out of time.

After that I held Priscilla calmly in my arms, swaying her gently. And looking into the hall over her shoulder. Down there, the disco had been going on for a long time already. The techno music hammered away furiously in the speakers and hundreds of figures jerking about in a wild dance cast hectic shadows on the walls. The techno suddenly broke off. Apparently the DJ had been asked rather crudely to put on something more cheerful for the masses. After a short pause, Tatyana Bulanova's voice started singing.

I spotted seven young dudes in the corner of the hall, separate from the main mass of people. Five of them were standing in a tight knot and seemed to be talking, but they were actually shielding the other two from everybody else in the hall – only not from me, because I was looking down from the ceiling. Those two were working on a girl from the senior class in school: one was holding her arms bent behind her back, and the other was feverishly fumbling for something under her little top. Then he pulled the top right up to her neck and stuck his ugly snout against her bare breast. The girl opened her mouth to scream, staring up at the ceiling with wide-open eyes full of despair, but her scream was drowned out. The young guy unfastened his trousers, stuck his hand up under the girl's skirt, deftly pulled off her panties and threw them aside. Then he lifted his victim up by the legs, pulled them apart with an expert movement, set the girl on his protruding member and started jerking about.

Priscilla distracted me from my contemplation of the scene.

"Let's clear out," she suggested. "It's too loud in here."

"Let's go," I agreed.

Surprisingly enough, I didn't feel the slightest sympathy for that unfortunate little girly. Put on something that covers you but doesn't hide a thing, and show up like that at a disco full of boozed-up teenagers – what could be more stupid than that? And stupidity, as everyone knows, never goes unpunished. I never could understand and I still can't, just what it is that these fragile little flowers are hoping for? That everyone will take pity on them and not pull them up by the roots, or trample them down, like weeds?

We set off deeper into the House of Culture.

"Let's find another way out!" said Priscilla. "Is there another exit here?"

"I reckon there ought to be. And I reckon I can imagine where it is."

We turned a corner and wandered into a dead end. The corridor ended in a wall with no windows and a single door that led into a cleaner's cubicle – a tiny little room with a sink.

There were empty buckets in there, and rags that stank of chlorine hanging up to dry on the pipes.

"Everything's just fine, follow me," I said. I walked into the room and found another little door, so small that I could only get through it sideways.

A narrow little corridor led us out into darkness. I spent a long time fumbling at the walls, trying to find a light switch, and when I found one, we discovered we were on the landing of a staircase.

"Let's go."

Priscilla held my hand tight between her palms.

We walked down to the ground floor: the door was locked. The stairs carried on downwards.

"Hmm, I didn't even know there was a basement in this building..." Priscilla muttered.

We walked down into the basement. The basement was a corridor too – a long one, cluttered with skis, sleighs, ice hockey sticks and other sporting lumber. Water pipes stretched all the way along the corridor, up under the ceiling.

The corridor was much longer than the actual building of the House of Culture.

"You know that legend, do you?" I asked.

"What legend?"

"Rumour has it that fifty years ago, after the war, when there weren't even any plans to build Petrochemist yet, on the spot where the town stands now, they built an underground town to use if there was a Third World War. They say some of the buildings in Petro are built right over shafts that lead straight to that town. Somewhere underneath us there are immense bunkers crammed with military equipment, an underground railway, residential areas, reservoirs."

"Is this reliable information?"

"Not really... Just an urban legend."

"Let's organise an expedition some time!"

"You're just full of great ideas today," I remarked. "They also say that everyone who ever tried to find that town either came back empty-handed or never came back at all. So there."

"But what's so dangerous there?"

"Some say huge swarms of man-eating rats, others say radiation."

"We'll find out everything sometime," said Priscilla. "Just don't say that I'm totally bonkers." She laughed. "Well, maybe I am just a little bit."

"Well, so am I," I admitted honestly. In actual fact, the most normal person I knew was Christina – and I wasn't anything at all like her. In our year and a half together, I hadn't had anything like that crazy stroll on Sunday night. "It's really great that I met you!"

"Destiny..." Priscilla said with a shrug. I immediately pressed her against the wall, and we lingered in the corridor for another half hour or so. Then I forced myself to move on after all.

"I've been wanting to ask you for ages... Why are you Crybaby?"

"An old school nickname."

"But where did it come from?"

"I'll tell you that some time later. A lot later."

The exit from the corridor basement was in the old park, surrounded by withered trees. There were some lights up ahead.

We'd covered half the distance towards those lights, when I froze.

"What?" gasped Priscilla. I immediately put my hand over her mouth.

Rubbish was burning in old garbage bins with flames a metre high dancing over these massive braziers, lighting up an abandoned ice hockey rink. A crowd was standing round the rink – about fifty guys of different ages and sizes. Most of them were on the short side and almost all of them were dressed in red and white with all sorts of variations: for instance, a red cap, a black jacket with a red collar and cuffs and dark tracksuit trousers with white stripes. Lots of them didn't have caps and their billiard-ball-naked heads were exposed to the wind.

"We're really in luck. It's the Doctors..." I whispered.

"The ones who cripple independent types?" Priscilla hissed when I took my hand off her face.

"Uhu..."

There was a loud roar as the whole lousy gang of them bellowed and flung one fist up in the air. The Doctors were greeting a young creep with a pointy face like a rat's, who had walked out into the centre of the rink. He waddled as he walked, with his shoulders slouched so he was almost doubled over, cautiously turning his head this way and that, as if he was sniffing out prey. The only clothes he was wearing were a white-and-red T-shirt and pale-blue jeans.

"We ought to sneak out of here quietly..." I whispered.

"No, come on, let's move a bit closer! I want to watch what's going to happen next!"

"Well, have it your own way." We moved forward and stood behind a thick tree, peeping out from different sides. The closest Doctors, standing with their backs to us, were only five steps away now.

Meanwhile another Doctor had skipped over the barrier and walked out into the arena. He was a bit taller, owing to his long legs, like the legs of a compass, but he was just as skinny: he was made up entirely of hollows – hollow chest, hollow stomach, hollow back between the shoulder blades sticking out under his shirt. This Doctor was wearing a white T-shirt and black fascist trousers with clown's braces.

The spectators roared and howled again, and then fell silent.

Compass took a broad kitchen knife in a cover out of the pocket of his pants. He theatrically bared the blade and flung the cover aside. His opponent, Rat, replied with a click – and the blade of a flick-knife slid out from his fist.

"What is this – Gladiator Wars?" Priscilla asked in a whisper.

"They've fallen out over something. A girl, maybe. I've heard they settle all disagreements within the group this way. Sometimes there can be three or four duels a night."

"Are they going to fight to the death, what do you think?"

"Hardly, most likely to first blood. But it could happen, if they both go berserk. They're animals!"

"A pity we haven't got a camera..." Priscilla whispered. "Fancy having something like this at home on video – to amuse visitors in the evenings."

Rat, small and fidgety, and Compass, as straight as a stick, slowly closed in on each other, circling anti-clockwise, sizing each other up. Compass roared and slashed wildly, backhand, with his broad blade – Rat jumped back out of reach of the blow. Compass jumped forward and sliced through the air, aiming at Rat's snout – Rat dodged away and used his free hand to grab his opponent's wrist. Compass instantly did the same. Locked together, the duellists started circling on the spot, as if they were dancing. They lashed at each other furiously with their feet, swearing obscenely.

"Let's bet. I say the tall one will win!" Priscilla whispered. I nodded.

"Okay. I say the little one will win, my sweet."

Compass pushed Rat away and lunged like a musketeer, pushing his right leg forward. His opponent squirmed out of the way and took a short swing, slicing open the back of Compass's hand – Compass dropped his knife.

Priscilla squeezed my hand tight. I didn't see the expression on her face, because I couldn't take my eyes off the two fighters. Their frenzied, bestial struggle was mesmerising.

Rat attacked, aiming for the stomach, but failed to reach

his target fast enough. Wounded Compass barked and smashed his hefty fish into Rat's teeth: the blow was instinctive, and therefore devastatingly accurate. Rat went flying backwards, but he stayed on his feet. Compass gave Rat a terrifying kick in the chest with one of his pole-legs that ended in the platform sole of a heavy boot. Rat howled as he went tumbling across the dilapidated asphalt surface, and I thought a blow like that had probably broken one or two of his ribs.

Compass dashed across to his opponent, like a footballer running towards the ball, kicked him and then gave a mewling howl when Rat grabbed his opponent's leg with one hand and stuck his flick knife into it right up to the hilt with the other. The lanky Doctor's leg buckled and he collapsed onto one knee. Rat grabbed Compass's T-shirt and jerked him towards himself, meeting him with a powerful blow to the chin that stretched Compass out flat.

Then Rat jumped up as if he was perfectly fine and threw himself on his fallen opponent. Compass squirmed about, pouring blood all over the arena, and Rat kicked him, cursing obscenely. Kicked and kicked and kicked...

At that moment some Doctor who had appeared out of nowhere grabbed hold of my collar, swung me round sharply towards himself and spat in my face, searing my nostrils with the stench of cheap alcohol.

"Spying on us, you bastard?"

I immediately pulled a little flask out of my pocket, said very clearly: "Sorry!" and fired a jet of liquid into the bloated ox's ugly mug. The Doctor collapsed on his knees, pressed both hands to his face and started screeching obscenities at the top of his voice.

Priscilla and I ran as fast as we could, with the hooves of the entire herd already thundering behind us. We came shooting out of the trees at a filthy, polluted pond and started running along the bank. The Doctors were getting closer. They couldn't see us through the darkness and the trees, but there were a horrific number of them, and they were running in various directions, whooping and shouting: "Stop, you cunts!" although they didn't know who these "cunts" were, or how many of them there were.

We made for the densest thickets, I ran ahead, covering my face with my hands to keep the branches of the dead trees from lashing me. We reached a clearing with old roundabouts that had stopped many years ago. In the gloom they looked like flying saucers abandoned by aliens.

I took Priscilla's hand and pulled her onto one of the roundabouts. She resisted, so I simply dragged her in under the rusty roof. We hunkered down behind a rocket on the platform.

The crowd went dashing past us, rumbling and roaring. The whole park was shaking about. Then the roaring and tramping got quieter and quieter. And after about a minute everything went completely quiet.

Priscilla nestled up to me gratefully with her cheek against my jacket. I stroked her hair and kissed her hot face:

"It's all right, my sweet. Everything's going to be just fine."

8.   [initial developmental period]

The outskirts of Petrochemist, a little street of rotten little houses. A gate in a wall, cobbled together out of planks of different lengths, and behind it a path (the width of the sole of a shoe) through thickets of half-withered nettles, three steps up onto a porch, and then an entranceway crammed with rusty buckets, boxes of nails and screws, tools and old magazines.

"No need to take your shoes off," Priscilla remarked without stopping. The living area of the little house consisted of a really small hallway, a purely symbolic kitchen, a small bedroom and a huge sitting room occupying three quarters of the house.

"Have you seen *The Arrival* with Charlie Sheen?" I asked when I walked into the sitting room.

"Aren't you tired yet of talking about films no one but you has ever seen?" Priscilla asked sarcastically, without condescending to ask why I'd remembered the movie. The reason was that in it aggressive aliens used these black hole generators. If you switched on one of those generators in a closed space, it sucked in everything inside that space. There was absolutely nothing in the sitting room of the little house – no carpets, no wallpaper, no ceiling lamps, no curtains, no furniture – apart from an antediluvian bed (the black hole generator obviously hadn't been able to cope with this ponderous, rusty heap of metal).

"They carted off everything that was worth anything," Priscilla explained.

"Why?"

"When my mother and father split up, my father lived here, then he moved to his mother's place and took everything with him. They gave this house to me, but I don't exactly live here, just spend the night sometimes."

In the hallway there was still a board with nails for our jackets. In the kitchen there was an old table and shelves with a few odd pieces of china.

"Like some tea?"

"I wouldn't say no."

"Then go for the water – the well's in the yard – and get the kindling from the shed. Have you ever drunk tea from a samovar?"

When I opened the door into the bedroom, little bells started chiming melodically: Priscilla had hung a few Japanese wind chimes in the entrance to the room, so they would greet guests with their simple music.

The first thing my gaze halted on was a huge photograph in a frame: a semi-transparent cloud against the background of a bright-blue sky.

Standing on the dry, cracked desk was an old black-and-white television, and on the wall above it was a flip-over calendar on a poster of Vrubel's painting *The Swan Queen*.

There was a grey cat lying on a stool, screwing his eyes up and making it quite clear how indignant he was because the light had been turned on.

The windowsill and the upper shelves of the bookcase were stacked with exotic plants whose names I didn't know. Their flowers were all different colours, large and so aggressively bright that they made my eyes smart. Not a room, but a genuine conservatory, an oasis, a blossoming island in the midst of a cold desert.

The other shelves of the bookcase had books on them.

"Do you like my sky?"

"Yes, very much," I said with a nod. "So you like Vrubel, then, do you?"

"Yes, I adore him," she admitted. "And Monet, and Degas... And especially Marc Chagall. Everyone in his pictures flies..." – Priscilla pronounced the final phrase quietly, in a special, sad tone of voice.

Now, who else of all the people I knew could have said that? People like Priscilla were gold coins in a heap of cheap coppers. (Basically, I don't know too much about artists. I was just trying to look clever. If Priscilla had asked: "And which artist do you like?" – well then, hey, I'd have looked a real fool.)

My little Christmas tree and I sat on the divan bed, cuddling up close to each other.

"We had a real entertaining time again today!" Priscilla snorted. "The second time the two of us meet – and everything goes wacky again!"

"That's why I like you so much!" I declared honestly.

"Yes... Just how did you put that degenerate out of action? Can I take a look?" And without waiting for permission, Priscilla pulled the little bottle with an atomizer spray out of my pocket. "What is it? It's not a gas spray, is it?"

"It's a perfume spray bottle. But it's filled with Ultron – a liquid for cleaning glass. You have to spray it straight into the eyes, from as close as possible, and the effect is instantaneous."

"And what is the effect?"

"That Doctor won't be able to see for a long time now. And if the burns are serious, he'll have to join the All-Russian Society of the Blind and earn his living exclusively by honest labour. Making switches and sockets and stuff like that."

"Don't you feel sorry for him?" asked Priscilla, aghast.

"Not in the least. Isn't he one of the brutes who broke our old drummer's arms?"

"Even so, it's cruel."

"Let me tell you a story, then you'll understand what's cruel and what isn't. It's something that happened in our school, in about the eighth grade. Basically, the only person who knows about it is Anya – my old classmate, who's our drummer now. So don't tell anyone. There was this kid in our class, a real weakling, totally downtrodden. He was afraid of his own shadow. And our creep and bastard in chief took a special delight in tormenting him. This bastard always wore a striped vest, so he was called Sailor. Sailor had the weakling really well trained... He beat him, made him bring money from home, once he took his jacket – but all that's only small stuff, really. One day he was smoking during the break and he called the poor wretch over and said: 'Open your gob and stick your tongue out, or else...' And he showed him his fist. The poor kid thought Sailor was going to stuff something disgusting into his mouth: insulting, of course, but not fatal. So he stuck his tongue out. And Sailor stubbed his cigarette out on the kid's tongue and just roared with laughter."

"You mean he didn't even try to resist?" Priscilla asked with her eyes wide open in anger.

"Of course not. When did you ever see patsies offering resistance? Their status doesn't allow them to do that. Or then there was this other time: a certain girl took a real liking to that kid, and a romance sprang up between them, kind of by accident, and he deliberately went walking with her where no one should have seen them. But Sailor found out anyway, and he ambushed them with his gang. Well, they gave that girl of his a good groping right there in front of his eyes. The poor little sod tried to object, but Sailor didn't even beat him, just spelled everything out for him loud and clear: 'What's up with yer, I'm yer mate. Not too mean to share a bint with mates, are yer?'"

"And how did it all end?" Priscilla interrupted.

"One time Sailor was sitting on a bench, and this miserable bruised and battered creature walked past him from the shop, with a string bag. Sailor yelled at him: 'Come on, get yourself over here!' and he started running and stumbled, and dropped the bag – he acted the whole thing out just perfectly! Then he jumped up and legged it, but the bag was left behind. Sailor walked over, and when he looked, he saw there were two bottles of vodka in the bag. He was a bit tight already, and he'd been wondering where to get more booze from..."

"Did he poison the vodka?" Priscilla guessed.

"What for?" I said with a smile. "You know what they make our special Petro bootleg fire water from? Acetone plus glass cleaner, and vinegar for the aroma. And then they stick on the label: 'Russian vodka', although it ought to read: 'Russian napalm'. So Sailor swilled it all straight down. It was early evening, it got dark soon, and they found him in the morning."

"Dead?"

"Much better than that. It all turned out just perfect. Apart from burning out all his insides, his brain was damaged too. He was in hospital for six months and came out a total moron. His parents put him in a school for idiots, and now he sweeps the streets in the mornings. He turned ever so quiet! If you're interested, you can go up and give him a kick – he won't mind at all."

"And the other one, the poisoner? Did anything happen to him?"

"Absolutely damn all. There were no witnesses. And who could find out where Sailor got the vodka from? Do you think there aren't plenty of accidents like that with fake vodka all over Petro? Nobody ever suspected a thing. The perfect crime, as they say. What do you think, did that kid do the right thing?"

Priscilla chewed on her lip and delivered her verdict.

"Absolutely. People like that Sailor don't deserve any pity."

"That's what I think too. That little kid... It was me."

"You!" Priscilla tried to move away, but I wouldn't let her. "And you... were you really the way that you said?"

"Yes. That's where I got my nickname."

"And how did you manage to change?"

"I haven't changed. I was just able to be myself after I finished school. After all, there was no one there anymore to tell me the way I ought to be. You can send me packing if you like..."

"No way!" Priscilla snuggled even closer against me.

"Then let's sleep. I'm as knackered as a horse."

Priscilla and I didn't even have the strength to get undressed. We put our arms round each other again, just like the last time, and plunged into sleep.

What did I dream about? That not very distant summer in the garden.

I relived the spiciest episodes of my life.

Regina and I used to spend the whole day sunbathing in the garden, among the ripe strawberries and gooseberries. I loved to lie on a bedspread laid out on the ground and leaf through books, every now and then plucking a berry from the nearest bush. Regina, in her bathing suit made of bits of string, was dozing on the next bedspread, and I was desperately trying to force myself not to think about the scene I'd spied on in the shed. But no matter what, my thoughts kept returning to it against my will, I felt aroused, and Regina's childish little body was enticingly close.

Then one day she slapped me across the back of the head and said:

"That's enough lying around, sleepyhead! Let's go and take a dip."

Two boards in the fence moved aside to reveal a dense tangle of growth. To make my way through it, I had either to duck down under thick, inflexible branches, or step over roots, or squeeze between the trunks, feeling the hard bark against my skin. I could barely keep up with agile Regina. Soon there was a bit more space, and Regina suddenly stopped and put her finger to my lips:

"Ssssh, kiddo!"

We could hear very interesting sounds. We took another couple of steps on tiptoe and lay down on the fragrant grass, like spies.

I saw that man again, with the receding hairline. He was lying there, stretched out at full length and a woman about forty-five years old was sitting on him, slowly lifting herself up and lowering herself back down. Even at her age she had managed to keep a trim figure, but age always tells, and it showed in the two deep folds in her face and her wrinkled breasts (too small to be described as "sagging"). The woman gradually moved faster and faster, moaning gently.

After a minute I felt uncomfortable lying on my stomach

– my erection was getting in my way, so I shifted onto my side, without taking my eyes off the sight. Then I glanced round and froze: Regina was gazing at my sex organ like a mother looking at a baby – tenderly, with her mouth slightly open. Her lips were trembling.

"Regina," I whispered in a halting voice.

She pulled back the foreskin and took my member in her mouth: I was seared by the intense pleasure of it.

"Regina, what are you doing?" I asked, unable to believe myself. What was happening seemed to me like a fall into an abyss – the kind it would be impossible to clamber out of again afterwards.

"What? It's just like nursery school," she whispered back and ran her tongue over me in a way that made me cry out and immediately bite my lip.

We heard answering cries: the woman was slowly gathering speed.

Regina freed her mouth and started working away with both hands.

"Don't have bad thoughts, kiddo! In Ancient Egypt the pharaohs always married their sisters."

"Yeah, and where are they now?" I enquired with my voice breaking. Regina plunged the foreign body into her mouth again, took it out and answered:

"Kiddo, I just feel sorry for you. You're sixteen, and you still haven't tried a girl yet. You're missing out on so many good things in life!"

I'd never heard my sis talk that way. She always behaved like a real prissy little miss... Maybe it was only at moments like this that she became herself?

"I saw you with that man in the shed..." I said, recalling the scene, listening to the woman floundering in pleasure and sensing that in just a second I would experience something I'd never experienced before in my life.

"Good for you... Close your eyes and fasten your seatbelt..." Regina grabbed my member voraciously with her mouth and started growling quietly.

Waves of delight ran through my body, one from the top down, another from the bottom up – and they met somewhere in the middle, bursting out in a hot fountain and making me arch up into a bow. I seemed to rise up above the ground that had been heated by my own body, and collapse back down again two or three seconds later.

"How long have you been doing this?" I asked inquisitively. It felt so good to lie on the grass, breathe the hot air and feel Regina's hot skin... But there was a painful ache in my soul. As if I'd been poisoned by rays of venomous sunlight and fallen hopelessly ill.

"None of your business," my sis replied and pinched me with her long nails.

9.   [secondary developmental period]

On Monday the youth page of *The Evening Petrochemist* carried my article (I had to cut it down to the minimum, or they wouldn't have given it enough space).

A LEGEND RETURNS

The youth rock band Adenoma, very popular in our town two years ago, has been revived with a new line-up: Crybaby (guitar and vocals), Priscilla (keyboards and backup vocals), Ferret (bass guitar), Ann (drums). The band is preparing for a big concert for all genuine connoisseurs of "heavy" music.

Basically, that's the entire article, and even then I had to strongly insist to get it put in the news column at the last moment. And so far the grandiose concert only existed in my imagination

– and in Priscilla's. To be perfectly honest, it was her idea to organise a supershow for all the "normal people" in our town, as she put it. That is, rehearse a long musical programme, find a sponsor, hire some good equipment... Priscilla was certain that your humble servant would organise it all, and how could he disappoint his princess?

That Monday evening I took my lovely lady to her first rehearsal in Ferret's garage – after a fantastic weekend spent together. I had no hesitation in taking Priscilla into the group when I found out she'd graduated from music school in piano, although I would have taken her in any case. I really needed my very own Yoko Ono, aka Linda McCartney, very badly.

In the garage a rather strange picture met our eyes: Ferret and Anya sitting at opposite ends of the space, staring gloomily at the floor – Anya on a stool and Ferret in the saddle of an old moped.

"Greetings, all. Allow me to introduce our new keyboard player and backup vocalist, her name's Priscilla.... Ermm... Why are you both so glum?" I asked.

Ferret and Anya looked at me morosely. There was a crimson bruise on Ferret's face and Anya's lower lip was twice the size of the upper one.

"Children, children, what can I do with you... " I said, shaking my head. "Well, what is all this? What started the fight?"

"Ask him." Anya jabbed her thumb in the direction of Ferret.

I remembered the rehearsal before the Evening of Horrors. Anya got tired very quickly hitting her drums and she was soaking wet. She had to take off her jumper and then her T-shirt, leaving herself in just a bra and thick woolly wristbands, demonstrating very clearly that she had no figure. However, this last circumstance hadn't stopped Ferret from ogling Anya avidly.

"He came on to you?" I guessed.

Consent was signified by silence.

I didn't say anything either. I just took Ferret by the throat, pulled him to his feet and slammed him hard against the wall. My hand closed tighter and tighter on his neck and puny Ferret wheezed, weakening rapidly.

I moved my face close to his ugly mug and asked:

"Any more questions, butt-sucker?"

The freak shook his head with his last ounces of strength. I unclenched my hand and Ferret slid down the wall. There were five blue spots left on his neck.

"You ought to smash him good and hard!" Priscilla advised me.

"I'd have done for him if we didn't need him. You can smash him for me if you like, Anya."

"And get my hands all filthy!" Anya snorted angrily.

Ferret coughed.

"This isn't a whorehouse. Keep your hands to yourself," I told him sternly.

"It's... Crybaby..." Ferret managed to force out through his wheezing.

"What?" (If he starts complaining, I really will do for him!)

"I'm sorry... I won't do it again..."

That's Ferret all over. Always knuckles under to anyone stronger, but at the same time he waits like a jackal for the right moment to sink his teeth into their throat. He has no pity for the weak: I've been told that the filthy louse has a little racket of his own on the side, and his "clients" are kids from the junior classes in school. There's only one approach that's effective against Ferret – you have to take a vicelike grip on him and never relax for a second. If you follow that rule, he becomes a quite manageable, even reliable little man.

"Don't say sorry to me, say it to Anya. And let's not have

any more conflicts inside the group! Anya, that applies to you too."

Anya flung her open hand up to her head in an army-style salute.

A fine army, I thought in annoyance. *Two dames and a freak. I need to find another guy urgently.*

"Listen to me, you freaks! Today I had a talk with the director of the Star. The result is that we've got less than two weeks to prepare, so from now on we keep slaving without any days off."

"But how did you manage to persuade the director of the Star? Didn't we have a little bit of friction there?"

"All water under the bridge. We agreed on everything. Entrance to the concert will be by ticket only, at least thirty roubles a head. The takings will go to the House of Culture fund. We won't get a kopeck. Personally speaking, that suits me just fine."

"Me too..." Anya said with a nod. "I don't lose anything anyway. But do you seriously believe there will be any takings? Yeah, of course, there will be some, somebody will come... But don't expect a full house!"

"Well, that depends on us. We'll have to print the posters and stick them up ourselves, ring round everyone we know... Critter promised to do a bit of hustling too. I'll handle the TV. Are there any more questions?"

"No, sir," replied Anya, holding her arms straight down by her sides. Ferret wheezed something, then lit up a dog-end that he'd squirreled away earlier.

Meanwhile Priscilla was studying a poster on the wall – it was a photograph of the Adenoma of the year before last, printed out large on a colour printer. On the extreme right – your humble servant, at that time with hair down below his shoulders, with his arms set in a cross on his chest. On the left – Buddha, a prematurely balding, plump youth with bushy eyebrows. In the centre – Smurf, a solidly built young guy with a broad face that was kind of puffy, but still pretty likeable. He had his arms rounds titchy little Angie and disgusting Ferret.

Apart from this poster, there was an entire gallery of pictures, drawn in charcoal or simple pencil on Whatman paper, hanging on the garage wall – they were portraits of all sorts of monsters: with twisting horns, webbed wings, three eyes, four arms, beaks and armoured shells.

There was also a poem that I once scratched on the wall during an appalling, total downer.

> *Shit never happens in a single dose.*
> *Relax for a moment, turn your back,*
> *And the shit hounds descend on you in a pack,*
> *Leaving you lonely and morose,*
> *Wretched and weary,*
> *Jaded and dreary,*
> *Sad, dismal, and all the rest of it.*
> *You shake your head that's aching and sore,*
> *And exclaim in wonder: "Oh God, my Lord!*
> *It's all just one big heap of SHIT!"*

"You really do look like a cry-baby in the photos," Priscilla whispered in my ear. "You've got such huge eyes, as if you're about to start blubbering any moment. And they're transparent, like little lakes... It even looks as if the water in them is trembling." Then she added in a louder voice: "Crybaby, where's your old keyboard player?"

"He's not just a keyboard player, honey. He's the founding father of Adenoma, the spiritual leader and author of half the songs, Ilya aka Smurf. We met at this guitar club they used to have at the House of Culture, and became friends. I used to drop round to his place sometimes, and we used to sit there, strumming a few songs. One time he sang me his own songs, and I sang him mine. That was how it all began."

Priscilla had already reached the Soviet-made electric organ.

"Am I going to play on that machine?"

"Uhu. Smurf found it in damaged condition at a jumble sale and bought it dirt cheap. Then he fixed it up himself – a real jack of all trades! That thing was better than it had ever been. But when he finished school, he scooted off to Moscow. So the old Adenoma went out of existence then. I've always envied that guy."

"Envied?" Priscilla echoed in surprise. "Can Crybaby from Adenoma really envy anyone?"

"Only Smurf from Adenoma. I felt really attracted to him, although there's a lot I hate about him. Ilya's arrogant. Ilya likes to be at the centre of attention and he can't stand to be ignored, Ilya's a born boaster, Ilya likes to change his point of view... Things that make people think I'm a narcissistic egotist, seemed charming and likeable when Ilya did them. And apart from that, Ilya could cure my depression without the slightest effort. He never enquired about my mood, and I never told him. We mostly chatted about music, discussed ideas for new songs, dreamed about what we do when we made the big-time... I only had to walk along the street with him to feel my mood soaring right up to the sky... I don't know what he's doing now, about a year ago he forgot I existed. I send him e-mails occasionally, but there's no answer."

And there were also some things I didn't intend to tell her: like, when Ilya was around I always felt like number two. Even though he and I were both "first among equals" in Adenoma, he was always the real leader. Ilya made the arrangements for all the concerts, Ilya got us the room in the Star through the local Department of Culture. He rejected almost everything that I composed, and he knew how to infect the rest of the band with his opinion. If not for him, our repertoire would have been about ten times larger.

"He should see you now!" Priscilla declared, shamelessly reading my mind.

"Oh, yeah? He'd grin and say: 'We'll see just what you can really do without ME!' To hell with him."

"Can I see the words of the songs?"

I dug out an old exercise book with words and chord sequences for Priscilla. She looked at it and drew her own conclusion:

"All the songs are very gloomy!"

"And why should they be cheerful?" I enquired. "We don't live in the Emerald City."

"You've got to write a new song. About how wonderful everything is! It can be a duet for us."

"Let's do it."

Then I let Priscilla look through our photo-archive – I gave her the album with photos from our old concerts, and I looked over her shoulder. Meanwhile Anya was warming up on the drums and Ferret had recovered and was strumming the strings of his bass, yelling at Anya from time to time to tell her not to hammer away so loud – he was tuning up, you see.

"Stop!" I exclaimed and grabbed Priscilla's hand just as it was about to turn the page.

"What?"

"Give it to me," I said. Forgetting myself, I grabbed the album out of her hands and stared hard at the photo.

It was a shot of the hall during the concert when we bashed out the *Pentagram* CD with five of our best songs. The camera had picked out a section of the front row, with our most devoted fans in it. Hey, lads, where are you now? In the photo they'd got up from their seats and their mouths were wide open as they howled in joy. Anya was there with them. To judge from the expression on her face, the delicate, fluffy dandelion in a warm sweater with the peace sign embroidered on it was squealing louder than all the rest. (Imagine if I'd told her then that in two and a half years she'd be a member of the band, only it wouldn't be Adenoma, but a de facto solo project by Crybaby!)

But that wasn't what had excited me – sitting there in the second row, behind our friends, was the stranger I'd met on the suburban train. No doubt about it, it was definitely him. I could never have confused that crafty face and those narrow eyes with anyone else. They were framed by long, dark hair held back by a ribbon across his forehead.

"Anya! Anya!" I howled – just you try getting a drummer's attention when he (or she) is hammering away relentlessly!

"What, Crybaby?"

"Come over here! Tell me, who's this guy?"

Anya gazed at the photo.

"Who – this one, with the long hair? I've never seen him before in my life."

"Are you absolutely sure?"

"A hundred per cent, Crybaby. Why are you so interested in him?"

"You remember the way we met on Sunday, in the Star, when the White Angels were there?"

"Well?"

"That morning I was coming back from the dacha garden with potatoes and I met this guy. He advised me to drop into the House of Culture at ten o'clock. So I did, and here's the result: I met you, then Priscilla, and now we've all resurrected Adenoma together. I get the feeling this cunning dude could foresee how it would turn out!"

"I tell you again, Crybaby: I don't know him."

10. [secondary developmental period]

The next day I went to visit another lovely female friend of mine, a Satanist – a perfectly normal girl, as a matter of fact, her Satanism amounts to nothing more than walking around dressed in black and listening to heavy metal rock bands that no one has ever heard of. She lives alone, rents a tiny little room with a shared kitchen. She studies in the same place I do, one year ahead of me, although she looks about fifteen. This girl with dusky skin and orange patches in her pitch-black hair has a rare and unusual name – Ruslana. She works as a reporter for PetrochemTV and, in addition, she presents her own little show – the ten-minute youth programme *Cuckoo*. Ruslana is an old acquaintance of our band, she once shot a feature about us and even argued with Smurf – one of his songs had these lines in it:

> *A man is dead, his soul is snatched away*
> *To Satan's realm, no more to see the light of day.*
> *See them roam the shadow world's dark, narrow ways,*
> *The final glimmers of his lost days.*

Ruslana tried to prove to him that Satan doesn't take human souls, she talked about reincarnation and said there was nothing bad or good in this world, and good and evil were just component parts of a single and indivisible whole. Basically, she's not really like a traditional Satanist as Christians see them – she doesn't recognise Christianity at all, Buddhism is much closer to her point of view.

When I arrived at her place, she was amusing herself by drawing yet another demon in charcoal on a sheet of Whatman paper. It looked like the monster out of *Quake*. The room smelled of sandalwood.

"Hi, Rusya!"

"Well now, look who's here!" She dropped the charcoal and clapped her hands, with happiness written all over her face. All her emotions are expressed boisterously and quite openly, so usually no one believes that she's twenty. "Sit down quick and tell me about things. I'm sorry it's so untidy here. If I'd known Roma was going to make my day with a visit, I'd have licked everything clean..."

I sat down in an armchair. A human skull stared at me from the top of the television with its empty eye holes. Ruslana dug it up out of the ground in eleventh grade when we all went on trips to green the outskirts of Petrochemist with trees and shrubs. (In fact, all the seedlings died within a month – flora simply can't take the air around here!) Our delightful dark-enchantress artist decided the skull was a greeting to her from the forces of darkness, cleaned the dirt out of it, and for some unknown reason called it Moisha. Ruslana simply adores it, she says it's her favourite man and kisses it every now and then, laughing at dumbfounded lookers-on.

"Rusya, I've come strictly on business."

"I'm all ears."

"I've resurrected Adenoma, I want you to do a feature for 'Cuckoo'."

"Resurrected it?" Ruslana exclaimed, as if that was unbelievable. "Just you?"

"No one else is going to do it for me. Of course, just me." In a few words I told her everything about the reunion, including the forthcoming concert.

"I get it, Rom. You'll have your feature."

"And another thing, Ruslanochka. Do you happen to know anyone who could play rhythm guitar in the band for us? I've completely lost the knack, somehow."

To tell the truth, I was simply fed up of standing on stage with a guitar. The singer in a rock band shouldn't suffer from muscular paralysis.

"We-ell..." said Ruslana, rolling her eyes up dolefully. "I suppose I can find someone."

"Well that's just wonderful."

"I've just got a nice letter from Yekaterinburg, from the witches there," Ruslana boasted. "They have this little idea about holding a role game, to do with the Inquisition. There'll be a dramatisation of a medieval trial, complete with all the details, and it will all end with an auto-da-fe. Wouldn't you like to go with me? You'd make a great warlock." Ruslana showed me her fangs and hissed, imitating a vampire.

"Get thee behind me!" I replied. "If I can play anyone, then it has to be an inquisitor. I'll roast the evil creatures on the flames."

"You don't want to be on our side? Oh, that's a mistake, Roma! We can fly! We can live for as many years as we like! We know how to have a good time, and do it in good taste. But what kind of life do you Holy Joes have? Tormenting yourselves with hunger, learning prayers off by heart from morning till night, masturbating in secret – what's good about that?" Ruslana giggled and flung a half eaten cake at me.

"You know, Rusya," I replied, dodging the sugary projectile, "I'm going to make a film on that subject one day. There'll be this group of enchanting girls and elegant young men, straight out of the TV serial *Friends*. Students from some university-type college, say. They all love hanging out with their friends, listening to good music, they're fine specimens, morally and physically, but they have just one little drawback, a tiny little one: they're vampires. And no matter how wonderful these young people are, at night they kill people and swill blood. And there's a vampire hunter in the film too – an austere young monk with sadistic inclinations..."

"Aha, so it's better to be vicious and hungry and do good than the other way round? What a tired cliché!" Ruslana remarked. "And dubious too. But all monks are profoundly flawed and inadequate little men. And the sympathies of the audience will be on the side of the ghouls."

"I don't doubt it," I countered. "So they'll be all the more indignant when this monk makes total mincemeat out of all the ghoulies. There'll definitely be a scene like this: the monk has a dream, he sees himself in the distant past, a thousand years ago. He seems to be riding through the night by the glimmering of lightning, at the head of an entire army. He and his men are all wearing loose grey robes and the hoods conceal their eyes. In the distance medieval castles and decrepit villages come into view, and there are hundreds of fires blazing along the road, with witches burning in them. And there are vampires and werewolves crucified in the trees. Just imagine that picture, eh?"

"Very engaging..." Ruslana agreed. "Did you write the part of the monk for yourself? You're not like that at all!"

"No, but I'd rather be like that than serve the powers of darkness. Honestly. All sin engenders death!" I reached into my pocket, took out the sticker I'd bought from the White Angels especially for Ruslana and stuck it on the mirror.

"That's a real classy sticker."

"I can't figure out why you're so stuck on all this Middle Ages stuff," I went on. "You dream about all sorts of knightly castles, but have you tried investigating what we have right here under our noses? Apartment blocks, garages, backyards, building sites – and there's a mysterious side to all of it. For instance, right now the two of us are in a standard nine-storey apartment building. Can you describe for me what's going on at this moment on the roof, in the basement, in all the apartments, in the sewerage system? Maybe something quite impossible to imagine. There's a secret to be discovered in every building."

"For instance?" Sensing an interesting story on the way, Ruslana clambered into an armchair and pulled her bare feet up after her.

"For instance, there's a story about a certain student hostel, where Anya used to live when she was studying at university. True, even she only knows about it all from the rumours. The point is that somewhere in this hostel there's a secret room, only two or three students know about it, nobody else, not even the supervisor has a clue. One of the guys living in the hostel found the room by accident, when he was hammering in a nail and discovered the wall was very thin. So he broke through the wall and found this little room with no windows, not even a room really, just an empty space. The space was created accidentally during the construction work: the building was put up during the period of Stakhanovite campaigns for increased productivity: never mind how slapdash and shoddy it is – just deliver a few days ahead of schedule and get a pennant as the best work brigade.

"So a certain famous hacker, an old school-friend of that student, moved into this room. He was only seventeen – he's twenty now – but the authorities were searching for him right across the country, he'd pulled so many big scams. This superhacker first tricked his way into the hostel – or got in through the window, maybe – and then his friend brought in his super hyped-up computer. They set it up in the secret room. And they put a mattress on the floor, with a couple of cushions from a sofa. And supposedly the hacker has lived in the hostel ever since then, for three whole years now. The way they disguised the entrance to the room was very clever: they moved a wardrobe and cut a door in its back wall. So you open the wardrobe – and there's the entrance to the secret room. Only no one knows what floor the room's on, or the number of the student's room."

"But how does he eat? Does his friend feed him?"

"He could feed as many people as you like, with the accounts he has in all the banks around the world! The hacker just transfers his money to a plastic card, and his friend brings him everything he orders. But he doesn't need much, just a bite to eat or an upgrade for the computer. He doesn't hack to get rich, he does it for the sake of art."

"And doesn't he ever leave the room, then?"

"Sure, they say he sometimes takes a stroll round the

hostel – not everybody knows everybody else there anyway. He'd have to go to the shower sometimes! But on the other hand, the superhacker's never left the hostel. What for, when he has an entire universe in the Internet? He lives a quiet life, he's not afraid of being found and arrested – how can they find someone in a room that doesn't exist? They say he's writing a programme for the end of the world. As soon as the superhacker activates it in the Internet, it's curtains for all the computers in the world, and that means for the world in general. But don't get hung up about it, no need to worry – it's just a legend..."

The week flew by like a bullet. Priscilla took leave from her flower shop and I radically neglected my studies – to hell with it! From morning till evening we hung out in Ferret's garage. Ferret joined us in the evenings – at the shady place where he worked, they came down hard on anyone who took days off. But then every time, after we'd been starving all day long, he brought us heaps of food that he'd bought on the way, at the 24-hour supermarket.

"Who did you kill this time?" I quipped – although, joking aside, I knew the ways Ferret earned his money were very far from honest. "A commercial secret," he used to say, pulling stuff out of his pockets – packs of quick-cooking vermicelli and biscuits, round boxes of processed cheese, little packets of instant coffee... "Well, Ivan Pliukhin wouldn't be Ivan Pliukhin if he didn't nick something. Rom, this is for you and me, fifty-fifty," he added, baring his rotten teeth, slapping me on the back and taking a bar of white chocolate out of his pocket with the air of a conjurer, or it could be crabsticks, frozen into a solid brick, or a microscopic little jar of caviar, or some other totally unnecessary piece of trash that he'd lifted from the shelf in the shop simply because he could. Ferret was definitely very proud of himself. But in secret I hoped that one day one of those little kids the filthy toad extorted money from would bring along their father or older brother, or the security guard in the supermarket would catch the petty thief in the act – in either case, Ferret would wind up getting battered so hard that next time he'd be afraid to nick what wasn't his... Empty dreams! This slippery git always made sure what he did was quite safe, no way was he ever going to get caught.

Soon the four of us were joined by a fifth – he was the guitarist Foma, aka Denis Fomin. I've no idea where Ruslana dug up this burly twenty-year-old layabout with long, long hair who played heavy metal. As I understood it, he'd been dreaming all his life of getting together a band in the classical heavy metal style, like Iron Maiden, but since his dream still hadn't come true, he was willing to play at funerals if necessary. He was sullen, uncommunicative and taciturn. Which made it all the more surprising that, as someone told me later, Foma used to earn a bit on the side at night as a systems administrator in an Internet club, and he was thrown out because he never came to work sober, and he was always blasting the entire club with terrible music that sounded like a tractor roaring, and every now and then he had fights with the clients and regularly cleaned out the till.

But it was gratifying that the guy accepted the basic concept without a murmur: quantity at the expense of quality. Our goal was to play as many numbers at the concert as possible. And, bearing in mind that just by warming up we'd have the audience in such a state that they'd happily jump about to the sound of scales, we could forget all about interesting melodic effects or fancy breaks without any regrets. Every new morning I brought another set of lyrics, Foma rapidly laid down a riff, Anya learned a new set of drum strokes that was hardly any different from the old ones, Priscilla stuck the gurgling sounds of the organ in somewhere or other, and we had a fresh masterpiece in the "addle-brain" style.

Overall, the atmosphere at the rehearsals was pretty tense.

"Crybaby, tell this rodent to stop drinking the mineral water straight from the bottle!" Anya demanded. "I won't drink any after him! And tell him not to come any closer to me than two metres, he stinks like an ashtray!"

"Why's she nagging at me, Rom?" Ferret complained. "I'm not doing anything to her!"

"So why are you ogling me all the time? I can't play when someone's inspecting me like I was the Venus de Milo or something!"

"What am I supposed to do, put my eyes out? I look where I want to look!"

I had to calm them down.

And apart from Anya and Ferret constantly yelling at each other for any stupid reason or no reason at all, my best friend took a dislike to Priscilla. I'd be standing beside my beloved, with my arm round her waist as she composed another break on the keyboards, and when I glanced in the direction of the drums I'd run into Anya's surly gaze, pinning Priscilla to the wall like a spear – and me with her for good company.

My young beauty made an honest effort to be friends with Anya, she tried to talk to her plenty of times, but Anya replied so coldly and reluctantly that Priscilla's desire to chat evaporated of its own accord. And even though the questions Priscilla tried to ask Anya couldn't have been more innocent, most times Anya didn't even listen to them all the way through.

"Anya, did you watch that programme yesterday on NTV..."

"I didn't watch anything," Anya interrupted in a dull, indifferent voice. "I only watch films on DVDs, my favourites, everything they show on TV is just lies. All those so-called 'reality shows', talk shows and all sorts of TV games with those heavenly prizes – they're performances, with good scripts and directors. All the music they put out on the box is artificial from start to finish –and that goes for the so-called rock, as well as the pop garbage. If it was genuine rock, they'd never let it get broadcast! The adverts are drivel by definition. Even the weather forecast is crap. Am I making myself quite clear?"

From the tone of Anya's voice it was clear that she'd delivered this monologue many, many times in her life.

"Well, maybe so," Priscilla said with a shrug, still smiling. "But what about programmes like *Animal Planet*? All they do is tell us about furry creatures: where they live, what they eat... Surely that's not lies?"

"Yes it is. Those programmes shouldn't be telling us about the creatures, but about how in five years time every last one of them is going to die out, and not only will we not be able to help them, none of us could even give a rotten damn. Argue with that, if you like!"

"Which films do you like?" Priscilla persisted.

"I could list them. But I won't. The titles wouldn't mean anything to you," said the drummer, pressing her lips together and gazing coldly at the keyboard player. (By the way, I didn't know which direction Anya's tastes had shifted in during all those years, but I did remember very clearly that in eleventh grade she used to cry over Kusturitsa's *Underground*.)

"All right, then..." said Priscilla, discouraged, and went back to her instrument.

I was completely at a loss to understand why it happened: maybe jealousy was involved, or maybe it was something else... I didn't ask straight out. Anya has high principles – she doesn't admit to a single one of her weaknesses. The only one who kept me smiling was Foma – to myself I called him the "Black Silence".

I ate at Priscilla's little house, and spent the night there too. Something incredible was going on: even though we slept together, nothing more serious than kisses happened between us. Sure, I wanted Priscilla like crazy, but so far I had enough strength and wit not to force events. The old libertine

Crybaby was afraid of losing the one who had made his life so wonderful.

"Why don't you tell me anything about yourself?" I whispered into my young beauty's ear in the darkness.

Priscilla laughed.

"What would you like to find out about me?"

"Everything."

"Ah, is that all?" she asked, mocking me.

"Ooh, you mean little girl!" I hissed and kissed Priscilla on the lips, long and intensely, after which I went on: "After all, I don't even know what school you went to, who your friends are, what you like in this life! I don't even know your permanent address!"

"Does that bother you?" The expression on my young beauty's face changed from crafty to concerned.

"Just a little bit."

"But why? Don't you feel good with me?"

"Very good..."

"You'll find out everything. In time."

"You have a surprise in store for me?"

"Let's say I do," she said with a gentle smile.

Where did you come from, Priscilla? I thought. *How did it happen that, entirely by chance, I met the girl I'd been dreaming about for so long*?

"What's happened?" she asked me another time. "You're all stressed out over something..."

"Everything's fine, sweetheart."

"Tell me. You can tell me everything."

"Last night a kid about thirteen years old was killed in front of our entrance. He'd been stabbed all over his body. In the news they said all the wounds were shallow, no single one was fatal. He didn't die from his wounds as such, but because they didn't get him to hospital in time. From loss of blood."

"And who did it?"

"All the signs are it was kids his age. They got drunk together, quarrelled and then they all stabbed one of their own with their feeble, clumsy little hands."

"It's dangerous to be a child in our town," Priscilla said in a quiet voice. "You might simply never reach the age of consent."

"Very many don't," I agreed. "Petrochemist is a special kind of place, a bad place. It's like some kind of black hole that sucks in human souls, and children's souls are just like little cakes for it. So the most important thing is to survive school. School is a war..."

"... a war of all against all," Priscilla concluded.

"If only it was. But for me it was a war of one against all. A war against the mob of unfeeling, pitiless bastards that tried to assimilate me, to dissolve me into itself. To crush me. No, nobody ever demanded anything from me – it would never enter anybody's mind to demand what was simply taken for granted. Spend time with guys when I've got nothing to talk about with them, drink with them, help them suss out the girls during the breaks, fight on their side and, if necessary, die with them, just to keep them company. And if I'd tried to explain that I found them and the things they forced on me disgusting, they would have made absolutely certain that I did die. After all, I'm really not the same as them, and I couldn't hide it."

"So what did you do?"

"I became a clown. Or rather, something more like a holy fool. I aped about in class, mimicked the teachers, during the breaks I sang songs, acted out scenes from films – I had everyone roaring with laughter..."

"Yes, that's obvious, even now. I often can't tell when you're talking seriously and when you're joking..."

"Nobody can. I can't always tell myself... But basically, I was in an advantageous position, strange as that may sound. On the one hand, I wasn't accepted into the general crowd or, rather, I was excused from it. But on the other hand, I had no problems at all. Who'd want to get mixed up with a total idiot?"

"But they did! You told me about Ignat..."

"That was nowhere near as bad as it could have been. Look at me now. No bits missing, and I'm in sound health! I always knew that if I survived until I finished school, I'd be free once and for all!"

"Crybaby, what about all the ones who didn't make it through school? So many teenagers die in Petro! What happens to their souls after the towns swallows them up?"

"They languish in captivity, feeding the town with their energy. The more souls Petrochemist gets, the more voracious it becomes. There's this legend... About a certain spot in Petro – you probably know it – the Benzolux plant. There are some abandoned half-built warehouses behind it. Between them and the wall of the plant there's a perfectly square little yard. The only way you can get in there is through one single gap between two bunkhouses, about half a metre wide, or even less... in other words, even someone who's not very fat has to go through sideways. And there isn't a single window overlooking that square – all the walls are blank. They say that on a starry night, if the sky is absolutely clear and there's no wind, at midnight the souls of everyone who has died in Petrochemist before reaching the age of eighteen gather in that yard. Imagine it, these golden silhouettes emerge straight out of the ground and swirl around in a crazy, blinding vortex that soars up into the sky, as if it's trying to break away. But it's an uneven struggle, the vortex collapses and the souls go back underground. They also say that everyone who has ever seen this vortex from close up has started aging with terrifying speed and died before morning as grey, withered old men and women. That yard is called the Bedchamber of Souls..."

When I showed up at home it was only for ten minutes at

the most. Once, when dad was in full possession of his faculties, he told me in passing that Christina was ringing ten times a day, and sometimes she came round in person and stood on the landing for a long time, waiting for me.

11. [secondary developmental period]

On the wall of the abandoned bunkhouse that Priscilla and I walked past with our arms round each other a preacher had been drawn in bright colours, writhing in convulsions – he had a purple jacket and two bull's heads, complete with horns. Both faces had blood-red, blazing eyes with no pupils, and both mouths were open in an insane howl. The preacher had one of his hooves raised towards the heavens, and the other was holding a thick telephone directory. On the right of this graffito were the words: CAUTION, SECT!

It was Saturday night. There was a whole week left until our concert.

"Crybaby, don't you get the feeling that Anya wants you?" the question was accompanied by a sincere, open smile.

I started coughing loudly – at first in surprise, and then from laughter.

"Anya, want me? Where did you get that idea?"

"What do you mean, where from? It stands out a mile!"

"Because she's always snarling at you? I don't think that's why exactly. You know, my sweet, I've always been her only friend. And now she feels like she's losing me..."

"Not just because of that. You know, whatever idea you might suggest, she's always on your side..."

"... The same as you, and Ferret, and Foma," I concluded.

"That's a different matter altogether, Crybaby. Ferret and Foma do what you say, because they accept you as the leader. Especially Ferret: just look how hard he tries to keep on the right side of you. But women are made differently. Anya's a very strong person. It's absolutely impossible to win doglike devotion from someone like her. But you've almost managed it..."

"What about you?" I asked in a gentle voice, to make sure that I didn't – God forbid – offend my little pussy cat. "What is it that keeps you beside me twenty-four hours a day? You're an independent individual, aren't you?"

My mystery girl replied with a smile that was tender and enigmatic:

"That's something you have to decide for yourself. If I chewed everything up for you and put it in your mouth, it would be just too boring!"

"Anything's possible, I suppose..." – it's pointless talking to Priscilla about herself, she just clams up!

"But as for Anya, Crybaby... Maybe you shouldn't make her suffer?"

"To avoid making her suffer, I'll have to abandon one or the other of you two beauties. Throw you out of Adenoma – hook, line and sinker..."

"Why? Nothing of the sort. Just stay back alone with her sometime and surrender!"

I couldn't believe my ears. I looked closely into Priscilla's face. I'd had similar proposals from Christina, she'd told me more than once that someone in the other group fancied me and then immediately asked: "Maybe you should take a lover? I give you my permission". But the look that went with this said: "Just you try it – I'll tear you apart, like a bulldog with a woolly jumper". But Priscilla was just waiting for my answer with the same smile on her face. What was this, another test of fidelity? It would be good if it was...

"Why would I want to do that?" I asked rather sharply.

"Think about it."

"And why would you want it?"

"I'm just curious."

"You're too curious altogether! I ought to shorten your nose for that." I laughed and gave her a little bite on her nose, eager to reduce a conversation on such a ticklish subject to a joke. To tell the truth, I was simply afraid of hearing something that wouldn't be to my liking. "And you're mischievous too!"

Priscilla laughed at that:

"That's why people like me."

The old single-storey stone house with cast-iron bars on the windows and a heavy door was tucked away between a nine-storey apartment building and the concrete wall of the Light Ray sports stadium.

"The children's library! I haven't been here in a thousand years... But why are we here?" Priscilla enquired.

"You're about to meet the finest people in our town, people who have been driven underground by an evil fate. I don't come here often, though. Just when I feel like a bit of pleasant company," I replied grandly and knocked. Ruslana opened the door.

"Here we are, Rusya!" I said.

Priscilla made a curtsey.

"Angelically magnificent, Roma. Come in."

The reading hall was in the basement. Our usual group had already gathered, and the premises were permeated with the aroma of natural green tea. One of the six people there was Anya, and she winked at me.

"There you are, Roma!" exclaimed Valerka.

"Roman!" said Yevgeny, raising his open hand.

Denis smiled from under the hair combed forward onto his forehead. Mashenka blew me a kiss.

"So now we're all together," Ruslana squealed loud enough for everyone to hear. "And there are more of us now!"

Priscilla introduced herself and was greeted with applause.

"Do you get together here often?" Priscilla asked me.

"Every week on Saturday night," I replied. "Rusya's mother works as a librarian, she takes the keys at the weekends.

"Are they all your friends?"

"More like acquaintances. I only hang out with them here," I said, shifting into a whisper. "I still know almost nothing about some of them. Basically, I'm not interested. Here everyone only says as much about himself as he wants to say."

Ruslana flitted across to us.

"And what do you do here?" Priscilla enquired.

"It varies," said the little witch. "We drink tea, chat, read poems, play games... The most important thing is that we take a rest from the cruel world."

"Play games? What games?" it was quite clear that my companion was never embarrassed in unfamiliar company.

"Today – whatever you suggest. That's the rule for newcomers."

Priscilla smiled mysteriously and looked at me. I realised she'd thought up another trick.

"I know a game. It's called 'Confession'. But I need a volunteer!"

"And I assume you'll choose me for that..." I chuckled. "Well all right, I'm ready."

"Ready? For everything?"

"For everything."

"Well, now you'll face a real test," Priscilla said altogether too softly. "Tell us all what you would never have shared with anyone. Tell us your innermost, most sacred secret. Tell us about your very greatest love."

"Oho, now that's interesting!" exclaimed Valerka, an enthusiastic young guy, extreme sports addict, acrobat and break dancer. "Well done, Priscilla! An excellent idea!"

"Yeah, yeah, spill the beans, Romka!" they all shouted in chorus. "We'll enjoy listening to that!"

"Okay, this is going to be just perfect," I said and waited for silence to fall. "This girl was called Zhenya. I met her at the Skylark health camp three years ago. I was sixteen and she was fifteen.

"How can I describe her? Perhaps the comparison might seem strange to you, but imagine the standard features of the heroine of a Japanese cartoon film in the anime style: huge transparent eyes (the originators of the style believe that they reflect the soul of the character), exceptionally long legs, luxuriant hair down to below her waist and incredibly large breasts – a real human-size Barbie doll. And Zhenya usually wore figure-hugging or, rather, figure-restraining clothes to control her excessively imposing forms. There was nothing wrong with her physical condition either, Zhenya wasn't one of your pampered beauties. When we met she'd been practicing gymnastics for many years, and she demonstrated her skills on the sports day that is held in every summer camp..."

"In short, you fell for the external appearance, right?" Mashenka enquired. This little lady was all of a quarter of a century old, but in my own mind I had dubbed her Old Woman Chapeau-Claque. What she had in common with that malicious granny was a snub nose, a hat and a thick umbrella.

"It's easy to say 'fell for the external appearance'," I objected. "Just to see Zhenya once can be enough to leave you miserable for the rest of your life. When I saw her, I wanted to howl out loud and roll around on the floor. She was always surrounded by a crowd of friends or, rather, admirers. Imagine it: they joke and blush, try to win signs of attention, they smile... but on the inside, of course, they're crying, they don't dare to suggest anything – for who can truly say of himself that he is worthy of her? Being around this beautiful girl was inexpressibly pleasurable and inexpressibly painful. I'll never forget the first time I experienced it, it was on the very first day of our group's stay at the camp. Zhenya was reading something, and one young lad started cautiously running the blunt end of a pencil down her back. Zhenya carried on reading, smiling, and I felt as if it was my back, not hers, and he was using a bayonet, not a pencil. Basically, I only ever spoke to Zhenya once. I was standing on the balcony, admiring the scenery, and Zhenya came out with her favourite book, *The Master and Margarita*, and asked me to read some of it out loud to her..."

"Romka, so what's the problem?" Valerka interrupted. "You're an interesting dude, and your appearance is well up to the mark. You should have tried your luck!"

"Ah, but the catch was that there was no way Zhenya's love was ever going to belong to me, or anyone else in our group. And everyone knew that, but it only made Zhenya even more attractive to us. She was a LENS."

"She was a what?" Ruslana asked.

"Four letters – L-E-N-S, they decipher as Levenson-Ergman-Nartov-Syndrome. Surely you must have heard of it? No, not a thing? Okay, I'll tell you in greater detail.

"Where did LENSes come from... You could say they were a gift from Perestroika. There were LENSes before that too, of course. I think they first started appearing in the fifties, when the efforts of the authorities were transforming the country into a nuclear dump at super-high speed, but no one was supposed to know about them. I suspect the LENSes were taken away from their parents, taught in special schools and forced to work in closed scientific research institutes, in order to exploit their high intellectual potential. LENSes are born into ordinary families and even now, by the way, cases are very rare. For instance, you couldn't find more than two thousands LENSes in the whole of Russia. Rumours credit the LENSes with magical powers – that's just lies and prejudice. The only way in which LENSes differ from normal people – apart from their innate talent – is the ability to communicate with each other telepathically. A LENS has two little golden whiskers –

antennae – on the back of his or her head. They use them to talk to each other telepathically. But telepathy is a gift we all have, we simply don't know how to use it. Incidentally, there might possibly be some other extrasensory abilities that the LENSes don't like to show off."

"And with people? Can they communicate telepathically with ordinary homo sapiens?" Anya asked.

"They can only pick up simple impulses from people – say, anger, curiosity, tenderness and so on."

Anya shook her head.

"And how do you know all of this?"

"There are all sorts of things going on in the world," I said instead of an answer.

"And did you see the golden whiskers on Zhenya's head?" Priscilla asked.

"Only a couple of times. Usually she wore a baseball cap with the visor to the back," I replied.

"And what if these whisker antennae are removed surgically?" Valerka enquired.

"Doctor Ergman tried doing that several times with newborn LENSes – they died."

"So is a LENS a mutation?" Valerka asked. "Or simply a pathological abnormality?"

"Neither of those. It's a gift from on high. The number of times in my life that I've regretted I wasn't born a LENS! LENSes are far more intelligent than normal people, they have a far stronger drive towards self-perfection, every aspect of their being is highly developed. And most important of all – LENSes feel and perceive everything far more keenly. They can easily distinguish the truth from a lie, good people from villains, it's impossible to exploit them – a LENS senses that straight away. They love everything and everyone, which means they don't genuinely love anything or anyone. In order to get a LENS to love you, you have to be a LENS yourself. Otherwise it would simply be awful, feeling like a botched fake beside a masterpiece. And you know what? I'm convinced that LENSes are a new race that will replace humans some day. Well, have I coped with my task?"

My story made an impression. Everybody in the room was sitting in silence with extremely serious expressions on their faces. Anya gave me the thumbs up. Ruslana expressed the general opinion.

"Ye-es, we could all do to become a little bit more like LENSes... Let's have a game of something else!"

"What, Rusya?" I asked.

"Let's play our favourite, associations. To start with we have to set the tables in a circle. Come on, guys."

"The four guys who were there, including me, plus Anya, who didn't really belong to any sex, dashed to carry out the order. When the tables and chairs were all in place, everyone took a seat. I sat down beside Priscilla, to explain the rules of the game.

"What next?" Priscilla asked.

"I explain for those who haven't played before. Everyone takes a sheet of paper and a felt-tip pen. Then one person writes a word on his or her sheet of paper – a noun, it can be a proper noun. He names the person this word is meant for, and that person has to write an association on a sheet of paper and then send it to the next person. And it's preferable if the association is oblique, it's more interesting that way."

"What do you mean by 'oblique'?" asked Priscilla.

"Let's begin playing, and you'll get the idea straightaway. Denis, you start!"

Denis picked up his felt-tip pen. In my own mind I called him Narcissus, because he was remarkably like a fragile flower – a morbidly pale youth with long, brittle fingers, as if they'd been specially created for playing the piano and were no good for anything else.

"Roman," he said and held up his sheet of paper with the word WAGNER on it.

"Look, Priscilla, he's written 'Wagner'," I said. "What should I write? What associations do you have?"

"You know, I'm not all that well up on classical music..." Priscilla said with a smile.

"Neither am I... Come on, anything at all."

"As a dilettante, the only thing I can come up with is *The Flight of the Valkyries*."

"Well okay, but that's too primitive, too head-on. Okay, I'll write NIEBELUNGEN. Yevgeny!"

"HITLER," Yevgeny wrote and said: "Anya!"

Anya started thinking, lost for a moment in an abyss of associations.

"What's Hitler got to do with anything?" whispered Priscilla.

I immediately recalled a documentary film about the German cinema and whispered back:

"The film *The Niebelungen* was made in the nineteen-twenties, a period of severe economic crisis in Germany. It was intended to raise the spirits of the nation. *The Niebelungen* was Adolf Hitler's favourite film."

"Now I realise what makes the game fun. You have to guess the way a person's thinking."

"Yes, interesting, isn't it?" I said and gave Priscilla a bite on the ear.

"Ruslana!" said Anya, holding up a sheet of paper with the word SKYSCRAPER. She was obviously thinking of that phrase of Hitler's that became mega-popular in our time, after the terrorist attack of September 11: "Just imagine how beautiful it is: skyscrapers and bombs!"

"FIRE," countered Ruslana. As everyone knows, they started building skyscrapers in San Francisco in 1875, following an enormous fire that left the city with a housing crisis.

"SALAMANDER," suggested Mashenka, directing the chain of associations towards alchemists and sorcerers in the Middle Ages. Priscilla continued the theme with "FAUST".

"Not very imaginative," said Denis and wrote "HITLERJUGEND".

"What keeps bringing us back to the fascists?" chuckled Yevgeny, a typesetter from *The Evening Petrochemist*, a gent of indeterminate age (with his little goatee beard and hooked nose, he was a spiteful leprechaun), and he traced out the name "ROMM". "Romka Mendeleev!"

I was stuck. The only thing I knew about Romm was that he shot the film *Ordinary Fascism*. But what did I know about the film? I tried to recall an article in the old *Literary Encyclopaedia* – I'd leafed through it once when I had nothing better to do. The only thing it said about *Ordinary Fascism* was that the distinctive directorial element was improvisation. "IMPROVISATION."

"Bravo!" Denis exclaimed.

"JAZZ," wrote Ruslana, deciding not to get too profound, and said: "Anya!"

She'll probably write either 'Queen' or 'Alisa', I thought, both those bands have discs with that title. But then, Anya's extremely unpredictable...

"FAECES," she held up, confirming my last thought.

The effect was impressive.

"How do you mean, 'faeces'?" Mashenka exclaimed. "Are you saying jazz is crap?"

"No, that's not what I meant. Take a sniff!"

"Yes, I can smell it now too," Ruslana confirmed.

Soon everyone in the reading hall had caught the foul, heavy stench.

"Look!" said Denis, pointing to a dark puddle creeping out from under the door of the next room.

Valerka glanced into the room.

"Motherfucker! Folks, I've got great news for you! The pipe's burst!"

"Anya, are there any buckets and rags here?" asked Priscilla.

"Yes, in the mop cupboard."

"Forget it, it's too late already," said Denis.

The faecal waters rose with incredible speed and the puddle spread wider and wider, driving the underground gamers back towards the exit. The stench was so bad that everyone was breathing through their mouths.

"There's nothing we can do, we'll have to go upstairs," said Ruslana.

In less than five minutes the sewage had occupied the entire reading hall. After a quarter of an hour the flood had risen to the half-metre mark, after another fifteen minutes it was a metre deep, and it stopped at that.

"Congratulations: now we have a swimming pool!" Mashenka joked.

We sat on the floor, surrounded by shelves of books – even on the ground floor the stench was unbearable.

"I'm afraid this gathering is over..." Ruslana observed. "I won't keep you any longer."

12. [secondary developmental stage]

A week after we started preparing for our supershow, I decided to drop into college after all, for the simple reason that missing seven consecutive days of study was grounds for expulsion.

In front of the steps I had another conversation with our aristocrat Oleg (he was wearing a new corduroy suit that was a perfect match for his favourite check cap, bought in Britain). He was sitting on a bench with some girls, mingling the dark, sharp-scented rings of smoke from his pipe with the sweetish smoke of long ladies' cigarettes. One of the girls from our group, Olya Varegina, was sitting on this refined libertine's knees, because there was no room for her on the bench. She wasn't even slightly embarrassed by the fact that he had been living with someone for the last three months, and she had no problems with her personal life either.

"Roman, wait a moment," Oleg said to me. I can't stand this lip-smacking snob, but I waited, out of pure curiosity.

"Roman, answer one question, please. What are you doing?"

"Why, do you have any complaints?" I enquired cynically.

"Our girls here saw a feature on PetrochemTV, they told me... (Olya and the other girls started nodding.) Roman, have you decided to play at Elvis Presley, or something?" Oleg asked in the same tone of voice as if I'd taken his Audi for a ride and smashed it up.

"I just don't understand what I've done to offend you!" I said with an air of bewilderment. I really love acting the idiot: the effect is deadly!

"Roman! You'll soon be twenty, and you're still playing children's games. What you're doing... What are you doing it for? It's only interesting to thirteen-year-olds! It's frivolous. Irresponsible."

"Yes, Roma," Olya squeaked in a shrill, mocking voice. "As if you had nothing better to do than amateur music shows."

The other hussies looked at me with the curiosity of a crowd of pagans waiting for a Christian to be crucified before their very eyes. Among the girls in our group I had the reputation of a perpetual Sloppy Joe and outsider who would never pull his socks up. The responsibility for creating this reputation rests entirely with Christina – she loves to mock me when she's chatting with the girls, pulling me to pieces, telling them how she's trying to make a man out of me, and how stubbornly I resist. (So the entire group knows how addle-headed and loutish I am, although I do offer some grounds for hope.) According to Christina's impeccable logic, by making me a laughingstock, she stimulates me to change for the better. Don't you just have to love women? They know precisely THE WAY EVERYTHING OUGHT TO BE and WHAT SHOULD BE DONE if everything's not THE WAY IT OUGHT TO BE. The unfortunate thing is that in my case all her knowledge about men isn't worth a bent kopeck, and all her attempts to break me in have the opposite effect.

"Oleg, Let me ask you a question. What does 'what are you doing it for' mean? Every day, for instance, you go to the toilet for a number two. But WHAT DO YOU DO IT FOR?"

Oleg drew the air in loudly through his clenched lips – the sound it made was like a long, sucking kiss.

"Roma!" Olya exclaimed strictly, wrinkling up her face in its frame of light-coloured ringlets.

"Your body, for instance, needs to eat and dump. But my body needs to eat, dump and sing on stage, and I never ask myself what I'm doing it for. If I want to do something, I do it."

"Roman, stop it," Oleg demanded. "I've had enough of your toilet bowl humour. And your flippant attitude."

Why, you stuck-up prig! What wouldn't I say to you if your daddy wasn't the director of Petrochemenergo!

"So?"

"Roman, you have to give up this nonsense and grow up!"

"Or you'll take me to court, will you?"

"All right, Roman. Let me try another way. Answer my questions. Question number one: Am I right in believing that you're going to hold some kind of concert?"

"Something of the sort."

"And I saw the place you rehearse in that TV programme... You play in a garage, don't you?" Olya asked derisively. "Why in a garage, when you could go straight to the garbage tip?"

When the peals of girlish laughter died down, I answered.

"The acoustics are bad at the garbage tip. And the smell's not so good."

I carried on acting the thick-headed moron. My advice to you is, when they try to dump you in the shit, pretend to be an idiot and plunge into the foul-smelling slurry yourself, without waiting for them to shove you in, and don't forget to pretend that you feel perfectly comfortable in the shit pit. It will disarm and confuse the enemy.

"You know, Roman, I can't tolerate dilettantism in any area," Oleg declared. "Hence question number two. Do you really think that anyone wants your so-called rock band? Apart from youngsters in the senior classes of school? And not even the best part of them?"

"So we'll play for the youngsters who aren't the best."

"Question number three. Suppose you do play this concert, what are you going to do afterwards?"

"I don't have the slightest idea."

"Precisely, young man!" Oleg tapped me on the nose with the stem of his pipe. You don't give a single thought to the future! You'll be twenty soon, and what do you have ahead of you, what do you have now? Nothing! If you don't take some thought for yourself immediately, you'll drag out the rest of your life in this filthy hole!" He swung the pipe round himself, as if he was taking in the whole of Petrochemist.

"Does that bother you so very much, Oleg? I'm touched," I said in a trembling voice, clutching at my heart.

Instead of acting the comedian, I could have struck up a serious discussion with our Oleg. About the fact that every place the erect primate known as homo sapiens had dumped his load was the same kind of cesspit. He would have started telling me about the differences between life in the provinces and in the capital, punctuating his argument with repeated references to "image" and "prestige"... And the girls would have gawped at him respectfully. There would definitely have been the question: "Surely you must be ashamed of yourself?" Me, ashamed? A person people have wiped their feet on (quite literally) since he was a child, and spat on liberally, and jabbed cigarettes in his face. How would you like that? In school I grew so thoroughly accustomed to all these procedures that I haven't felt any need to possess prestige in the eyes of other primates for a very long time. I can manage with very little. As a certain song by an unknown artist puts it: "I can walk down the street with a lame mulatto girl."

He would have told me: "Grow out of these infantile complexes, work for your own future". Guys like Oleg, who are preparing to take over their father's business some day, are very proud of working for their own future... Stupid people, can you really not see that there is no future? Why am I the only one who understands that? And you've grown so rooted in your humdrum routine that you accept it as the only possible version of reality. Something that has always been the same and always will be. Live this way, or not at all! Destroy yourself with a computer, a mobile phone, a fourteen-hour work day. Let the nuclear fallout settle – say: "Fallout? What rubbish! It's just snow". And go and do what you're paid to do. Only it's not a prestigious profession, or car, or laptop will help you live to a ripe old age, but a rucksack, a cagoule and a brace of pistols. Take all this and slip off to somewhere in Siberia, wait there for the chaos to start. At least you won't have long to wait, I know that for certain. The crowds will die, the isolated individuals will survive – that will be how it all turns out. I could spend the rest of my life wandering the roads of a world run wild, playing music for myself (it's a shame a guitar is such a cumbersome device, I wonder if I could learn the harmonica?), fighting off brutalised humans and at night feasting my eyes on the radioactive glow blazing in the sky.

That's all I could have said to Oleg, and he wouldn't have understood a thing. (Now Priscilla would have understood, but my conversations with her still hadn't touched on this controversial subject.). As it was, he took my defensive clowning for the real thing. At least, he reacted to it in dead earnest.

"Oh, God, I couldn't care less about you! It's Christina I'm thinking about, and you should think about her too. Such a serious girl, stuck with such a – pardon the expression – numskull!"

I lashed out at my opponent with a verbal uppercut.

"You don't need to worry about her any longer. I'm leaving her today. I already have someone else. Did you all hear that?" I know that one of Christina's favourite theses goes like this: "He (that is, me) is my cross, and no one else will ever take him on". Meaning: "He's no fucking use to anyone except me, and even I can barely stomach him... But since it was me he came to... the things we do for love!"

It worked. The girls gasped. Olya put away her smile. Oleg hesitated for a long time with an expression of dismay on his lordly face and then gave it up as a bad job.

"Do what you like, Roman. Please yourself. I wash my hands of you." His voice made it quite clear that he had tried his best to appeal to my reason and, having failed to find even the rudiments of any such item in the degenerate bonehead Romka Mendeleev, he was feeling aggrieved to the very depths of his soul.

Behind my back I heard a flurry of agitated conversation between the girls: the detonation of my information bomb had set the stagnant swamp heaving.

I walked past Artyom.

"Good morning, Artyom!"

Large, bulky Artyom raised his eyes from his crossword

and waved to me with his gel pen. There, look at that, if you please. As Scott Fitzgerald said: "If the whole of society is solving crosswords, then it is doomed."

The showdown with Christina took place beside the same window with a view of the trench and the main heating pipeline. The Bus Driver was scampering over the mountains of dug-up earth, earnestly manipulating his imaginary wheel.

Christina, suspecting nothing, looked at me malevolently, as if to say: "Now you're in for it, you little straying alley-mouse, prepare for your severe, but just, punishment". I mentally begged myself to be adamant and cold, although I felt genuinely sorry for this hard-headed, narrow-minded girl.

"What have you got to say, you monster?"

"Well, nothing special, Christie. I'm leaving you."

In a year and a half Christina and I had been through all sorts of things, but I'd never said anything like that. She didn't believe I would ever say it. Well, of course not, I was no more than a free supplement to her own intelligent, serious self...

You should have seen the way her face crumpled and shrank! She changed from a hard bitch to a fragile little girl in a single instant.

"Altogether?" Christina couldn't believe her pale-pink ears.

"Altogether," I confirmed absolutely calmly. "I don't need you anymore."

It would have been interesting for me to listen to her objections, but all Christina could manage was incoherent exclamations.

"No! It's not true! You can't... I won't... Don't..."

She was about to burst into a flood of tears, I had to get a move on.

"Christie, you have to understand me..."

She shook her head desperately, as if she was shaking off invisible insects:

"I don't want to understand anything!"

Clear enough. I had to act harshly.

"You featherbrain!" I said with a frown. "Don't even think of clinging on to me! I'm a monster. Leave me alone, all right? Just leave me alone!"

I swung round and headed for the auditorium. Christina spent the entire lecture sprawled over a desk at the far side of the hall, with her little face flopped in her hands, and I dispassionately scraped my pen over my notebook, all the time thinking: "Go on, go on, stare away..."

In the evening when I arrived for rehearsal, I found a crude cross daubed in fresh red paint on the door of Ferret's garage, with the caption: ATTENTION! HOUSE INFECTED. I knocked and shouted:

"Guys, it's me!"

Ferret opened up, looking gloomy.

"Hi, Crybaby. Do you know what kind of folk art this is?"

"I can guess..." I said, nodding seriously. "The Doctors find someone who lives in this house undesirable."

"Exactly," Ferret agreed. "Fucking Soviet Youth League... But don't you worry just yet. They never snuff anybody out straightaway. Usually they give the victim a week or two to clean up his act and reconsider his views on life."

13. [tertiary developmental period]

During our usual nocturnal wallow, Priscilla jumped up off the divan bed and exclaimed angrily:

"How long is this going to go on?"

"What?"

"How long are you going to make out that you're innocence personified?"

I liked the way she put the question.

"Why, do you have any better ideas?"

"I could find some!" Priscilla said in a loud whisper.

"Aha!" I exclaimed gleefully. "You want me so bad, your temples are all cramped up tight?"

Priscilla almost choked on her laughter.

"So very self-confident, what a joke! I just feel sorry for you, that's all: you keep prodding me with your erection all the time..."

These scathing words jerked me out of idling mode. I pounced on the girl, pressing down on her with all my weight.

"How do you like to do it, Crybaby?" Priscilla asked, instantly going limp.

"I like something spicy, my sweet."

"Get started!" Her fingers tickled my stomach.

"Are you sure? You won't regret it?"

"No I won't, not if you manage to surprise me!"

"All right, you asked for it." I switched on the night lamp, climbed off Priscilla, opened the wardrobe, rummaged through its contents and picked out a bright summer frock with a knee-length hem. "Yes, that will suit. Now I'll go out, and you put it on."

"Well, if that's what you want... But what for?"

"We're going to play. You're an innocent little girl and I'm a lecherous guy. You've wandered into my place by mistake, and then I turn up. I start pestering you, and you don't know how to react, your arms and legs are paralysed by fear."

"But can I cry?"

"Yes, in fact you should."

Priscilla looked into my eyes with the gaze of a little predator.

"Come back in fifteen minutes?"

"Fifteen minutes?" I listened dubiously to my body going crazy. "That long?"

"You can wait!" she said and pushed me, protesting, out of the room.

"Okay," I sighed. I walked round the kitchen and felt the samovar – still hot. I splashed out some tea for myself and sipped it, trying to drink as slowly as possible, which wasn't easy.

So that's it, my beloved Priscilla. Now I know you're mine. You won't get away. And I'm not going anywhere either. Why would I, if I've managed to find everything I was dreaming of?

What I was feeling was... It wasn't my usual feeling of a whaler who has harpooned himself a fine large fish. I was aroused physically, but mentally I was perfectly calm, perhaps for the first time in all my nineteen years. All I had to do now was rejoice in life. There was nothing to be afraid of anymore, I'd managed to defeat my bitterest enemy – loneliness. For the last year and a half I'd been the loneliest person in all Petrochemist (after Guerukha, of course). I don't mean in my so-called "personal life". Sex has nothing to do with relieving loneliness, on the contrary, there's something fatal about it, a certain brutal heartlessness. I don't remember the Latin words, but the saying is that "all creatures are sad after copulation". Sex only heightens the sense of desperation.

Without noticing it, I came round to an old idea of mine – to publish an erotic magazine. There's always a demand for cheesecake, just as long as there are teenagers, smelling of sweat and grease. The important thing is to find a sponsor for the first issue, after that we can keep going on adverts. All the photos can be downloaded from the Internet, and I'll write the texts myself: porn stories, letters to the editor from readers wanting to share their intimate experiences and personal ads from various gays, swingers and all sorts of sadomasochists looking to hook up – that's just in the early stages, afterwards genuine correspondents will turn up. Sitting in the office all day long, ferreting through porn sites and getting paid for it – that's the life!

I loitered in the kitchen for a little longer and then knocked impatiently on the door of the little bedroom.

"Yes, yes, who is it?" a thin little voice replied.

Standing behind the door, with her hands clasped behind her back, batting her eyelids, was a little darling about twelve years old. A polka-dot frock, two pigtails decorated with white bows, a clumsily made up face. If I'd met her anywhere outside this little house, I'd have taken her for Priscilla's younger sister.

"Hello, girlie," I smirked, feeling something seething and frothing up inside me, searching for a way out.

"Hello, nunky," said the silly little goose, leaning her head to one side.

Without hurrying, I stepped closer to my precious darling, suddenly transformed into a demure little child, gulped loudly, ran my damp palms over her cheeks, her neck, her shoulders. I clasped my hands together, jerked Priscilla toward me and grabbed her lips between my teeth.

Priscilla pulled herself free with a squeal.

"Ouch! What do you want?"

"I want you, my little one," I said and started throwing off my clothes. My young beauty gasped, squeezed her eyes shut and covered her face with her hands. I jerked her towards me, squeezed her close, licked her neck all over.

"Don't! Don't!" Priscilla squeaked, slapping me on the cheeks.

"Silence!"

Priscilla gave a loud gasp and stopped resisting, paralysed by fear.

"There's a good girl. I'll buy you a pair of slippers like Cinderella's." My hands were kneading the girl from behind, just below the waist. "And you know what else? A new dress!"

I grabbed hold of the material on Priscilla's shoulders and jerked down hard. The moth-eaten frock split apart with a crack, and there was nothing at all under it.

I lifted Priscilla into the air and laid her out on the divan. She snivelled very realistically. I squeezed her breasts – crudely, as if I was kneading dough – and licked her stomach ravenously. Eventually I stuck my tongue in the place that smelled of rotten canned fish.

Priscilla gave a loud sob, then started scraping her nails over the sheet and moaning sweetly in pleasure, slipping out of her role.

"Oh, Crybaby..."

"Do you know how I amuse myself, my little one," I asked when my mouth was free. After the cunnilingus my tongue was tingling ever so slightly (I adore that sensation!), "I lure stupid little bunnies back to my place and screw them!"

I unpacked the condom I always take with me when I leave the house, stretched it on good and tight and proceeded to the endgame. I turned Priscilla face down, put my hands underneath her, lifted her up and entered her (noting, as I did so, how very unvirginlike my innocent victim was!) I grabbed hold of my darling's pigtails, like a horse's reins, and started moving, revelling in her shouts.

About twenty minutes later I stretched out on the bed and Priscilla settled down on my shoulder.

"Yes, Crybaby, that really was something else. I've never had anything like that with anyone before..."

"Like what?"

"Original. And wild."

Why you spiteful little thing! I know that's not what you meant!

"I was hoping you'd say: 'It never felt so good with anyone else as it did with you'." My hand slid over her wet little stomach.

"I'll say it some time. Do you know any other interesting little tricks?"

"I know lots of things. If you fall into my hands after

the concert, you won't escape alive! And by the way, how do feel, with the concert coming up? You haven't ever performed anywhere before, have you?"

"Yes I have... I graduated from music school! I played in all sorts of competitions – at district level and provincial level..."

"But you realise the crowd that will come to the Star is quite different!"

"I'm not bothered. With you it'll be great!"

"My darling..."

Our lips locked together.

14. [the tertiary period of development]

"Crybaby, look at this!"

I glanced out into the hall, parting the curtains ever so slightly.

We had insisted that half of the seats must be removed for the concert, so that the audience could cut loose whatever way they liked best. Now the freed-up space in the hall had been filled up by people: T-shirts and baggy hoodies with various rock insignia, collars, chains, garishly painted faces, insane hairstyles. Blue-grey clouds of cigarette smoke. And almost no one older than seventeen – those who were a bit older had taken seats, but there were no more than about twenty of them.

"Where did so many independents come from in Petro?" I asked in amazement.

"They were always here, they just didn't show their faces," Anya replied.

"I never saw so many at our earlier concerts!"

"The folks here aren't just from Petro, they're from all over the district," Critter hissed lazily. He was behind the curtain with Adenoma, as our most devoted fan. "I dragged along whoever I could. Phoned round everyone."

"Did they take long to persuade?" I asked in surprise.

"With the stories that are going round about you, persuading someone's no fucking problem."

I looked at the clock.

"Right, soldiers, it's time. Everybody off the stage. Lights!"

The hall at the Star has one unusual feature: the lights there don't go out at a stroke, but slowly and mysteriously, like in a cinema. As the lights got dimmer, the hall got quieter and quieter. Total silence arrived together with total darkness.

"Curtain!"

The curtains parted. A flash of dull-red light illuminated the empty stage. There was a mike on a stand in the centre, with a guitar and bass guitar lying at equal distances away either side, and the drum kit was standing behind. The organ was over on the left, disrupting the general symmetry, with a second microphone beside it.

"Annie, you're on."

As soon as Anya appeared on stage, the audience started roaring. She looked really awesome – we all did, in fact.

Two days before the concert I'd rummaged through the House of Culture's costume store and picked out a few things: about twenty intense black uniforms which had symbolised fascist uniforms in May Day parades and historical plays performed by the local theatre studio although, to be quite honest, their design had nothing in common with real fascist uniforms. They were more like the uniforms worn by the arch-villain's henchmen in some old James Bond movie. Each of us chose a uniform – apart from Priscilla. There wasn't one that fitted my honey bun. She had to make do with her own tattered jeans and a black T-shirt. The only other thing needed to complete a really brutal stage image was to create visual uproar on our heads with the help of sugar water – the result was a gang of droids from a Japanese cartoon film.

Anya took her place at the drum kit and started playing a slow rhythm. The bass drum stood out loud and cheerful, reverberating through the microphone so that it sounded like a huge heart. Scatterings of bright orange and yellow squares, triangles and diamond shapes started creeping across the drapes behind her.

"Foma – go! Ferret – go!"

The guitarist and bass guitarist walked on from different sides, picked up their instruments and started up together.

"Go on, sweetheart." I wanted to press a long kiss on Priscilla for luck, but it turned out short – my beloved tore herself free and dashed out on stage. The little organ soon started croaking away.

Anya suddenly rattled out a short percussion solo, driving the speed of the rhythm up several times, and as soon as she hit the cymbals, the front man came flying out onto the stage – that uncouth, self-obsessed lout, Crybaby.

I grabbed the mike off the stand and howled: "Well, did you miss me?" Then I launched into *The Final Day*. Even through the rumbling of the drums and the heavy guitar riff I could hear the crowd in the hall howling – they remembered the song. The silhouettes that I could make out in the semi-darkness started moving, jumping and writhing about. I warmed up quickly and halfway through the song I was leaping around the stage like a stoned toad. It felt like someone had attached springs to my shoes. Foma and Ferret moved their entire bodies simultaneously – it looked like they were bowing over and over again, or hammering in nails with their foreheads.

The first number in the programme rushed by in two minutes.

"Thank you, Petrochemist!" I shouted.

The hall was howling. Before it could settle down, we played another three aggressively depressive tooth-rattlers, all of them composed in the week before the concert. I flipped completely and totally knocked myself out, so I hardly had any breath left for the last song. As soon as it was over, I filled my lungs with air to pronounce a single phrase:

"The next song will be sung by our incomparable Priscilla."

It was the first time Priscilla had ever sung on stage, but she wasn't worried at all. The song, called *Coloured Balls*, was from our old repertoire, only Smurf used to sing it.

> *People are different-coloured balls,*
> *Down the steps they hop and skip,*
> *Roly-polies with gaping jaws,*
> *And trundle off on their daily trip.*
>
> *They trundle on in a jostling throng.*
> *Through the snow and wind and rain.*
> *The little balls roll off to school*
> *The big ones off to work again.*
>
> *The student balls wander about*
> *In search of any kind of food.*
> *Red balls hold rallies, rant and shout*
> *And want the president removed.*
>
> *A lot of balls are coloured green,*
> *Preserving Nature is their end.*
> *A blue ball rolls down the dirty street*
> *Trailing after his little friend.*
>
> *Rapacious brightly coloured balls*
> *Rampage the district on the loose*
> *Devouring all they come across,*
> *And if they must, each other too...*

After *Balls*, we hit them with another three high-energy numbers that we'd written and our rehash of the old number

Music Bound Us Together by the band Mirage ("They try to persuade me, but I won't listen: they'll never break us apart!" I howled, squeezing Priscilla tight against myself). That was followed by a duet by me and my princess called *Only the Good Things*, and to wind things up we played that super-mega-hit of all times, *Mendeleev Rock*. Those who know me well are aware that the title is primarily a dedication to wonderful me, and only secondarily to my famous namesake and his table of the elements.

"Thank you! Thank you!" – I was so hoarse, I couldn't even hear myself through the microphone.

The hall carried on heaving up sound for ages. About two minutes after the final chords, the incoherent rumbling that was still going on gradually took the form of a chant: "A-de-no-ma! A-de-no-ma!" The lights came up, and I jumped down off the stage into the hall. I was immediately surrounded from all sides, people shook both my hands, slapped me on my shoulders and back.

"Out of sight! Great stuff!"

A lanky chick with a mohawk hairdo licked my nose like a dog. Didn't I amuse myself with her after a gig a couple of years ago, after getting her drunk first? I think her nickname was Baby May. The incident flashed past in front of my inner eye with the speed of an express train...

...The mayor of Petrochemist at the time, Kharlampiev, an energetic individual and entrepreneur, decided to organise a full-scale Youth Day on 29 June. In those days no public event happened without our Adenoma in its classic line-up. We were the warm-up act – not the main dish, more like the salad. The main turns were supposed to be bands from out of town. Kharlampiev didn't invite just anybody, he lashed out on a grand scale and brought in "stars", who – terrifying thought – actually made video clips! To be precise, the boys band Kids out of the Box and a girl singer with the imposing name of

Wynona. Does anyone at all remember who they are? Some musical shops have shelves labelled "Sale", and anyone who wants can find the pop compilations from two years ago, buy them for a third of the original price and learn all about them.

On the posters they wrote: "Straight from the Music TV hit parade!" It wasn't even a lie. Kids out of the Box did once appear briefly in the hot twenty on that TV channel, at about number 18, with the clip *Hot Summer*. So a huge gathering was guaranteed for our performance. They built a stage on Labour Square, beside Telecommunications House, opposite the local government building.

The event kicked off at midday. As soon as Adenoma took the stage and started tuning up, I noticed a black wedge of underage punks, led by Critter, forcing their way through the crowd to get close to the stage. There were about twenty of them altogether. I spotted Baby May straightaway – it was hard not to notice that long-legged heron in a T-shirt and shorts, wearing a collar and ghoulish makeup.

As soon as we launched into the first number (there were only six of them), the punks started a brawl or, rather, they started jumping about, trying to shove each other hard with their shoulders. Some of them call this the "slam", some call it the "pogo". But that's not important. The point is that soon the pigs made their way through to the brawlers and pacified them with their truncheons. May was the only one they didn't have to pacify. She spent the entire concert calmly standing by the edge of the stage and studying me.

It was hot enough to boil your brains – we'd put a few bottles of cold mineral water in the shade and sluiced ourselves off with it after every number. From the stage we had a clear view of every single spectator: most of them were teenage girls wearing almost nothing – or maybe there weren't all that many of those girls, I just didn't notice anybody else? Whatever way it was, I had only one thing on my mind.

I wasn't a virgin any longer, but unfortunately I didn't have any experience of seducing fair ladies. It was the perfect time to begin. For starters, I chose something on the simple side. While Adenoma were performing, I kept looking in May's direction and winking, and in the breaks between numbers, when I could free my hands of the guitar, I blew her kisses. After the concert she became mine in the basement of a concrete building heated to incandescence by the sun. I lured my heron into the dark space under the stairs (some anonymous well-wishers had left a wooden stool in there). She kept droning ecstatic compliments into my ears, about how the way we'd played was "bastard f... ing incredible", before I shut her mouth. I kissed this black blossom long and tenderly on her lips, then sat down on the stool, unzipped my trousers, and she straddled me, after pulling her shorts off together with her panties. Then there was a bit of a hitch: May couldn't figure out where to put those stilts of hers and we had to move the stool.

May sniffled loudly as I stroked her skinny legs and bit her on the neck.

After we'd done everything, May jumped up off me with black lipstick smeared over her face, walked out from under the stairs, forgetting to put on her underwear, leaned against a wall flooded with hot sunlight, and I think she burst into tears. I decided there and then that I'd had enough of her (a little bit of a good thing...), gave "Miss Punk Rock" the slip and went to join the other guys in the band, who were feasting at our keyboard player Ilya's place. My colleagues greeted my account of what I'd done with laughter and applause, but of course, I was the one who laughed loudest – without a single twinge of conscience...

... Maybe it wasn't Baby May at all. I didn't get a good look at her: the faces around me kept changing, I remembered many of them from the old Adenoma's gigs.

Valerka pushed his way through the crowd and appeared in front of me.

"Now that's a show! Attaboy Romka!"

"Romka-a-a!" someone bleated in my ear – that had to be Queazo.

"Crybaby! Far out!" shouted Buddha (Buddha?), reaching out his arm that didn't bend since it was broken.

The tears were running down my cheeks, I felt so good.

On that dark evening in late autumn we tumbled out of the Star House of Culture as one big crowd: five musicians and an army of rock fans. And then we all froze, as one man.

Standing along the concrete wall opposite the Star were the Doctors. Identical young thugs in identical gear: red caps or bare heads, white and red jogging jackets and tracksuit trousers. Nobody moved, they reminded me of a long row of statues, assassins guarding the entrance to an abandoned ancient shrine. The Doctors' response to the concert had been to gather all their forces in order to annihilate in one fell swoop everyone who dared to dress, behave, talk or think differently from them.

Our crowd quickly closed ranks. Standing at the very centre, I involuntarily became the leader. Anya and Ferret stood on my right and my left. Priscilla hid behind my back.

Anya slowly took her hand out of her pocket with a knuckle-duster on it and her features sharpened, especially the chin – it was ready to jab into human flesh, like a wedge. Really, how could she have changed like that in two and a half years? She was a real Terminator now.

Critter tugged a piece of pipe out from under his jacket. Ferret reached into his pocket, but I grabbed his hand – I knew what he was reaching for, and I realised the weapon wouldn't be needed. At a rough guess, there were about seventy Doctors, but we had at least a hundred and fifty battle-worthy personnel units, not counting women and children.

So I took the first step towards our enemies. Everyone behind me repeated the step. Another step, then another. As soon as we'd covered half the distance to the concrete wall, the Doctors pulled back slowly, with obvious reluctance. They were clearly disappointed to see that, instead of a bit of amusement, they were in for a full-scale battle royal against an enemy outnumbering them two to one. The action played out in total silence. We advanced without hurrying, the Doctors backed away without hurrying, then suddenly they turned and left without saying goodbye, English-style. The entire brigade turned into some narrow lane and a second later every last one had disappeared. We were left facing a completely empty, dimly lit street.

At that point the silence came to an end and we all doubled over in laughter. The girls squealed triumphantly, Foma chortled heroically, Valerka shook without opening his mouth, Priscilla snorted through her nose, Queazo jangled like an alarm clock. Anya jumped on my back and gave me a smacking kiss on the cheek – it was the first time she'd ever done that. Then she made way for my adored Priscilla. Ferret took a step towards Anya, hoping for something, but she showed him the knuckle-duster. Then our bass-player thumped me hard on the shoulder in his usual stupid way (I'd been favoured with that mark of attention so often that evening, my shoulders were aching) and shouted:

"Crybaby, we saw them off! We won!"

You won't believe it, but I couldn't think of any objections to that.

15. [crisis]

I was sitting on a bench in our bathhouse at the dacha and Regina was lathering me with a soapy sponge, moving lower and lower.

"If only mum and dad could see us..." I said. "I can't even get my head round that."

"So how do you feel when you think about it?" Regina asked.

"It gets me going," I confessed.

"I noticed," she agreed, slowly massaging my manhood, as stiff as a tyre spanner, with the sponge. "Me too."

"Do you at least understand that we'll never wash this off for as long as we live?" I asked.

"It's you who doesn't understand, kiddo. You'll never merge with anyone else the way you do with me. Never trust anyone, sweetheart. People betray you, Roma. People use each other. It's all different for us. Because brother and sister are a single whole in every possible sense. Their love never ends. And we'll always be that single whole, as long as we live."

I felt myself melting from pleasure and the heat, and in the absolute silence Regina's insinuating voice hypnotised me.

"You and I are spending our last summer together, kiddo. Very probably you won't ever see me again. Do you think your depraved, perverted sis has decided to screw her own brother as an afterthought, because she's tried all the rest? If that's what you think, I'll bite through a certain something of yours right now. Remember: you'll screw with others, but with me it's UNITY. No one else will ever give you that... but it means you won't be able to rejoice in life. Learn to get everything you want, kiddo."

Regina straightened up, took a tinplate basin of water and sluiced me down, washing off all the lather. Then she put her arms round her neck and straddled my thighs, nestling against me. She rose and fell, rubbing her hard nipples against me, kissing me tenderly on the lips.

I stroked the bulges at the bottom of Regina's back, then hugged them more tightly and started working with my arms, increasing the rate of friction. Regina threw her head back, crying out in abrupt bursts – I think she was swearing because her feelings were too intense. A minute later, when the semen poured out, she howled and immediately tumbled off me with a sound like a croak. She'd fainted: the lack of air and searing heat had done their work. I carried Regina out into the cool anteroom, she was as light as a little doll. I laid out a tattered blanket there, set my sister down on the floor and sat beside her. It seemed to me that she smelled of blood.

Regina half-opened her eyes, smiled and patted my cheek. I felt so good, and at the same time so vile that the tears gushed from my eyes in a torrent.

The next morning found Priscilla and me in her little house – on the divan bed. The electric fire was switched on, because we had nothing covering us except a padded blanket.

I had woken before Priscilla and, lying there between those four narrow walls, I was thinking through an idea I'd had for a video clip for a lyrical love song. The action takes place in a little house like this one. Priscilla's drinking tea; I come to visit with a bouquet of flowers. We sit at the table, talk and laugh, and I play my guitar and sing her a song – the same one that the clip is for. Then she kisses me on the cheek, I say goodbye and leave. The final sequence in the clip shows me walking out of the little house, and then the camera rises high and higher, until it has a bird's eye view of the whole town or, rather, what's left of it. Apart from our little house there isn't a single building still standing: just ruins and more ruins, and in the centre of the city – a deep crater.

Priscilla stretched like a cat. She screwed up her eyes with an affected smile that stretched from ear to ear.

"Good morning, pussycat!"

"... Morning," Priscilla yawned.

"I hurt all over, sweetheart," I complained. "Especially my back. After the way you scratched me with your nails..."

"I hurt all over too," Priscilla replied. You torturer..." She gave a mock sob.

"Any complaints?"

My young beauty shook her head with that familiar touching smile.

"I know from myself that performing in public does your head in totally. It did in both of ours," I said.

"You were just great on stage!"

"Correction: WE were just great."

The cocktail of a colossal concert and bestial sex with a girl I really loved – I'd never had that before... And what's more, nothing like that would ever have happened while I was with Christina. To be quite honest, Christina's figure is much better, and my princess's body is a bit pudgy, with distinct rolls of fat, but perhaps that's precisely why Priscilla aroused me far more powerfully. That gave her a special zing.

"Do you feel good with me?" I asked.

Priscilla nodded.

"Do you want it always to be this way?"

"Always?"

"Always, my darling. Let's always be together!"

A shadow seemed to run across Priscilla's face and it darkened slightly.

I realised I'd said something wrong, and added hastily:

"Do you think I'm fooling you? You're wrong. I want you very much. What do I have to do to make you believe me?"

Surely she's not going to mention lawful matrimony? In principle, why not, I could consider that possibility too... In any case, it won't happen until I've taken care of my studies. So I still have two years!

"You see, Roma... I don't want anything from you."

"Nothing but me, myself?"

"No, nothing at all. I don't want you to think we owe each other anything. And I don't want you to get used to me!"

Well now, this is a fine turn-up! I almost shuddered, but then I thought: *What if she's testing me, what if she wants to hear what I still haven't said yet?*

"You know, Priscilla, you're special to me, and the way I feel about you is special."

She pulled off my hands that were creeping over her body like tarantulas and exclaimed in a rather loud, shrill voice:

"You don't even know me properly, you can't say that!"

"What I've already found out is quite enough."

"And wasn't it the same for you with other girls?"

"Absolutely not. I can say that for certain."

"And what's so special about me?" A note of sarcasm had appeared in her voice.

"Everything. You like the same things I do. You're as insane as I am. I think we're an ideal couple, Priscilla."

"There, you've said it all..." she said, turning sad. "All you see in me is crackpot Priscilla, who can abandon everything for the sake of some insane idea like yesterday's concert, but in actual fact I'm sweet little Tanya, quiet as a mouse, butter wouldn't melt in her mouth. And don't say anything to me about love. You fell in love with Priscilla, not with me. But what will happen when you stop being infatuated and you see the real me?"

"I'll like you however you are!" I objected. "Want to bet?"

Priscilla gave a broad, broad smile and beamed as bright as sunshine. *Everything's going to be fine*, I decided. My heart suddenly felt lighter.

"Imagine it, sweetheart: in ten years' time we're lying on a bed just like we are now, looking at each other. And you're smiling. And we both know that after another ten years it'll still be the same. Love and eternity – isn't that great?"

"Yes, it's great, Roma. Let's get dressed. Our autumn holidays are over. It's time I went to work and you went to college."

"Okay."

While we were getting dressed, I watched the news on PetrochemTV. The film crew had only shown up at yesterday's concert for ten minutes, and the feature on our performance was even shorter, a minute or thereabouts – all because it was someone else reporting, not Ruslana. They showed the House of Culture for about five seconds, us on stage for about fifteen seconds, and the raving fans for about thirty seconds. The commentary was piss-poor too: like, there was this concert, Adenoma performed, everybody enjoyed it, la-di-da, la-di-da. Anya had a point after all, when she said there was nothing but drivel on TV. But not even that could spoil my impressions of the concert. In any case, I'd already put together a long article in my own head for *The Evening Petrochemist*.

I didn't know what was going to happen to our band after this, but I was absolutely certain the people of Oblivion really needed us. We would keep improving, there was certainly room for that, do a few gigs now and then, then we'd see. No matter what, some day we'd clear out of this concrete garbage tip.

Priscilla and I walked out of the little house and flipped.

"Do you see that?" I whispered.

Serious-faced Priscilla gave a faint nod.

Overnight the first snow had fallen, scattering a thin layer of small white grains over the withered nettles and the roofs of the tumbledown houses nearby, and the heaps of broken brick, and the mud, and the asphalt, and the shit. In less than a day, this blindingly white snow would become sickening grey sludge, but in the meantime we were looking at an unfamiliar new town.

"Happy First Snow!" shouted Priscilla, suddenly livening up. She collected a handful of fresh snow from the railings and flung it so it sprinkled all over me. I got my own back by doing the same – Priscilla squealed.

I instantly skipped up close to her, grabbed the collar of

her coat, pulled her towards me and snatched a kiss almost by force.

"Crazy lunatic!" she laughed, struggling to free herself.

"Look who's talking!" I remarked and added, "Everything all right?"

Priscilla nodded.

"That's great then."

We walked together as far as the gate and out of the street of single-storey houses. Then the dotted lines of our tracks in the snow parted and went in opposite directions.

"Be seeing you!" I said, giving my sweetheart a smacker on the cheek.

"Bye-bye!"

I set off to the College.

Oleg was standing in front of the porch, knocking the ash out of his pipe. He greeted me reluctantly and didn't say anything. Thanks, dude, you're growing in stature in my eyes.

I walked into the small hallway with the turnstile.

"Cheers, Tyoma!"

"Roman, hang on," the athlete said with a broad smile.

"What is it?"

"My little brother was at your concert yesterday... Did you run into a few problems?"

"Everything's fine, Tyomich!"

"If anything happens, call on me. Just don't go looking for trouble yourself."

"Whatever you say. Thanks in any case." I shook his huge hand, the size of a hefty iron.

There was seven minutes left to the start of the lecture. I looked for Ruslana, she usually waited for me by the window, in her black cape, with a chain round her neck with a tin skull hanging on it. They'd already covered over the heating main, and its location was indicated by a long thawed patch in the blinding white snow.

"Hi, Romochka!" our local Satanist exclaimed and started gabbling:

"I was at your concert yesterday, it was something out of this world! I really loved it, Romusik! Better than in the old days! I did a little drawing." She unfolded a sheet of drawing paper, and there was Adenoma, as Nazi monsters with guitars held at the ready. "I'm sorry I didn't stay until the end. Work, you know, things to be done..."

"Rusya, where were you in the hall? On a seat?"

"Yes, I don't jump about in the thick of the crowd. I'm fragile, mustn't be tilted."

"And dear Rusya, did you happen to see this young man?"

I stuck the photograph of the long-haired guy under her nose.

"Sure, I saw him. He was older than everyone else, lots of people saw him."

"Know anything about him?"

"Maybe I do. Why are you interested in him?"

Once again I ran through the story of how this person had radically changed my life, without even meaning to – or did he do it deliberately?

Ruslana gnawed on her finger.

"Hmmm, if it's really what I'm thinking... I congratulate you, Roma. You've been brushed by the wing of an angel."

"What do you mean?" I asked.

"You were lucky: you met the Phantom."

"What Phantom?" I realised I was about to hear another urban legend, which, to my shame, I didn't know.

"He's the phantom of Petrochemist."

"He seemed quite alive to me," I chuckled.

"He is alive, only he always shows up in the right place at the right time. I know lots of people whose lives he's saved."

"Kind of like Batman?" I imagined the scene: a dark night,

a gang of freaks out of their skulls on booze catch a chance passer-by, knock him off his feet and are just about to start flailing at his skull, back and chest with their heavy boots, when suddenly the Phantom appears with his hair and the flaps of his coat fluttering, like some gigantic predatory crow, and disappears a minute later, leaving the mutilated bodies of the marauders lying on the asphalt.

"Not exactly, Romochka. He doesn't batter anyone with his hands and feet. It goes like this. Suppose you're walking home late in the evening, and he suddenly appears out of nowhere and strikes up a conversation with you, for instance: 'I'm not from round here, will you show me to the station?' While you're showing him the way, you chat, and since he's a very charming person and good to talk to, you get caught up in the conversation, and twenty minutes go by before you remember that it's time you were going home, and you say: 'Sorry, I have to go now, I hope we'll meet again...' You get home and discover your apartment has been reduced to dust by a domestic gas explosion. If you'd got back fifteen minutes earlier, you'd have been burned alive. That's what the Phantom does."

"So what is he, then, a fortune-teller?"

"Fortune-teller, telepath, medium, psychic. Call him what you like, it all comes down to the same thing. And another thing: he doesn't help just anybody, he's selective."

"How does he choose who deserves to be helped and who doesn't?"

"No one knows. So you can be proud he chose you."

"Okay, okay..."

I headed for the auditorium with my thoughts in a tangle. Christina was waiting for me there with a face on her that would have softened Shamil Basaev's heart. She'd committed another outrage on her hair without any rhyme or reason – this time it was perm and highlights.

"Do you like it?" she asked in a slightly breathy voice.

"You are as lovely as a mountain chrysanthemum against the snow," I lied listlessly, with a brief glance at her hair. I was thinking about the conversation I'd had with Priscilla that morning.

There had already been times when the latest young lady I'd been seeing "on the side" from Christina hinted gently that we'd had our fun, but we shouldn't overdo it. But those were girls whose virtue was really easy, I only spent time with them so I wouldn't feel so sick listening to Christina's hysterics, and they only spent time with me to have some fun with a pleasant young guy and push off as soon as his money ran out. But I could only dream of a girl like Priscilla. I was certain she wasn't a slut, wasn't I? So what was the problem? Why didn't I suit her? She couldn't be feeling disappointed with me so soon, and I hadn't offended her in any way.

Then I noticed that Christina was still standing there beside me.

"Well, what else?"

"Roma, don't you want to talk to me?"

"Let's give it a try," I said with a shrug. "Relate."

"Can it be somewhere else?"

We made our way out into the corridor to our favourite window. I was prepared to miss part of the lecture too, as long as we dotted all the i's."

"Why?" Christina asked with just her lips.

"Because," I snapped.

"It is to do with me or something else?"

"Definitely to do with you."

"What do I have to do to myself? A plastic operation?" Poor Christina started rubbing the freckles on her face, as if she wanted to tear them off, together with the skin.

"What's your appearance got to do with it, Christina? Do I really seem that primitive to you? Do you think I'm only interested in your appearance?"

"But what did I do wrong?" asked Cristina, holding back her sobs.

"Nothing, it's just that we're not suited to each other."

Yes, I agree, it's a strange thing to say after Christina and I had been in a relationship for a year and a half.

"You don't have any of the things I like in girls. And I only realised it just recently."

"I've seen you once with your new tart. There's nothing good about her."

So she'd been following me too! Why, you paranoiac, Christie!

"You don't even know her, you can't say that!"

"Why Roma? What did I do?"

And that was when I started getting a bit of a handle on the situation. My poor Christina was convinced that the reason I'd started this whole business with Adenoma and Priscilla was a personal thing, it was all just to get at her, to teach her a lesson for treating me badly.

"I love you, do you hear?" said Christina, decisively staking her claim to me.

"What of it?"

"What about her, your tart? Do you think she can give you as much love as I do? She'll dump you as soon as she gets bored."

The most hurtful thing was that perhaps Christina was right. I recalled my conversation with Priscilla that morning and summoned up all my defensive forces.

"Well, maybe I don't want to be loved? I want someone to UNDERSTAND and not make any demands on me. But can you boast that you understand me? The number of times you've told me: 'I love you'. Has it ever occurred to you that the more often you repeat those words, the less they mean?"

"But Roma... If you leave me, I'll just die!"

Is that your only argument?

"You won't die," I replied calmly.

"But all the same, it won't be me anymore!"

"That's your problem," I concluded coldly, hammering the final nail into the coffin of our romance. "Don't pester me anymore, okay?"

As soon as our classes were over, I went to Concord Street. To the flower shop.

16. [death throes]

I jumped out of the route taxi minibus and dashed off along the street at full speed.

I found the little shop without any trouble and walked in the door to the song sung by its springs. I was expecting to see the same kind of splendour as in Priscilla's room, but there's no way plants can live in the centre of our town. The flowers gathered together in the cramped room were sickly, withered, boring, only the cactuses looked at all sprightly.

A stodgy lump of a woman who I didn't know was loitering behind the counter.

"Hello," I growled churlishly, sensing that something was wrong. "Where can I find the girl by the name of Tatyana?"

The woman turned her deadpan face towards me.

"She left the job." And she added gravely: "Yes".

This was a blow to the solar plexus.

"What do mean, she left?"

"She left the job. Yes. Two weeks ago. Yes. Took her wages. Yes."

"She won't come back here again?"

"No."

The expression on my face must have been very funny.

"But what made her leave?"

The woman puffed herself up and said nothing, glaring straight into my eyes.

"Confidential information?" I asked, getting the idea. "All right, choke on it! Yes. And go screw yourself. Yes."

I leapt outside like a scalded cat. So, so... Priscilla had tricked me: she didn't take leave, she resigned! I didn't know yet what that meant.

A little while later I opened the dilapidated gate, slopped along the waterlogged path in my boots, ran up onto the porch and knocked – the door wasn't locked and it swung back.

"Sweetheart, I'm home!" Without taking my shoes off, I ran across the kitchen and pushed the bedroom door. The only sound it made was a creak. The wind chimes didn't greet me with their jingling – they weren't there.

Holy smoke! When did she manage to do this?

None of Priscilla's things were left in the bedroom: no flowers, no books, no calendar with reproductions of Vrubel's paintings, no piece of sky, no decrepit TV. An empty wardrobe, a divan bed with no cover on it, a naked desk – the room had become like the rest of the house. Empty, cold, unwelcoming... And there was no note or farewell gift for me.

She had decided to play hide and seek with me. Or rather, to disappear forever. Now I knew for certain that final conversation wasn't accidental. She'd decided to get rid of me, but she couldn't tell me to get lost in so many words. And she was right, I wouldn't have gone anywhere if she had. But why – who's going to explain that to me? WHY? What did I do wrong?

I ran out of the house and set off, panting for breath, along the filthy street, dashing along so hard that I ran into Fast Foot. The basket case jumped out of the way and let me past with a polite bow.

Priscilla, my charmer. I hate you!

I set off for Anya's place. She was my last chance.

"Come in, Crybaby," Anya said and nodded. She was dressed in the old rags she usually wore at home. "Something's happened... I need to talk to you."

"And I need to talk to you. Okay, you go first."

After all, it's best to start with the easy part, and I didn't expect Anya to come out with anything that would knock me into a heap.

"Crybaby, I probably won't be able to play in Adenoma any more. I'm going away. I'm sorry."

How about that? She knocked me into a heap after all.

"And why's that?"

"Last week I got an e-mail from friends in the Regional Ecological Centre. I've been offered a job in the Filimonovsky Wildlife Reserve... And I have to save up for my studies next year..."

"And you decided to leave?"

"Why not? There's nothing to keep me in this rotten dump. And I think you'll survive all right. Just imagine what the natural scenery's like there! It's a dream."

"When are you leaving?"

"Soon, my friend. Tomorrow morning."

"And can you do one last good deed for me?"

"Even two, sweet Crybaby."

"I need Priscilla's home address urgently."

Anya raised her eyebrows into question marks.

I sketched out my last morning with Priscilla for her in broad strokes. Anya frowned.

"This is bad. Worse than you think."

"What's wrong?"

"Remember, you asked me once to find out all about her?"

"Well?"

"If you don't want the horse to trot, don't gee it up. There was one little thing I didn't tell you then... Priscilla or, rather, Tanya, has a fiancé. Let me stress that: not some boyfriend or other, but a man with whom she intends to tie the knot in the very near future and live with him in joy and in sorrow until death do them part... and all the other abracadabra."

"Why didn't you tell me?" I screeched.

"Why frighten you prematurely? All sorts of things happen in life – that's your favourite phrase, isn't it? She might have left him for you. There's always a chance, although in this case it wasn't even equal to zero, it was a negative value."

"But why? Who is her fiancé?"

"Some kind of manager, I think... he's twenty-five, works in Petrochemenergo, a terribly busy young gentleman. In theory, I could find out Tatyana's address... But it won't do you any good! If, as you say, Tanya's taken all her junk out of the house, then she's probably moved in with you know who."

I grabbed hold of her elbows.

"Anya, even though you're not a woman, but some sexless God-knows-what, I appeal to you as a woman. What does it mean? You know, Priscilla was really crazy about me."

"Firstly, she's not your Priscilla anymore, she's Tatyana, and that's the last time I'll say that," Anya corrected me sharply, pulling her arms out of my grip. "And secondly, our modest little boy, what makes you so sure she was crazy about you?"

"She told me lots of times that she was crazy about me and what I did, and she's always dreamed of going out with a rock star..."

"So what? Infatuation isn't love. Maybe she was delirious about you, maybe she still is, but that means absolutely nothing. If you want to know how I see things, it's like this: Tatyana's facing a long period of stable, regular life, so she decided to have one final fling. To play a few childish games. To live a crazy life for a little while."

"Why just a little while?"

"Did you think she could abandon such a desirable man for the sake of this, how can I put it, not to offend you... mess! It's only in fairytales that the girl abandons the king for the shepherd."

"You know I believe in fairytales, Anya. I thought she did too, and we'd be an ideal couple. What we had was magical."

"You know, Crybaby... It's still not certain that you turned her head. The way you are.... It's not possible to say unequivocally that you're bad or good. For me you're a romantic, a fine person and my friend. But to someone else you're a spineless, featherbrained waste of space!" Her voice was suddenly severe. "You're always adrift somewhere on the astral plane. Have you already told Tanya all your fairytales? About your brother who was killed, although he never existed? And about Sailor, who you supposedly poisoned with bootleg vodka, although he's still alive and perfectly well? And about the underground city? And about... I don't know all the other stuff you've made up! And I won't even mention the LENSes – that's too crazy even for a story the morning after a pissup! Why do you lie all the time? What do you do it for?"

"I don't lie," I snapped back. "I make up stories, Anyuta!"

"I know you make up stories. And you believe what you tell people," said Anya, relaxing a little bit. "But how are other people to know that?"

"Maybe I see what other people don't notice?"

"But then you stubbornly refuse to see a fact that's absolutely obvious to everyone else. You're stuck in your childish complexes. For your information, there is another world – the world of adults – but the door to it is barred and locked to you."

I didn't reply to that.

"You really are a good person, Crybaby. There's something pristine about you. You're not like all the other ball-carriers. (That was Anya's name for all men without exception.) They're all high principles and bluff. So proud, always trying to prove something to someone... But you, you're just the way you are and you don't get uptight about it. Everything will work out fine for you. But not here and not now. You have to understand, Crybaby, you have a lot of wonderful qualities. Perhaps, and I emphasise, PERHAPS Tanya feels the same way about you as you do about her, and it's important for her to keep that magic. With her chosen life partner, everything will be very ordinary and very banal. They'll quarrel over trifles, and have loud rows. But you, the Magical Boy, have lit up her life for two weeks, and then gone back to your own magical country. And she will always remember you and love you, and for her you will always be magical. So why am I saying this? Don't even think of chasing her. Don't even think about it. Keep yourself busy: write songs, play computer games, watch TV until your brain's numb, work, study, bang your head against the wall. If you go running after her and beg her to come back, you'll only make things worse for yourself. You'll rip the wound in your heart wide open. Now come here."

She clasped me in her arms. I hugged my faithful Anya with both arms and wept bitterly for my dead dream. She stroked my hair.

"Cry as much as you like, Crybaby," my friend said seriously. "I won't throw you out. Just don't pour alcohol into yourself or slash your veins..."

A sudden thought made me pull myself out of Anya's arms, grab her hand and tear off the wristband that she never took off when I was with her.

Just as I thought, there was a dark scar under it. The scar that had killed my beloved fluffy dandelion and created the new Anya – tough, angular, harsh, with a boy's hairstyle.

"Did something like this happen to you? Is that why you changed? Did you drink? Did you try to kill yourself? Is all that why they expelled you?"

Anya just nodded to all my questions.

"They even put me in a loony bin for a whole month," she said quietly.

We embraced each other again. Anya looked at me with genuine pity.

"I really don't want to leave you at all..." I couldn't hear any emotions in her voice. "I'll miss you."

"Me too, Anya... I envy you. I could just drop all this shit right now and go with you."

As I left, I kissed Anya's cheeks, salty from my own tears.

I wasn't the only one blubbering that evening. At home I was greeted by loud howls and sobs, emitted by my totally blind drunk dad, with his face nestling against the top of the kitchen table and his entire alcohol-soaked body shuddering.

"What is it this time, you old devil?" I asked.

"Oh God, God..." my father moaned. "The boy... How could they do it? He's not to blame for being born like that... Eh? What they did to him... Begging on the street..."

Clear enough. He'd remembered that story *Little Fool* by Bunin again – about how this wanker of a seminary student had his way with a Down syndrome girl and they produced an incredibly ugly child, and later he was thrown out of the house, together with his mum, and they had to live on charity.

So, what would you like me to do? If the old soak was roaring and turning the air in the flat blue with obscenities, my fist would soon stop his mouth, but as it is... he's disgusting, but pitiful too.

Half an hour later the phone rang.

"Ferret on the line," the receiver grated repulsively. "Where did you get to, I've been calling all evening!"

"I got to wherever I got to. State the essence of the matter."

"The essence of the matter? Get yourself together and come to the bridge."

Well, well! Even this butt-sucker is good for something.

Ferret and I met on the bridge.

"Cheers, Romich!" he said, slapping me on the shoulder blade.

That habit of his has really pissed me off.

"You rodent, touch me again and I'll break your jaw!"

Ferret just grinned with his rotten teeth.

"Come off it, have you heard what's going on in town?"

"What?"

"The Doctors have gone on the rampage. They've decided to pick on everybody who went to the concert one at a time. Imagine it, they even gave our Foma's kidneys a good battering! And Critter and his guys got smashed up by a couple of docs too."

I couldn't believe my ears.

"How come? I thought they wouldn't come after us again!"

Ferret answered maliciously:

"You're too naive, Romka. They'll only stop coming after us when they're all in their graves. Anyway, this is the point: today at midnight there's going to be an almighty rumble, Doctors versus independents. What do you say? There are so many of us now! We'll hold a St. Bartholomew's Day Massacre for the red-and-whites, with the execution of the Streltsy in the morning!"

"What, you want to drag me into this business?"

"What do you mean, 'drag you in'? You and me were dragged in ages ago. Who did we hold the gig for, after all? For all the normal people in our town, you said so yourself! But if we don't smash the Doctors, there soon won't be any normal people left."

"So what if we played a gig, Ferret? Music's one thing, but gang battles are something else. A concert's fine, but I don't play these games."

"What games, Crybaby? That's bullshit. I don't understand you at all. What kind of game is it when good young guys are getting crippled?"

"Don't you yell at me, you halfwit!" I barked. "And don't breathe in my face! You can do what you like, all kill each other if you want, I couldn't care less! I'm not getting involved in this!"

"What's wrong with you? Have you got problems or something?"

"Yes, maybe I do..." I didn't try to deny it, because it was written all over my face anyway.

What kind of problem is it?

There were lots of problems, but I only mentioned one:

"Anya's leaving town!"

He smirked.

"Is that the whole problem? So, let her leave. We'll find another drummer!"

"Nah, that's not the point... She's my best friend..."

"What? Friend? Well, Romka that's a real good one!" Ferret laughed.

"Why?" I didn't get what he meant.

"What friendship can there be with dolls?"

The way Ferret rendered it, "dolls" sounded as foul as any word possibly could, and it didn't mean "individuals of the female sex" but "walking slits".

"No one can be friends with dolls," I declared scathingly, "but with lovely ladies, they can!"

He burst into laughter again. "Oh yeah, ladies! The only friends you have are ladies, Roma!"

"Ferret, you're like a little child! We're not in kindergarten any longer – why do you care who I hang out with?"

"Because you're not enough of a man! You'll turn into a lady yourself soon!"

Sure, of course it would be better to become a wonderful specimen like you!

"So what? It wouldn't hurt if we all had a bit more woman in us!"

"What? Crybaby, straight up, I don't understand you at all, what are you blabbering about?" asked Ferret, starting to feel alarmed. In his opinion, I'd just suggested homosexual lovemaking.

"Let's put the question this way: What do you want from me, Ferret?"

The animosity in my voice was so obvious that Ferret paused and shifted into a different tone of voice, soulful and slightly sycophantic.

"Crybaby – or Roma, whichever you prefer – this is what I want to say: there have been plenty of little misunderstandings between us, but that's all trivial stuff. Romka, you're my friend."

"Didn't you forget to ask if I want to be your friend?"

"What do mean, want? You are my friend."

I had to introduce a little clarity.

"Ferret! Have I ever, even once, called you my friend?"

"Romka, you and me play in the same band!"

"So what? There's a different name for that: partners, colleagues... But a friend is someone you'd do absolutely anything for."

"Romka, I'd do absolutely anything for you!" said Ferret, slapping his hand against his hollow chest. "I'd bite anybody's throat out with my bare teeth for you! And if they knock my teeth out, I'll use my gums. By fuck, I would!"

"That's good, probably, isn't it?" I enquired.

Well, what else could I say! If Ferret was even a little bit less of a freak than he was, I could have believed him. Basically, I'd been taking a risk from the very start by warming this hyena cub in my bosom, but what could I do – where was I going to find another bass-player? Bass-players are much rarer beasts than guitarists, especially in our reservation for retards. The same reason had forced us to keep Ferret in Adenoma before. Although Smurf had always been blissfully ignorant about this particular gentleman. He even believed that Ferret would change when the wind of childhood stopped playing in his arse. How naive! Petrochemist has never changed anyone for the better yet.

"Ferret, I don't want to be rude, so I'll say something else. When you get right down to it, I've got nothing against you, I like you just fine... but we haven't got enough in common for friendship. We're different kinds of people. Admit it!"

"So who do you have lots in common with? The ladies?" Ferret grinned. "Say what you like, Romka, but you're not just friends with that doll of yours, Priscilla, are you?"

"The relationship between Priscilla and me is none of your business..." I growled through my teeth.

"What is it, something not right between you and her?" Ferret said brightly after a moment's thought. "Dumped you, has she?"

I said nothing and silence, as usual, was taken for consent.

"Well I hope you gave her a good shafting at least once."

Without making a sound, I smashed Ferret in the teeth – I swear it just happened, I didn't will it – and I caught him so neatly that the rotten louse was laid out slantwise across the bridge.

I looked down on Ferret's prostrate figure.

"Ivan!" I said with feeling, breathing heavily in my rage. "I'm not beating you because you're a filthy, idle jerk, but because it will be good for you. It's better if I do it than anyone else. Although you won't get any smarter anyway..." I took Ferret by the collar, jerked him to his feet and whacked him heartily on the ear. It was slightly disgusting to soil my hands on this vaguely humanoid creature.

Ferret went flying away and hung there, bent over the parapet.

"Hey, don't you even think of falling," I yelled, dashing over to him.

"Ii-ekh!" Ferret barked, suddenly swinging round and

kicking me between the legs. A million Christmas trees lit up in front of my eyes and I doubled up in pain.

Two seconds later something came flying towards my face. I instinctively put my fist in the way. Crunch! My hand howled, and so did I.

Ferret hauled off to take another blow. I jumped a metre backwards. The thing clutched in the bass-player's skinny paw sheared through the air with a whooshing sound.

Ferret made a few more furious attacks, and I jumped further and further back. Finally I was able to see that his weapon was a homemade nunchaku – two wooden bars joined together by a long, thin chain.

We froze, crouching in combat poses.

"Why do you run, why do you run, eh, you little cunt?" Ferret ask spitefully, whirling the nunchaku around clumsily in front of him. There was blood snaking down his abominable face.

"What, were you going to go to the rumble with that nunchaku? They'll stick it up your anal orifice and pull it out of your mouth!" I said instead of answering. My left fist was weeping violently, my crotch was throbbing with pain, I was like a wounded beast. I had the brutish desire to break every single one of Ferret's ribs and teeth, and I would have done it, if not for the nunchaku.

"You ungrateful turd!" Ferret growled, coupling every more or less decent word with two or three swearwords. "I talk to you as a man, as a friend, like my own brother... And you – you traitor! And queer! You stirred this whole business up, and now you're pissing yourself? You've betrayed all of us, not just me, you're worse than the Doctors! If your brother was alive, you'd hand him over, tripes and all! I'll tell everyone how you ditched us! When we're finished with the Doctors, we'll start on you, don't you worry... Anyone who's not with us is against us! We'll have a word or two with you..."

"Wipe your ugly snout," I advised him.

"Attack me, you little cunt!" Ferret howled.

"After you," I replied.

Ferret came dashing at me.

"Ekh! Iekh! Ekh! Iekh!" he barked out, trying to catch me with the nunchaku. I kept jumping back, and when the latest blow was reaching the end of its swing, I was finally able to counterattack with a foot to Ferret's stomach. He leaned over towards me and I immediately jumped at him, knocked him off his feet and fell on him, pressing him down with my knee. I tore the nunchaku out of his hand. Ferret immediately reached into his jacket. I flung the nunchaku aside, grabbed hold of the hand and pulled it out – it was already clutching the little pistol. Ferret struggled to point his "rod" at me, but he didn't have the strength. I easily pulled his hand aside and smashed it against the asphalt a few times, forcing him to drop the weapon.

"Hey, you, wanted to shoot me, did you?" I said, putting Ferret out with a final heavy punch. Let him lie there. I kept my "war trophies" – the "cricket" and the nunchaku. I'd been on the lookout for something to replace that stupid bottle of Ultron for a long time. I even went as far as to rummage through the pockets of this soldier fallen in battle to get the other three cartridges. I found money too – three crumpled ten-rouble notes, a brand new fifty and a bit of small change. I expropriated the lot. He hadn't earned it anyway!

Battered, bruised and sick at heart, I wandered aimlessly through the labyrinths of Oblivion, until I came out onto brightly lit Marx Avenue, right beside the pharmacy. In the window ablaze with orange fire there was a glowing advertising placard devoted to new homeopathic remedies for male ailments. The biggest letters on it spelled out a slogan: "GOODBYE, ADENOMA!"

I had to survive until tomorrow somehow. Insomnia was already standing behind me, grinning and pulling faces. The night ahead frightened me. I know what it's like, talking to ghosts for hours on end, tossing and turning on a fiery-hot bed, clenching your fists... going over the same moments again and again, and crying because you can't change anything anymore. And I wouldn't get away with just one sleepless night. Or two, or a week of them. Yes, yes, Macbeth has murdered sleep. And now Macbeth won't be getting any more of it... In comparison with my present state, all my previous downers were like a gentle breeze.

I merged into the flow of people and drifted along the street with them, passed the open door of a domestic appliances shop, then went straight back: coming out of the door was the signature tune of a certain well-known TV comedy show.

Okay, I'll take a look, take my mind off things. For two minutes. Or three.

I glanced in through the door. Five people were already standing in front of a gigantic television with a superflat screen. A wiry, shaggy-haired comedian appeared and the subtitles informed us: Semyon Shaferman, "Surname".

The comedian started in a trembling, affectedly uncertain voice:

"I... I... I'm not a very interesting person, and you could say there's nothing remarkable about me... Apart from my surname, of course – oh yes, indeed! That's for sure... Oh, the beatings life has given me for that surname... I remember, in geography at school, the teacher used to open the register and say..."

The comedian's face turned stern, his eyebrows knitted together, and he continued in a hostile bass voice, running his finger across an invisible register:

"'Right... Who's coming up to blackboard... Who will it be... Anisimov? No... Krabova? No... Martyshkin... Murunov...'" – and then the comedian-teacher's face lit up and he exclaimed joyfully: "'Siskin-Piskin!'"

The viewers laughed. I grinned, despite myself.

Semyon Shaferman continued in the trembling voice of a failure:

"And so I creep to the blackboard, cursing myself for not having learned my lessons, and my surname, and my dad, who left me that surname. (The teacher's gleeful voice.) 'Right then, right then, let's have a listen to Siskin, our own Piskin!' (A failure's voice.) So there I am at the blackboard, standing there and speaking out manfully... (A totally downtrodden voice.) There are rivers in Siberia, they flow and they disgorge... (A pause, the teacher's voice, reproachfully.) 'Siskin-Piskin!' (The failure's voice, with a hysterical ring to it.) There are many, very many rivers in Siberia... They flow and they disgorge! (An even longer pause. The teacher's voice, indignantly.) 'Siskin-Piskin!'"

Shaferman lowered his head and lapsed into shamefaced silence, then he was reincarnated once again as the irate teacher and thundered:

"'What am I to make of this, Siskin-Piskin! You haven't learned the lesson again, Siskin-Piskin! This is gross disrespect for the subject and the teacher, you Siskin-Piskin you!'"

At every mention of the hero's surname, the audiences on the screen and in front of it writhed about in hysterics. Shaferman the teacher covered his face with his hands, he was about to burst into tears:

"'Oh, come now, Siskin-Piskin!... How can you do this, Siskin-Piskin? (Lowers his hands helplessly and sighs heavily.) Ah, Siskin-Piskin, Siskin-Piskin...'"

Shaferman continued in a trembling voice:

"But my trials and tribulations only really started in the army..."

"Romka! Cheers!" Someone slapped me on the shoulder. It was Valerka, dressed too lightly for the weather: light jogging jacket, wide-legged jeans, a rapper's bandana and trainers.

"Good evening..." I shook the hand held out to me.

I only knew Valerka very slightly – from our underground club in the old library. I knew that he was supposedly studying in the evening institute and worked as a trainer in a fitness centre (the same one where my "ex", Christina, abuses her body for two hours three evenings a week). Why he wasn't in the army yet was a complete riddle to me.

"What's wrong, Romka?" was the first thing he said.

"'Siskin-Piskin!'" Shaferman yelled in a sergeant-major's voice.

"Why?"

"You look really down in the dumps! Your face looks like you had every disease that exists. What's happened – maybe I can help?"

"You're not looking any better yourself, actually," I replied. "As pale as a snowman."

"'Siskin-Piskin!'"

"Everything's just dandy with me," Valerka said guardedly, although I could see perfectly well he was shuddering, like he was freezing. I gave as good as I'd got:

"I'm doing just fine too."

"Ah, my friend, that won't do at all," Valerka objected. "Tell me what's up with you, and I'll say what's up with me. How's that for a deal?"

"'Siskin-Piskin!'"

"Okay. Only let's get out of here."

"'Siskin-Piskin!'" The exclamation rang out behind our backs.

Outside I told him everything.

"So this is the way things are: the girl I love has done a bunk, the band's fallen apart, my best friend's leaving town... Otherwise everything's just great."

"My situation's pretty wonderful too. You know what's been set for zero hundred hours tonight?"

"I know. Only don't tell me you're going to be there!"

"I am, Roma. Look, I decided to take a wander, walk up an appetite, get it?"

"Valerich, it's sheer idiocy!" I exclaimed. "I didn't expect this from you. How come you got sucked into this? You're a perfectly normal kind of guy."

"So what If I am normal? Like it or not, something has to be done about the Doctors."

"So you've given in to mass hysteria, have you? Better go home, Valerich!"

"Listen, Romka, I'm not trying to persuade you to come to the rumble with me, am I?" said Valerka, as guardedly as ever. "Don't worry about me, I've come through worse. I'll have a drop of beer, and then I'm ready for the Doctors, or the resuscitators, or the pathologists! I'll give them all a whipping."

"If you haven't got anything to do for the next couple of hours anyway, come with me," I suggested, fingering the money I'd taken from Ferret in my pocket. "I'll stand you a beer."

"I can buy my own beer... But where do you want me to go with you?"

"A certain spot where I haven't been for a thousand years. Only I need to buy a few flowers. Do you know where I can do that?"

"Flowers? At this hour? Valerka rubbed his chin. "The only place I can think of is the souvenir shop in the 24-hour supermarket, beside the magazine counter. Only the flowers are artificial, you know that."

"That'll do," I said and nodded.

... The cemetery is inside the town limits, with construction sites surrounding it on all sides.

"They say this place will be a car park soon," I said, walking beside the fence. "First they'll flatten everything here with a bulldozer, and then they'll asphalt it over and steam roller it. I expect they'll choose an appropriate name: 'A Better World' or 'Eternal Haven'. And at night the rides will drive off by themselves and race around the town... This is our spot, Valer."

I leaned down over the grave and put the plastic flowers on the headstone. I stood there in silence for fifteen minutes, without my cap, leaning against the railings. The wind tousled my hair. I actually did start feeling better. The problems didn't go away; I just froze, like a computer, disconnected from the entire world. Valerka stood beside me, serious and thoughtful, then opened the little gate in the railings.

"Where are you going?"

"To have a smoke."

"Smoke right here. She doesn't mind."

"She?" Valerka ignited his cigarette lighter, lit up and held the little flame close to the headstone. "Who is she – Regina Mendeleeva?"

"My sister. She died from the poisoned sunshine, when I was sixteen."

"Sorry, I didn't catch that – what did she die of?"

"Heart failure."

"I didn't even know you had a sister. You tell us so many interesting things about yourself, but you never mention her."

"It's not something I can tell anyone about. It's sacred..."

Sacred, hmmm I'm not sure that's a word that can be used here. Regina was anything but holy.

"She changed me... No, more than that – she created me, the way I am now."

"The cool dude Romka?" Valerka asked with a smile.

I didn't try to explain anything.

"You know, Roman, I'm feeling a bit better. How do you do that? It's like I'd drunk some kind of magic potion."

"You haven't drunk it yet," I retorted. "We'll stock up on beer now..."

"I'll tell you what, Roman," said Valerka. "Do you know my address?"

"Na-ah. We don't really know each other, if you think about it."

"Well then, we'll fix that. Have you got a pen and paper?"

"Sure I have."

One thing I never leave the house without is writing materials. A little thought could pop into my head at any moment – an idea for a song or something else.

"Jot down my address and mobile number. Do you remember my surname?"

"Siskin-Piskin?" I suggested. No other name came to mind.

Valerka took the notepad and pen out of my hands:

"If you're feeling strung out tomorrow, haul over to my place. I'll tell you how we fucked those Doctors over, and we'll figure out a few things... We'll set your life in order."

"I'll hold you to that," I said, miming as if I was shooting Valerka with my finger. "Well, if that's the way, you know what... Take this piece of trash, it'll come in useful." And I took out the nunchaku.

"You keep it, Romka," Valerka said with a smile. "A nunchaku's a crude two-dimensional weapon, but in a fight you have to think in three dimensions."

He opened his jacket, and hidden underneath it was a long chain, folded over several times.

"Well, go for it," I said encouragingly.

We went to get the booze.

17. [clinical death]

At eight in the morning I said goodbye to Anya. My Anechka. All her bits and pieces fitted into a rucksack and a sports bag.

The bus station is the dirtiest place in town, just the way it should be. The platforms are cracked and dilapidated. The waiting room – a tin hut – is boarded up. And then there's the human mishmash. There's no place more crowded in Petrochemist. This is a place where anyone can see that in our town there isn't a single person over twenty who's in good physical or mental health. The town has failed to kill them off quickly, and in revenge for their stamina, it makes them die by one teaspoonful every hour. The people cough as if they're about to throw up all their innards. They're wrapped in dozens of sweaters and scarves. They have swollen, cracked, asymmetrical faces and watery eyes, dark flaking skin with wide pores, sores crusted over with dried scabs. Not a single decently dressed person there, they're all togged out just a little bit better than street bums. Why should they bother about their appearance, if the town has already mutilated them?

There were tables beside the platform, with brain pies, which were brooding over how grisly this life can get. Beside them the heart pies were suffering from human indifference. I won't say anything about the liver pies – they were spasming acutely from all this foulness.

> *Feet set deep in mushy filth,*
> *In their black galoshes.*
> *Souls awash with slushy shit,*
> *White snow-sprinkled faces.*

That was what my mood was like. And incidentally, that was also the beginning of a new song. Only I didn't know what to write about after that. My perennial problem: I come up with a quatrain, but I can't compose anything to follow it. I've said everything I wanted to say.

"Anya, look, the Bus Driver's turned up. He'll take you all the way to the nature reserve without any changes!" I joked when I spotted the celebrated psycho.

Mirthless Anya put on a smile.

"You thought up names that really fit those crazies!"

I shrugged modestly.

When she had her foot on the step of the bus, Anya swung round sharply and raised her index finger to my face:

"Promise, Crybaby!"

"I promise, Anya."

"Good boy!" she said and gave me a peck on the forehead.

The doors closed with a hiss right in front of my nose. Everyone knows you kiss corpses on the forehead.

From the bus station I went straight to College. I greeted Artyom rapidly as I passed through the turnstile and headed for the auditorium – to pretend to take notes on the lectures. In the corridor I was stopped by Oleg jabbing the stem of his pipe into my belly.

"Well Roman, are you satisfied? Christina's collecting her documents."

"What documents?"

"From the dean's office. She's transferring. She can't bear to see you every day."

"A-ah... I thought something had happened..." I said with a nod and wandered on.

Oleg caught up with me, champing furiously.

"Roman, I despise you. You've brought shame on the girl! You know who you are?"

"Siskin-Piskin," I replied in a tone that implied the question was rhetorical. Oleg staggered back when I looked straight into his clear eyes. I think he realised I wasn't very god company today.

I wonder what he expected to hear? If it was repentance, then for what? I had no intention of going back to Christina, although the thought did pop up every now and then. Go to her cap in hand? Screw that! That would make her feel like the Queen of the Universe, she'd mock me into the ground, and enjoy it, ridicule me from head to foot, make me crawl on my knees from the Krivitsky Ravine to Concord Street, and then reinstate me in the position of her beloved – in the absolute certainty that the permanence of our relationship had acquired a monolithic character. And there'd be nothing left for me to do but trivialise myself down to her level and live by the same stupid rules as she does. No thanks, spare me that!

And then I met Ruslana – miserable, with red eyes and a slightly puffy face. They'd called her at one in the morning, dragged her out of bed and sent her off to the edge of town, to the wasteland, to film the scene of the bloody battle between the Doctors and the independents.

At the wasteland Ruslana saw about six ambulances and a long line of small police jeeps. Their flashing lights cast multicoloured glimmers on the rusty skeleton of the truck and the motionless bodies lying all around. In response to Ruslana's question, one of the guardians of the law informed her that, according to provisional figures, there were about eighty participants in the fight left on the wasteland, and at least twenty of them were fatalities. The others had run off as soon as they heard the sirens. There were so many that it was impossible to arrest them all, but even so about twenty individuals had been detained. It was the first battle on this scale in a decade. And in addition, the officer mentioned that he personally had seen a monkey dressed in rags. It was making its way across the wasteland, searching the badly injured young men, when it was caught in the beam of a policeman's flashlight and dashed off.

The cameraman shot the bleeding boys in close-up. It was a terrible sight: slash wounds that looked like open mouths, eyes poked out and teeth smashed in, hair matted together with blood, the white stumps of bones protruding through torn sleeves and trouser legs. Ruslana found Critter among the victims of the fight, with a clown's makeup smeared across his face: they'd shoved a two-foot metal shank into his stomach. He wasn't likely to survive with a wound like that. Soon a bus arrived – there were so many wounded that the ambulances couldn't cope.

Kids with injuries of varying degrees of severity carried on arriving at the in-patient department of the town hospital all morning: they were the warriors who had fled from the field of battle even though they were seriously hurt, and been forced to seek medical assistance. The wounded arrived in such great numbers that all more or less healthy patients were evacuated from every department of the clinic as a matter of emergency.

Ruslana found Valerka in the hospital too. They'd broken his right arm and a few ribs. But even so he was feeling cheerful and he told Ruslana what he'd seen with his own eyes.

In all about four hundred people gathered on the wasteland, in two crowds. The independents were pretty much the same bunch as at the concert, but the advantage of numbers was with the Doctors: they'd managed to strike an alliance with all the local vocational college students, even the ones who were devoted rock music fans. (Most likely, many of the new recruits had been crudely bought or primitively frightened.) Most of the independents had made up their faces with war paint. Both sides were heavily armed: chains, knives, metal shanks, bricks, lengths of piping, tyre spanners. They handed bottles of drink round from hand to hand: vodka, beer, fortified wine, home brew. The warriors drank to raise their spirits, and the empty bottles became weapons as well. When they were half-tanked, the independents started singing in chorus: "Arise and dress, be on your way, for this is your final day! Your final battle has arrived, you will not leave the field alive!" The song was addressed to the Doctors.

The battle ahead was not like the usual settling of accounts over a debt not paid in time or a carelessly spoken word, it promised to be a bitter battle to annihilation. Both the independents and the Doctors hated their enemies with a visceral hatred. So there weren't any of the detailed discussions on the gang code that every showdown usually starts with.

Without any preliminaries, the two crowds threw themselves

at each other and clashed, the young guys beat each other with pieces of metal, stuck knives into each other, knocked their opponents to the ground and stamped on them, rolled about clinging to each other, like bears. Bricks flew overhead. The battle quite quickly fell apart into a series of duels: everyone found himself an opponent, and once he got the best of him, went looking for another. As an experienced gymnast, Valerka handled his long chain with virtuoso skill. He managed to put four Doctors out of action before three of them finally knocked him down and started working him over. Just then the sirens started sounding, and they saved Valerka from certain death: Doctors and independents went dashing off, working their legs as hard as they could and merging into a single stream.

Petrochemist had wept a whole month's worth of bloody tears.

"So who won?" I asked.

"No one. A Chinese Draw – all the pieces wiped off the board. I don't think there'll be any more large-scale battles like this for a long time – both sides need to lick their wounds..." Ruslana replied, closing her red eyes. "Ah, my head's splitting... They gave your Ferret a bad beating too. He arrived in a foul mood, brought a bottle of some kind of booze with him. He got plastered quickly and started yelling louder than anyone else – saying that first he was going to flatten all the Doctors, and then that lousy little bastard Crybaby. I saw him in the hospital today. I only recognised him from his physique and his axe-shaped earring; they'd turned his face into a bloody pulp. I stopped to look and see if it was really him. I stood there for a minute, then the nurse came, checked him and pulled the blanket up over his face..."

"You know, I don't feel sorry for him at all. Not him, or Critter, or any of the rest..." I said thoughtfully. "They're all idiots. Were. You know, Rusya, if you figure it out, the whole sorry mess is because of me, because of our concert..."

"That's not true, Roma!" Ruslana squealed nervously, banging her little fist down on the windowsill. "It's not your fault! You didn't call those idiots to the wasteland. They went there themselves, of their own accord!"

"Exactly. That's just what I'm saying."

The tears poured out of Ruslana's eyes, her face wrinkled up and she started crying loudly, like a child. She'd seen a lot of things that morning.

That evening, after doing my work mechanically and indifferently (I wonder how many mistakes I missed?) I realised I had absolutely nowhere to go apart from home, to the eternally whingeing alcoholic. Nothing made any sense anymore, there was no one around who could ease my suffering. There was no one at all that I could simply spend the evening with, without touching on any painful subjects. Anya had cleared out. If I knew Ruslana, she wouldn't want to see me right now: if she was at home, she was trying to sleep and forget what she'd seen. Natasha was probably working or taking a rest after work. I could call on Angie – but with her babe-in-arms she didn't have time for anyone... Dammit! The late Ferret was right when he said I hung out with dolls a lot more than guys. I enjoy their company much more. And I don't regret it at all! Why is that? If I was gay, it would all be clear...

If I shared these thoughts with Anya, she'd be bound to say: "It's just that you're stronger, you're not looking for a collective that you can hide behind, like a wall. Spend time with the people whose company you like best, and to hell with anyone who objects." Anya idealises me in lots of ways. Or maybe she's just paying her tribute of gratitude from school. Apart from me, no one in the class treated Anya normally. Even when they battered her face for her at the disco, no one stuck up for her. I had to rake apart the crowd of screeching, drunken hobgoblins and drag poor Anya out – of course, I came in for a mauling too – and take her back to my place to daub green disinfectant on her bleeding cheeks.

It had got dark without me realising it. I wandered along the streets, not noticing how one changed into another.

> *A night perfumed with freedom,*
> *Hearts beating a jagged rhythm,*
> *With raging turmoil in my brain*
> *I go to look for yesterday...*

Priscilla... I was thinking about her again. Maybe she's sprawled out with her manager right now. He's stroking her on the back, like a kitten, and she's arching up and stretching. "Where have you been for the last two weeks, Tanya?" he asks her. "Far away," she answers. "In a parallel world. I had a different life, and my name was different too. It was strange there, and great, but I won't go back again." "I don't understand," says her little fiancé, getting nervous. "Where did you really get to?" "I just went to my grandmother's place! Why, what did you think?" "You're a real daydreamer, you are!" he laughs in relief. "A-a-ah, afraid of the competition? Don't worry, I'm all yours. I won't disappear again."

Ah, Siskin-Piskin, Siskin-Piskin... What a total fuck up!

I suddenly got this feeling, familiar, but inexpressible. I don't know how to explain it. I used to get the feeling when I was a kid, when I wandered into the deserted corners of my home town: the abandoned stadium, the park, the ruined church. I wandered about all on my own and imagined the most incredible things, I did battle with imaginary bandits and villains, mostly stolen from various different films. For me Petrochemist was a kind of post-apocalyptic town, half-dead, where power belonged to the forces of evil. And actually, that's what it really is.

Naturally, I regarded myself as a lone wolf, a champion

battling the dark hordes. My constant companion, oddly enough, was sorrow. Not because no one went with me on my walks: I had more than enough friends, but I'd stopped initiating them into my game as soon as I realised they couldn't follow the way my thoughts moved, they didn't understand. My hero was always sorrowful: not aggressive or withdrawn, but precisely sorrowful. His victory – that is, mine – was always clouded by something: either my imaginary girlfriend was killed (I didn't have any real ones in those days), or my former friends turned their weapons against me... It was precisely this feeling of something mysterious and fantastic, and at the same time sorrowful that had gripped me. There was no despair, no fury, only profound sorrow.

"Have you called an ambulance?" someone barked in my ear. I recoiled, demonstrating the instantaneous reactions possessed by all children of Petrochemist. A fist, weighted with a knuckle-duster, came hurtling towards my face, I jerked to one side, but the metal just caught me and scraped my cheek raw.

I pulled Ferret's nunchaku out from under my jacket and smashed the Doctor on the jaw. A nunchaku's a pretty hefty item, all the same! Three more Doctors sprang up where the first one was lying, one was immediately sent flying off to the side, the other two jumped back. Three more ran up and joined them.

We stood there facing each other in the space picked out of the night by the light of a streetlamp: me with the nunchaku at the ready and five Doctors, crouching like boxers. The sixth one was rolling about in the dirt, complaining about his broken jaw. The seventh looked bored, lying motionless with one darkened cheek.

I heard footsteps behind me. I quickly moved back to the wall and pressed my shoulder blades against it, to avoid an attack from behind. There were eight of my enemies, not counting the two who had been put out of action. The Doctors usually move round the town in large herds: if this encounter had taken place a day earlier, before the showdown on the wasteland (in my own mind I called it the Battle of Oblivion), I'd be under attack from at least thirty thugs by now. But no matter how many of them there were, it was clearly too late for medical intervention. Nothing was going to get through to me now.

"Well, musician? You're fucked, you and your Prostatitis!" said one who was as skinny as a coat hanger, and they all started cackling. I recognised the skinny one. It was the outrageously resilient Compass: his right hand bandaged, a half-healed lilac bruise on his chin, his left ear cleft like a stray dog's.

"Come on, try it!" I encouraged him. "Meet Jackie Chan!" The scrape on my cheek was bleeding freely. I could sense that after they'd been through the Battle for Oblivion and felt various solid objects on their own skins, the Doctors were afraid of the nunchaku. They kept their eyes fixed on my weapon. That lent me courage, because I didn't know a thing about the martial arts. I could be quite certain that I was indeed fucked, but the question was: What losses would the Doctors suffer in the process?

"Who's first? Pissed yourselves, have you?" I wasn't afraid of anything anymore, I really wanted to provoke the lowlifes into attacking and lay another couple of them out.

The Doctors loitered on the spot, waiting for something, and it came – a white Zhiguli 9 drove into the narrow street and hurtled straight at my shaven-headed adversaries. They darted out of the way and the car braked, digging up the earth with its rubber hooves.

The door swung open.

Like a Jack jumping out of his box, an object of very considerable size leapt out of the car and started flailing like a windmill, smashing the Doctors down rapidly and ruthlessly, like a giant beating pygmies. The drunk teenagers went flying through the air, smashed into walls and flopped heavily into the puddles. Compass fell first, doubled over by a blow to the kidneys from the side of a hand.

Five of them were laid out, and two managed to get away. The giant grabbed the other one, the scraggiest of all, by the scruff of the neck, raised his fist, which was the size of the Doctor's weedy head, to the Doctor's conk and started talking. He talked for a long time, very colourfully, and the essence of what he said was that anyone who so much as looked askew at Roman Mendeleev would have to deal with a member of the paratroop forces and, if necessary, more than one. Then the giant pushed the midget away and stepped back with an expression of disgust on his face.

"Would you believe it, Roman! That young whelp shit his pants!"

The nunchaku fell out of my hand. The inhuman strain came to an end, and so did my final strength. It was as if a puppet's strings had been cut – I tumbled down onto the asphalt, close to fainting.

The giant hurried across to me.

"Artyom..." I wanted very much to hug him. For want of anything better, I hugged his legs.

"Romka, how are you?" Artyom asked anxiously.

"Everything's fine..."

"Shall I give you a lift home?"

"Yes, if it's no trouble."

"Hey, what do you mean, 'trouble'?" and he set me on my feet without any effort and led me over to the car.

Epilogue. [reincarnation]

We managed to find a sticking plaster in Artyom's first-aid kit. I stuck the torn skin on my cheek together crudely, wiped the blood off my face and neck with a handkerchief and wiped my hands – on my trousers, because there wasn't a dry spot left on the handkerchief.

"Maybe I should take you to hospital? Roma, how are you feeling?"

"No, no, everything's okay."

"The things that are happening in Petro, fucking incredible! Have you heard about the rumble there was last night? Real battle action! I only found out today when I watched the news on the box. Turned out my little brother was there too, at least he came away in one piece. When I found out, I gave him a clip on the head..."

Lit-up street lamps flickered past outside the windows, and huge metal frameworks, like cages for a whole brood of Godzillas.

"It's a real miracle you were driving past!" I remarked.

"Nothing really miraculous about it. But it's a strange story, all right."

"What do you mean?"

"Well, I'm driving down a completely different street, going to do a few things, when I get this text message; THEY'RE BEATING ROMA MENDELEEV ON FRIENDSHIP STREET. No signature. Well, I really stepped on it! I thought I'd be too late. Do you know who it was? I haven't got a clue. He knows me, and you!"

"I'm afraid I do. Stop now, please," I said.

"But you don't live here, do you?"

"No, I just..." I didn't have enough inspiration to lie. "I want to walk back."

"Are you sure?"

"Artyom!" I said with a smile, mimicking boundless optimism. "Believe me, I know what I'm doing. I really want to."

"Whatever you say."

I squeezed his massive great hand in both of mine, and

limped away rapidly. I looked for a place where I could get away from everyone, and I found it – the old Light Ray stadium.

On the wall beside the rusty gates I saw some graffiti that stamped themselves into my brain at the first glance: in the background – standard, cement-block apartment buildings, in the foreground – a horrible child, looking like an embryo. Naked, wrinkled and pale-yellow, with two heads. On one face both eyes were covered over by membranes, on the other they were wide open, and they were black, with white pupils. Below the child's feet were the words: THINK AGAIN.

I walked in through the open gates, passed a half-ruined grandstand (all that was left was the brick framework, the wooden seats had rotted and fallen apart ages ago), cut across the running track with pale grass breaking through its asphalt, and walked out onto the football pitch, lit up by the windows of the nearest nine-storey apartment block.

I took out the small pistol I'd grabbed from Ferret and set it against my temple.

"Hey, Phantom, now how are you going to save me," I chuckled to myself.

"Romka!" a jolly voice exclaimed behind me.

It was just too incredible altogether. I must have flipped already – never mind, it's more interesting this way.

I swung round. There was the Phantom, standing about five steps behind me: bareheaded, a ribbon across his forehead, the same long coat.

"Well, what were you going to do?" he said with a reproachful smile.

"Haven't you guessed? I want to exhibit my brains."

"What for? Who needs it?"

"I've got a different question, my dear Phantom," I said acidly. "What the hell do YOU want from ME?"

"I want you to throw that toy away. If you press the trigger now, you'll destroy your soul. Don't shoot yourself, Roma!"

"I'm not going to, I've just had a better idea." I pointed the little pistol at the Phantom's chest. "If you're really a phantom, you've got nothing to be afraid of. But if you're not, this is going to hurt!" I told him, starting to shout, feeling myself hating the Phantom more and more intensely every second. "Hands up!"

Still smiling ironically, the Phantom raised his hands. With an air as if he was saying: All right, if you insist, I can put my hands up.

"Stand still!" I ordered him. "Answer: who are you?"

"A man, just like you."

Tell me more lies, you snake!

"Why are you haunting me? Why did you introduce me to Priscilla – that was all your work, don't deny it!"

"Because, Roma," the Phantom sighed. "Because. Because I felt sorry for you."

"Sorry for me? But everything was all right."

"All right doesn't mean good, Roma," the Phantom retorted.

"Everything was excellent!" I howled.

"Everything wasn't excellent, Roma. You know how I see the world and people? The world is darkness, and people are lights. Some of them are candles, some are lamps, and some are beacons. You, Roma, are a beacon, and I wanted that beacon to shine at full strength..."

I interrupted:

"It seems to me you couldn't give a damn for me. You're not a human being, you're Oblivion! You stirred up this mess so that more people would die! You don't help people, you destroy them. The way you've destroyed me, and everybody who was killed in the fight on the wasteland. And you collect the souls... And when I peg out, you'll grab my soul too! But first I'll make a hole in your belly and see what happens."

"You're clueless, Romka! Absolutely clueless... Surely you

understand, it's not the town that kills us, we kill each other! That's something we humans do, isn't it? I'm not a demon or a ghost – just a man who was lucky enough to be born slightly different. And as for you – I wanted you to become stronger. And see the word differently. It's very easy to feed yourself stories all your life, about how you live in a place that's bewitched... but this is a perfectly ordinary place. Tell me, Roma, why do you want to kill yourself? Because of the band? You'll put a new group together. Because of the guys who were killed in the fight? That massacre would have happened sooner or later anyway – suppurating abscesses have a habit of bursting. Because of the girl? You'll find another one."

The bastard's grin stretched right across his ugly mug.

"You don't understand... Priscilla's not just any girl, she's my Yoko, she's the life I never had and now never will have... You know, it's like I've been irradiated. It feels like nothing makes sense any more, I'm going to die slowly of leukaemia, in torment. You understand all that, don't you, you fucking telepath? Explain why you did it all!"

"What did I do?" the Phantom asked with a smile. "Nobody dragged you to the Church of the White Angels by force. Do you think I planned everything that's happened to you over the last three weeks from start to finish? No way, I'm not God Almighty! I just gave you an opportunity, and you decided whether to take it or not. And you did all the rest yourself too, I only gave you a nudge. Your life was all mouldy, and I just wanted to show you that you need to take the maximum from life."

Honestly, he was just begging for a bullet!

"The maximum? I feel lousy right up to the maximum!"

"Lousy is better than nothing. It's better to suffer than to be indifferent to everything. You've got lots of new opportunities ahead of you. You feel lousy? Well, that's an incentive to overcome this condition. You feel unhappy? Try to become happy again. At least recall the guys who were killed last night on the wasteland or crippled for the rest of their lives. You could have shared their fate, but you managed to keep out of it and save yourself for something better – so don't rob yourself of this chance! Think well about what I've said, and you'll see that I'm right."

"Maybe I understand what you're talking about, dear Phantom. I won't shoot you, if you tell me at least one reason why I can't do it."

"Okay, I'll tell you. The cartridge in Ferret's pistol is a blank."

"What?" My arm sank down of its own accord.

"Surely you don't think anyone would give that psychopath a gun with live rounds?" The Phantom smiled so broadly that his mouth and eyes turned into three slits. "By the way, don't forget to visit Baby May. All her friends are either dead or in hospital. Find her. She needs care and attention more than ever now, my friend! Be seeing you." He swung round with a flap of his coattails and headed for the gates.

I watched him go, then turned towards a large panel of plywood that still bore the faint outline of the Olympic rings and the faded words: "O SPORT, YOU ARE THE WORLD!" I aimed at the white dove of peace and squeezed the trigger. There was a fine bang all right, but no bullet hole appeared in the plywood.

"Bastard freaks!" I snorted, flung the pistol into the grass and walked towards the exit. It was only then I realised my hands were frozen, and I stuffed them as deep as I could into the pockets of my jacket. The skin was sure to split now. When I got home, I'd have to look out that old tube of baby cream.

"Siskin-Piskin, Siskin-Piskin..." I muttered dull-wittedly as I walked along. "Can't get the damn thing out of my head."

When I reached the gates, I'd already composed the ending to my finest fairytale.

The five of us were racing along in a small bus. Almost all

the space was taken up by the dismantled drum kit that bounced and clattered every time the vehicle hit a bump. The windows were hot from the summer sun. Ahead of us was the first road tour in our lives – a series of gigs in various towns. Not in big stadiums yet, just small clubs.

I was sitting in the back of the bus, hugging Priscilla, who was snuggling up against me. On the next seat Anya was combing out her luxuriant silvery hair with a wooden comb. Foma was dozing opposite her. Ferret was smoking standing up, blowing the smoke out through a small open window. Just recently our freak had acquired a girlfriend, who promptly set about making a man of him: Ferret had started wearing clothes that were new, washing his hair twice a week and buying only good cigarettes.

"You see, my sweet, I told you we'd win!" I said tenderly and tickled Priscilla's neck with my tongue. My princess opened her eyes and presented me with a smile.

"Thanks for everything, Crybaby."

Outside the windows of the bus, magnificent lakes framed by lush green trees flowed into each other, glittering and shimmering, casting bright spots of sunlight on us. It was hard to believe that we had only left Petrochemist an hour ago.

"How are you doing, princess?"

"I'm so happy, I could blow my top. I just can't believe it. What's going to happen next, Crybaby?"

"I don't know," I admitted honestly. "In any case, that's a new fairytale."

Pavel Kostin

Rooftop Anesthesia

For Lena and all of them

Most urbanites like their heat hot. They enjoy the sun's dusty violation of their defenceless bodies. They enjoy an oppressive noon in June, with all its excruciating urban trappings: sizzling hot tarmac, grey foliage on half-dead trees, headaches. They really like it.

Although, of course, they don't admit it. And, what's more, as soon as this kind of pestilence sets in, the endless whinging about "the heat" starts up in the buses and the offices. The city folk pull long faces, squinting aghast at the blazing street through the patterned glass and wheezing hoarsely about their suffering. Ha-ha! Wasn't that you just a week ago, peering up at the grey mother-of-pearl sky, invoking the heat to descend on this town? And now what? There it is, your heat, it's finally shown up! I know, next comes the talk about sea and sand and a suntan. That's no answer, honourable citizens! It's time to define your position and accept responsibility! Either heat or rain, all right?

But I know what I want. I hate heat. In any of its manifestations. Sand doesn't make the air any cooler, and water doesn't take the heat out of the sun. Sweat, dust and heat make it hard to think. And the beach... it's just another garbage tip, only bigger.

My name's Peter. I appreciate rain like no one else does. When the sky's grey, I find it easy to breathe. It's physiological. Maybe some kind of sickness: I haven't had myself checked out.

I'm nineteen. I'm an atheist. That's not particularly important, but anyway... I'm a loner. I suppose. In questionnaires people write: "I prefer to be alone". What drivel you write, comrades. If you "prefer to be alone", you simply are alone. In the most extreme case, that's simply what you are, a solitary by nature, and no one's really bothered about what you "prefer".

So what else can I tell you about myself? I'm tall. Quite cute from some angles. Hair – light, mind – dark. Eyes – blue.

I've started this story because these days the solitude that I "prefer" has become a problem. Screw the anxiety and depression – they're just ghost-ideas! But this morning – on this scorching Tuesday the 4th of June – the moment suddenly arrived when I needed other people. I repeat, nothing to do with anxiety and depression. Those words are fakes. What's the point of rummaging through your memories and endorsing every one of them "lonesome" or "not lonesome", if you can simply get up and go to a place where there are people? If you don't, you choose it all yourself. You "prefer to be alone".

I'm a thrill-seeker. Not in the sense of sex without condoms, but extreme sports. Not skateboards, or bikes, or roller skates, nothing at all exotic. I invented my own sport. Urban extreme, heard of it? No, of course not...

The triumph of freestyle, that's what it is. All the adrenalin you could want, the beauty of danger is present to some extent, and there's plenty of scope for applying agility.

It's hard to explain the gist of it straight off, just like that. Every single operation has its own gist, that's the whole point. One day it's one thing, another day it's something else. Night, rather. I go out at night, because it's more convenient. And there's no lousy sun at night.

Right, stop there. Now you'll go thinking I'm some kind of psycho, with a knife, rope and Vaseline neatly arranged in my sports bag. Never. I'm an urban freestyler, and even though there is a rope in my bag, it's not intended for tying up brown-eyed schoolgirls. I usually tie it round myself to stay safe.

Like tonight. The current operation has been worked out in every detail, rehearsed twenty times over (conceptually) and, as always, it will go smoothly. Fanfare, applause! Sure, I'm still nervous anyway. You'd feel nervous too. That's what adrenalin does, that's what extreme's like, it's the reason I'm an urban freestyler. Tonight I'm going to climb to the top of our tallest building and climb back down it. I'll climb up the staircase, then climb down an entirely different way, and it'll be frightening. Or rather, it's frightening now, it won't be frightening later, but you get the idea.

* * *

I walk across the dark yard, stealing closer to the entrances. The building from which it is ordained that I shall make my extreme descent today, is downtown, near enough. True, it's abandoned, but that doesn't blight the idea too much, right? My trainers make no noise. My T-shirt doesn't rustle. The adrenalin is gradually stoking up a blithe fury. "Blithe fury" is one of the key concepts of urban extreme. I'll describe it in minute detail sometime.

But let's get back to our abandoned buildings. It would remind you of a seventy-metre-long concrete cock. An uncompleted Soviet construction project. "Soviat", as the feckless brown-eyed schoolgirls write in their classes at school. The lump of concrete is surrounded by a nominal fence. On three sides of it there are a parking lot with its Asian owners, a square with a heap of little shops and a construction site with a dog. The dog's called Laima, but I don't like her. I'll go in on the fourth side. Not that I'm afraid of the nomadic tribesmen or broody Laima. But on the "civilised" side there are bright streetlamps and house lights, and in urban extreme cutting through the light is considered inelegant, I've just decided that.

After skirting casually round the parking lot, Laima and the light, I walk another thirty steps or so away from the building. Then I move to the side, across the grass. As far as the fence and then further. The grey planks are grey with an internal greyness. Their colour has absolutely nothing to do with the night. My long, faint shadows creep along the fence. I am distinctly aware that from the windows of the houses opposite I can be seen clearly as if I'm on stage. It's an unpleasant feeling, but not fatal. I'm a homeless hobo, good townspeople, got that? I turn the corner and run smack into darkness. The light disappears – the fence is blocking it. This is where I'll get over. Moving with secret-agent exaggeration – I have to have my fun! – I look for a handy section. The fence is flimsy, my main concern is that it might collapse with me on it.

I reach the corner. I go back, examining the planks, all equally manky. No need to hurry – it's night. Well, this might as well be the spot... Right then, let's record it. I put the bag on the ground and open the zip.

My video camera's old. But on the other hand, it's cheap. I digitise the picture manually, through the sequence: VCR + PC + TV card. I shoot the historical piece of fence for fifteen seconds, then take out my still camera. I have to be more careful with that – the flash. The equipment is put away in the bag. I take out my mittens and put them on. Yard keeper's mittens, tattered but as sound as dumbbells. The bag goes over my shoulder.

Foot up on a board set crosswise. Mittened hands grab the top of the fence. Heave myself up, one foot on top, jump down.

One, two, three and we're over. I look round at the empty lot. Nothing new has appeared since I examined it through binoculars the day before yesterday. Garbage and clutter. The concrete monstrosity's doors and windows are black holes about fifty metres away. To settle the trembling a bit I pull the mittens off and take out the video camera. Another thirty seconds of historical garbage, clutter and concrete. Up on top there are red lamps. Almost like light-emitting diodes in the darkness. For planes.

There's supposed to be a watchman around here somewhere. Just to be on the safe side, I freeze again. The silence of night in the city... Cars honking in the distance and the wind murmuring gently. I fondle the personalised notepad in my pocket. Personalised, because my name's written on it in big letters. The coolness of the night caresses my body under my black T-shirt. I want to freeze on the spot and stay there, listen to the night. A remarkably pleasant feeling.

All right, let's go. I run in short bursts, hunched over slightly. Only from close-up do you realise how huge our city's major relic is. A mountain. A Colossus that dwarfs human beings. Once you know its shape and you've registered its silhouette as a backdrop, behind the rain, behind a friend's house, behind the eyes that you love, you inadvertently start thinking of it as just a picture. Wallpaper behind the countenance of everybody's life. And it's only when you merge into the wallpaper yourself that the realization of the city's true proportions hits you.

A shot of the relic from the bottom up. A black and grey plain with little red lights in the distance. A dead aerodrome. I walk inside. It stinks of just about everything. No surprises there. I wait for a minute – impenetrable darkness shrouds my eyes. It's an incredible process, I've always marvelled at it. My pupils dilate, and very soon I can make out the stairway and the predatory lengths of steel reinforcement rods snaking out of the walls. I remind myself to do something about getting a torch, smile and the nervous tension immediately eases. It's this little joke I have with myself. Every time I swear I'll buy a torch for the next one. And I don't buy it – for good luck. I've been lucky so many times without a torch, I'll be lucky again.

I walk carefully up the first flight. I take out my mobile

phone and prss the keyboard by touch. The display lights up and a pale white patch appears on the wall. There's my light – all hail progress! Now softly, softly across to the next stairway. Speak softly and step soundlessly. The landing is dotted with broken bottles. Mustn't step on the glass – no fun in that! Here I squat down and freeze. Listen. After a few seconds, the mobile display's backlight goes off.

Silence and darkness. I can't hear the cars any more. I can't hear the city at all: only the strange sound as the wind squeezes its way in through the blank window apertures. Silence. A little bone in my foot cracks. I look at my watch. The glowing green lines indicate about seventeen minutes past one. Time – I have a whole wagon load and trailer of it. More than that. Two wagons.

There's no one in the building. If there is, then he's hunkered down like me, not stirring and not breathing. Somewhere in the distance, in a different world, brakes squeal. In the silence the shrill sound jangles my nerves. My heart takes a steep dive, I feel dizzy. I shake myself, put on a disdainful grin. Come on now, what's wrong with me?

I switch on the mobile's backlight and move on. Onwards and upwards. There are twenty floors in the building. Enough to get tired and do a little thinking about life.

"Why do I do this?" – that's the question you're bound to ask yourself sooner or later. It doesn't bring money, glory or fame. It doesn't particularly improve my physical condition (although there is a bit of that). It takes a heap of time and makes me excessively secretive for no particular reason. It's a sport – that's a good answer. Only totally useless. What fucking kind of sport is it, if I invented it myself? What do I take as a victory, or a defeat?

I've no problems in the logic department. And so: if you do something that has no point for you, you do it to achieve some other "external" goal. That is, if you hate your job, you don't go there to work, but to earn money. Who can argue with that? Or try this: if you don't love your girlfriend, you don't go out with her for her sake, but in order not to be alone. Religion? Dead simple: you go to church, although you don't believe, in order to appease your conscience. But I still don't know what my problem is. Here's a juicy example for you: a circus that's absolutely empty; a clown walking around in the ring, giving a funny performance. Do you know what he's doing it for?

If you do, you're smarter than I am. I don't have a clue. I am that clown, with the minor exception that I'm also a bit of an acrobat. This is my fourth operation. The previous ones have included walking across a river on the lower girders of a small bridge, photographing the town from the top of a tower crane and a totally experimental crossing of the roof of a sports complex, going up the fire escape on one side and down on the other. Now I'm going to entertain the empty big top with a vertical descent from a height of seventy metres.

No, seriously, do I really need this?

I stop another couple of times along the way to shoot the decor. My heart's pounding like a wild thing. As I caress the buttons of the camera, I can feel how wet my fingers are. I smile. "Word of honour," I tell myself, "that's not a nervous smile! Word of honour." And it seems like I'm right. I'm just poking fun at myself. I stroke this smile good-naturedly over my trembling fingers and the cold trickles from my armpits.

My legs ache. Twenty floors. Four hundred and eighty steps. The higher I go, the cleaner it gets. A graphic stairway of time. On the lower floors they booze almost every day. They get up to the fifth floor once a week. Anyone who climbs up here, right to the top, doesn't do it because they need a drink.

There's an ominous droning above my head. They've installed a mobile phone network mast on the roof. Not exactly good for the health, but it shouldn't kill me, I joke to myself.

The upper landing. A ladder brown with rust, a trap door

and a padlock. I breathe out sharply and then immediately remind myself that this has been provided for. I reach into the bag and then think: I ought to shoot it... I let go of the handle and start looking for the video camera...

Stop.

Let's not get flustered. A wagon load and a trailer. Two wagons. I squat down and wait for the little white window of the mobile phone to disappear. I look at my watch: the mountain was conquered in twenty minutes.

It's quiet here too, but in a special kind of way. I can hear the wind very clearly. The sounds of the black Colossus below me rise up with the warm air, as if they're rising up a chimney. I hear the rustling of the rats and the abandoned building as clearly as through the funnel of a megaphone. A building like that, and not a single ghost. Real estate simply going to waste. Ha-ha-ha. After I photograph the ladder, the lock and the stray bra in the corner, I take a hydraulic cutter out of my bag, lift it up over my head and set the crude cutting jaws round the loop of the lock. In the darkness the sound of the lock striking against the trap door sounds like a loud crash to me. I squeeze harder.

I can't see a damn thing. The steel is either crumpling or it isn't. There's absolutely no way to tell from the handle of the cutter. I light it up with my phone. There's an ugly fold, like some strange organic form, on the silvery loop of metal. I grip it again and squeeze to finish the job.

I hear a melodic clang. The lock turns over and hangs the other way round, ignoring my attempt to grasp it. I can't hold the cutter up with one hand; it describes a crooked arc and slams into my knee. Ouch!!! In the first instant I remember a million things. Then I just focus on keeping my facial muscles still and silent. There's a strange pleasure in that – holding the pain inside myself. It's not a fracture: just a stupid knock, but painful, and the worst part is the first few seconds. Even so, it's not good just before the descent.

I put everything back in my bag and pick it up. I take hold of a brown crossbar and feel sharp flakes breaking away under my fingers with an unpleasant, quiet crunching sound. I set my foot on the first rung, slowly and deliberately. It seems all right. I lift myself up a little bit. Bearable, if not pleasant. Higher. Trying to distract myself from my throbbing knee, I remove the lock from its loops. Later I'll throw it in the river. Fingerprints and such. No one needs my fingerprints, even as a free gift, but I'm acting the cautious spy. I enjoy it.

I feel at the surface of the trap door with my left hand. It yields surprisingly easily. After a brief pause, I open it.

A second of shock and surprise. It think it's daylight up there. I blink to clear my eyes and realise it's a lamp. You know, the kind made of thick glass, covered with wire-mesh. Lulled by the darkness, my unsuspecting eyes are stunned by the light for a second. That's why I thought it was the sun.

Crash! I almost fall off the ladder. My heart sinks into my boots. When it swung open, the damned trapdoor smashed into the metal sheeting of the roof. But I don't think even this clatter should reach all the way down to the bottom. I clamber out onto the roof. The glow of the lamp illuminates metal boxes and antennae behind barbed-wire mesh. The bright light cuts off the panoramic view, and I can't believe I'm seventy metres above the ground. I can just barely hear a vibrating drone. I walk over to the dark edge of the roof.

That's where the city night is! The entire city is laid out in front of me. The tiny five-storey apartment buildings, and the high-rises way off in the distance. Lights and headlights everywhere. When I make the descent, it will be deserted down there. But when you see it from above, the entire city is moving. As if you're looking into a magic mirror and you can follow every inhabitant separately. The yellow blobs of taxis taking someone home. Or to visit someone. On the edge of town the fireflies of headlights drift along in pairs. Slightly faster than they ought to. If I listen closely, I can make out the roar of a powerful engine. Or is it an illusion? It's about five kilometres away...

Sometimes I feel like I don't have a partner, sometimes I feel like my only friend...

I slowly lower my bag onto the roof. Something inside it clangs quietly. How should I shoot this? How can I convey the coolness, the wind, the sensation of it? I wince, realising that on video the only sounds will be the droning and interference.

It's all down there. The entire city. I record it all with the camera, realising perfectly well that there, on the tape, all this will just be a background. Wallpaper the viewer can't merge into.

Mastering the fear, I set my foot on the low metal-rod barrier. The genuine abyss is lost in the darkness of the night. That is my city! That is my domain! The great sovereign lord "I". I breathe in the scent of the miraculous.

I take my final panoramic shot before the descent. I know the night city will disappear on the tape. There'll be nothing left but strings of coloured lights. And not a single person. My empty amphitheatre.

I walk away a couple of steps and stamp on the damp roofing felt. My leg's all right. My watch shows ten to two. I uncoil a blue rope a hundred metres long. There's a hook on the end, with a pair of rings dangling behind it. After tying a few secure knots, I hook the rope to the metal rod. I go down on my knees. Below me is a blank wall. The adrenalin shimmers all the colours of the rainbow. I feel the tingling of blithe fury in my legs. After making sure there's no one down there, I clutch the rings in my wet palm and toss the folded rope down. It twitches silently, filling up with a living energy in my hand. I feel it swaying through its entire length, gradually calming and settling down.

I switch the video camera to Record and stuff it into the

side pocket of my bag, then close the zip as far as I can. The lens sticks out like a cat's head. I throw on the straps and fasten the Velcro pads. I've got gloves on my hands. Have I forgotten anything? There are two swivel hooks on my belt. I click on the rings. With my back to the abyss, I take a step backward. The rope trembles tautly in my hands.

It's terrifying, damn it!

Oh, it would be beautiful to jump backwards in long leaps, like a SWAT team in the movies... My absentee audience would probably appreciate it. But I'm not a special forces officer. Right? So I'll do it the best way I can. I put one foot over the barrier. Then the other. I take a tight grip on the rope and start slowly leaning backwards.

It's harder than I thought it would be. The edge of the roof has been left behind forever. The light of the lamp is cut off by the black border of the edge and it looks like some alien star rising from behind the horizon.

A step down. The rope obediently slips through my hands. I move my feet a little lower, changing the angle. That way there'll be less pressure on my wrists. Another step. And another.

It looks like I'll cope all right. I've always coped before and I will now. It's still too soon to look down. Still way too soon. The bag sways in time to my sheer vertical steps. I just hope the camera's picking up more than the grey wall of the relic! But we'll come back to that later. Right now, a step. And another step. Precisely and regularly.

Not many people get the chance to see this concrete from so close up. You might think, so what – it's concrete. But no one's seen it so close up for fifteen or twenty years. Right in the centre of town – and there it is. An abandoned wall. A dead shrine of the dead. I could touch it...

The dawn of the alien star retreats upwards. Now I can make out the stars. The stars straight ahead of me. I'm canted over and the world is canted over. The town is behind me, the stars are ahead of me. I ponder a superbly important question. Will the tape record the stars? Step by step. Carefully.

The hook! Damn it, the hook!

It has my fingerprints on it. A wild thought of going back. I brush it aside. I'm not that desirable. Who could be bothered with this nonsense? Who's even going to look for those fingerprints anyway? My brain automatically provides the reply: the mobile phone equipment. My hand freezes for a moment. No. We carry on down. I'm a regular guy: never been booked, never been prosecuted, not in the files.

I can glance down. Half the distance has been travelled without incident. Fingers crossed! Forty metres off the ground.

After another ten metres or so I experience an unexpected effect. Every step sets me gently swaying from side to side. Like a pendulum. I remember the tread on my trainers. If they slip it will be very upsetting. And then I suddenly explode into laughter. The jokes I tell myself are too funny altogether. I stand there, perpendicular to the grey square, at tenth-floor level, stooped over and laughing silently, with my eyes staring wide, trying to make myself shut up. It's nerves, I know, nerves. A sudden weakness flares up in my bruised knee. My stomach's trembling. That'll show up as jolting on the camera.

That makes everything even funnier. A step down. A spasm of laughter. A step. I'm my own audience and my own clown. With that thought the laughter suddenly disappears. My jaw clamps shut. Down we go.

Warning: laughter can kill. If you suddenly find something amusing thirty metres from the ground.

A minute later I look round. The ground is fifteen metres away. Below I can vaguely make out lumps of concrete that have fallen off something. The bottom is emerging from the gloom. If I've just been on the surface of the town, why not call the ground its bottom?

I could easily jump down, but I maintain my rhythm, stepping down to the end of the wall and then off it, as if it's a step. There's solid ground under my feet. I'm back down below again. I look up. Now the Colossus looks far more... familiar. And the red dots aren't light diodes any longer, just ordinary red lamps, casting light and shadows. In my black T-shirt and trousers I must have looked like a cockroach on a white sheet of paper. Only a blind man could have failed to notice me. It's a good thing no one's called the police.

They haven't, have they?

I detach the swivel hooks. Set off to the fence at a run. The adrenalin shock is starting to wear off, and this is expressed in the urge to run, talk, do something. I flit over the fence and trot towards the street opposite me.

The time on my watch is a quarter past two. I'm an ordinary person now, in an ordinary city.

* * *

The morning is magical. The dense grey sky doesn't let through a single ray of sunlight, and the asphyxiating heat of June is hidden behind the clouds. On a morning like this I want to go out on the balcony and take a really deep breath. Now that's an indisputable sign of a good mood! The damp town is like some calm, self-confident creature. I'm prepared to associate with a damp town even during the day.

I live in a room in a communal flat with my cousin. I could live with my parents, but what for? We don't really have much need of each other. Money? I put up posters, do sales promotion jobs, sometimes load scrap metal. Quick and relatively well-paid, though exhausting. My flatmate Sergei's still dozing. Now there's a real ace when it comes to filtering money out of life. I always owe him. He looks like an innocuous kind of guy. But his nose for business is something else. There's always a sign on our door: SINGLE CIGARETTES SOLD.

He used to work in the tyre business. You're probably clued up on that. Changing the tyres on people's wheels. Only not actually taking them off (though that would be a good earner), but selling them to clients. He used to walk around with a pile of grey, sickly looking photocopied questionnaires and pester motorists indolently with stupid questions like: "What make of tyres do you prefer?" and "How often do you chaynge your tyres?" (chaynge – that's what it said in the questionnaire). And all the motorists indolently sent him to hell. The cunning marketing move here was that the survey was carried out in the name of a tyre company. It was assumed that the thick-headed motorists, flattered by this dollar-driven attention would go dashing off to buy precisely those tyres. One and a half roubles per questionnaire. Ah yes, if a client who had been questioned should take it into his head to call in for some tyres, my friend was supposed to be paid a hundred dollars. For purposes of identifying clients who had been surveyed, he had to find out their name.

I told you they sent him to hell, didn't I?

He was chalking up twenty roubles' a day, but then he went to the market and bought a database of car numbers stolen from the State Road Traffic Safety Inspectorate. When he saw an expensive-looking car with worn tyres, he wrote down the number. Then at home he copied the name out of the database and filled out the questionnaire. "Which make of tyres do you prefer?" – "I always used to use... but sometimes I chose... Now, for the summer, I'm going to put on..."; "What gives you the most satisfaction in tyres?" –"Reliability, comfortable driving, good-quality tread." Ten questionnaires a day. A dead cert.

They soon got his number and booted him out, but he'd already raked in a good five hundred on his scam.

I always envied his innate ability to see money where I can't see it even if I stare my eyeballs out. He knew how to make money out of nothing, and he knew how to make contacts too.

We're quite similar to look at – he's light-haired too, only he has brown eyes and thin lips. But we're quite different on the inside. He'll never keep quiet about something he doesn't like. He has no priorities in life. He's willing to argue himself hoarse if he's been short-changed by ten kopecks. I'm different. I won't let ten kopecks bother me. I won't argue over most things in this world, I couldn't even care ten kopecks for most things.

Well, to each his own. I'm in an excellent mood. Yesterday everything went just great. I know exactly what I'm going to do today. What else do I need for happiness?

Well then, I know for absolute certain what my next operation is going to be. I've got a pretty good idea where it's going to be. I already knew that yesterday. The only catch is that it needs at least two people to pull it off. Three would be better.

Sergei's not in the running. Not because he doesn't have a clue about my nocturnal hobby. He simply won't do it. What for? – That's the answer he'll give. So I have to find myself two people. Suitable people. And I know where to look.

* * *

The journey to the uni takes half an hour. There are prospective students jostling at the entrance, greedily devouring the notices with their eyes. I elbow my way through the garrulous gathering. My route lies down to the second floor. The Internet room. I walk in without knocking, third year, after all. It's almost empty. In an open closet to the right of the door, the server is droning away on a low note. Droning like... My eyes are blinded by a flash of darkness, a roof, red lamps. I get a sour taste in my mouth and my bruised knee aches. Oh, that's good...

I plump myself down at the first computer and drop my personalised notebook on the desk. I type in the address of our municipal site. And after that, a forum. That's my hunting ground, where I set out my traps.

Do you know what an Internet forum is? An amusing sort of gimmick. Let's suppose you have a question. Zum Beispiel "How high can the average rabbit jump?" or "Where can I sell an old television?" You enter this here forum and write a message like this: "Dear friends! For purposes of writing a scientific paper (novel, letter to the woman I love, complaint to the public prosecutor's office), I desperately need the answer to the question: How high can the average rabbit jump?"

After that you can quite safely proceed to a second forum, since you'll completely forget the address of the first one (in fact, you've probably forgotten it already, if you ever even knew it), just as soon as you close the window. After repeating the experiment, write down the address of the forum and come back a day later.

During that day a multitude (sometimes thousands!) of people will visit that forum. Hundreds will read the theme that you started. One in ten of those will feel the desire to write an answer to your question.

Accordingly, having come back a day later and read the answers, you will discover:

A. That the average squirrel can jump a metre into the air.

B. That this is not true, and the average squirrel can't jump at all.

C. That both these statements are untrue, and you can read about the life of squirrels at squirrel.ru.

D. That you can easily earn up to $$$10,000 a month, all you have to do is buy the formula.

E. That in a scientific article (novel, letter to the woman you love, complaint to the public prosecutor's office), it would be better to write about the common wombat, not a rabbit.

F. That you are distracting people from serious business with your stupid questions about rabbits, that your questions attest to your exceptionally low level of intellectual development and you should immediately desist from asking idiotic questions in order to avoid major unpleasantness.

G. That you, "Deer Sers", can acquire scrap metal for self-pickup from a depot in Khabarovsk.

Eventually, somewhere in the dense thickets of this forest of passions, someone of a laconic and sceptical turn of mind will pitch this at you: 60 cm. Voila. The answer's yours.

Now do you understand what a forum is?

Sometimes certain people linger in a forum longer than others. Sometimes they become its regulars. As they learn the names, in time they start to regard each other as friends. Virtual friends, no more than that. This binds them even more strongly to the forum. They discuss new films, makes of car and the subject of the prophecy of Gethsemane in the Gospel according to St. Matthew. And so a rather distinctive regular get-together takes shape, bringing together the most varied kinds of people. And I intended to search for my future companions among them.

It wasn't going to be any kind of blind date, either. It's hard even to imagine how much a forum can tell you about a person. It's literally as if you were working side by side, only more so, get it?

Imagine it, on Monday in the forum they discuss their favourite dish. On Tuesday – whether it's okay to date two girls at the same time. On Wednesday, Thursday, Friday – Liza Minelli; how high the average rabbit can jump and mobile phones respectively. And nothing that's written gets erased – anyone who's feeling curious can read it all, no problem.

By consistently gathering information on a person with the pseudonym "Off-Roader", for instance, you can learn more about him than by trailing him for years. Compile his answers, write up the style a bit and you'll have a dossier that would be the envy of any secret service.

Actually, as far as the individual with the pseudonym "Off-Roader" is concerned, you wouldn't be likely to find out too much. That's my pseudonym. And I don't write all that much in the forum. I prefer reading. It's clear enough why – you send in some eminently worthy response, and some idiot will say all sorts of nasty things about your opinion, and about you as well.

But now it's time. The time has come to find out how high a rabbit jumps. And I write my question.

"Dear friends.

I have a proposal. Team members required for a unique, unforgettable, if ever so slightly dangerous pastime. The financial outlay is minimal. There's no need to go anywhere – it's all within the city limits. Nothing crude, no role-playing, nothing criminal. If you have something unusual inside you, if your heart knows how to dream, if you don't like cowardice, join me. Details in private correspondence.

Adult status, a love of the night and good basic physical condition are desirable."

I reread what I've written. It reads an awful lot like an advert. In a sense, that's exactly what it is. I send it. I'm surprised to notice that my palms are wet. I don't give a damn. Let them write snide remarks. For the next operation, I need two people. I stand up and stretch. The girl at the next computer glances disapprovingly in my direction. Uhu. Like I've got nothing better to do than look at what you're doing in the Internet.

I catch the eye of the class supervisor and nod to him, can't remember his name. So I don't talk to him. I glance away and pretend to be desperately interested in the make of the monitors.

Just waiting or not doing anything in public is a big problem. If only I could sit down in a corner and have a think about something. Think for ten minutes, fifteen, half an hour. Ah, but no – sit down on a chair and gaze into empty space, and in a few minutes the glances are bound to start. Just what business is it of yours, citizens? Is it really hard to imagine someone simply doing nothing? Thinking about life? Or not thinking?

I go back to the keyboard with a sigh. I'll check what I wrote and go. No point hanging around here. I've done what I promised myself I would.

And there's already one answer. Some stupid nonsense, most likely. Sure enough. It's a certain Nemo.

"Query: Do you need a team to support your pastime, or are you suggesting a bit of fun in order to assemble a team?"

Stupid nonsense. No point in replying to anything like that.

I'm out of here. I have to take a look at what's happened to the rope I left on the Colossus. The memory of the silvery hook with fingerprints on it is bothering me.

* * *

The rope's not on the building any longer. Whoever cut it down, they're not likely to have raised much of a ruckus. I recall something that happened to the local anarchists. They decided to stage a political "act of protest". They got hold of an immense sheet of white canvas from somewhere, scrawled "The state is the people's prison" on it and hung this rag over a massive advertising hoarding at dawn. No doubt they were expecting a sensation, a scandal and an armada of cars with blinking lights.

By lunch time a journalist from the local newspaper called the police station and asked what the reaction of the authorities would be. The police were surprised and asked: "To what?" The journalist informed them with some disappointment about the outrage committed on the hoarding. The police promised to get into the matter.

By the evening the anarchists took the sheet down

themselves – the "act of protest" was quite clearly a flop. I only found about the whole thing from the sad article by that same journalist. Between the lines I could read a provincial yearning for scandal.

After walking round the Colossus on all sides, I change course and move in the direction of the sports shop. I'm interested in equipment. It's quicker by public transport, but I like walking.

Suddenly I feel a fierce heat. Like a burn. My back starts warming up, as if someone's focusing the beam from a crooked lens on it, trying to roast me. I look round.

Just as I thought. The sun. This beautiful day didn't stay beautiful for long. It's going to prod me in the back and weigh down on my neck, the hot sweat all over my body is going to shout out: Scrrartch yourself! (*sic*) Unbearable!

"Young man, may I have a minute of your time?"

I stop dead on the spot and look ahead. Was that meant for me? Yes, it was... But who talks that way nowadays? A girl. Young. Not tall. Dark hair, slightly plump face, although she's not fat. White blouse, light-coloured jeans, white trainers. Looks too stylish. She's twirling an audiocassette box in her hands. I watch, entranced, as she strokes the transparent plastic ribs with her fingers. She has very light skin.

"May I ask you a few questions?"

I start recalling one or two things about girls and young men like this. Sergei told me about them. And there was something about an audiocassette too...

I look at my watch with an air of being extremely busy. I run my thumb round the dial, as if I'm figuring out how much time I have. I recall the coolness of the night, the green lines in the darkness. The hands are white now. My thumb leaves a damp trail on the glass. It's hot, damn it. I don't want to talk to her.

"Young man, what do you think about pre-marital sex?"

I've run into a pushy one here. A couple of minutes later it becomes clear what she wants. Her name's Lena. She's a member of the youth movement City Initiative Plus. According to Lena, the organisation brings together young men and women who are concerned about the moral state of young people these days (quote). The whole thing feels like something she's learned off by rote. Almost word-for-word.

Lena is eager to have a talk with me on the subject of morality and ethics. No need to worry, girl, I wouldn't make a good lead singer for the Sex Pistols. Her face is very expressive. Especially her eyes. Grey. They positively speak to me. I wish I had eyes like that. But then they probably teach them that... at the training sessions, damn it. Lena lectures me. The audiocassette box twirls in her hands. The rosary of the new age. I look harder and see the name of the group. Fresh stuff. Churned out by the producers just this year. I wonder if they choose the cassettes themselves or the organisation hands them out? If they're handed out, that gives away the target audience they're aiming at. And I'm not in it, sweetheart, I'm not in it.

"Poverty, criminality, the insecurity that many young people feel," Lena hammers on, "all these are, as you realise, a result of the sharp decline in morality that our country has suffered in the recent past. Our organisation brings together a majority of young men and women who are concerned about the moral state of young people nowadays."

Right, she's already said that. I take hold of her hot elbow. Lena instantly shuts up and jerks away. Is she afraid of me, then? An unpleasant feeling. I grin and guide her along in my direction, toward the shop.

Lena calms down and carries on singing her tune. I don't mind. I listen carelessly to her words about the need to promote a high level of morals. A whole bunch of high-sounding words. Recruiting. Promoting. Outreach. Shiny bait for young people, drifting lazily on the lake of the city summer.

From time to time Lena glances at me from out of the corner of her eye. But she doesn't stop lecturing when she does it. Sometimes I reply with a grin and adjust her direction with her elbow. After fifteen minutes, Lena invites me to attend a meeting of their organisation. I knew it was coming. I turn my face away to hide the sarcastic smile and shrug.

Lena stops and places a card in my hand. There's a new victim waiting for her round the corner. We say goodbye. You didn't manage to rope me in. You picked the wrong target.

"Peter, stop," Lena says as I'm already leaving.

Now what? I turn round.

"Didn't that get through to you? It didn't, did it?"

I shake my head slowly. She's very perceptive. Or at least smarter than I suspected after the parables about zombifying TV serials. The jury's still out on zombification... Lena sighs.

"You know, the reason I'm doing this isn't... it's not for City Initiative Plus."

That name still sounds rote-learned. You can't throw the words out of a song. Testing out new methods on particularly resistant specimens? Lena senses my suspicion.

"I'm just training. This is my field practice. Not for my studies, for myself."

We spend the next half hour sitting on a bench by the lake and I listen to this girl's absolutely incredible story with my mouth wide open.

Fasten your seatbelts, this is really something.

Lena wants to found her own religious sect, get it? There you have the dreams of young people nowadays! Not a dance group, not a music group, not even a fan club. The girl wants to set up her own sect. What's so strange about that? A perfectly normal desire. Everyone wants to get ahead these days.

She sees her place in the sect as prophet and implicit leader. The property of the sect's followers is controlled by the leader of the sect. He also has unlimited power over the disciples.

Lena's answer to my question about the philosophy is that it hasn't been worked out yet. Right now she's practicing by trying to convert followers to City Initiative Plus, occasionally moonlighting for the Jehovah's Witnesses. The philosophy isn't the most important part, Lena assures me. It's not a matter of the philosophy. It's just that she has this dream of being the head of a sect. Some people dream of getting to be the director of a tobacco company, why not dream of being a prophet?

I can't find any counter-arguments to that.

Half an hour later, we part company. Stunned by this new fact in my picture of the world, I move on towards the sports equipment shop. Finding new routes is especially amusing. The city inside most urbanites' heads consists of the well-trodden streets. I think that's something left over in the sub-cortex from animals. Animals always follow the same track to the waterhole. People always get to places using the same streets, pavements, bus routes. When I close my eyes, even I sometimes see the daytime city as a tangled bundle of avenues and roads.

Time how long it takes a bus to get to the place you want. Take a map and a ruler. Measure the distance as the crow flies. You'll be amazed. And the avenues? Now there's a real invention for you. The urbanites are so used to moving along these straight lines that they have a "straight line" in their heads, assembled out of avenues and large streets, leading them home, to work or to the hairdresser's.

Trace out their route on a map, and it will look like a jumble of zigzags. Side streets! That's the answer! Side streets, alleys, courtyards! If you really want to walk in a straight line, take the trouble to buy a detailed map of the city (you know, with the numbers on the buildings). Then at least once try blazing a trail through the small squares and courtyards.

The way I do. At first I was astounded when I turned off a rumbling avenue into a little green courtyard, cut across a couple of quiet streets and found myself on another avenue. An avenue that in my head was located forty minutes away by bus, on the opposite side of town. I've amazed my companions like that more than once.

Up on top of the Colossus, it's all laid out in front of you. The streets and side streets are parallel and intersecting straight lines. Down there on the bottom, the town grows up over your head and hides its major arteries behind the buildings. All you can see is walls on all sides. The sun over your head. It makes me think of a terrarium. During the day I have to hide away, off the streets, in order not to turn into a snake. It's incredible, but most of the urbanites do the opposite. And yet only a few steps away there's a green, enclosed yard.

When you walk through the fresh green yards, your thoughts are fresh too. The urbanites rushing along the avenues switch off, like phones that have lost contact with the operator. They're stuck inside themselves. Thoughts about yesterday and tomorrow clack through their eyes, like figures on a meter at a petrol station. And they can't breathe.

Lena got what she wanted from me, after all. A brilliant job, I must admit. I agreed to become the first disciple of her sect. Not bad going, eh? No defined charter, rights, rules and regulations. Not even any philosophy! In fact, neither of us has even the slightest idea of what we believe in! And she already has her first disciple.

This girl will go far, I'm telling you!

The sun has disappeared. Well that's just great. There's still a couple of kilometres to go to the shop.

I got something from her too. She agreed to be introduced to the concept of urban extreme. A girl's even better. There's nothing wrong with female company. I take the map out of my well-scribbled notebook and look at the address written on the back of it. Not far from my communal flat... if you know the short cut, of course.

* * *

When I get back home, I find Sergei's not there. Out having a good time, probably. So all right – I have to transfer last night's video recording to the computer hard disk. I switch on the old VCR and spend a few minutes admiring darkness studded with the white tops of plastic bottles. The grey contours of walls in the circle of light from the cell phone. And also – a starry sky. And the abyss over the edge of the building. The recording has turned out excellent, and the sound of my own heavy breathing sets my heart pounding faster.

That was probably the most dangerous operation I've done so far. The next one will be a bit gentler. And what's more, I'm not planning on pulling it off all alone.

I look through the night's photos on the screen. Great stuff.

A key tries to turn in the lock. Then Sergei opens the door and smiles in greeting. I smile back at him. He walks in and two of his mates walk in behind him. Looking well-oiled. The last one's holding a plastic bag, with the neck of a vodka bottle sticking out of it.

I ignore their appeals to join them and go to get washed. After last night I feel desperately sleepy. Coming back into the room, I find them dragging the table into the centre.

"Ah... if anyone here is opposed to this action, let him speak now or forever hold his peace!"

They laugh. Alcohol robs people of their reason.

I feel insanely tired. I flop into bed.

* * *

In the morning, I'm woken by Sergei groaning.

"Water..." he moans, half-joking, half-serious.

In order to decompose one litre of alcohol, the liver requires one thousand and one hundred grams of water. And then the products of decomposition have to be expelled from the body... I pick up a half-full bottle of mineral water off the table and hand it to my suffering friend. Sergei sucks on it greedily. People often create their own problems, don't they?

On the other hand, people just as often see problems where there aren't any.

On the way to the university Internet room, I start thinking about the organisation that Lena was propagandising yesterday. What was that question I was asked in the forum? "Are you putting a team together in order to have some fun, or are you inviting people to have some fun in order to put a team together?" It wasn't really all that stupid, if you applied it to that youth organisation scam. Surely they aren't really all that bothered about the state of morality, are they? Actually, they couldn't give a damn about morality! They want to get a team together. The leaders drill the divers, and the divers go and fish people out of life, the lousy creeps! The leaders know perfectly well that the organisation is only interesting to young people for as long as young people are unhappy. As soon as someone becomes self-reliant and starts to see life as it really is, he doesn't need anyone's advice and encouraging get-togethers any more. It doesn't take a great brain to guess that the organisation's viability depends directly on how unhappy its members feel subconsciously. And they probably dip into their pockets too. For the membership fees. The more young people are in need of "support", the more money flows in. It's a business too. Not much worse than Sergei's swindle with the tyres.

Yesterday Lena claimed that wasn't her way. No disguised psychological dependencies. An honest sect with honest adoration of the prophet. An idea as pure as the tear of a young novice nun.

Oh-oh! There's a full house today. All the Internet computers are taken. A girl I don't know is sitting at "mine" and fiddling around, doing some kind of garbage. Of course it's garbage. She's not using the web, so why the hell doesn't she sit at any of the other machines?

I circle round her like a crow and sit down on my favourite little chair. To wait. No, I mean it, why do people come here? If I didn't need the Internet, I could quite easily stay at home. Well just look, over there! That way! A free computer without an Internet connection. Go over and sit there. What difference does it make to you? I drill into her back with my eyes. Wish I could drill right through it...

After twenty minutes the girl realises that I'm not sitting here to admire her graceful forms and features. Aha, good girl. She smiles at me and leaves. Okay, I forgive you.

I load the forum page. I've received about twenty responses to my proposal. Not counting the obscene proposals and ecstatic acceptances, bristling with smilies and spelling mistakes, they all come down to wary clarification of the circumstances of the action. These people are not taking any chances. I can't write to them about urban extreme, and the operations and the night, just like that. They won't understand. They won't believe it.

There's nothing else for it. I go back to the very first reply.

"Query: Do you need a team to support your pastime, or are you suggesting a bit of fun in order to assemble a team?"

I open the "Participant Information" page.

Right then, Nemo. His short file in my transcription:

Twenty-one, student, Aquarius... A regular on the forum (more than seven hundred messages). Interests: fishing, foreign languages, equestrian sport.

What are you doing sitting in the forum if you've got unusual interests like that?

I launch "search for all messages from the participant" and start reading them from the beginning. Everything he's ever written on any subject is all herded together here. All the messages about food, girls, art, mobile phone rates, etc. However, I'm interested in his way of thinking.

Half an hour later, I can say that I'm intrigued. Not exactly over the top, but he's an interesting character. I'll quote a few passages, so you can understand what I'm talking about.

"You don't like red caviar. So okay. But why do you write: I bit into it once and this disgusting sticky, salty liquid spread over my tongue. You must admit, you could write the same thing about ice cream – disgusting, sickly-sweet rubbish; or about kebabs – repulsive carbonised pieces of burnt meat. It's not a question of what one thing or the other is, but of how you perceive it. So okay. Perhaps your rejection of red caviar is based on precise sensations of taste that you yourself experience. But that doesn't mean that everybody experiences them, or that the infamous red caviar really is disgusting. To sum up: Why insult a perfectly good food product? ☺"

"I'm not claiming that N is a useless film director. I'm not claiming the opposite either. I didn't feel I'd fallen in love with his film. But I didn't feel I hated it. I didn't feel anything at all. That was what I didn't like. Throughout the film, I sat there calmly, analysing what was happening on the screen. This person does this, that person does that. So okay. But when I want academic reading matter, I'll reread my old favourite, *Capital*☺. A film should engross me! I want emotions! After all, this is art."

"What difference does it make to you who it will be? Life is a zero-sum game. If someone wins, someone loses. If someone receives something, someone else loses it. And in the process, each of them does everything they can in the given situation, no matter what they say about missed opportunities. Psychological resources are just as important as any others. You're fated to win or lose this time round, the only thing you can choose is your perception of the situation and the people around you."

"I don't prefer a forum to real interaction. A forum is a certain freedom in expressing your own thoughts, which is not at all determined by the content of those thoughts, but exclusively by their form. In real space I wouldn't launch into long, wordy discussions or deliver a ten-minute monologue on the War of the Roses. Here I can do that, without inconveniencing my readers too much. Anyone who doesn't like it can simply scroll down the page."

The long and the short of it. Gift-wrapped with ribbons on. It was the last argument that hooked me. It would be strange to go out "on patrol" with a garrulous comrade who's just waiting for a convenient moment to blast your ears off. It would be especially inconvenient if done while suspended in mid-air with the asphalt twenty metres below.

Possible options for my new team have already begun taking shape in my mind. All that's left is to lure them into urban extreme somehow without managing to convince them that I've totally flipped. So we'll write letters. Here's our correspondence below.

"Dear Nemo!

When I saw your reply to my question in the forum, I must say, I was impressed. It distinguishes you advantageously from the mass of others who don't make much of an effort to monitor the quality of what they're writing.

My reply: I am assembling a team, in order to have some fun. My hobby is a truly enthralling activity, real class. I call it urban extreme. Not in the sense of sex without condoms, but genuine extreme. No skateboards or criminal activity.

I pull all kinds of interesting extreme stunts. I need two people for my next operation. It will be fun.

If you're interested, write. But you have to promise me not to divulge anything. In any case, let me know if you will take part or not.

WBR, Off-Roader."

"Greetings, Dear Lena!

I'm writing to remind you about myself. Remember, we

met yesterday at the lake? The weather was sparklingly sunny and summerishly warm. You recruited me to your religious organisation. And I promised to tell you something about my hobby.

So I'm telling you now. I go out at night. I don't actually just go out, it's more like I make sorties. For instance, I once climbed up the fire escape of a sports complex, walked across the roof, and then down on the other side. That sort of thing. Now I'm planning another sortie, but I need two people to make it work. Tell me what you think about this.

Be seeing you, Peter."

"Chears.

Call me supreme master, since you've signed up. Very interesting. Not inviting me on a robbery, are you? Somehow I don't quite get what it is you want. What kind of sortie is it going to be?

Supreme Master."

"Greetings to you, Supreme Master Lena!

The gist of the next operation is as follows: a cable is stretched between two buildings on Lenin Prospect. It is attached at both ends. Two people crawl across from one side to the other, and one person goes the opposite way. They go in turns, because one is always making sure the cable's safe and the other one who's free is recording with the video camera. The person making the crossing is secured by a swivel hook attached to his belt. It's impossible to fall, get it? But it should be a little bit frightening. Enough to twinge the nerves a bit.

So now I've told you everything. Write.

Be seeing you, Peter."

"Hi, Off-Roader.

I can't imagine a more up-beat offer. My head starts filling up with all sorts of crazy theories about stealing bodies from the morgue. Or is that my morbid fantasy? I accept your terms: I promise to keep quiet, you tell me about it.

Fire away, Nemo."

"Dear Nemo!

No dead bodies. My hobby is nocturnal operations that generate adrenalin. I'm assembling you for a high-altitude crossing. To explain: a cable is thrown from one building to another. We scramble across it. One person films it all. Interested?

WBR, Off-Roader."

"I'm interested. Give me your contact details."

"Hello, Peter dear,

You surprised me. Never had buzz like that before. I graciously accept your courtesy.

As for the buildings and the ropes. I don't know how to crawl across, but I can film things. I have a camera.

Supreme Master."

* * *

And so our team came together. Not straightaway, of course. Everyone came to the meet separately. And we stayed separate the first day. Maybe only Lena found her niche immediately, but that's her personality, and anyway she immediately stared trying to lure Nemo into her net. At first he was worried about what was going on, but when he found out I'd only just met Lena too, and she'd hauled me in, he relaxed. Eventually we both started calling her Supreme Master, and she seemed to get real pleasure out of that.

Nemo turned out to be a short intellectual with post-modernist pretensions by the name of Alex. White mobile phone, Almodavar, martini with apple juice, stuff like that. Genuinely not inclined to deliver verbose speeches in real space, he managed to express a huge number of emotions with a sparing but eloquent range of expressions. When lifting his left eyebrow towards his chestnut-brown hair, he could vary the angle of his half-smile slightly so that contempt, approval and the desire to drink another martini with apple juice were all located within a few millimetres of each other. After "Nemo" it was kind of hard to call him by his real name.

For our next meeting, we all went round to Lena's place, and I brought along the video of my previous operations. Lena was positively entranced by what was going on and, seeing how impressed people were by the kind of thing I did, I felt... pride? Vanity, perhaps. Sinful or not, it's an incredibly good feeling. As he watched my trainers and the reflections of lights in the river dangling in the video shot, Nemo remarked:

"I don't know how dangerous this really is, but it looks magnificent. Where are you going to distribute this?"

He was totally surprised when he realised I genuinely didn't have any plans for my tape. As if urban extreme was nothing more than an excuse for posturing in front of the camera. But he also got incredibly wound up and started thinking up plans for the best way I could promote myself publicity-wise. He shuffled the possibilities this way and that, and his shroud of intellectualism slid off him like sand off a stone. His eyes glittered and his hands, which had been dumb so far, started fluttering all around the room as he moved about it.

"We'll do some promo material! No, first we'll make a site!" Nemo scratched the back of his head with the gesture of a total non-intellectual.

His suggestion was to give our activity extensive exposure. Not just when the chance came up, but as extensive as possible. To really go for it, remember about it during the operations, compute the photos and the composition of the camera shots.

Irrespective of the content of these ideas, I liked the emotional energy that had unexpectedly surfaced in him. I had no idea how a cold snob would have behaved up there on the roof. But I couldn't afford to get carried away – right now Nemo had forgotten about everything but the external aspect of urban extreme. He hadn't even given a thought to the sweaty palms and trembling hands.

He suggested establishing an urban extreme squad and calling it something with real oomph, like "Da Freeze TylerZ". Then making a website. Putting our photos on it, writing our sporting bios. Putting out info about the operations, the planning, and then – reports. Including photos and videos. Blanket stylisation in the youth style. A touch of eroticism. A glance at Lena left him perfectly satisfied, unlike her. And me. Eroticism? Who was going to shoot it – him?

The craving for fame was blazing in his eyes. He could see himself signing skateboards. Nemo was already running through possible pseudonyms for us and had just decided that Red October or Silent Hunter would suit me, when Lena stopped him.

I didn't interfere, I sat on the divan with my feet pulled up under me, toying with my notepad and listening to both of them. For reasons unknown, I got a tremendous kick out of all this blather. Lena got up and declared that she was the one who decided what to do. She menacingly reminded us that she was still the Supreme Master and she decided the fate of the order singlehandedly. By "order" she meant the three of us. Alex was taken aback, but I'd twigged from the start where this girl was heading and I wasn't even the tiniest bit surprised.

Eventually they accepted a compromise. In my view it was biased in Lena's favour. Symbols, logos and such were hers. The philosophy (still not invented yet) was hers. The charter, rules and lifestyle were all decided by our Supreme Master, possessor of Universal Knowledge and pretty ankles.

I couldn't give a damn for the philosophy. I had my flame of blithe fury up there on the roof, and that was all I needed.

Then I producd a plan of the operation, which I had taken the trouble to draw this time, since I had associates, and the two of them prodded and poked at it for a while. I saw uncertainty in their eyes and there were no substantial objections.

Eventually we decided to divide things up. I was responsible for the operations as such (I should think so!), Lena for the philosophy of the organisation, and Nemo for promoting the squad, as he stubbornly continued to call our "sect", despite Lena's protests. I just smiled. Sect or squad, what difference did it make? It was all the same up there. Lena offered that we made suggestions about our philosophy, if we had any, and I promised to write them both e-mails about blithe fury.

As I was saying goodbye, standing in the hallway of Lena's soft-toy of an apartment, I asked her for a date that evening. Alex realised what was what, but he didn't say anything; just smiled. That all-knowing smile of his filled me with a helpless, pitiful rage.

* * *

That evening Lena and I had our date. Not my idea of fun, I must tell you, especially if you fancy the girl. Really gives you the jitters. You spend the whole evening making sure you don't screw up and your young miss doesn't get bored. I took her for a game at the billiards club. She didn't object, and I could understand her – I'm not the best of company when it comes to lively conversation.

At first I felt awkward. Lena wasn't saying anything, so I ordered her a cocktail and taught her to play nine ball. I was thankful for the remarkable way she understood everything straightaway. We played nine ball for an hour and a half and Lena actually won now and again. She smiled at me a lot, and I smiled back. It came out rather phoney, and I was aware of that. She understood my unease, but with all the people-handling skills she'd acquired in those vampirish schemes of hers, she managed to keep things going quite well. It was just that I hadn't been on many dates, that was where the problem lay. I suppose you have to get used to it, so that you can start enjoying it. I was starting to get used to it. I drank a couple of beers to relax myself a bit and give myself something to pass the time when it was her strike.

Then I suggested we should stop and she agreed. I tried hard to spot any tell-tale signs of relief on her face, but I didn't find any. She just smiled and shrugged. I decided not to tempt fate or strain my wallet and just see her home and end the date on that. A smile and a shrug. "Why not?" I wonder if those gestures mean "It's all the same to me?" or "If that's what you want?"

It wasn't until I came out into the night that I felt I was where I belonged. We walked through the dark city without speaking, and yellow lamplight lay in soft blobs on the asphalt. Every streetlamp was a bright globe against a backdrop of blackness; each one created an entirely tangible sphere of light. Those globes left misshapen fingerprints on the sparse low clouds; like a photo negative of a shadow theatre. We came out onto the main bridge of the city, and I decided to risk it and took hold of Lena's hand. Without any kind of hidden agenda at all. I realise what a load of nonsense all this holding hands is, especially nowadays, when the TV gives us a different kind of slant on everything, but I just liked it. A warm little palm. At first I thought I'd be ashamed of my damp fingers, but then the gentle freshness of the night cooled them off a bit and everything was fine. Some citizens we came across, a couple of strangers, were actually touched when they looked the two of us over. That was fine by me – just an ordinary young guy and his girl strolling through the city at night. What could be more normal? And I'm that young guy. The night filled my lungs, and I looked around on all sides, trying to memorise this moment. From here I could see the tallest buildings in the city, including the Colossus, and at that moment, as we walked up a rise, a crazy idea flashed through my head, a wild plan for an operation, I smiled.

All in all, the evening turned out just dandy. I shook her hand when we said goodnight and we parted company.

* * *

First thing next morning I settled in at the uni and started vehemently expounding the concept of blithe fury in e-mails.

"It's not fury in a pure form. It's a powerful emotional lift, but a lift that is definitely contrary and cuts through obstacles. That feeling of a victory that is close, or actually even within reach, extended through time. Like any other feeling, it's hard to explain in words to anyone who hasn't experienced it, and extremely easy by using examples and analogies. So to start with, I'll try to describe the common, everyday occasions that give rise to blithe fury, and only then proceed to detailed exposition of the nature of the phenomenon.

"Imagine to yourself that you need to go somewhere on the edge of town to get some ludicrous item – a thermometer, an alarm clock or a padlock. You don't want to do this, you remember how far you'll have to go to get there, jostling in the crowds, going round the shops, choosing this uninteresting item. And what's more, the rain starts pitter-pattering outside, and soon the windows of your flat are awash with taut rivulets of water. Bad luck!

"But you have to go, no matter how futile and tedious it might seem. That item is indispensable. And you walk out outside. You shudder resentfully under the dripping canopy over the entrance, adjust your collar and walk out into the rain. The rain is pouring down, it feels like a head-on shower. The wind whistles, the tyres of cars go swishing by. And then, as you push your way forward through the wind and rain, this errand starts to get a grip on you. And the stronger the headwind blows and the torrent lashes, the more furiously you want to confront it. Soon you find you can easily tear the dense, wet day apart, cutting through it, and the increasing resistance only provokes your fighting spirit even more. Blithe fury lives in moments like that! A hurricane blowing against you, but you just force it back even harder and more furiously with your shoulders, and all this filthy splashing mess gives you a feeling of joy and satisfaction. Keep moving forward! Keep tearing through the wind!

"Or another example. You're losing. It doesn't matter at what. Chess or football, or a computer strategy game. And you already realise the situation's not so great – press the flush, gentlemen, it's all over; but suddenly it grabs you. Fight back! Just one thought in your head – don't give in, fight on to the last breath! And the passionate drive to hold on for at least another minute is so strong that it far outstrips the feeble desire to win at the start of the game. You invent plans furiously, and every second won from defeat is your victory.

"What is the essence of this phenomenon? A subtle vibration of the elements or a reflection of the joy of victory? The craving to feel a significant part of the process? The desire to have tangible opposition, in order to feel your own strength? I'm inclined to think it's the latter. Everyone wants to feel that he is strong, brave, confident, but not everyone knows how to feel strong. Blithe fury is the natural gratification from resistance overcome as it arises. Pushing back the wind, hanging on for another minute and... doing something risky.

"And that brings us to urban extreme. Up on the rooftops, you walk through the wind and rain in the same way. Cutting through resistance. You conquer walls and come out right on top, in order to look down on the city and feel that you're up at the surface again. Well, of course, it's frightening. But if you step over your own fear, it becomes very agreeable. Very.

"I almost always experience blithe fury when I start an

operation. I savour the operation coming up; I'm absolutely terrified, naturally, but I'll step over that. And I start wanting to move faster, make a dash for it, get started – I even have to restrain myself and remind myself that there's no hurry...

"I think that without blithe fury, urban extreme makes no sense. That's what it's designed for. Without it, everything loses any meaning at all. Except perhaps for the physical exercise and the development of skills (good for what?). Consequently, I have assembled a team for the next operation, and not conducted an operation in order to assemble a team.

"Blithe fury – that is the motive force and the end product, the cause and the effect of urban extreme."

* * *

After writing my letters to Lena and Nemo, I pushed the keyboard away and tapped my fingertips on the desk. The shaggy little blue monstrosity in a helmet who was stuck on the computer monitor goggled his empty little plastic eyes at me. I shot him with a finger and left.

It was time for me to go to work. That was what I called it. Work consisted of me and my team-mates riding out to some deserted spot outside the city. There, under the appreciative guidance of our "boss", we loaded scrap iron (rusty pipes, cars, metal booths of some kind) into a three-tonne truck. Then it was all delivered somewhere. The earnings were pretty good for a day's work, only you had to put yourself through hell. Hour after hour of heavy, monotonous labour. Dirty work, with absolutely no prestige attached. The kind people describe as "only for the money". But this final argument outweighs everything else. And so I went on these dubious excursions time after time. It was Sergei who got me the job, and occasionally he arranged such expeditions himself.

We assembled at an old car park on Thursdays. Usually five or six of us. Half of them don't even speak Russian. They don't need to. Get there, fling what they show you in the truck, get your money. No need to talk to anyone.

This time we set off to the suburbs in a truck with green sides along a bumpy track that had forgotten when it used to be regarded as a road. When the truck reached a fence eaten away by rust, it smashed open the dilapidated gates without stopping and drove through onto asphalt that had settled and warped with age, covered with puddles. A two-storey brick building beamed at us with its broken windows. On all sides there were garages with their doors wide open, and that was where our booty was lying.

How do people find out about such places?

The truck backed up to the first garage. We got started.

If you perform boring, unpleasant work for longer than half an hour, your head fills up with thoughts of its own accord. You can forget what you're doing, where you are and what you need all this for. You automatically register that everything's going as it should, your hands count off the work they've done, but you're far, far away.

I knew I shouldn't imagine things about Lena. But it's always the same. A girl only has to show the slightest liking for me and I start imagining that she's in love with me. My problem is that I believe in the images of people that I conjure up in my mind. Is that pathological? I only have to think about something a bit, and other people's thoughts that I imagine become real in my eyes. I do all their thinking for them, instead of going and asking. But when it comes to making things real, people and their thoughts are almost never like my ideas about them. That's probably the reason I'm so unsociable.

I'm not like everyone else. At least that cheers me up. My urban extreme is a phenomenon, not an action. I don't do it in order to be different from the urbanites: it's part of me. I'm an urban extreme thrill-seeker. That's more important because I've managed to step over my isolation in order to prepare for the next operation. I've got to know people. Gone out on a date with a girl.

All for the sake of urban extreme.

After a couple of hours of work, the knee I'd bruised at the Colossus started to ache. I did my part of cleaning out the last few garages with my teeth gritted. I felt a lot worse than in those minutes when the same knee was hurting, but the canted-over city was spread out like a net below my back. A more uncomfortable position, a forty-foot sheer drop and deadly danger, but that's still not it. Up there the beginning and the middle and every step meant something. Here the only thing that mattered was the result. An important difference.

After we'd filled up the truck, we crawled up like dung beetles onto the rusty heap of metal. With its appetite satisfied, the truck crept off in the direction of the city. Almost everyone on board seemed pleased. The heavy work was behind us, there were a drink and a rest ahead for the drudges. But I wasn't smiling. My leg was hurting badly, and all the rest of it...

Nemo was probably right. I ought to promote my urban extreme. Do videos, photos, website. Give blind fury its due. Let the rusty iron rust.

A sign flashed by on the shoulder of the road – we had entered the daytime city. Our truck with green sides drove out onto a normal highway and stepped up the revs. The fresh breeze blew away the sweat.

We were approaching the city. Envoys of entropy, harbingers of the food chain of the new age.

* * *

That evening Lena bestowed upon us the basic ideas of our sect.

It was quite interesting in places, only I didn't take it all in. I don't know where she dug up most of the postulates. Chances are the philosophy of our sect was compiled from dozens of various different teachings and branches of philosophy, extracted from the books that she'd taken it into her head to read at bedtime. I don't think she invented it all on her own, just staring up at the ceiling.

Well then, listen. According to the teaching of the Supreme Master, Good exists in the world and Evil exists in the world. In the form of potential energy, both Good and Evil are contained in people, and both are also contained in their actions in the form of kinetic energy. There are the following forms of transition from kinetic energy to potential energy and back. If someone does Good to you, the quantity of Good in you increases. The greater the quantity of Good in you, the stronger your desire to do Good. And vice versa. If someone does the dirt on you, you become more evil. Do Evil to someone else, and you will be liberated. Do Good to an Evil man and the amount of Evil in him will be reduced, and the amount of Good in you will be reduced likewise.

"And what if someone does good to you, while you're in an evil mood?" Nemo asked.

"Then equal amounts of Good and Evil are destroyed," Lena replied, with a nod for greater solemnity.

"And where do they come from?"

"Supreme Master! From nature," said Lena, raising two fingers. "Some people are lucky and some are unlucky. Disciples."

An interesting idea. But so far we've been operating with positive magnitudes. What if we sneak into the minus zone? If a Good person does Evil, the amount of Good in him should increase! So I asked about that.

Lena thought about my question.

"Such is the harsh law of life."

Nemo soaked it up. It's quite obvious to me that it's total nonsense. I don't give a damn. I'll worship the Brahmaputra if necessary. We're going on the operation next week, there's no place for scholastic dispute there.

"And how does this apply to our... sect... Supreme Master?" Nemo asked.

"We must do good to others. It will be worse and worse for us, but we are going to do Good, disciples. And with our death all the badness will disappear. And so we will make the world a better place."

So that's cleared up, then. Call her Supreme Master, and everything will be okey-dokey. We went on to talk about our promotional activities. Nemo examined this question far more thoroughly. First of all a heated argument sprang up about the name of the team. Lena masterfully pressed home the religious side of the question, shamelessly abusing her title and position as Master. Nemo objected reasonably, employing the terms "target audience" and "focus group", reducing Lena to a state of embarrassment. She had a pretty good grasp of that stuff too, but the dream was more important. It made no difference to me. The name wasn't all that important up on the rooftops.

"But it's very important down here," Nemo said with a nod, and Lena reluctantly agreed.

Lena wanted something like "The Brotherhood of Good" or, at a pinch, "Good Balance". Nemo suggested "Roof Dancers", "BeaTin' Hearts" and, with a nod in Lena's direction, "City Angels". He insisted that a title like "Order of Equilibrium" would make it hellishly difficult to find a chocolate bar of fizzy drink manufacturer to sponsor us. They went on arguing for a long time before I latched on to the general idea. I suggested taking what we were going to do, naming it in Nemo's style and swapping one of the words for a synonym in order to get a religious meaning.

So that was how the name of our sect was born: "City Extreemerz" became "Apostle City". It made no difference to me. So "Apostle City" it was. It sounds pretty okay.

The second point was the "general concept" as Nemo called it. According to his plan it ought to look like this. A site is opened on the Internet under our name. The site displays detailed information about the team ("Sect!" – "Okay, sect..." – "Supreme Master!" – "Okay, sect, Supreme Master"), our photos, bios, beliefs. The sect's elaborated philosophy concerning nocturnal operations and its religious rationale. Why, what for, our purpose in doing it.

But that's only the basis. Afterwards, as we prepare for the net operation, we work out a plan and put it in place. What we're going to do and how. A gutsy name for every operation; for instance "Junction Attack" for the next one. Nemo squinted at us after he said that and looked pleased: he'd managed to squeeze his idea in.

After that came the operation itself. Maximum video and photo shooting. Soon after the operation a report is prepared and posted on the net. Attached to the report are a detailed description of the operation and all the photos. An edited video clip. Operations are sorted by date.

According to Nemo, all this ought to earn us fantastic popularity.

Lena agreed with the general substance of the idea; the only thing that worried her was how exactly the religious activities of the sect would be linked to our nocturnal operations.

"Directly," Nemo answered. "The nocturnal activities of the Apostle City sect are its religious activities. In order to attract as much attention as possible to our movement without resorting to coercion, psychological manipulation or intrusive missionary activity."

Our Supreme Master was satisfied with that answer. She and Nemo went on to discuss the sect's visual image. I grinned. With an approach like this, it looked as if there was a real chance of filling up our empty circus with spectators. Filling it up especially for the clowns. But that was Nemo's job. I started feeling a bit nervous when I saw him coming up with a whole heap of ideas for his area and basically handling the whole thing effortlessly. I wasn't sure I could maintain a fitting level of operations for all three of us. Previously I'd done this alone, and then only three times. Before that, I hadn't had any proper preparation. You could say I came to urban extreme by chance. Or maybe I didn't. Somehow life just took a turn in that direction, especially after school.

How I got into uni is a different story altogether. No sweat, naturally. It's easy enough to get in anyway, so for me it was a walkover. Well, I studied for six months in the first year. Course notes, classes, vodka.

Then it got boring. I wanted something else. I started looking around. It turned out that almost everyone had a hobby. Something that occupied a greater or lesser place in their lives. I didn't have a hobby like that, and I made a conscious decision to acquire one.

At first, being extremely interested for obvious reasons, I decided to go in for picking up girls. Girls are always interesting. I studied the theory, read the books, talked to the specialists in this line. The specialists looked down their noses at me and tenderly explained the details.

When it came to the practical application, things broke down. I wasn't getting anywhere at all. Of course I knew why. I couldn't explain properly everything that I had to get across to the girl, and that put a real damper on things. On the other hand, I found that reassuring. It shot down the theory, and not my application of the teachings and precepts.

Whenever I met a girl I always tried to show how good and intelligent I was, and how I understood everything, but I always felt terribly uncomfortable about the whole process. I still haven't managed to get rid of that uneasy feeling even now. Every date I had usually ended with me reaching out to the girl for a kiss and getting absolutely nowhere. I changed tactics and alternated moves. Sometimes I gazed intently at the girl for a long time. She would start looking back intently at me, trying to make out the expression in my eyes. Then I delicately moved a bit closer and started stroking her hair. The girl would usually lower her eyes. I started the final approach, aiming for a kiss on the lips. And then she would move away, say brightly: "See you" and run off into her entrance. Sometimes this would happen earlier, during the hair-stroking stage.

The sudden cavalry charge was another gambit widely employed in the hope that at first the girl wouldn't realise what was happening and then afterwards it would be too late. I didn't give any hint of my motives for seeing her home until the final moment. We would say goodnight, even half-turn our bodies away from each other, and then I would throw myself on the unsuspecting girl like a tiger, with my lips thrust out. Credit where credit's due, their reactions were astounding. Or had they only been pretending not to suspect anything? Oh, women, the devil's own vessel. Just millimetres before I could clamp my lips on their sweet little lips, they managed to turn aside, and I scored a shameful miss. I even managed to frighten some of them, one was so frightened she threw her hand up and I ran into the edge of it so hard, my eyes started watering. She apologised for a long time afterwards, and she could hardly stop herself from laughing.

The next variation was force. On the principle that a well secured patient requires no anaesthetic. The dubious nature of this method was adequately offset by the protective mechanisms of the facial muscles employed by the girls. Grasping the head of my experimental subject firmly (but gently!) in the region of the ears with the palms of my hands, I would close my eyes and reach forward to kiss her. A few seconds later I would discover to my amazement that I was kissing her on the cheek although, bearing in mind my unsuccessful previous experience, I had aimed for the lips.

How did they manage that? One day I ran straight into two hands braced against my chest. Not a very pleasant sensation, I can tell you. It's damned humiliating.

And the most common outcome of all was the most banal. I would smile in farewell, reach out to give her a peck, going for the lips as if by accident. I would kiss her on the cheek. We would smile sweetly at each other again and part forever; and I would walk home nursing my messed-up feelings and an appalling inferiority complex. Ever since then I don't try to steal a kiss on a date. Everybody's good at some things and bad at others. I was no good at kissing goodnight. That's not the end of the world, if you think about it.

I went on dates for three or four months and then happily dropped the whole business, deciding that love would come along on its own and meet me on the bumpy road of life. Deep in my soul I knew that wasn't the way of things at all, but there was nothing I could do.

The next attempt to find myself was in the martial arts. Several of my fellow students literally used to rave about that stuff, gradually replacing normal Russian speech with a peculiar blend of Hollywood jargon and Japanese terms. It went so far that I could hardly understand them when they were talking to each other. Naturally, it wasn't the slang that attracted me. Or the possibility of smashing in the teeth of some drunken hoodlums in an alleyway, concerning which I had serious doubts. Or even the ability to control yourself and manage your life, which every last one of our sportsmen promised me, and which I doubted even more. But I wanted to be so carried away with it, like them, that it would seem like something important.

After visiting various different classes for a couple of months I realised sadly that this too was not for me. At the end of the training sessions everyone went home, and that was the end of their studies. It felt like many of them were actually waiting impatiently for the end of the session, as if someone had forced them to come and pay the money that was due to the trainer. I picked up a couple of useful skills but then it all ended. I never did get to glimpse the promised depths behind the training session, the throws and kick-ass stuff. My hobby has to be my life, but this started and ended in strict conformity with a timetable on a page from an exercise-book pinned up in the changing room. I didn't find the chance to pump up my muscles or acquire the ability to fight tempting in itself. At least not enough to forget about everything else for the sake of it.

The fine arts didn't work out either. Amateur theatricals were a non-starter. I couldn't draw. I thought writing poetry was boring, and the passion for it looked very strange to me. So I launched my next assault on music. The guitar.

Learning the basics turned out to be rather easy, only I had absolutely no use for the basics. I wasn't planning on singing, damn it. Maybe if I'd got some kind of satisfaction out of it right from the start, I could have got the knack of music-making and been relatively successful, but it wasn't to be. I didn't take my guitar to lectures, I didn't have any friends. Who could I play for? Should I go out in the streets and stand there in front of the urbanites with my cap turned back-to-front? I wasn't ready for that then, all right? Maybe now, after the Colossus and the bridge, but then – absolutely, definitely not.

Anyway, I gave up the guitar too. Again after a couple of months, without ever really learning anything. So having failed to find my life outside the university, I started getting bored. The lectures started to pall. I began to find it tedious going to the same old subjects and listening to the same old people. I'd more or less got into the groove of study, and I wasn't having any difficulties keeping up, but I'd lost any sense of satisfaction from solving complex problems.

I started feeling fed-up with the stuffy lecture hall, the swirls of dust patterning the beams of light and my fellow-students' backs. Every morning I thought about yet another identical dusty day lying ahead, and I plodded off again to listen to lectures, feeling incredibly bored. In my mind, the very concept of a day became firmly attached to the dust in the lecture hall. I didn't know how to shake all this off.

Then I started going out walking at night. Just walking. At night the air's cleaner and the heat's cool. And then again, there were no blinding rays of sunlight striking me in the eyes, and no crowds of citizens scurrying around the streets at night. In some places this looked dangerous, and it was, but I simply tried not to stick my nose into anything.

And one night, out of sheer curiosity, I carried out my first operation. I was walking along the street beside the sports complex. A long way ahead of me there was a group of drunks hooting with laughter and I could hear bottles clinking. As I already said, the last thing I wanted was to get involved in anything, but I didn't want to go back home – the night was way too beautiful. I saw a fire escape ladder and walked over to it. I looked up. The first rung was really close – jumping up to grab it was no problem. The building itself didn't look too high, either.

I suddenly realised I really could do this, and my heart immediately started beating faster. I felt afraid, but then immediately this exhilarating tingling started up in my legs – afterwards I christened it blithe fury. I couldn't take my eyes off that ladder leading upwards, and the next moment I realised there was a different world up there. I realised I was standing right on the bottom of the town. All those levels running up! After that I couldn't leave. I jumped up and grabbed hold of the ladder. I hauled myself up easily and started crawling higher. The ladder reverberated as I climbed up it, but I wasn't afraid any more. I was too hyped up.

I scrambled up onto the incredibly wide expanse of the sports complex roof and looked round at this grey field that suddenly seemed boundless. At night it had no boundaries, and I felt very small.

I set off, and every step was the first. I imagined what I looked like and almost laughed – the picture seemed so fantastic. Like a man on the moon, I walked across an uninhabited grey desert absolutely alone, with the lights of the city shining around me and up above – the stars. And all this had been so close! How often I had walked past it and never suspected that a different world began only a few meters away. A world that wasn't like the day; a world where everything was different; a world where it was legitimate to be solitary.

I liked this world a lot. I cut across the entire roof of the sports complex and regretfully clambered down an identical ladder at the opposite side. With every step on the way down I could feel the magic being left behind. But even so, I realised that going back wouldn't bring me the emotions that I'd just felt. On the contrary, deliberate attempts to summon them up would consistently diminish the taut energy of the sensation, and sooner or later force me to get used to it. And then I would lose this world of my own that I had only just acquired.

Next morning I seemed to switch off from reality. The only thing I could think about was what I had experienced the day before. I wanted more. In order to protect this supremely valuable memory, I decided not to concentrate on it. I thought up a name – urban extreme.

I decided to plan and prepare every subsequent operation in detail. I observed sites through binoculars and figured out the possible obstacles. I bought equipment and calculated how much time an operation would take. And while my mind was busy with the calculations, I could sense the really important thing. Up there.

I already told you it made no difference to me what our team would be called, didn't I? I expect that now it must be clear why.

Having discussed things that were incredibly important from their point of view, Lena and Nemo came up with one idea in common. That was to use black robes. Similar to the kind that priests wear. I immediately opposed it, gauging what it would be like trying to manage ropes and swivel hooks in cassocks. I advocated my usual tracksuit trousers and T-shirt with trainers. They both eagerly reassured me that it was only a detail of the image.

Lena liked the use of churchy accoutrements for its own sake. She claimed most sects were always happy to use robes in black or some other colour. As if it gave the sect some kind of official status. In this connection, I enquired whether she was intending to register our organisation with the appropriate authorities, but she just shrugged that off.

Alex found the robes attractive because they looked mysterious and "generally cool". He was planning to take lots of shots with figures in black robes standing with their arms folded in "gimmicky gestures" (that's a quote too) and holding all sorts of "glittery things", by which he meant swivel hooks, blocks and hooks.

He promised that no one would be forced to put on the robes during the actual performance of a mission. He intended to take most of the group photos with these robes. And since the lion's share of our photographs were going to be taken up on the rooftops, now I could count on having to pack black dressing gowns into our bags as well.

I didn't know how they were planning to change back and forth during an operation, either. Now I'd have to time how long it took Lena, for instance, to put her robe on and take it off, and then include these calculations in the detailed plan of the operation. I didn't really object to making things a bit more complicated. We could go with the robes.

When they'd had their fill of tittle-tattling, they decided the main points had been settled and the details could all be fitted in. They couldn't have looked more delighted. As if they'd erected some kind of monument to themselves with all their theoretical disquisitions. In the evening we decided to celebrate the creation and confirmation of the sect's official philosophy. Lena and Alex swapped names of discotheques and clubs for a little while and then settled on one that had opened just recently.

It was all the same to me – I didn't understand any of this. All those clubs and discotheques were as like each other as advertising clips. Okay, there's the lighting. There's the layout of the tables. The name? And the visual style? But even so, it's all the same. You can take your bearings from the type of people who visit an establishment, and the prices. But the best thing to do is just go to the club that's closest geographically, and not clutter your brains with dozens of names.

We piled into a taxi and got to where we wanted to be. Just as I was expecting. Stylish design, TV monitors on the walls. Why do urbanites go to these clubs? What the average urbanite, who turns up at such a joint is looking for is beer and nuts. But beer and nuts can easily be bought for a third of the price in a shop. So what's the idea? Come on, explain it to me! Maybe the booze there is exceptionally good? Like hell it is! And then, there are all these forums where you read messages seething with indignation from urbanites about such-and-such a club serving the most repulsive beer that this urbanite has ever tasted in his life. Surely it couldn't be the need to be with other urbanites? After all, the whole day is already spent in the crowd, associating with other people, what's required is a rest from them.

No, there's something wrong with the city in the daytime, if people rush back into the crowd again at night. I don't care. What difference does it make where you drink?

We ordered our first mug of beer. Or rather, I ordered one. The Master toyed with a cocktail which, in my opinion, was only bought because of its name, and Nemo stirred a martini with apple juice. Whenever I come to a new place, it always takes me a while to get used to it. Take a look around. Think through a couple of questions about the air-conditioning and lighting systems. It's only after that, when I've merged into the environment a bit, that can I try to relax.

These two didn't share my views on R and R at all.

"How are you doing?" asked Nemo.

I shrugged.

That was the end of questions for reflection. Lena and Alex starting jabbering.

"You know, I don't like my course," Lena told him. "We're not learning to do anything. All of us think the same. You can study for six years, it's still useless. It would be easier to read it all yourself. The lecturers don't teach us anything. What can she teach me? Only what she knows how to do. And who's she? You know, guys, everything good that I've ever learned, I taught myself!"

Nemo had a very attentive expression on his face. Sometimes he nodded to me. Then Lena turned towards me and looked at me meaningfully with her grey eyes, painstakingly articulating every syllable with her face. Is that to show that I'm in the conversation too? I already knew I was in it. I was listening.

"What are you studying to be? I forget."

"A psychologist. Sociology, influencing people. Small and medium-size groups."

I knew who she was studying to be. The leader of a totalitarian religious sect, that was her special subject.

"I'm going to be an economist. I'm hoping to find a good job when I graduate. In fact, I'm hoping to find one sooner than that," Nemo smiled.

I can't be bothered worrying about all that stuff. I'm studying to be a techie: a local networks administrator, systems administrator, technical support manager, call it what you like. It comes down to the same thing: maximum time spent with computers, minimum time with people. Will it be easy for me to find a job? I don't know. The demand's there. But I'm afraid. Seriously, I'm afraid. Not like when I'm up on the rooftops, this is different. Not even a whiff of blithe fury about it. Semester after semester recedes into the past, and nothing about me changes. Guys I know in their senior years graduate and get jobs in the shadiest damn places. Hardly anyone gets a normal job. One they can live on. Best not to think about it. I prefer to feel my fear up on the roof.

But then, you have to start a family, don't you? We've had these social norms implanted in us, haven't we? I don't take myself as an example, but what the hell are other guys supposed to do with these social norms? A family? Children? An educated individual understands his responsibility for children. That's why he won't have any.

So is everyone else as cool as cucumbers in the freezer? Like hell they are. I don't believe it.

"One of my friends has her own travel firm. She's the general director..."

"Whose business is it?" asked Nemo, screwing up his left eye in a flashy move.

"Hers. Her own private firm. Her parents' gift, but she's in charge of everything."

Nemo nodded and drew a pack of cigarettes out into the light of day. He looked down rapidly. I could see he was thinking. "The same age as me... Am I too late already?" Yes indeed. The perennial "they". "They" manage to buy themselves an apartment and a car. Get married twice and divorced one point five times. When you're nineteen, or twenty-one, and you hear that that someone the same age as you "has his own business", a strange feeling comes over you. A desperate gut feeling. As if you've thrown this round away. And it's all over for you now.

It doesn't come over me. I don't give a damn. I've got urban extreme. Nemo shrugged the thought off too. He looked up and to the right. He recalled all his successes and achievements. He did the right thing. How else can you fight against other people's successes? I don't know what I'd choose. My dreams are pretty thin on the ground. I'm already doing what I want to do anyway.

As the time passed, my companions got drunk. Nemo started slurring his words. Lena started bumming cigarettes off him, although she hadn't smoked before that. I tried to keep up with them, only I couldn't manage it. I kept forgetting to swig my beer. I wasn't bored, I don't know how to be bored when I don't have to do anything.

Anyway, the evening was winding down. I think Nemo was running out of money. He gave me a searching look. I suggested calling a halt. Nemo backed me up almost delightedly. Lena could have partied on, I sensed it.

* * *

So there are the three of us, walking along the street at night. Nobody's talking. I'm not feeling even slightly awkward, but Nemo seems to think everyone's bored. He keeps cracking jokes that either aren't funny or are just crude. Lena laughs, sometimes too much – it's the alcohol. We reach Alex's place first. Without the slightest regret, he waves and disappears into the entrance. I envy him slightly. If I was in his place, leaving a guy to see a girl home, I'd imagine all sorts of wild stuff.

We still don't talk. The two of us. I take Lena by the hand, Lena doesn't mind. She even squeezes my hand tighter and starts swinging our clasped hands backwards and forwards. Her white skin seems to glow in the darkness. Her entrance. We say goodnight. I kiss her on her dainty cheek. I start moving away and then I feel that she isn't moving. It's like I'm paralyzed for a second. The darkness in front of my eyes starts pulsating slightly. Against the background of darkness, the left side of her hair glimmers with the reflection of a street lamp.

I slowly shift to the left. My cheek rubs against hers. I feel her warmth and her hair. Then I kiss her on the lips.

The first thing I realise is that it's a hell of a long time since I kissed anyone. I'd forgotten that smell and that taste. The erection starts straightaway. I just can't get the rhythm of the lips right. Lena tries to fit in with my clumsy efforts. We just about manage to commit an act that could rightfully be called a kiss. I can't go on – I'm so appallingly nervous. I'm afraid that if we keep going, I'll be bound to do something even worse, I'll do something scandalous or wrong. So I smile at her and leave. She turns away almost at the same time as I do.

Holding my breath and trying to keep the rhythm of my steps steady, I listen tensely to the silence. She didn't laugh. So everything's probably all right. I walk out into the street and head for home. My heart's pounding. I agonisingly wind back through the last few minutes with Lena. Frame by frame. Did I do everything right? I didn't screw up anywhere, did I? Maybe I ought to have shown her up to the apartment? Who does she live with, her parents?

Stop.

"There's nothing crasser than the stab of an opportunity missed."

She's bound to think I was rushing things. Or that the way I kissed was wrong. Who needs a guy who still can't kiss properly at nineteen? I try to convince myself there's nothing terrible about that as far as girls are concerned. I imagine Lena with a girlfriend I can't see, talking about me. "You mean he doesn't know how to kiss?" – "Why, what did you expect?" – "Well, that's no great problem, you can teach him, right?" – "You bet I will." The girls giggle and start throwing cushions at each other.

I've no need to be embarrassed about the fact that I can't kiss. I couldn't get it right from the very beginning, all right?

All those parties at uni are such garbage. You can see from a mile away who's got the hots for who. Then the music starts darkness, primitive lighting. Teasy-squeezy dancing.

I never did like those dances. I always felt absolutely awful. Everything in slow motion, couples dancing, and I'm standing there, out of it. I don't give a damn about being out of it, it doesn't bother me at all, it's normal. But there's this little voice in my head, whispering to me: "Invite someone..." it gnaws at your bones – that feeling that you should be like everyone else and invite someone to dance. That you shouldn't stand there all on your own. You should make an effort to be popular. You shouldn't stand in the corner with a gloomy expression on your face and your arms crossed. Should. Shouldn't. Should. Shouldn't.

And you walk over, with a comical grin spread across your frontispiece, to the opposite side of the frontline, where the girls are gathered together with boredom written all over their features. And then they say no. Wave you off with a negative gesture. Shake their heads slowly, turning their eyes away, as if you'd asked them for a smoke, not invited them to dance. You walk back, feeling relieved.

Sometimes something even worse happens. Someone says yes. For sure, someone not highly desirable in terms of the generally accepted ratings. Otherwise, why would she say yes, when the others said no? Out of pity? Naturally, you can't dance (where could you have learned?). And the two of you start circling cluelessly, too fast, getting ahead of the rhythm, and your stuttering steps get it all wrong. You feel like your entire class is watching you and laughing in its heart at your grotesque efforts.

But you have to do it. You have to. And when the music ends and you smile and nod at your partner, thanking her for the dance, it feels like you've done your duty. Done what you had to. Now you don't have to worry any more until the end of the party – you've beaten your drum. Do what you have to do, no matter what – that's the gist of it.

I was always invited everywhere, but I wasn't popular. I even remember this one time when a certain girl got totally bombed and I'd put a few away as well. We kissed. The real thing, heavy suction and even spray, damn it. I pawed her a bit, it was just like a first date's supposed to be. Although I suppose it wasn't a date, just a party with booze, but it still counts. Technically speaking, everything was fine. I even started anticipating and woke up in the morning in a good mood, imagining how the two of us would carry on from there and all that kind of nonsense.

But she didn't give any sign. She didn't come over or sit on my desk or tell me what yesterday evening meant to her. So that was where our relationship ended. Tough shit, my friend. She was just drunk.

What about Lena?

I put the idea out of my head straightaway. I dumped any ideas about her ages ago. Que sera, sera, I don't want to give myself the jitters trying to guess the future.

I hurry along the dark night street. A yellow half-moon is flying through the clouds.

* * *

The next day we exchange e-mails and texts. Everything's agreed. The operation is set for the following night. I present something like an estimate for the equipment that we'll need. I've persuaded Lena and Alex to let me prepare everything for them, apart from the clothes. The last thing I need is to discover half way through the operation that they've forgotten their equipment.

I look through the budget in my personalised notepad and call round to Alex's place. "Hiya, cheers!" says Alex. Then he spends a long time fiddling with the page of calculations. I can see he's short of readies. He asks me to lend him some money. I agree. I have money as a result of the raid on the rusty garages. Alex hands me back the notepad with a sigh of relief.

Lena opens the door. I look her in the face intently. The black hair is slightly mussed, scraps of dreams still hover in her eyes. She gives me a questioning look. I wait for about three seconds. Four. Then I take out the notepad with the budget in it.

I wasn't hoping. I wasn't, not even for a second, honestly.

Lena examines the listing of gear indifferently. We've agreed to share all costs equally. For the time being. Only for the time being, because in a normal sect the disciples pay in all the money and the leader controls it. But our Supreme Master takes a realistic view of things, she understands you have to take one step at a time. Later on the disciples will sell their apartments and follow their leader to the ends of the earth. But for now it's even Stevens, everyone pays a third. The operation hasn't turned out cheap. But it's not provocatively expensive either. About the same as if we'd had a serious session in that club yesterday. If we'd really pulled the stops out.

Lena glances over the notepad page once again and goes back into the apartment. I hear her asking her mother for money.

After a while Lena comes back and hands me the money. The precise amount. I fold the money up carefully and put it away in my pocket. Lena waits. She's wearing a washed-out T-shirt with a faded design and tracksuit trousers. Touching yellow socks. I raise one hand in farewell and feel for the door handle behind me. The door swings shut behind me. An old-fashioned door, upholstered with red imitation leather, tacked on with brass tacks. The tail-end of the nine in the number has broken off.

And the rage I feel for that door is just terrible. I could just throw myself on it right now, tear the damn thing to shreds, kick it and punch it... Something inside flares up and I start feeling feverish. I'm overflowing with potential energy now. If only I could let it out... I experience a ferocious masochistic pleasure from reining it in by force. I start walking down the stairs.

* * *

My room has been transformed into a military depot. Equipment for the imminent operation is laid out across the beds. I'm packing the bags.

The bags are the first things that require attention. The fundamental and primary quality of a bag for urban extreme is convenience. The second is maximal holding capacity. Convenience is more important. You realise that for real up there, when a shapeless bag starts swaying on your shoulder and smashing against your arms that are already trembling anyway. I've selected longish sports bags approximately 40 x 30 x 30 cm. The kind people say are bigger inside than out. If necessary, the bottom can be unzipped, and the bag becomes another 10 centimetres deeper. We're going on the operation at night, so accordingly the bag's colour is black. The small maker's name is no problem. Two fabric handles that fasten together with a soft flap with press-studs and one large strap to hang the bag over your shoulder. The length of the strap can be adjusted, but it's too soon to do that now – I'll set the length when the bag's full.

A few items from the mountain-climber's arsenal. Strong, blue nine-millimetre ropes, in coils of a hundred metres. Shiny metal hooks attached to their ends. Seamless steel rings slide freely along the ropes.

Knives stylised to look like army issue. The appearance doesn't really matter. What is important is for the blades to be ringing sharp. They have sheaths and covered handles too. On no account must the knife fall out of your hand.

The hydraulic cutter. Looks like a pair of garden shears,

and about the same size, only heavier. A terrible object. Cuts through almost anything. Principally required for getting rid of padlocks hanging at appropriate and inappropriate points on all target sites where we might carry out the next operation.

Binoculars in a case. Good for preliminary reconnaissance and assessing the situation on the spot. Not very likely to come in handy tomorrow, but have to take them – a handy item.

First aid kit. I take it just in case. I realise perfectly well that in a case of critical error in practically any of my operations, the first aid kit will be absolutely useless. And the last time, when I hurt my knee with the cutter, I didn't even think of stopping to bandage myself up. But the first-aid kit lends a certain legitimacy to my actions, it rounds out the set of items that I carry around in my bag.

Detailed map of the city with the numbers of the buildings written on it. I carry it with me almost all the time.

Digital camera with a flash. I check to make sure I've downloaded the shots from the memory into the computer. You never know when you might need another shot. Optical zoom x4: preview screen. I always check the batteries, and check them again just before I leave. That would be really upsetting – to have an operation screwed up by two little batteries.

Mechanical watch. Its main advantage is the large hands that glow in the dark. There are plenty of cheap electronic ones around nowadays, but this one feels more reliable. The strap is leather and it encircles my wrist with a firm grip.

Torch... I can't help smiling. There are three of us now, but I still haven't bought one. For luck.

Clothes. I'm conservative on this point. Black tracksuit trousers, black T-shirt or polo-neck. Convenience comes first. At night it's almost impossible to see someone dressed in black standing absolutely still in a poorly lit area.

Assorted snap-on belts with swivel hooks. As a safeguard, not for aesthetic reasons. Gloves with open fingers. In order not to skin your hand on the rope and still feel how tense or slack it is.

Soft grey trainers. Close attention must be paid to the patterned soles: it's no fun if your foot slips off the wall dozens of metres off the ground.

Everything's ready.

* * *

Half past one in the morning.

We walk quickly along my route through the nighttime city. A clear sky, luminous blue-black. A white half-moon. I lead the way though the alleyways and courtyards, the guys follow me. I feel exceptionally confident. I look round occasionally to make sure everything's all right. I hear their irregular steps behind me. Lena's stride is shorter, and every five or six steps she has to take a couple of skips. Nemo's walking normally, but his movements are fidgety. He keeps adjusting his strap all the time and smoothing out the side of his bag, although I arranged it perfectly.

Fortunately, they've had enough sense to dress properly. The three of us are all in black, as if we're draped in a pall of impenetrable darkness. Nemo's wearing a T-shirt and black jeans. Lena's wearing a tank top and loose pants. She's pinned her hair back with a clasp.

We pass through a quiet district and advance towards the centre, where the goal of our operation is located. Two five-storey buildings standing close together on an avenue. The rustling tyres of occasional cars. Grey buildings drifting past us, windows glinting. The swish of our steps sounds out of place; sometimes a shard of glass screeches quietly under the soles of our shoes. Equipment jangles as bags are adjusted on shoulders.

I occasionally glance at Lena, concerned that her shoulder might be aching from the weight. Our Supreme Master is making an effort not to drop back by a single step, hunched over and trying to grasp the bag exactly like a handbag. It's an amusing sight. Calm night all around. We're moving through summer coolness, and we have a goal.

The house that's our starting point is at the end of the courtyard. We cross the yard and walk up to the fire escape ladder leading to the roof. Some urbanites come towards us from the direction of the avenue, and I stop by the ladder. Nemo and Lena stop uncertainly beside me, not knowing what to do. But there's no need to do anything. We're simply a group of people waiting for a friend. Nobody will ever think we intend to clamber up this fire escape. No normal person would ever get an idea like that. Alex and Lena gaze into my face intently. The urbanites walk by without paying the slightest attention to us.

I wait for another minute. Lena and Nemo wait too, tensely, following my movements. My experience with previous operations has made me an incontrovertible authority in their eyes. They've never done anything like this before, and to them it seems as if they're in a critical situation. Right now they trust me absolutely, and that increases my own confidence in myself. They sense my confidence and intuitively trust me even more. Now they'll do what I tell them to do without even thinking about it.

Tonight I'm the leader.

I walk right up to the ladder and look up. The bottom rung is two metres above the ground; dead easy to reach. When you look up from below, in the darkness the sequence of thin iron pipes merges into a continuous vertical fence. The half moon is hanging above the distant edge of the building. I jump up and tap the ladder. A quiet metallic sound.

I point at the ladder, looking at Nemo. He walks up, exaggeratedly brisk and cheerful. Jumps without even taking aim. Doesn't realise he should grab with one hand and keep hold of the bag, so it smacks against his side with a dull thud.

Something in the bag clanks. Nemo hangs there on the bottom rung. Then he jumps down. Rubs his side.

"We should video this. Video ourselves walking up to the building and the ladder," Nemo says.

I nod. Lena starts taking out her video camera. She has a digital DVcam with a mini screen – much flashier than my old eight-millimetre job.

"Move back..." Lena whispers loudly. "Move back..."

She waves her hand at us, as if she's afraid we didn't understand her. We obediently step back.

"Round the corner." Surging up from a whisper, for a brief moment her voice pulsates deafeningly loud.

We move away another ten steps. On Lena's abrupt command, we start walking out. Nemo assumes a deliberately dashing air. He tries to look like a fearless extreme sportsman moving silently through the city night. He's totally useless, although just a moment ago he was doing great...

"The robes..." Nemo suddenly remembers when we're halfway there.

Lena presses her lips together. I curse to myself. Figures in black robes will definitely attract attention in the middle of the night. And what if the police notice? And we have real gentleman-burglars' tool sets...

Nemo's feeling nervous too. He's plainly afraid, but he still asks for a shot with robes. Just one. We could perfectly well have taken this shot anywhere else in the city, in a quiet courtyard on the outskirts, without taking any risks. But I'm getting hyped up. I agree. We jog back to the entrance and feverishly unzip the bags, groping for the crumpled robes. The knife comes flying out of Nemo's bag and clatters nervously on the battered asphalt. Lena walks up to us quickly and squats down. Her right eye's looking into the viewfinder of the camera. Her left eye is screwed tight shut. She presses a button on the matte side of the camera. The red light on the front panel goes off.

We all freeze. Someone's walking through the yard. The entrance is separated off from the yard by bushes. Nothing terrible will happen if they see us, but none of us are going to budge. It's dark. We're all in black. The bushes are between us and them. The urbanites walk past without noticing us or even glancing in our direction. A magic feeling, believe me. No one can see us or hear us. We're part of the night. Our mood soars sky-high. Every movement seems honed to perfection, impeccable. I'm the first to take out my robe and put it on. The cool cloth feels pleasant slipping over the skin of my hands.

Lena peeps out from behind the bushes and runs out backwards, taking small steps, holding the camera with the lens trained on us. We look round too and walk out round the other side of the bushes. We walk round the corner of the building, straight towards the little red lamp under the lens. My feet are rushing me. I want to get it over with. It should look realistic on the tape.

Nemo walks straight up to the ladder without stopping. No, damn it! You have to take the robe off. A figure in a black robe, climbing up a fire escape... Has he totally lost it, or what? It's too late to stop him. Lena's filming. She's there inside that viewfinder, completely absorbed. Her face on the outside is tense but blank. Alex raises his hands. The sleeves of the robe slip down, exposing his arms to the elbow. This time he gets it right and jumps, reaching up to grab with one hand and holding the bag against himself with the other. He grabs the middle of the rung. He lets go of the bag and grabs the rung quickly with his other hand. The sleeve of the robe gets trapped under his hand, he unclenches it slightly and the sleeve slides down almost to his shoulder.

Nemo pulls himself up and grabs hold of the second rung. He starts climbing up rapidly. The ladder drones very faintly when he moves his feet. The blurred black figure moves quickly up the wall.

Nemo creeps to the top and clambers adroitly onto the roof. He disappears for a few seconds, then a white face framed in the black flame of a hood appears above the ladder.

I wave my hand: Get away from the edge of the roof! I'm really worried we might be seen. Nemo disappears. I turn towards Lena. Her face is glued to the camera, as if she's drinking out of it with her eyes. She's totally petrified, shooting the empty edge of the roof.

I grab hold of her bare elbow and she shudders. She takes the camera off her face and looks at me enquiringly. I draw her after me into the darkness, away from the building. At first she dawdles, doesn't understand, looks up to where Nemo is. I squeeze her arm harder, almost drag her after me. She gives a cry. The camera dangles from her wrist on its strap, with its lens pointing downwards. The red recording lamp is glowing feebly. In the darkness I stop her and pull off her robe. She doesn't resist. Suddenly she gives another cry. Her hairgrip is left in my hand, and the thick tangle of her hair cascades down in dark waves. Lena looks at me reproachfully. But it seems to have brought her to her senses. I take off my robe too.

We cross the yard, walking parallel to the main avenue, but on the other side of the building. We walk over to the other building. The bottom rung is broken off the fire escape ladder here. I turn towards Lena. She's looking at the ladder with a question in her eyes. I walk up to the ladder and lock my hands together.

Lena walks over. I go down on one knee in front of her, looking into her eyes. Lena sets a trainer with surprisingly prominent ribs on my hands and twists it in. She leans lightly against my shoulders. Her bag is pressed against my ear.

I lift her up. The zip of the bag slips coldly across my face. For a second my hands jerk to one side and a panicky thought flits through my mind: We're going to take a hard tumble! But

I take a step back. Holding her weight in my hands is hard. Suddenly the heaviness eases. I look up.

She's grabbed the first whole rung and is looking down at me over her breasts. Her tank top has ridden up, and her white stomach is glowing in the darkness. I adjust the lock of my hands and help her pull herself up, Lena clambers onto the ladder and creeps upwards without looking back.

I follow her trim little figure with my eyes. I notice Nemo watching us from the building opposite. I give him a thumbs-up – all in order. Then I climb up after Lena, watching her legs working away.

After I climb onto the roof I take a look round as usual. Lena walks over to the edge of the roof step by step and looks gingerly down. The breeze swirls her dark hair, and it covers part of her face. It's beautiful. I set the bag down quietly on the roof; I want to take the camera out. But the zip squeals and Lena turns towards me. The enchantment of the moment evaporates. Then I simply start limbering up. Nemo watches us from the opposite roof.

For the first few minutes up on the rooftops, I don't want to do anything. I want to stand stock still and stay here forever. Breathe in the pure city night, free of the burnt odour of the day and the dusty sunlight. The light of the city streetlamps creates incredibly gentle, caressing colours. I become gentle and caressing too, I melt. Sometimes it feels so good it sends shivers up my spine.

Lena waits while I stroll dreamily round the roof. In the centre I throw my head back and look up at the stars. I feel slightly dizzy. The sky is absolutely clear, only there are far fewer stars here than on the Colossus – it's not so high, and the city lights are much closer. That's called light pollution. What a very apt term.

Out of the corner of my eye I notice Nemo nodding questioningly to Lena. She shrugs, squinting sideways at me.

I smile at them reassuringly and stride confidently towards my bag. I open the zip fastener. Lena catches on, quickly gets out the camera and starts shooting me, moving the lens from side to side. I take out a rope. A knife. I hook it onto my belt. I take hold of the end of the rope and walk towards the booth in the centre of the roof. The door is locked with a padlock on the inside; impossible to open. Not even the hydraulic cutter would be any good. But I don't need to get inside.

I wind the rope round the reinforcement rods protruding from the booth on both sides. These metal rods are the basic reason why these two particular houses, and no others, were chosen as the site for holding this operation.

The knot draws tight. My rope anchoring is absolute heresy from the viewpoint of real mountaineering, but it ought to hold us anyway. I click the hook end of the rope onto a ring protruding from the wall. In the darkness the rope seems almost black. I imagine how the rope will stretch when it takes the load. The knot will shift a little, pull tighter... My breathing speeds up. The onset of blithe fury.

I hear a faint whirring and turn round in bewilderment. It's the sound of the camera as the lenses move further apart for greater magnification. Lena walks round me in a half-circle, with her face glued to the viewfinder. For some reason I slap the knot with my gloved hand. Tug on the rope twice. As if that shows its real ability to bear the load.

I get my camera out and photograph the roof. I take a couple of shots of the panoramic view. Five storeys is nothing really, but the lights of night always look spectacular. I take a snap of Lena with the video camera as Lena videos me.

I go over to the rope and calmly uncoil its loops. This will probably be the most difficult moment of the whole night. Crossing from one building to another at a height of twenty metres.

Twenty metres of emptiness.

I pull out thirty metres of rope. Cast an appraising glance at the far side. Nemo's standing on the edge and looking at me. As if he's forgotten what he has to do. I wave to him: Get back! He doesn't understand at first, but I can clearly imagine him reaching out by reflex for the rope that has fallen short and falling. Frantically clutching a rope that is fifteen metres too long. I gesture to him again: Get back!

Nemo moves a few steps back from the edge. And so do I.

I loosen up my shoulders. Heft the hook, feeling its weight. Not enough. I wrap a couple of turns of rope round it. I coil up the rest and clutch it in my fist. Take aim again. I straighten my arm out completely.

I swing my arm round. Two circles, three. I fling the hook up and away, paying out the rope with my left hand. It's not going to reach! But the hook describes a wide arc and lands on the opposite roof. Nemo pounces on it like a kitten on a bow of ribbon tied to a string, but his pounce looks comical: the hook's not going to creep away – the rope's too heavy.

I sense warmth on my left. Lena's moving up on me with the camera, trying to catch Nemo and the rope in the lens.

I carefully set my hand on the cold skin of her stomach and move her away from the edge. I feel her muscles trembling delicately under my touch.

Nemo starts slowly pulling the hook his way. I raise an open palm towards him: Stop! Wait! I check to make sure I haven't forgotten anything and go over to the fire escape ladder – to climb down.

Tonight I'm the leader. Tonight I have to take responsibility for everything. I feel confident, strong and daring when I run across the empty courtyard. I feel important and indispensable as I listen to my own quiet footsteps. I deliberately jerk my arms sharply as I run, leaving the sound of sliced air behind me in the darkness.

I easily jump up and grab the first rung of the ladder that

Nemo climbed twenty minutes ago and soon clamber out onto the roof.

On the opposite roof Lena is zealously videoing every metre of the rope. The little red eye flies through the night, leaving a thin, blurred trail in the black air. I walk up to the rope and wave my hand, trying to attract Lena's attention. She stops using the camera. I take hold of the rope and lift it to the height of my head. If I simply tug on it, the rings will slither down from that side and the rope will stretch out to its full length, touching the asphalt on the bottom of the city.

I gesture for Lena to do the same. Then I start drawing the rope towards me. Lena pays it out from the other side. I look to see where Nemo is, but he's already guessed what to do, and is gathering the rope into coils, leaving the end with the hook free.

The rope creeps across from one roof to the other. Two figures connected across a chasm by a nine-millimetre thread. I can't see Lena's eyes, all I can see are her white hands working away and an occasional glimpse of her white stomach.

Eventually the rope has all been pulled over. Nemo carries it across to the booth. The booth is further from the edge at this side, and the rope reaches another twenty metres across the roof. Nemo lashes the rope round the metal pipe of the water heater and pulls, hand over hand. The rope whistles as it slithers over the pipe. Nemo draws it tight and loops it round again. Pulls it even tighter. Starts tying knots. I don't interfere, just watch. In the meantime I take out my camera and switch it on. When Nemo has finished. I hand the camera to him.

Now we have a taut line. It's attached slightly higher on this side than on Lena's, forming a slight incline. Not dangerous, but noticeable. I touch the rope to test its tension and something silvery slides quickly down into my hand from the knots. I grab it instinctively.

I'm holding one of the metal safety rings.

It's a sign. I'll go first. I squeeze both hands round the ring and hang on it, bending my legs up. The rope barely even gives... it gives a bit and then stops. I swing to and fro, tugging furiously, trying to stretch it even further. Better now than halfway across. But there's no more movement.

It's time.

Working smoothly, with no fuss, checking my abdominal muscles, I lift up my legs and wrap them round the line. Nemo watches my movements intently from a distance. I can almost hear the lens of Lena's video camera whirring to extend my hand right across the screen.

A flash. Nemo taking a photo. I pull my stomach up to the rope and feel for the swivel hook with one hand. Pull the ring towards it. Move my hips forward and click my belt to the ring at the same time.

I'm attached. I slowly unfold my legs. My entire weight is transferred to my belt, and it presses painfully into my back. I let go with my hands and immediately slide at least a metre down the rope. I lose my balance and start slumping over with my legs up in the air. I quickly grab hold of the rope and stop myself. If I didn't grab hold, I would have slid head-down as far as the chasm. Maybe all the way across. But that isn't the important thing.

My primitive safety system works.

I throw my legs over the rope. Look at the sky. Start pulling the line towards me. The ring lets it run through freely, and I start moving. Stars above. Streetlamps below. I won't even see when the roof ends if I only look upwards. If I don't know when the chasm begins, then there might as well not be anything there. I edge my way through the city night. One shoreline is left behind, the other still lies ahead. Suspended over the bottom of the city, up at the surface. The firmness of the rope feels pleasant under my hands. I clutch its ribbed surface more tightly than necessary. I can feel its firmness. Its reliability.

I'm up among the rooftops now. Here it's clear what I have to do. And the only thing I depend on is the firm reliability of a dead rope.

On along the supple bridge between two buildings, above the city. Counting the metres, straining harder than necessary in order to feel my strength.

Silence. Regular heaving. A clear goal and clear means. This is happiness. It's right here. Up among the rooftops, under my hands. So simple and quiet and dark, without any cheering or shouting.

I could just check my movement, transforming my movement into strength and stay here, looking at the stars. Breathing in the precious air of the night city the way a fish breathes water. Live purely here and die soon.

I start feeling pressure in my fingers. The angle of the rope is increasing. Nemo didn't get it perfectly taut, and it's stretching under my weight. The angle is increasing, that means I'm getting closer to the edge of the chasm. I hear footsteps there in the chasm, very close and my heartbeat fades away with my breathing. Then I realise they really are steps. There's Lena's face, only half a metre away from my own. And the black lens of the video camera. I made it.

I'm on my way down again.

Now there clearly is a roof below me. I wasn't moving anywhere, it just appeared. Sprang up as Lena's footsteps transformed it from the chasm it had just been into a secure piece of concrete covered with tar.

Turning as far as possible to face the camera, I unclip the swivel hook and spring down off the rope. I rub my slightly chafed hands. Lena videos everything. I walk up to her and put my hand over the camera. Lena looks at me questioningly.

I point to the rope. She slowly turns her eyes to look at it.

She looks and looks. I can see she really wants to have a go. Try something new. The tongues of blithe fury are licking at her. She's got the tingling. But she's afraid, afraid!

I walk up to her and nudge her towards the rope. She moves submissively, as if she's in shock, as if she's shamelessly drunk. The rope touches her cheek. Her face trembles. She turns her head in slow motion, scraping her delicate skin hard against the coarse, rough material. She does this so thoughtfully that I even want to go up and put my hand over her defenceless face. I help her get up onto the rope. Her face is intent and focused. I click on the swivel hook. Tug on it about twenty times. It's secured. I'm feeling nervous too, all right?

I carefully lift her up. The rope slackens. I almost carry her to the edge of the chasm. Lena gasps fitfully and adjusts her grip on the rope. Then again. And again. I stop, lowering my hands. She gazes fixedly at the rope. Hurries on with jerky movements. I'm concerned she might get tired. The line starts to sway. I grip it tightly, to makes things easier for Lena.

Now I can feel her body. Feel her movements. She's hurrying. She'll get across even quicker than me. But she doesn't know that. All she sees is the line in front of her. Chances are she's not even thinking about how far she's already gone and how far is left.

I didn't think about that either, did I...

But I glided, and she's wallowing. Come on, Lena!

Kinetic energy, potential energy... Where are your Good and Evil now, Supreme Master?

I feel a new trembling. On the other side Nemo has also spotted the swaying and taken hold of the rope. We hold Lena over the bottom of the city from both sides, and she doesn't see herself, or us, or the stars, or the city, or even the night. "Keep moving!" is what Lena's thinking. It's harder for her – uphill.

Her black silhouette creeps over the chasm in little jerks. Her black hair sways like a broad, trembling ribbon. Now I can see how much emptiness there is below us. How far down it is to the bottom.

The opposite roof is already under Lena. She doesn't notice it, doesn't change her pace. Nemo grabs her by the shoulders. Unclips the swivel hook. Lena jumps down clumsily, almost falling. Goes off a bit to one side and sits down. I'm afraid she's going to be sick. Although that's no big deal, of course. Let her... It's no big deal. Lena sits there, looking down at her feet and breathing heavily.

Nemo has taken off his robe. He strokes the rope. Climbs up onto it. Shifts his grip for greater comfort and ends up on top. I follow his movements. The video camera whirs quietly in my hand. He's lying on top of the rope. His right leg is bent at the knee, with his foot on the rope.

Nemo starts cautiously moving his hands. The slope slithers under him. An interesting method. He's not looking at the stars, he's looking at the ground. It must be more frightening that way. He doesn't jerk like Lena and he's not relaxed like me – he's a bit jittery, but well in control of himself.

After crossing the centre of the precipice, he stops and rests. Sets his chin on the line and looks intently straight ahead. He looks down cautiously and I involuntarily follow the line of his gaze. A little grey cat is sitting on the asphalt, watching us. Its eyes glitter and its tail flicks to and fro.

I smile. After his rest, Nemo carries on moving, shifting his right hand forward.

He loses his balance. His face contorts. Like a cat washing itself, he stretches his left leg out sideways and jerks out his arm. The rope sways wildly. Nemo balances, his body shudders in sharp spasms beyond conscious control. He freezes. I hear him give a brief, gasping laugh. On the other side Lena has fallen to her knees with her hands over her mouth.

Then he tumbles sideways. A long, fateful tumble, sweeping his spread hand through the air in a devil-may-care arc.

It's very frightening – that fall of his. For all that long time, I watch his extended hand and try to recall if he clipped himself on or not. Did he clip himself on or didn't he? Then comes the realisation – I didn't see – he was on the other side... I don't even know...

Nemo swings round on the rope and dangles by his arm. His legs curl round the rope. His hips bounce against the rope, without moving more than a few centimetres from it. Lena screeches pitifully.

Nemo soars left and right like a pendulum, with his free hand making ludicrous gestures, trying to restore his balance.

I hear a dull creaking sound behind me. The feeling of relief slips away, washed off by a new wave of despair. I force myself to look.

It's the knot of the rope. The excessive vibration has set it rubbing hard against the metal and creaking. A second later the creaking grows fainter. Then it stops.

Nemo dangles soundlessly above the chasm. Lena kneels on the other side with her hands over her mouth. Her eyes glitter, like the cat's eyes down below. Silence.

Down below the cat starts meowing.

"Meow!" says the cat, looking at Nemo. "Meow!"

After thirty seconds of cat-accompanied silence, Nemo carries on moving head-down. As he negotiates the final few metres, already over the roof, he starts laughing. Then more loudly, almost hysterically. I want to help him get down, but something stops me. I'm surprised to find the camera in my hand.

Nemo jumps down. He's not at all subdued. He's bright and bouncy. He jumps up and down on the toes of his trainers, muttering. Slaps me on the shoulder.

"Did you see what I did?" Nemo keeps repeating excitedly. "Did you see that?"

I wave to Lena and tug on the rope. She gets up and starts

untying it. It's hard for her – the knot is pulled tight. She uses her knife.

On the way back they both become incredibly talkative and laugh at every little thing, almost getting hysterical.

It's the adrenalin. A serious strain on the nerves almost always makes you want to jump about and laugh. Feels like I'm still affected. I remember Lena on her knees on the other side of the chasm, covering her mouth with her hands.

Nemo keeps suggesting we go and get rip-roaring drunk, but I'm categorically against it.

The night is black above us, silvery clouds hiding the moon.

* * *

"Keep that!" Nemo shouts, jabbing his finger at the screen.

I'm doing the montage. Lena's wearing a short skirt and she's standing with one leg deliberately thrust forward elegantly. Her left arm is across her chest, her right hand is twirling a cassette close to her neck. Lena occasionally nibbles at it. Her grey eyes are filled with the abstract curiosity of a boss watching as work she doesn't understand is being done.

When the video was downloaded to the computer, Lena declared that the clip had to incorporate the idea of our sect. Exactly what idea, or how, she didn't actually say. That was as far as her ideological prescription went.

Nemo is sitting on a chair he has turned back to front. His hands flutter across the monitor. Every now and then, in a fit of inspiration, he starts beating his heels on the legs of the chair, grabbing my personalised notepad off the table and tossing it up in the air.

I grin as I carry out his wishes. My job is pasting things together.

Once you've siphoned the video into the computer, you have to process it and then weld it together in a decent clip. No one's interested in watching Lena moving hand over hand and panting for two minutes on end.

The task is to produce a watchable twenty-minute clip. Nemo's all fired up to make a masterpiece about how hyper-cool we are. He insists on the black robes showing up in every shot, as if the number of black robes guarantees, if not victory at Cannes, then at least the assured adoration of the public. I start feeling afraid that in the end the clip will turn out like a tale of monastic life. "Welcome to the Apostle City Monastery."

What's montage? Montage is lies. All hail progress – bits and pieces of the material that's been videoed are shuffled about in any way that takes your fancy. We put the shots with robes, taken down below, in the middle. Which means that we strode around in those idiotic sacks all night long. It also means the roofs in our city are covered with asphalt. But no one's going to notice that. And even if they do, who cares anyway?

If they constantly bombard us with all sorts of faked-up videos on TV, why shouldn't we do the same thing? The viewer gets the quality of viewing he deserves. Since the viewer is already tamed and used to spoon-feeding, why should we sweat – let the urbanites eat what they're given. They'll watch the crap, we'll make it, and everybody will be happy.

It turned out even better than I expected. A perfectly coherent video about how we walked until we got there. Climbed up, climbed down and walked again.

"Great!" Lena complimented us, coming over.

Strangely enough, Nemo paid greatest attention to the opening screen and the screen before the final credits.

"The way characters are presented is more important for the way they're perceived than the actual characters are. It doesn't matter who your character is, what's important is the way you present him. The image of Superman or a total jerk isn't created by what they do, but by how you show them."

He makes us take photos of ourselves. Wanders around the

room in ovals for a long time, examining the setting, and Lena and I dodge his sweeping glance, skipping out of the way of his zealous attention. After rejecting closed curtains, Alex stops beside the emptiest wall of the room I share with Sergei.

He grabs Lena and shoves her towards the wall.

"Sit down," says Nemo.

Lena feels uncomfortable like that. Nemo says Lena can go down on one knee. Lena blinks and says she's wearing a short skirt and that would make too much visible.

"That's good," Nemo declares. "I want the panties to stand out in the shot."

Managing to persuade Lena, but not me, he sets her in the centre. I find the sight of Lena's smooth knee and neat leg incredibly disturbing. Nemo stands me behind her and tells me to put my hand on her shoulder, and her to put her arm round my leg.

What an agonising thrill a matter-of-fact touch can be! I'm afraid to move, I can feel her warmth. It seems to me that Lena's pressing against me in a special kind of way, as if she's trying to communicate her feelings to me.

I must be hopelessly backward. These are the kind of feelings a fifteen-year-old boy has.

On the other hand, what else is left to me?

Sometimes, when I'm thinking about some couple in love or watching some film where the characters love each other, I feel envious of everyone in the world who has a girl. After all, there are so many of them, aren't there? I think: "Why not me?" One of those questions it's best not to ask, probably.

So many girls, and not one of them mine.

There's nothing else left to me.

Nemo takes ages setting up the digital camera facing us. Then he stands beside me. He puts his hand on Lena's shoulder and she winds her arm round his leg.

Agh, that really hurts!

The camera cheeps for twenty seconds and then blinds us. Nemo checks the photo.

He twists and turns Lena, who no longer feels so embarrassed, this way and that, then me, swooning at the smell of her, stands in the front and at the back, checks out "humorous" and "amusing" shots.

"Letters," says Alex. "I need big iron letters."

The big iron letters that Alex needs, which means we all do, are for the photos just taken. Alex wants glittering highlights. He wants contemptuous facial expressions.

"More haughtiness in those glances!" says Alex.

And we search for photographs in which we're looking at the camera as if our necks are hurting. We do the titles "Apostle City" and "Urban Extreme" in big iron letters. And we add in the kind of highlights that could blind someone. I add them in.

We write the text together too. I write, Nemo dictates. He insists on using slang everywhere. "Assault on the heights, descent, run in" and other stuff like that. Reading it, our modest operation is transformed into an incredibly dangerous and well-paid campaign, full of stunts and mind-blowing adventures. Nemo calls the ropes cables. He calls Lena and me warriors. Lena doesn't mind. Warriors can perfectly well be members of a sect.

Whatever you say, Supreme Master!

Out of all this we (I) make a website. It's easy. Putting it on the Internet is free, you just have to produce it yourself. Any idiot can do that in five minutes. Sometimes I get the impression that's what they spend most of their time doing.

The new hobby for idiots – filling the Internet up with themselves.

So we decided to join in. The two almost ordinary young guys and a girl who were messing about on the rooftops of the city yesterday are now, through the magic of technology and

Nemo's imagination, being transformed into boundlessly cool, public, extreme thrill-seekers.

Register with the search engines, site catalogues, banner networks. In a few hours the first visitors on the prowl in search of cities and religion will stumble into our site. They'll see our photos and watch our video. They'll read our story.

It's easy to get public exposure. It's much harder to become interesting. Ah, and yes – it's even harder to want to do that. For me. Could I have done it alone? I wouldn't have been prepared to tell all and sundry about myself. I'd have come up with a bunch of reasons: problems with the law, lack of time, reluctance to acquire admirers. What difference does it make? I wouldn't have done it.

But if everyone wants to do it so much, why not?

* * *

After that operation the three of us started spending more time together. In a certain sense, Lena and Nemo became my first real friends. When I had nothing to do, I went round to see them. Sometimes they came round to my place. Just like normal people.

Human company is addictive. While you're alone, you don't know a thing about this. There's just the world and you. When you toss a coin, it lands heads or tails. But in any case it lands. If you want to learn to do press-ups, you start doing press-ups. You do five press-ups, then ten, then fifteen. The day comes when you can do a hundred if you need to. A predictable result. You and the world.

All my obsessive attempts to guess other people's thoughts and actions in advance proved absolutely useless. I tried, I honestly did try, but it was all a waste of time. It applied to everything and every situation, even the most ordinary. I looked up at the sun and tried to guess what Lena would put on today. I computed her actions, imagining her twirling in front of the mirror. I assessed the heat and forecast to myself that she would put on a little top and a short green skirt. I could already see the skirt in front of me. But she put on a T-shirt and shorts. Orange.

My notepad was full of the possible ways Nemo could say hello. I was expecting him to walk up to me and Lena and say: "Hi, guys!" or "Greetings, dear friends!" Then I'd take out the notepad, smile and show him I knew how he was going to greet us. But I kept getting it wrong. I just couldn't guess right. Then I started writing down several different possible greetings at once. But even so I couldn't guess, Nemo thought up something new every time. Obviously he must have got himself a notepad like mine and written down different ways of saying hello in it, so he wouldn't repeat himself.

It's hard to say what we did. A bit of everything. Why do people get together? When Nemo and I first met, he asked me what I wanted a team for. I was totally certain it was for urban extreme. But now we had one successful operation under our belt. We didn't have to see each other so often in order to prepare for the next one. But I still kept going round to see them.

I showed them our city. They lived in it too, but they didn't know it through and through. I couldn't walk on a summer's day, and night time didn't work out, so we decided on a compromise and walked in the evening, when the sun had already faded, but it was still etched on the pale sky.

I liked the fact that I knew the city. I wanted to teach them, but at times I suspected what I really liked was the fact that I knew the city better. I used to catch myself not showing them all the walk-through courtyards, alleys or narrow little passages between the buildings. The city was mine for as long as they knew it was.

I only had to close my eyes, and all its wide avenues, streets and courtyards blossomed in front of them in a tracery-work pattern. I could imagine one district or another. The city was bigger than me, but I knew all of it. It's a very pleasant sensation. The Minotaur probably felt the same kind of joy as he wandered round his labyrinth. He knew where the right turn was, and where this passage would lead. And no one apart from him knew that. He reigned supreme over his labyrinth, not because he was mighty and powerful and he had horns, but because he knew it like the back of his hooves. Anyone else would get lost in the labyrinth. I thought of the city as my labyrinth, and Lena and Nemo tacitly acknowledged that. That was what I liked. Nemo knew how to be original saying hello, and Lena wore green shorts... or an orange skirt, but I knew the city. We all had our talents.

At first it was hard to make sense of Lena. I thought about the sect, the crazy ideas about Good, Evil and weird energies. Urbanites could only see desires like that as a deviation from the norm or an irrepressible desire for glory. Once I got to know her a bit better, and talked to her about all sorts of nonsense, I understood what was really important.

All this stuff about the sect, the Supreme Master and her passion for converting people was just a screen. She was good and intelligent. She studied the methodology of recruitment and went to seminars with meaningless names. I had to look really hard to see her from the inside. But from the outside everything was in good shape.

They say for a girl it's her appearance that's important. You can be clever and determined, with an accurate assessment of your own capabilities, any kind of girl at all. But if you're a beauty, the world opens its doors in a far more welcoming way. When a girl's beautiful, she grows up with the idea that she's wanted. And if she has even a smidgen of brains, she'll do all right in life, that's the bonus. And it's easier to see that from the outside.

Lena seemed attractive to me. Maybe I'm not the world's

greatest expert on girls, but even I could see that. Not a glossy poster beauty though.

Lena knew how to take care of her shiny black hair and light skin, and how to make up her grey eyes so they looked bright and clever. She had excellent control of her clear, resonant voice, she knew how to laugh and smile, and her teeth were whiter than white. Her body... a ticklish subject, but... yes, everything was fine there. Breasts that weren't too large, a flat stomach. Slightly full hips, but then no one's perfect. I could assess all this without any hormonal hysteria, because there was no chance for me and Lena. Someone else could have thought she was a real beauty. Someone else who had also never been popular, but still hadn't given up hope of finding himself a match.

Behind all the talk about the sect, her anxieties sometimes slipped out. Once or twice the thought flitted through my mind that the Supreme Master act was a screen against life. Like when she mentioned another girlfriend and spoke about her family life this time, not her business. I think that's a sensitive issue for all girls. It wasn't so obvious with Lena, but I could see she was concerned because she wasn't married, and there weren't even any prospects on the horizon.

Lena wasn't hung up about it, that's for sure. When the three of us went to discos, young guys or men sometimes came up to her and asked for a dance; afterwards they tried to pick her up, but they never got anywhere. She joked with us, picking out the weak points of her failed admirers and mocking them caustically. We laughed, but sometimes I imagined myself in their place. I don't know what Nemo was thinking, but he probably did the same.

I saw the way she eyed those guys, summing them up. I don't think she just rejected them out of hand. It's more likely she just wanted to get the maximum return from using her body, appearance and character. A perfectly normal desire to break the bank.

Although she spoke disparagingly about her studies at college, Lena studied diligently and even felt slightly ashamed of it. I heard pride when she spoke about the top grades she'd earned so easily for trivial subjects. But she never admitted that she'd had to work for those grades, or even sit down with the textbook for one evening. The important thing for her wasn't the grades, but the fact that she'd been able to get them without any effort, whether that was true or not.

And that was how she behaved outside. In a shop, she would charm the sales attendant with her psychological tricks, getting him to give her his complete attention and ignore all the other customers. His attention wasn't all that important to her in itself. But she could get it easily, and that seemed important to her. She valued that about herself. So if this trickology ever failed, she took it very hard. As a blow to her self-esteem. Maybe that was why we got to know each other. If she'd managed to convert me with a mere half-turn of the millwheels of her eloquence, she'd have forgotten me straightaway.

We just walked. The three of us. I taught them the city, and I learned a few things from them, especially from Lena. I was astounded by her eloquent gestures and facial expressions, so much clearer than mine. I tried to learn to feel at ease with people. It just came naturally to Lena. Sometimes I wondered how things would have gone if I'd learned to communicate with people the way she did. But then I drove those thoughts out of my head. I'm different, that's all. My place is up on the rooftops.

Sometimes we dropped into clubs. I even started feeling comfortable in some discos. There's a strange thing! I started to appreciate the virtues of deafening music and the absence of any need for conversation. You simply hurl yourself into the crowd and move to the music, giving it all you've got. It's not important to know how to dance, you just have to shake about a bit.

Lena and Alex sat down at a table, and I went dashing straight to the epicentre of the music. Where there were no conversations, no discussions, nothing. "Right on. Right on," the phrase echoed round my head, while the bass guitars ripped the pressurised air to shreds. Maybe my twitching and jerking looked totally ludicrous from the outside, but I couldn't give a damn, all right? My goal was to get so tired in the next five minutes that it'd be hard even to walk. And then even more tired in the five minutes after that. And so on.

Sometimes we arrived too early, and the dance floor was empty. Now there's real scope for cutting loose! I don't understand those urbanites who wait for the crowd to get thick before they dance. It's a really amazing process. At first the space is totally empty. Then one or two people stand cautiously on the edge and start stamping their feet, pretending to make conversation at the same time. Like, they're up to anything, not really dancing. Then others join them. The dance floor doesn't fill up from the centre outwards, but the other way round. Then people who don't know each other at all stand in a circle at the centre and start tramping away together, gazing at each other with mindless, empty eyes.

An empty dance floor was ideal for me. After one of the slow numbers or a long block of dancing, the crowd would break up and go back to their tables, and the spots of coloured light creeping around the floor became visible. Then I would dash out into the very centre and start churning the air wildly, squeezing litres of sweat out of myself. And immediately all the others would come dashing after me as one man, completely surrounding me.

More often than not, the only ones who understood my fancy jerks and jiggles were Lena and Nemo. I saw them smiling as they looked at me, and I smiled back. Most people thought I was drunk, stoned out of my mind or gay. But sometimes I caught interest in the eyes of the girls following the frenzied diction of my body. That really spurred me on. But what could I do in that dense, pounding air? Only dance even more frenetically. Once one of them actually came over and asked what my name was, and I answered by showing her my personalised notepad. Then I pointed to our table, telling her to take a seat, only she walked away.

Seriously though, I find it hard to remember what we did, apart from the operations. Various stuff. Could you describe it? Young people nowadays have damn few ways of spending their free time, and most of them look actually like ways of killing it. And they mostly involve the use of alcohol. The same old horses... just grazing together, that's all. Eating the grass.

So, in a sense, the three of us were like horses. We grazed together, and nuzzled each other's faces, metaphorically speaking. That suited me just fine, but it didn't always suit Lena, and especially Nemo. I could see that. They wanted more.

I thought those were good enough times, by no means the worst in my worthless life, but Nemo was fretting over not doing the right things and not getting anywhere. I sympathised with him. He could expect something more than simply eating grass in a meadow in the company of other horses. With his abilities, he could be eating roses in the company of unicorns.

It was amusing that Alex's image as an intellectual only took over when he wasn't carried away with enthusiasm or was feeling rather uptight. When he totally relaxed in our company, all those martinis with apple juice were forgotten. And when he was giving orders about where to cut the video, tapping out a disjointed rhythm on the chair, he could quite easily swear a blue streak in a whisper – something that he completely, totally, absolutely never allowed himself to do. Even when he almost fell during the operation.

On the whole, Alex was normal, more normal than Lena and me. It's just that there are different ways of being normal. There are normal alcoholics. Normal plumbers. Normal world chess champions. And that's why I regarded Nemo as a normal intellectual. He watched the films he was supposed to watch, read the books he was supposed to read, and was smart enough to start laughing before the end of a familiar joke.

Alex never aspired to the role of an unacknowledged genius. Certainly not. A bearded intellectual licking his lips over Weininger's *Sex and Character* – oh, no, that wasn't for him. He didn't have his head up there in the higher realms, and he appreciated the pleasures of the flesh far more than the banquets of the intellect. He wasn't always willing to show this, but it was still pretty easy to read it in him. He wore his fashionable sunglasses with delight and never sank to the level of pronouncements about how he despised pop culture.

That niggardly range of facial expressions had presumably been picked up from films, or maybe from one of those books. I never saw it of course, but I strongly suspect that sometimes Alex practiced in front of the mirror to perfect his meagre emotional response. But when he'd drunk enough, he could quite easily laugh with real gusto and lie on the table and smack his open hand up on the pint of beer that had replaced his martini by the end of the evening.

Nemo could discourse perfectly sensibly and reasonably on any subject at all. He might know absolutely nothing at all about the subject, but he could still hold a long, confident conversation about it. The irritating thing was the way he shifted from one point to another. For me the ideal conversation is one that employs unconvoluted positive or negative statements. He skipped from one argument to another, using the sounds of the words, rather than their meanings. It sounded convincing, but it was actually total gobbledegook. A couple of times he and I discussed good and bad movies when Lena was there. Lena swallowed the hooks of his verbal acrobatics and in the end I just gave up, realising that every time I was only arguing the point at issue for my own benefit. Nemo was more interested in a smooth form than a precise understanding of what was happening on both sides of the conversation.

He always took care of his appearance. He wasn't some sleekly pampered character out of a boys' band, but even so. I got the impression that he ironed his T-shirts. Polished shoes, a mobile phone washed with neat alcohol, in a case. Shaved armpits, even.

The touchiest subject for Alex was money. He wanted money. He wanted a lot of money. And he didn't know how to get it. He thought a lot about "the others", but that was no help to him at all. He was involved in some dubious kinds of deals, getting customs clearance for automobiles, but that brought in a lot less than he'd been expecting. He constantly had his ear to the ground and he scoured the jobs sections in the free newspapers, pretending to me and Lena that he was looking for a set of wheels.

But he had a determined grip. I had no doubt that he'd get what he wanted in time. I envied, with an envy mingled with doubt, his ability to discover something in urban extreme that I had never looked for in it.

Sometimes he used to come out with complaints about all the hugger-muggery that went on, and how you couldn't break through it without "contacts", and so on, but I never backed him up in these conversations, even though I agreed. Once I objected that we had urban extreme, and up there on the rooftops everything was different. Nemo replied that we had to get everyone else to realise that, but I couldn't see what everyone else had to do with it.

It was easier for me. I didn't have to think about any future. I didn't have one looming up on my horizon. When you have no tomorrow, you can live today calmly. Live for urban extreme. Or, if you're lucky, graze in a green meadow with the other horses and nuzzle each other's faces.

* * *

The site did its job. Someone had already discovered that we existed. About ten people. Seven totally ignored us, deciding that we were liars or idiots. One wrote a short, angry letter in which he called us nitwits and also, for some reason, "Satanists", and signed himself "Seraphim". Lena latched onto him and wrote a long reply, in which she challenged him to a debate about the sect's ideas. She was hoping to lure him in, assuming he actually cared, but he didn't answer. She signed herself "Supreme Master" and I think he was just frightened off. If she'd put "Lena" under the bottom line, she would have had a chance.

The other two got interested. And they wanted to know more. I was afraid they'd turn out to be even greater idiots that the obscure Seraphim, but Lena wasn't bothered by that. And what's more, she'd recruited another pair on the city streets during the day. Conversion was proceeding far more briskly, now that she had something to offer apart from abstaining from sex before marriage. All four of them turned out to be teenagers between fifteen and seventeen. Lena told us she'd tried not to push Good and Evil and all those energies of hers, but put the emphasis on urban extreme.

Naturally, it could have been our distinctive image, pushed so insistently by Nemo, that caught their interest, but I suspected that the main reason was the Supreme Master herself. Lena was wearing summery clothes more and more now, and smiling quite deliberately at her victims. And anyway, she herself told us once that the most effective recruiters were young girls. It was easy for them to win young guys' trust, and the girls' too. I don't know what our recruits were hoping for, but they enjoyed being in the same room with Lena, that's for sure.

I myself had only the vaguest idea about the new recruits' involvement in the operations. Lena based the development of her religious plans on them, plans unburdened by any connection with reality. It seemed like Nemo was the only one who had a clear idea of what he needed them for, but I tried to keep out of all this. He remembered them all by name and he taught them to tie knots as a way of making good on Lena's promise to introduce them to urban extreme. He himself only learned to tie the knots the day before the class. I had to help him. But on the other hand, under the eyes of the new "disciples" Alex looked cool and confident, winging the string onto his hand with a dexterity that was still as green as grass.

These young guys, or perhaps the plans for them, made me feel ashamed and disgusted. The only one I singled out was Dima, a lad about sixteen. After the first meeting, which I sat through off to one side, burning up with shame at the content of Lena's sermons, he declared that from now on his name was Demon. Everyone forgot to call him that, and he used to get offended, thinking we did it on purpose. It seemed like Dima really did believe all the hogwash the other twosome fed him. At the third class he had the guts to ask when we were going on an operation. And he really was interested in the knots and equipment. The other guys took turns seeing Lena home after meetings, hoping for God only knows what. I suspect they even fought over her, but then they set up some kind of timetable.

The half-hour meetings were pretty tedious. Lena smiled as she pontificated about her ideas, honing her skills. At the second class, the guys started getting bored, but she came up with the brilliant idea of forcing them to make notes and alternating the religious bullshit with lessons on knots and ropes. Things started to go better. She convinced them that the title of Supreme Master wasn't for real and was only used as a convention. At the start of the next class she talked about the previous one, as if she was checking their homework.

At the fourth class I was horrified when I started to realise the young guys were falling for it. It was ludicrous, but they believed in it more than she did. Lena gave them a hobby and promised them urban extreme. And they all found her sexually attractive. It worked.

* * *

The idea for the next operation was again chosen by me. I'd already thought a lot about this much earlier, and I'd amassed a heap of plans worth carrying out. The next thing we were going to do was a diagonal descent. It's simple – the rope is secured on a roof and then it's secured to the ground about forty metres from the building. We go down the rope from the roof to the ground. We could do it tomorrow if we wanted.

But I had another idea. Not nearly as simple, but considerably more attractive.

I don't recall exactly when this crazy idea came to me. Exactly when I realised it wasn't a joke. I'd like to think I deserve the credit for it. You know the way it is sometimes. A chance phrase turns up in conversation and immediately evaporates. And then you recall this phrase, and you twist it this way and that, it puts on the flesh of detail, and there you have it – a new idea.

A crossing from the TV tower to the Colossus. Sounds awesome, doesn't it? Three hundred metres, at a height of seventy to one hundred metres above the city centre. In actual fact, there wasn't anything new in the idea of a crossing as such, many operations were crossings, but the scale of the figures was ecstasy-making.

The three of us thought about this crossing together. We calculated the time, the metres, the speed. But not in earnest. None of us thought it was possible. The obstacles to implementation were already apparent at the planning stage. A line four hundred metres long? No one would let us stretch it right across the city, would they? But it was interesting. A perennial subject. Before our first operation together, neither

Lena nor Nemo would have understood what we were talking about. Now they interrupted each other in their eagerness to discuss the video and photo options, and Nemo forgot his manners, and Lena forgot her disciples.

Suggestions came up, Nemo sketched clumsy plans of cable attachments and pulleys on paper. Suspension tackle for the camera. He promptly came up with solutions for secondary problems, running through highly detailed calculations of time and possible videoing schedules. For fifteen minutes they would completely forget that it was a fantasy project. Then one of them would sigh: "No, no, no", as if we'd been planning to go through with the crossing tomorrow.

I took almost no part in these arguments: I listened carefully, though. Theoretically it could be done, oh yes. But in practical terms, it was impossible. The Colossus and the TV tower acted like pillars, staking out the centre of the city, boundary markers on the north and the west. A good quarter of the extended line would run above all the buildings, and high up too. So high that the city would be no more than points of lights down on the very bottom.

In principle – I repeat, in principle! – I knew how to do it. A distance of three hundred metres – five hundred taking into account getting round the buildings – that's a two-minute run. A winch on the Colossus, a winch on the TV tower. Two people on the winches, one down below. That was the main problem, tensioning the line. The fact that the urbanites might spot us. Once we were up there, we could decide everything between ourselves, and it would be nobody's business.

I knew how to do it. But I didn't go shoving my oar in. Not that I didn't want to do it (what an achievement!), I was awash with blithe fury. Sitting quietly on one side and listening to Lena and Nemo arguing, sometimes I could have raced to the table and feverishly dashed off on my notepad the elementary solution that was pounding in my head.

But there were a few other things too. Apart from the supposed impossibility of making the operation work, and the danger, and the amount of work required. I tapped my fingers on the notepad, watched the Supreme Master scratching her beautiful knee and pondered.

What would we do afterwards? After those three hundred metres at the height of a thirty-storey building? We wouldn't be able to plan any operation at all without being aware of its insignificance and futility, its daylight primitiveness, compared with the crossing from the TV tower to the Colossus. It was an upfront apotheosis, and after it there would be nothing left.

That was why I always let them discard the idea. And that was why we settled on the diagonal descent.

* * *

The sect was growing. But the changes in my life were only just putting out shoots.

I've never been afraid of exams. Nothing surprising about that. You can only be afraid when you have something to lose. Or you can fail to get something. Whether or not I got an education wasn't all that decisive. But better to get it than not, and I mean the fancy piece of paper, not the torrent of knowledge, cascading into your head (ha, ha!)

Take the average urbanite, for instance. He goes to his college, has a good time, and acquires an area of expertise. He hopes. In the fifth year he starts looking for work. That's when he discovers everything's not so jolly. I've never wanted to repeat that stupid mistake. I don't hope, especially since I had an excellent incentive not to.

I regard education as something you should have. An attribute. Like my mobile phone. An achievable end in itself – thanks for that, at least. To study, you just have to do it. No special attitude, no luck, no hermitical seclusion. Studying is simply an occupation. One of. "Wheredyoutakelunch?" – "In the cafe on the square."- "Wheredyoustudy?" – "In the college beside the square." I took urban extreme more seriously. What you don't control in yourself is what makes you special.

Parents could be either mysterious or entirely comprehensible to the very tips of their fingers. It all depends on the attitude you take to them. I didn't try to understand them or get close. As a kid it was all simple. You had your parents and yourself. You didn't have anyone else. Then you grow up and you start to get the idea. One fine day a mind-blowing flash of realisation flares up in your brain and a terrible, frightening world opens up behind your parents.

Then you start realising why it happened, and what the point was. And you feel ashamed of yourself. And of them too. It's not your fault, after all. Later you realise it's not their fault either. And then comes the clear realisation that in general it's nobody's fault, and everything's arranged the best way it possibly could be, if you don't look too hard.

My parents wanted to see me. In the cafe on the square. Okay, if I have to, I have to. After I left home we started seeing each other more often. Not that I really did leave home. It's just that one day I thought it would be interesting to try. I asked myself: "Will anyone feel better if we don't have to look into each other's eyes every day?"

Things were easier for us. Easier for me. And that means for them; I'm their son, they love me more than anything in the world. Somehow I realised it with incredible ease in time – the fact that it's possible to love someone quite incredibly and be ashamed of them at the same time.

Literature's to blame for it all. Most teenagers go through a stage when they sincerely believe that their parents don't love them. Or couldn't give a damn. What rubbish! Open any book and it tells you as plain as day that all creatures love their offspring more than anything else in the world. And people are no exception. But no, the same misunderstanding is repeated time after time in every generation. What's going on here, eh?

At least I'd read all of those books. And I knew perfectly well that my parents loved me more than anything else in the world. Right then, so everything's just great. They didn't even have to convince me that they always did what was best for me. I knew that myself. From the books. We never had any conflicts – a blazing row would have looked as comical as hell. I bit my lip and reminded myself of the history of mankind. Mankind's older than I am, so who's more likely to turn out right?

They were sitting at the white table outside the cafe. I spotted my father's back just as soon as I glanced round the corner. His straight back, which he had carried through life, in spite of me, was sticking up above the chair. I didn't recognise mum straightaway, she was sitting half-turned away from me, with her head lowered slightly, telling him about something. No doubt about the wild life of her girlfriends.

My father's an accountant. And a very good accountant, at least that's what he says. Spectacles, wallet, no cigarettes. And he knows how to make all sorts of thingamajigs out of paper too. That's the warmest memory of my precious childhood: little paper ships, planes, birds. And windmills. But I didn't regard the windmills as the genuine article: they weren't made just out of paper, a stick and a nail were also required. And you needed scissors as well.

Even now I'm still really good at making little ships, planes and birds. Only no one knows about that.

My mum's generally on the small side, a petite brunette. I can easily imagine how they ended up together. My tall father, my little mum. What more could anyone want? A great combination. Genuinely beautiful girls only waste their lives, always looking for a better candidate, afraid of backing the wrong horse. That's why beautiful women are unhappy. Don't be born beautiful, be born happy. As you can see, I read all those children's books diligently back in my childhood; a most uncommon occupation for children. But then, I had to kill the time somehow.

I entered from the right and circled round so that they wouldn't have to twist their necks out of joint. We said hello. Lots of smiles. I ordered something to eat.

Studies, health, money, whatever. My parents were never the kind who panic and get embarrassed, not knowing what to talk to me about, or in general what to talk about with someone twenty years younger than them. It's an acquired skill.

Naturally, they don't know anything about urban extreme. Having reported on my life, I listened attentively to the story my father was telling.

"And her daughter, Ira... it is Ira, isn't it?"

"Yes, yes, Ira..." mum replies absentmindedly with an intent expression.

"Right, Ira... Ira, she got her a job with a provider. On the Internet. She earns quite a lot for a student. Nine thousand a month."

"Ooh, well I never..."

"That's because she knew someone, of course. You didn't think it was her brilliant brain, did you?"

My father laughs, glancing sideways at me. I smile politely. I listen carefully while he tells mum about the successfully fixed-up Ira. It's their way of trying to help me out. An excellent way of telling someone something unobtrusively. Especially me. It looks like there's a dialogue going on, but the information's all flowing one way.

It's incredible, but my sainted parents genuinely believe that I can set myself up in life like the majority of urbanites. I assume that all these innocent stories about the children of the neighbours of their dead school friends are intended to show me the path through life.

Surely it's obvious that if they can spot all this, then so can I... Most people find it harder to see an opportunity than to make it happen. With me, it's the other way round. And unfortunately, that's not because I see the opportunities so easily, it's because I just can't make them happen.

I'm not under any illusions about being able to achieve anything in life. I know I can't do anything in the daytime.

I forget to maintain the right series of expressions. For about half a minute my face expresses fixedly polite attention. My father realises that Ira's not going to leave a lasting mark in my heart, and that makes him furious. He restrains himself, but he's seething in helpless fury anyway. He raises his voice sharply on his final words and can't resist shifting his gaze onto me.

"You have to think about the future while you're still a student, all right?"

Then he blinks and lowers his eyes. A long, long half-second pause.

"Your father and I went to the cinema yesterday," mum says affectionately and entirely off the point.

For the rest of the meeting I listen to them telling me about black actors in a Hollywood movie. It's uncommonly interesting.

When we leave, they pay for me. I could quite easily have paid for myself, but I have to give them a chance to do something nice for me.

* * *

A day before the operation, I decide to take a stroll round the shops: to buy a cassette for the video camera and a couple of things for home. I always used to go to the same shops.

The hot sun was scorching the swathes of dust on the city asphalt. Urbanites walked towards me, hurrying about their business. I was going about my own business too, like a normal urbanite. Camouflaged. I carved my way through the courtyards and streets, trying to keep moving in the shadow.

I dropped into a shop and made straight for the stand with the cassettes. There turned out to be loads of them – about twenty different kinds, with different markings and abbreviations on the covers. I'd seen all this before, only I'd always thought: What difference does it make, no one's going to notice the finer points of quality, I'm not a professional cameraman.

But there are different markings on the covers! And they mean something, don't they? So I asked the salesgirl, who was friendly at first, what was what, and she even managed to explain the whole thing to me in general terms. Then she turned ratty, because I got finicky. But there was no help for it. Once I'd waded in, I had to get things clear. In the end I bought a tape that suited me, which turned out to be almost the cheapest.

I wandered on through the daytime streets. The yellow sun beat down on every glittering object in the city, skipping across the aerials, windows, shop windows and leaping into my eyes. Across the mirrors and wheel hubs of cars. The urbanites' watches and spectacles glittered. Even non-reflecting things glittered: the leaves of the trees, the plastic of the shop doors and even the very asphalt.

The sun infiltrated everywhere, it spilled across the bottom, like sunflower oil, slowly poured out by the rays of the Orb of Day. And I walked through the thick of it.

It occurred to me that I needed sunglasses. But then I decided that sunglasses weren't such a very important thing. What difference did it make where I bought them? All I had to do was stay in the centre, and sooner or later I'd come across a brightly coloured stand, glittering with glass, with a bored salesman in a cap standing beside it.

So I set off through the centre. When you walk along the central avenues, you don't think about how far you have to go. The distances aren't measured in kilometres, or even in the number of streets. The distances are measured in time. By the watch on your wrist. You measure time, not space, with your steps. The walking distance from one shop to another is not half a kilometre, but ten minutes. No matter how far you've walked, you're still in the same place – a central avenue.

Seven minutes later, I came across a white stand hung with blazing garlands of black and coloured glasses. Many of the spaces were already empty – the sun was blazing hot even for run-of-the-mill urbanites. Beside the stand was a salesman in a cap and shorts, not wearing dark glasses.

I walked up and cast a proprietary glance over this splendour. I wanted to buy black glasses.

"Do you need any help?" the salesman pounced affably.

I leaned my head to the right and took aim.

"This is a good style," said the salesman, butting into the process of my artistic deliberations.

I tried them on. Someone with a small shadow stopped beside me, and the salesman switched to him. I looked at myself in the mirror. Excellent. Quite excellent. I could smile, my smile was no longer a grimace to protect me from the sun. The city shed its blinding colours and the sun went out.

I looked pretty good myself. Black glasses. A fashionable style, I think. Not too eye-catching, but elegant. I looked the part perfectly. No need to be ashamed to walk down the centre of the pavement.

"Four hundred roubles," said the salesman, assessing my financial situation with unerring accuracy.

I took out the money and handed it to him. I'd done a deal.

I felt great. I wasn't forcing my way through the city sunshine. I was sauntering along. Perfect mimicry. I can easily be like them. But what about the other way round? I'm an urbanite. But I can see a lot further. If I can see a lot further, why remain just an urbanite?

These commonplace tinted lenses remove the boundaries of light and shade. Blinding sunlight and plain, simple light blur and mingle. The black squares on the streets disappear, and so do the bands of sun-scorched dust. In these I can look up at the rooftops during the day, without being afraid of going blind. Oh, wretched urbanites! Oh you, for whom spectacles are merely an item of dress! Look through your lenses. Black glasses are a particle of the night.

In black glasses it's far easier to walk along the avenues of the day.

That day I called into another couple of places and did a few things. I had my photo taken in a studio – for no particular reason, just in case. I bought a Pepsi at one of the city's kiosks. I dropped into the uni and had a proper snack in the canteen. And for that I took the black glasses off.

Towards the end of the day, it turned cooler. The day started melting away. The sun stopped being hot. The evening breeze flew in and the roasting ceased. I took the black glasses off. It proved quite possible to smile even without them.

I was elated. Even during the daytime.

She sees my good deeds and she kisses me windy...

* * *

That night we made our way there by taxi. In my heart of hearts I still couldn't accept it. My nerves were unsettled by Nemo's obstinacy, and the involvement of urbanites in urban extreme. The taxi-driver didn't give a hoot, he didn't see anything strange in a group of two young guys and a girl with big bags. When all's said and done, this was nothing compared to some things a taxi driver sees at night.

But even so. Urban extreme is urban extreme. You walk through the night-time city, you breathe the night air, you get used to solitude. Isn't that the essence of it? The satisfaction of breathing. When you walk to the spot, you're already charged with a different energy.

On the last operation, Nemo had been as nervous as a rabbit. He didn't know what to do, so he had just repeated everything after me. But tonight he didn't want to go there on foot. He said walking took too long. He said it didn't make any difference.

The building from which we were going to make our descent was the last one in the city. After that came an open field, and the city ended. They were building detached villas there, but the lights of the city came to an end on this building. So I thought of it as the last one. I could have chosen any other one, but we needed those square metres of empty space to stretch the rope into. Forty metres diagonally down from the house to the point of contact.

The walk to it was an hour and a half, following my routes. Nothing to it, I'd have been quite comfortable with that. But Nemo started saying that walking for three hours at night was incredibly tiring. I tried to argue with him, make him understand, but how can you argue with him? And Lena didn't say anything. The Supreme Master.

During the day, when it was almost evening, I'd come out here to examine the surroundings and set up an anchoring point in the ground. It was an elementary anchoring point – a pointed metal spike one metre long, hammered into the ground at an angle of forty-five degrees. I rode here on the bus, like an urbanite. But travelling here at night like an ordinary person – I couldn't get my head round that. It bothered me. Nemo remained absolutely calm. He said we'd write in the report that we got here on foot, and we'd edit the storyline accordingly.

* * *

We climb out of the cab three hundred metres from the building we need. I wait until the taxi's out of sight and start walking into the shadow, away from the streetlamp.

"We have to video this!" says Nemo.

I actually shudder. His voice sounds too loud for this night. Lena reaches into the bag and pulls out the camera. The robes. We run the way Nemo tells us to. He videos it. Having videoed the scene with plenty to spare, Nemo turns off the camera but doesn't put it away. He looks around, trying to find good shots. His long shadow is calmer than he is. Then, without bothering to take off his robe, he sets off towards our target. I watch him go for a few seconds. I take my own cassock off. Lena hesitates a bit, but then takes hers off too. I feel immense satisfaction at this tiny decision. Nemo calmly walks along the lamplit side of the street, not even noticing that we're lagging behind.

And then I see a man walking along. Walking slowly towards an entrance on the other side of the street. Looking at the figure in the black robe. At Nemo.

I freeze. Lena freezes, catching my glance.

That's it. It's happened. The urbanites have noticed us. I can already hear the screams. I can see the jostling crowd pointing fingers at us. Someone laughs. I can hear swearing. The police arrive. The end of the operation. The end of urban extreme. The end of our team.

Nemo turns his head and notices the man walking along. Then calmly turns away and carries on walking. The man keeps his eye on him for another three or four seconds. And that exhausts the incident.

I come to my senses and run to overtake Nemo. He's still turning his head this way and that. Looking for classy shots. I walk behind him. I'm not feeling nervous any longer. It turns out no one's really interested in us. The urbanites couldn't care. That changes the night. The solitude disappears.

If we don't have to hide, we're a part of society, right? We trail after Nemo. There's the building. Lena starts climbing up the ladder. Nemo goes after her. I'm about to climb up too, but Nemo gestures: Where are you going?

Ah, that's right. I drew up the plan myself, but now I've forgotten it a bit. It's a strange operation today. It's putting me off my stride. I run round behind the building. I wait.

Now Nemo's supposed to attach the rope up there and

then drop it down to me. I look for the spike in the ground. I see a white plastic bag in the distance – that's how I marked the spike, so I wouldn't have to search for it at night. And it doesn't attract any attention.

Behind my back is the city. In front of me is nothing. The isolated streetlamps of highways leading off and away. A moonless night, and the blackness claims all the colours. A dozen or so random windows are lit up in the building, and the pale yellow light divides the darkness off from the city even more forcefully. At night in this building, all you can see in the windows is your own reflection. It's like a still, black ocean, with you standing on a glass beach, facing eternity. Ten steps forward, and you could get lost.

I hear a rustling sound above me. My heart leaps in surprise and I dart to one side. I realise immediately what an absurd thing it was to do.

It's the rope being lowered by Nemo, touching the wall and tapping against it. The black silhouette in a robe moves. I can't see the hands, only the silent figure changing its outline. The rope creeps down as far as me. As if trying to make amends for my foolish fear, I reach for the rope without waiting for it to reach the ground.

I cautiously pull the rope towards me. It yields. The black silhouette is still silent. I take the rope across my shoulder and set off into the darkness.

Step by step the golden glimmer of the city disappears. The ground under my feet becomes uneven; grass roots. The rope chafes my shoulder noticeably, binding me to the city.

The light disappears. I can only see the stars and the streetlamps, equally far away. The grass crumpling under my feet rasps loudly, clutches at my ankles. I walk towards the white plastic bag as if it's a beacon; there are no other reference points. I walk towards the beacon, pulling the entire city behind me as if it's on a towline; hauling it towards the distant streetlamps. The white spot stands out against the darkness, expands, sways on the waves with my steps.

It turns into a plastic bag. I stand there, looking at the big nail hammered into the black sea. The spike protrudes twenty centimetres. Enough. I throw the plastic bag aside and squat down. I pull out a couple of metres of rope, not strong enough yet to turn round. I tie a knot. Another one. And another.

I step on the spike, hold my breath and turn round.

The city blazes with lights above me, like an immense ship. The gigantic flank of its hull seems to be drifting past me, and I am lost in the boundless sea of darkness. Everything is over there. Black chimneys, aerials, people's lives.

On the city there are black figures standing motionless. Nemo and Lena. The yellow light of the windows highlights them like statues.

Nemo waves his hand to me. I look round for the plastic bag and wave it through a semicircle. Right – left. Right – left.

The statues come to life. Even from here I can see Lena aiming the camera. Nemo says something to her, I can't make it out. They start circling round on the city, as if they're doing a dance. Lena is facing Nemo. He climbs up onto the rope with his feet forward. And climbs back down. The same thing two or three times. Every time I feel the spike under my foot tense and the earth hiss.

Nemo climbs up onto the rope. It looks conclusive. He clicks on the swivel hook. Looks down along the line. I can't see his face, but I know he's looking at me. He drags things out. Deferring inexplicably. Starts the movement. The spike pulsates under my foot. For the first few metres he is in the light of the blazing windows on the top floor and momentarily becomes a human being. I can suddenly make out the folds of his clothes, his hands, the glow of his face.

He moves towards me, descending. The descent goes easily, he holds on tight to the rope in order not to start slipping.

After about twenty metres, he becomes a shadow against the background of the windows. He plunges into the ocean of night, diving to where I walked over the bottom.

A couple of minutes later he is nearly at the end. He is almost the height of a man above the ground now. Nemo looks at me and the white plastic bag in my hand. He lowers one hand and touches himself between the thighs. After a moment I realise he's unlatching the safety catch. Then he lowers his feet and hangs above the ground by both hands. The white face looks down. He opens his hands and drops soundlessly, folding down into a squat. The spike zings, but I'm the only one aware of it. Nemo breathes out noisily and gets up.

He pushes the hood back off his face and comes across to me. Now I can see that he's smiling.

"Have you got a torch?" he asks

I shake my head. Nemo frowns.

"Why not? How can we manage at night without a torch? Did you forget it? It was the same last time. We won't be able to see half the camera shots."

As if I didn't know that. How can I explain to him? About the torch, about luck? About the most important thing in urban extreme. I walk towards the house, going back to the light.

"Don't you forget the torch next time!" says Nemo, shattering the silence behind my back.

I walk to the fire escape ladder and jump up to grab the first rung. Clamber up onto the roof. There's a surprise there for me: only the camera is waiting – Lena's already making her descent. The camera is standing on the concrete barrier, with the recording light blinking. I squat down on my haunches, pick it up and look for Lena in the viewfinder.

Her slim figure is wound round the rope. She's not going down like Nemo. She lets go with her hands, skids a couple of metres and closes her hands again. She goes faster like that. I can hear the shrill scraping of the swivel hook along the rope.

She gets there quickly. Stops about five feet off the ground. Nemo walks over and supports her from below. Takes her in his arms, like he did the last time. I couldn't care less. I have to video it.

I'm the last to go. I put the camera into the bag and look round the roof. Nobody has forgotten anything. I set my foot on the barrier. My usual habit – now I'm at the top of the cliff.

I climb up onto the rope. Look at the sky. My gloves squeak over the ribbed surface of the line. I take a deep breath in. Starting to feel sad.

I shift my hands, slip downwards. Glancing along the rope, I understand why Nemo dragged things out. Halfway along, the line merges into the blackness; I can't see any more of it, as if comes to an end, attached to an invisible point on the sky.

The glow of the city disappears again. And now I'm alone! Alone in the middle of the night, genuinely alone, on the surface of the ocean of darkness, swaying on its invisible waves, I listen to the voiceless breaking of its waves. I could just nestle against the line out of the city into nowhere and stay here!

Minute after minute goes by. Everything is behind me and there is nothing else – no anxieties, no problems, only my heartbeats, one after another. Time flows on.

"Hey!" Then again, louder: "Hey!"

It's from down below. Time to go back.

"Peter! Peter!"

I make the descent. A minute later I'm down there.

"What happened to you? Did you get stuck?"

I adjust the bag on my shoulder. We walk into the city. We walk through invisible gates and then the lights are not just ahead of us, but all around. Nemo takes off his robe. We come out onto a street, and then a crossroads.

"Well, excellent!" Nemo declares cheerfully. "We'll be saying goodnight then!"

I stand there, not thinking about anything. Urban extreme

has shrunk to minutes and seconds. A taxi takes us round our various places, and we don't talk inside it. Nemo disappears. Lena slams the door. I pay the taxi driver.

The black sheen of the mirror-smooth windows, a shroud of vague regret over my soul.

* * *

I happened to turn up at the next meeting with Sergei. The gathering was at the lake that day, and it happened to be on his way to some place he was going to.

He had a disagreeable habit of ogling every girl we came across, following the movements of their bodies with his eyes and make blatantly vulgar remarks. He'd say: "Look at the ass on that bitch" and other comments like that.

But he's a good guy, all the same.

When we reached the spot, it turned out I was the last to arrive. Sergei was about to leave, but he spotted a piece of rope in Nemo's hands, tied into yet another useless, cunning knot. He nodded to Nemo and Lena – they'd met a couple of times at my place. Sergei couldn't care less who they were. He only asked: "Is she yours?" – and that exhausted the subject.

"What's this you've got here?" Sergei asked, nodding at the audience.

He probably thought we had a knot-tying club. Flustered by the suddenness of the question, Nemo held the knot out and told him what it was called.

Our new disciples didn't say anything, but then Lena took a step forward and started expounding. She told him about Apostle City, about urban extreme, about the sect and even about Good and Evil. Our "sectarians" listened to her with their mouths hanging open and their eyes glued to her vigorous facial expressions. With Sergei there, I felt terribly embarrassed by all this drivel, but then I was amazed to see that he was interested.

When she finished, he started asked enthusiastically how

many disciples we had. Lena gestured round eloquently at everyone sitting there. Sergei's interest waned noticeably, but then he asked how we attracted new guys. Nemo joined in, pricking his ears up at this unusually dynamic interest, and he gave Sergei a brief outline of the site, the video clips and the reports of the operations.

I didn't take part in the conversation, although I knew Sergei well. He surprised me again by asking for Nemo's phone number. After that, everything went back to the usual pattern, and I even forgot about this episode.

Three days later Sergei showed up at the appointed time for the next meeting at the lake. He was carrying a large bag, like ours. Nemo and Lena acted like this was perfectly normal. Seeing how surprised I was, Nemo turned to me.

"The guys are ready!" he said. "Today we're going to prepare for initiation."

I looked at Lena, since she was supposedly the one who answered for the "guys". She didn't object. Okay then, they know best, this sect business isn't my baby after all.

Soon after the meeting started, Nemo announced that all the disciples were ready for the initiation to become full members of Apostle City. He explained that the initiation was due to take place during the next operation, when the brand new disciples would "work on the safety system".

The disciples were really delighted at this news, in fact they were ecstatic. The most delighted of all was Dima, who had been dying to go on an operation almost from the start.

At this point Sergei stepped in. Nemo introduced him as "a friend of Apostle City" and said that he dealt in sports equipment. Sergei opened his bag and started taking out T-shirts.

The T-shirts were black, with Apostle City logos on them. The same logos we'd made for the site. The young guys gazed at the T-shirts with hungry eyes and reached out for them with greedy hands.

Sergei named the price.

I smiled ironically. Nemo watched the disciples attentively. Lena stood there with one leg pushed forward, looking thoughtfully at Nemo. I'd already realised how things would end when they told Sergei about everything.

The guys instantly fell silent and started glancing at each other. One of them looked at Lena. She smiled at him. He smiled at her. And reached for his money. In my view the asking price was too high.

The other three said they didn't have any money with them.

"That's all right," Sergei said with a smile. "You can pay later."

"You're practically Apostles already," Nemo added.

He was very good at talking to people in that cheerful tone of voice. You had to give him that. The guys immediately relaxed and grabbed all the T-shirts. Nemo exchanged glances with Sergei. Not with me. With Sergei. But I couldn't care less.

"When you start taking an active part in the operations, you'll need gear. But we'll help you get it," said Sergei.

Then Nemo started telling them what it meant to be "a genuine Apostle". He talked about the operations, about urban extreme; he told them how we did it. He structured his phrasing very competently. It turned out just like the operations reports on our site. Made us look like genuine heroes. Nemo described in detail how he almost fallen during the crossing from one roof to another, and it sounded as if he'd done something really heroic, risking his life. He didn't say anything about the safety hook.

I realised something had changed. Nemo was eulogizing urban extreme far more lavishly than he used to. Lena also spoke about the ideas of the sect, about her being the Supreme Master, about Good and Evil. But the guys liked the T-shirts far more. Nemo said that today we, the initiated, needed to discuss a few questions together.

When the kids had gone, I glanced regretfully at Lena and I asked what it was I'd missed. Nemo answered straight out that the organisation needed money and he ("they" – he corrected himself, after looking at Sergei) intended to make a profit on Apostle City. I thought it was a dubious idea to go fleecing the new disciples, and even Lena backed me up. She was concerned about the popularity of the sect. Who'd want to join an organisation that was going to leech off them? There were plenty of those already, everywhere you looked.

Nemo and Sergei reassured us.

"It's only for the beginning," said Nemo.

"You'll have a share," said Sergei.

I shrugged. The sect wasn't my idea.

* * *

That evening I saw Lena home. The disciples had all left, Sergei went dashing on along his verdant pathway, and Nemo didn't even offer.

To understand what happened that evening, I'll have to explain what had happened inside me.

I always used to think of myself as firm and unwavering. As if nothing inside me changed, and I stayed the same as I was the day before. A self-contained individual. I would be the same the next day. And the next year.

But the first time I climbed up onto a roof, the rock inside me trembled. It changed. Something original appeared inside it. The fine cracks that had crept across the smooth surface ages ago now ran together. I became more than just a shell, a defence against a hostile world; I became the independent bearer of something like a seed of life. From now on all my actions were no longer merely an attempt to keep up with everyone around me.

Before then my life was like a race that I had no chance of winning. Or even ending up in the leading group. I was stuck in the middle crowd. You know the joke: a Chukchi and a geologist are walking across the snow. Suddenly this polar bear appears! The Chukchi hastily starts putting on his skis. "What are you doing?" says the geologist. "You can't move faster than a bear!" – "I don't need to move faster than a bear," the Chukchi replies. "I need to move faster than you."

That's the way I used to see everything. We're running a long-distance race, and the world is chasing after us, gobbling up the ones who fall. We have to work and work, be successful in order to be as good as all the rest. In order not to fall behind. Or else...

But when I saw the city down below, saw that light, breathed in that air, felt that freedom, I suddenly felt so good. None of it made any difference to me, I couldn't care less. Yes, there was something going on down there, the lucky ones had their own firms at the age of nineteen, the urbanites scurried about. But I was here, looking down on my city, and I sensed the blithe fury. Here was my joy! The thing that meant the most to me! Right then, at that moment, I didn't feel anything: just the night, just the night all around, just the city down below, and all the rest of it was ABSOLUTELY NOTHING TO DO WITH ME!

Like a drug. Better than a drug. Urban rooftop anesthesia.

I only realised this the day I put on my dark glasses. When I realised – horror of horrors! – that I was beginning to like looking like the urbanites. I simply hadn't believed that I could: I'd never be able to be like everyone else, I'd always be lagging behind, trying to catch up with the urbanites who were speeding away from me on their skis, with the world clacking its fangs right behind my back.

But once I put on those sunglasses, I realised that I could. Easily. Easy as ABC. I also wondered if they could be the same as me.

And I thought: But why would I want to be the same as everybody else?

I came to know the lightness of being up on the surface of the city. I realised I could do something else instead of running in a straight line. I didn't dance and I didn't play the fool for the empty auditorium. This isn't slapstick. I don't do it for the non-existent audience. I do it for myself, because I like it. I like to walk through the city the way that only I know how; I like to dance the way that only I dance. I like being up on the surface of the city. *I* like it.

And that started changing everything around me. I wasn't obliged to go up onto the rooftops of the city. I wanted to. I wasn't obliged to see Lena home or kiss her. Or have sex with her in a doorway, so that I could answer the question "Is she yours?" with a casual nod. I... well, let's just say I found it interesting, all right?

I started finding it very interesting just to look around.

And I looked around that evening. Twilight. Backlighting from the advertisements, flickering and flashing on before the municipal streetlamps: car headlights coming towards me and the roar of engines ahead of me. Lena walks along, looking down at her feet, and smiling, and swinging her handbag. Sometimes she shifts her glance onto me, but immediately turns it away when she notices me not responding. She tries to conceal this movement and it looks like a semicircle with her head, as if Lena's got a stiff neck – very amusing.

We stepped onto the bridge. And the streetlamps blazed up ahead of us. All eight hundred metres of stone suddenly ignited with yellow fire. The vault of orange streetlamps tapered into the distance ahead of us, jerking the bridge out of the darkness of night.

I looked at Lena. She was admiring the lights, just like me. I waited until she noticed my glance and looked at me.

"We ought to snap that," said Lena. "For everyone." Then

she thought about it. "But a photograph is either before or after..."

It was quite bright on the bridge. We discussed Nemo's projects. Lena didn't like the idea of collecting money from disciples at that level, but she agreed with Alex that we did need money. Then she started telling me how she saw the way ahead for our sect. At moments like that, Lena really does become the Supreme Master. And it doesn't matter that it's impossible, unreal, Lena. I felt and saw that very clearly now.

She spoke about political backing, an army of recruiters, and I just stared. This time she was wearing short khaki-coloured trousers with a green blouse and sandals. And she was carrying a black handbag with a lot of white metal on it.

Lena has slim, clearly defined arms and hands. Long, slim fingers. She could have played the piano, only I knew that she didn't.

She told me things about the disciples that I hadn't noticed. About the sports qualification that one of them, Misha, had. About Dima's brother, who was killed. She knew their sorrows. She knew their grief.

The bridge came to an end. It carried on blazing behind us. Building after building was left blazing behind us. We walked along the blazing avenue to her house, and the smoky-grey city night surrounded us.

"Oh, there's no one home," said Lena, looking up at her windows.

Then I kissed her. It worked pretty well. With the rhythm and all the rest of it. What a delicious taste! Kissing is really great! Thoughts swirled about inside me, in the darkness of me, where her damp lips lived.

Then it was as if she started falling backwards. I drew back, let go of her delicate hands, looked into her face.

Lena took half a step back and stood there; one foot was still with me, the other wasn't. Stood there with her eyes half-closed, looking down at the beige-coloured asphalt between us. She nodded ever so slightly, to herself, almost imperceptibly; in surprise, as if she was saying: "So that's it..."

The handbag slipped off her shoulder and down to her hand. There was a jangle of white metal and it started swaying to and fro. We both looked at that handbag. Our short shadows were like cats' shadows.

Lena adjusted the handbag and put it on her shoulder. She seemed to want to say something to me, but she didn't say it; or was that her way of saying goodnight? Then she turned round and walked into the black entranceway. The grating of the drain by the entrance clattered, the wooden door thudded.

I stood there for a moment, and then another, and walked away. I felt really good. I wasn't hoping for anything and I didn't want anything. I was just remembering that sensation of focused attention on my lips. The small shoulders in my hands; the smell.

I thought: Maybe I should go back?

I stopped and looked up at the silvery clouds of my city. At least seven minutes, that's the test. Then I went home. I promised myself to remember that night forever.

It was the last night of the old urban extreme.

* * *

The next morning I put on my night-dark glasses and set off to the old car park. There was supposed to be another trek for scrap; another raid on rusty metal. The city helped me along my way and the urbanites coming towards me were on the same wavelength; I could look at their faces without any fear. I forgot all about the heat, merely wiped the sweat off my face every now and then.

The dusty car park was congested with old cars: their day was just beginning. There were specimens here that you could only find in post-nuclear fantasy movies. The fact that the bodies were covered in rust and the autos were thirty, forty or more years old didn't bother our local drivers, after all, sometimes they could "pull in" the value of their old rattle-traps in a single day – and sometimes the car was despatched to the scrap yard that same day.

Here it was hard to tell if the owner had dumped his car or not – they all looked pretty much identical. I once saw a little guy, who was obviously from the Caucasus, clamber into a rusty skeleton on wheels. I thought he wanted to nick the seat or something else out of it. Thirty seconds later the skeleton started up and calmly pulled out of the car park under its own power. I was the only one who was surprised. External appearances were irrelevant to the unpretentious activities of the local inhabitants; they distributed crates of strong drink of dubious origin to kiosks or made raids on heaps of scrap metal out in the country. This car park was an absolutely perfect illustration of the expression: "any means to an end". And the end, naturally, was money.

I looked around for "my" truck and set off towards it, skirting round the incredibly toxic-looking multicoloured puddles. I took off the dark glasses – I had to keep a sharp eye out, there was rusty junk lying all over the place: off-cuts of pipes, spare parts deformed beyond recognition, rusty nails. Step on one of those, and you could say goodbye to your foot. But the local workers hopped and skipped around without worrying at all about that, thinking of nothing but the time.

On every outing the membership of our team changed by about half: some had been deported, others had begun their annual drinking binge (the most common reason), and still others had died of cirrhosis of the liver. Junkies couldn't make the grade – a body wasted by drugs is in no state to work.

From my experience of working with these people, I had come to realise that alcoholics are extremely smelly and sociable individuals. They only need to learn another alcoholic's name in order to understand his inner world, his spiritual nature, his secret dreams and aspirations. The yellow eyes of my colleagues were always aglow with the readiness to slap someone on the shoulder and commiserate. The laconic laments about life before downing a drink were like caresses before sex for them. And when a drinking companion died, they took it very badly, and quite often they were left sleeping with their mouths open on the withered grass outside the city, because they couldn't wait for work to be over before they drowned their sorrow.

"Pete!" the boss roared. "Do you know where Tolka is?"

I didn't have any idea who Tolka was. For the boss – I don't know his full name, only his patronymic, Afanasievich – this car park was his entire life. In the eddying swirl of disappearing faces, I already seemed to him almost like a master craftsman of Russian scrap-collection and, therefore, a man worthy to be his assistant.

"Today you're going to Nestyanka," Afanasievich informed me in a loud voice. "Today you'll count what we take; I'm off to the Young Pioneer camp across the water – they say the storage tanks are going begging."

I nodded. Being appointed tallyman meant a steep hike in the money due me, but also the need to give orders. Apparently, in all this time Afanasievich hadn't realised who he was dealing with. But what an absolutely splendid career!

I put on the dark glasses, swung round and set off home.

"Come back!" Afanasievich yelled after me in a booming voice, and the gloomy Caucasian types studied my stride, trying to figure out the cause of our conflict. I didn't take off the dark glasses as I skirted round the multi-coloured toxic puddles and the rusty nails, heading for the brown pillars of the gates.

I didn't go back there again.

* * *

Everything in our sect started changing by leaps and bounds. Nemo and Sergei were always solving problems and coming up with ideas that I didn't understand. As a result, even the concepts of the Supreme Master started to look stable and reassuring. Then Nemo suggested going on an operation the next Tuesday. Did I say "suggested"? He simply set the date of the operation. And he suggested that Lena and I should invent it.

I objected on the basis of: What point was there in deciding to set out on an operation if we didn't know yet what it would look like? Nemo shook his head and announced that the substance of the operation was a secondary consideration, or absolutely downright unimportant. After that he told us all to sit down and think, forbidding us even to think of the TV tower and the Colossus.

We sat down in my communal apartment and started thinking. In the half-hour allocated to us for this task, we had to come up with a specific concept and its implementation and also, preferably, the plan of operation. I twirled my notepad in my hands and waited for the idea to come flying into my head of its own accord. Lena put forward several ideas, but each one of them turned out to be no more than a repetition. Nemo confidently declared that we didn't want any repetitions – we already had operations like that on the site. I was with him on that point – the uniqueness of each operation was part of the concept of urban extreme. Repetition would have destroyed the idea of fresh experience. I started liking Nemo again.

I suggested postponing the plan of operation until something simply occurred to us. But Nemo categorically stated that "everything's already been decided", leaving me totally perplexed. I tried again to squeeze out at least one idea, but nothing came to mind. It had always happened spontaneously, of its own accord. Having to come up with an idea intentionally, as if we were obliged to do it, seemed more like work than pleasure to me. So I told them that I couldn't create operations to order. They couldn't come up with anything either: and I even felt slightly proud of that, although that kind of pride was clearly pretty close to gloating.

After we'd struggled on painfully for ten minutes longer than the time allotted, Nemo banged his heel against his chair and suggested I should describe my solo operations.

I thought for a moment and started with my very first innocent stroll across a roof. Nemo dismissed that as too simple and "hard to present". Then I went on to the descent from the Colossus and the crossing of the river. Nemo decided it was too far down to the ground from the Colossus and "the visibility was bad".

"The bridge, Peter! We'll do that."

I blinked and reminded him that we'd just been talking about the need to avoid repetitions.

"But we don't have it on the site!" Nemo declared, smiling out of the corner of his mouth. "So it would be a first... and then, only you did it. We haven't experienced it!"

Well, he was right about that. They hadn't been there. I remembered the bridge, and the first thing to stir in my memory was the black, glittering water below me.

The preparations for that crossing had taken longer than the crossing itself. I really didn't want to fall in the water in the middle of the night, so I took serious care with the safety measures. I climbed up the metal structure right to the top of one support, secured the rope at that side, climbed down and threw the weighted rope across the river. I walked over the bridge in a perfectly mundane fashion, picked up the rope and secured it symmetrically at the other side.

I came back, although I could have started from that bank – I came back for luck. I put the strap round my waist, clicked onto the security rope and set off sideways, shifting my hands along the iron girders.

What made this crossing different from the other operations was its damp, subterranean atmosphere. Even dozens of metres away, I could feel how cold that black water was. The slightest sound produced an echo that resounded hollowly under the concrete vaults. The cold wind was loaded with a chilly dampness that it was blasting from under the bridge, and I was right in its path. There were no streetlamps shining here, their yellow light streamed down from above. But my eyes grew used to the darkness, and it was painful to look up. This crossing was more like a stroll under the vaults of a cavern than an excursion through an industrial building.

Nemo said that now he'd get started on the preparations. Whatever that meant, I got started on the preparations myself, as I understood them. Equipment, cameras, plan. Just before the operation, Lena and I started seeing each other more often. I did my best to make it happen as often as possible. Still, it never worked out so that I saw her home, and I didn't really know what I should do, I was worried about seeming too pushy. A couple of times I invited her out on a date, but she couldn't make it – she didn't have any spare time after studying for her classes and working for a voluntary organisation.

Nemo and I started seeing each other much less often. He disappeared off somewhere with Sergei, and sometimes Sergei simply passed on his greetings and a promise to show up the next time. Eventually Lena had to ring him and remind about the sect meeting the following day, just three days before the operation. Nemo promised to come.

The next day the group was all together. They were all wearing our T-shirts, each and every last one of them. After rattling through a discussion of the Supreme Master's ravings in one minute, the disciples took their seats to wait for the news of the forthcoming operation, in which they had been promised the chance to participate. Nemo welcomed them all and got down to business.

"Congratulations once again, guys! This Friday is the operation. And you're all going to take part in it." The delighted disciples started buzzing. A delightful sight.

"This is the operation: a crossing of a river that you all know. By bridge. Under the bridge! I'm not sure that you're all prepared for the danger, guys, but there's someone I want to involve as a participant. The others are handling the preparations for the operation. I've got your contact numbers. I'll get in touch with each one of you and tell you the details of the operation. What do you have to do? You have to bring your friends with you. Lots of friends. As many friends as possible, guys. Invite everyone within reach. We'll show this city who we are! The Apostles of Apostle City!" he bellowed.

"Apostle City!" the disciples shouted ragged and uncertainly, smiling self-consciously.

I had this strange desire floating around inside of me to get up and... I don't know. Smash a bottle against the concrete, if I'd had a bottle in my hand. Give the stone kerb a hard kick.

First urban extreme had lost its solitude. Now it was becoming public. But I calmed down. "What did I expect?" I thought. The decision had already been taken when we made the site. I had to prepare for fame, ha-ha.

But even so, I didn't like it at all. It was strange to feel uneasy before an operation.

That evening Dima walked Lena home. The timetable.

* * *

On the night of this operation we didn't even gather in advance. The day before, Nemo simply told Lena and me to come to a certain spot a couple of hundred metres from the bridge.

That night I call for her and we walk calmly to the spot – Lena listens to me when Nemo's not around.

I don't notice how it happens, but suddenly we're walking along an avenue under the rays of the orange streetlamps.

Coming to my senses, I take her by the hand and remind her about the special route. She doesn't object; right now she does everything as I say. The last few small streets before the meeting place are almost entirely unlit. The buildings stand close to each other, no lights can be seen in the distance, and the city is like a little village, with us walking along its only street. It's hard to believe that if we climb up to the third floor of these buildings, we can spot high rises, the fiery trail of the city's main bridge, the TV tower and the Colossus. In fact, the TV tower and the Colossus are visible from almost every point of the city. We can't see the city lights. There's black mud under our feet instead of asphalt. But on the other hand, through the narrow overhead cranny of the street we can see the stars surprisingly clearly.

Darkness all around. We hear music, muted by distance. I even confuse the courtyards, getting my count wrong by one and discovering that Lena and I are already there. Footsteps ring out in the gloom, and we swing round in unison towards the sound. The shuffling across the asphalt gets louder and louder.

A figure in a black robe emerges from the darkness. Walking toward us: the hem of the gown flutters and flaps. The dull light reflects off the smooth cloth; there's no face. A fearsome sight, but strangely fascinating. Nemo gently pushes back his hood as he walks along. What a poser.

"Howdy-dowdy!" he says at the top of his voice. "Let's go!"

We ask him where his bag is. He hasn't got anything apart from the robe that he's wearing.

"It's all there already. Put your robes on!"

Lena and I exchange glances and reach into our bags. Nemo dances on the spot.

"Oh, what a night this will be!" Nemo says quietly to himself, gazing at the end of the street.

Once he's sure we're ready, Nemo hurries towards the passage between the houses. Without stopping, he orders us to put our hoods up. We follow Nemo across the dark yard very quickly; the way out to the bridge is on the next street.

The music gets louder. We're almost running. My heart starts pounding. My palms get wet. Lena hurries along on my left, looking down at the ground; I can hear how hard she's breathing.

We're greeted by the bright orange light of the bridge. And loud music. And a crowd of people. Standing along the river, on both sides, is a crowd of urbanites, about five hundred people altogether. Black figures are swarming over the supports of the bridge on both sides. Looking closer, I see Dima, and I realise they are our disciples. The rope is already thrown across the river, trembling. On the side of the river closest to us I see Sergei; he's standing at a table. There are T-shirts and equipment on the table. I think he's selling beer as well, involuntarily I slow down. I want to go dashing back; unto the darkness. Nemo hurries towards them confidently – there are only thirty metres to go.

We haven't really been noticed yet, but a few people are already looking at us and shaking the people next to them by the shoulder. Then Sergei sees us.

"And here are the heroes of this night!" he howls, drawing out the words.

The hastily trained disciples turn, catch sight of us and start yelling. Hearing so many shouts, the crowd of urbanites is confused at first. But then a reflex response produces a scattered bellowing in separate little groups.

Lena and I involuntarily slow down. I feel likes someone's pulling me back by the ankles. I want to stop, and then inconspicuously disappear. But Nemo's striding forward quickly and confidently, deliberately exaggerating each step. The black material flutters; the orange light of the streetlamps glimmers on the sleeves. And we despairingly follow him. The abhorrent music roars.

He reaches the crowd, and the crowd parts before him. We follow Nemo into its open throat. All around there are strange, unfamiliar faces, and the gaze of their eyes seems to press Lena and me together. They stare at us with burning curiosity; they look up from below, trying to peep under our hoods. They're so close; they could reach out their hands and touch us. We hear an occasional clap of hands. One person is clapping behind the people standing close to us.

Finally the music is muzzled as Sergei switches off the tape deck.

I automatically lower my head. The folds of cloth caress my cheeks, hiding my eyes from all the people surrounding me. All I can see are Nemo's feet, stepping in broad strides.

He walks up to Sergei's table and shakes his hand briskly. Then he walks over to the support of the bridge and throws his head back, looking at our young guys fiddling with ropes up above. With his hands on his hips. Acting as if there's no one else here.

"How's it going?" he asks, clipping the words short.

His voice has turned unfamiliar and abrupt. The crowd doesn't fall silent, but he doesn't care. Lena and I stand behind him. I stare down hard at the ground. Lena cautiously looks around, glancing at all this and at me.

I'd rather not be here.

"It's all done, Nemo!" shouts Misha, one of our young guys.

He looks intently at Nemo, but occasionally his gaze shifts to the crowd. I can see he's feeling uneasy too.

Nemo turns round. Gestures to us almost imperceptibly: "Make room!" We almost jump aside, out of his way. We step away and turn round, like him, and automatically end up standing on either side of him. Nemo throws his arms up and the black sleeves slip down to his elbows. His bare arms protrude out of the blackness like white branches.

"Let's begin!" he shouts loudly.

The crowd falls silent and then immediately responds, more confidently now. Nemo throws back his hood with a well-rehearsed movement. I notice that now all eyes are fixed on him. Those eyes grope at his face, as if expecting to discover some unusual kind of deformity. There are almost no smiles.

Since Nemo has arranged everything theatrically, the urbanites are waiting for the show to continue. I suddenly realise that perhaps we're supposed to take our hoods off as well. I don't take my hood off. I glance stealthily at Lena. She looks at me too and also stays under cover.

Nemo lowers his hands. He walks over to the support and throws off his robe. He clambers up with exaggerated confidence, in full control. I sense all the gazes fixed on him and on our backs. Nemo picturesquely slaps one of the disciples on the back, moving aside to the right so that everyone has a good view of it.

They hook him on. He tugs at the iron girders, checking to see if they might come away. Turns toward the crowd. A shadow covers him from above, his face is almost hidden from sight. Suddenly – thwack! A bright circle of light illuminates the darkness under the bridge. For a moment we can see the green streaks on the concrete. Then the circle flits across to Nemo, accentuating the outline of his figure. The face with a broad smile turns matt-white. Astounded, I look for the source, forgetting about the crowd.

Sergei is holding an immense torch, the length of his forearm. The blinding white eye makes Sergei himself almost invisible. My retina retains a blurred imprint of light.

"Apostle City!" Nemo shouts.

The disciples repeat it after him.

"Children!" Nemo shouts. "Don't try this at home!"

He laughs loudly. In parts of the crowd people laugh in response. I'm almost certain Nemo prepared that joke in advance. Only the answering laughter isn't because of the meaning, but because he laughed himself. No one seemed to understand about Apostle City.

Then he starts moving. He walks sideways along the iron girder. Taking long steps. After a few steps he's above the water. The crowd all fall silent as one man. Deathly silence. The white patches of torches quiver on the black water. Somewhere a bottle clinks. I can hear Nemo's footsteps along the metal. The spot of light creeps after him. The light is bright, but the only thing that glitters is the steel security ring on his belt. The metal of the bridge is rusty, it doesn't reflect light. "That would make fine scrap!" – the idiotic thought flashes through my mind.

The rust flakes away under Nemo's trainers. Large pieces plop into the black water, shattering the reflections of the torches into fragments that instantly fuse together. The sound of a car driving towards the bridge can be heard in the silence.

The water under Nemo comes to an end. Dima meets him at the other side and grabs the rope. Holding on with one hand, Nemo half-turns towards us and raises his open palm in a gesture of greeting.

"Applause!" shouts Sergei.

He starts clapping loudly. He's switched off the torch now, and I can see a video camera lying on the table in front of him. The silence collapses. And the applause rings out. Nemo claps. I realise he could have astounded some people, the way I astounded him in my time. Someone whistles discontentedly and Dima instantly turns towards this whistle in silent indignation. There is fury on his face, as if he hates the people who whistled. He turns towards the whistlers, and the whistling stops.

Nemo climbs down the support. People in the crowd say

something to him. He smiles and answers, looking into their faces. Then, with a strangely anxious air, he looks round, searching for us.

I suddenly feel afraid. My heart leaps up into my mouth. I hesitate and hesitate, and realise that in another moment Lena will step forward. But I can't allow that, can I? I can't, can I? I just can't, all right?

I dash forward. My stage entrance. I stand there, facing the support. Should I take off the robe or not? A spot of white flares up in front of me and in it I see my long, gawky, motionless shadow. "Too soon, Sergei, too soon!" I think helplessly. My defenceless back is irradiated with light and the gaze of millions of eyes.

I look up. The disciples are watching me expectantly. I'm an object of emulation for them. Gritting my teeth, I start climbing up. After a couple of metres I realise I've forgotten to put on my gloves. Go back down? No, no! In this light that's impossible! I keep climbing.

The disciples meet me. I nod to them. I nod again. Now they seem like dear comrades-in-arms. They belt me up and click me on. Unable to put on a smile, I chuckle inwardly when I see the knots learned at the sect meetings. Misha tests the anchor points with serious concentration. Then he looks at me expectantly. At first I don't understand what he wants.

Then I realise. I have to go. So I go. I've been this way before, along the same route, already seen this rusty hollow in the second girder, this piece of black, knotted-off cable of unknown origin. But now I'm not in a cave, I'm on the top of a skyscraper. A huge black monkey. I'm Kong Kong, and the machine gunners have their searchlights trained on my back. The skirts of the robe sometimes get hooked round my legs – I have to pull it out. My hands hurt. The rust crumbles under my fingers and, as I shift my grip yet again, I notice in the light how brown my palms have become. The light in front of my eyes blots out the bridge's repulsive innards – moss, waterweed, tattered trash, sewage.

"So is that it, then?" someone shouts.

I shudder. I look to the right, at Dima. "He's close," I think, "close". Dima's looking down furiously. I carry on. They whistle. I carry on. Another minute at the most.

Dima cries out in fright. I turn round, startled, to see what's wrong with him. He's looking down, past my back. I try to make out if he's all right.

An explosion only a metre away from me! A silent inward scream. An empty bottle breaking against the rusty iron of the bridge.

A ringing sound in my temples. No air to breathe, and a squealing in my ears. The concrete vault in front of my eyes is suddenly a photograph put there to block off my vision.

A bottle. Nothing but a bottle. Someone threw a bottle. Some fool. Dima's shouting words of annoyance. I can't make out what; I'm looking straight ahead at the photograph of the concrete vault.

The photograph is gradually filled out with depth. I breathe in dampness. My weak legs come back to me. "Well, a good thing it wasn't..." I think, and immediately want to laugh hysterically. It's passed off now. I hear them calming the troublemakers in the crowd. I have to move on.

I reach the end in a half-dream, Dima meets me and looks into my face.

"Peter, are you okay?" Nemo asks from the ground: "Dima, how is he?"

I wave my hand abstractedly with a detached air, as if to say: Simply mind-blowing. The light disappears and I immediately feel a sense of relief. I move over to the support and clamber onto it. I sit down on the damp concrete with my feet braced against the iron. I don't want to climb down. I'm resting.

I close my eyes. Pain pulses in my hot hands. I open my eyes and see the world in a new way.

The crowd is down below. Someone's leaving. No doubt the ones who were whistling. Others dribble after them. New spectators have appeared too. Chance passers-by are standing some distance away, looking up. A young guy and a girl. A group of young people. Suddenly it all reminds me of a stage set. Sergei's selling beer. One of the people who've just walked up asks the spectators something. "Movie..." I hear a scrap of talk. Nemo's talking to people down below. The disciples are tightening up the rope. From my position they look as if they're fixing the gear in a lift shaft. The iron joists conceal their faces. Lena walks up to the bridge support across the river from me.

Lena.

Frail, even under her robe, small, with slim arms, she climbs up the support. I watch, entranced, as they clip her on. She walks towards me. I'm glad the light isn't on me now. And immediately I curse myself for that thought. But all the same, it's such a relief...

I look at the girders from where I sit, and from this angle the span is very small. It looks as if she has no distance at all to cover. She hurries. Our sweet Lena's little steps.

She falls precisely in the middle. Falls. Her right foot in its little trainer searches for support in empty space, with her right leg inexplicably straightened out. She braces her left foot against a girder, hanging on the safety line, hunched over, swaying, her legs splayed wide, clutching at the rope with her right hand.

I hear the air hiss out of Dima's lungs. Exclamations down below.

She's in real trouble. She tries to reach the girder with her hand. I see her fingers are rusty, like mine. I sense death.

She grabs hold. Pulls herself up. Clambers back. Carries

on quickly. Dima meets her, unclips her. My eyes meet hers. A few seconds earlier both of us were more afraid than we had ever been in our lives. We read this in each other's eyes. We're closer now than ever before. I've never felt like this when I look into a girl's eyes. We're closer now than when I kissed her. I see the huge pupils of her glowing grey eyes. If we were alone, we'd have had sex. Rough. That very moment.

Lena tears her eyes away. She climbs down. In the crowd they yell.

"Excellent!" says Nemo. "Come on, Dima!"

Nemo's voice is not so confident now. It trembles slightly. Either Dima can sense this, or he's feeling the same thing as me. I don't even know how I'm going to climb down. My legs are like cotton wool. There's a roaring in my head.

Dima looks at Nemo. Looks at me.

"Well, come on, Dima! Demon, come on!" Nemo shouts loudly and encouragingly. "Peter, buck him up a bit!"

I grin, closing my eyes. Nemo, Nemo... I want to slap Dima on the shoulder, but I hammer on the girder: Come on now. Aha.

Dima doesn't move. Then he shakes his head.

"No," he says, "no, next time."

Nemo quickly turns away and waves to Sergei. The light goes out; darkness.

A few minutes later we climb down to the ground. Nemo raises his hands in greeting for the last time, says briskly to us: "Let's go!" and walks away quickly. We follow him. Lena asks about the equipment, but Nemo replies that the disciples and Sergei will see to everything.

I recover my senses. The adrenalin does its job. I jump about, feeling my living body. Up, up! The show's over! So, where shall we go? Where shall we go, eh?

But Lena says she has to go home. We leave Nemo; she goes off in a taxi.

I decide to run all the way home. At the end of the route I get really tired, my chest is tearing apart, my lungs are wheezing.

That night I sleep like a log.

* * *

When we met at the usual spot by the lake, Nemo and Sergei were working figures on notepads. They were laughing happily. The notepads trembled in their hands, the ballpoint pens scratched. Summer was still as pushy as ever. The heat was scorching.

"Howdy-hi!" said Nemo. "We're just counting..."

"Congratulations," said Sergei. "You covered your costs yesterday. And made money too."

Then he told us that, strangely enough, the largest receipts were for the beer. The T-shirts were far less popular, but about ten of them had been sold.

"And the publicity," Nemo declared. "The publicity's invaluable!"

They gave me money. When Lena arrived, they gave her some too. I have to admit, there was more money than I was expecting. Less than at the scrap yard, but still good.

The disciples arrived. Dima was sombre. He kept looking at the water of the lake and took almost no part in the conversation. After the greetings, when a few minutes had gone by, he put in a few brief words.

"I'm sorry about them, yesterday, those... They got pissed, the jerks..."

I looked at him and thought of how tormented he must be by the desire to change everything and walk across that river after all.

Nemo consoled Dima. He said, if not for them, the operation wouldn't have taken place. What point was there without spectators?

Dima smiled, as if he was feeling better. But I knew where

his pain was. He hadn't walked across the river. He hadn't done it. And he had no chance to change that now.

A pleasant melody started to play. Nemo reached for his phone. He looked at the screen, knitted his brows. Took the call. While he was talking, everyone stayed quiet. Lena stood there with her arms crossed, gazing off into the distance. I tried to catch her eye, but she eluded me.

"... that is interesting..." Nemo leapt to his feet in the middle of a phrase.

Everybody looked at him. He didn't cry out, he didn't change his tone of voice, but the sudden surge of joyful anticipation and suppressed exultation in it made it clear that something had happened. He hastily shifted into a laid-back pose, planting his feet wide apart. He spoke, and his vowels invited us to admire him.

He finished. Slowly switched off his phone. Slowly attached it to his belt. He tried to conceal his smile, but it kept rising to the surface, like a little yellow plastic duck in foamy water.

"Did anyone give my number to anyone?" he asked us all, no longer hiding his genuine smile, with his teeth glinting.

"I did," Misha said cautiously … "They asked for it, they were thinking of joining..."

"Come on, tell us..." Lena demanded.

"Our TV news wants to do a feature on us!" he blurted out, laughing and clapping his hands, and his voice rang with such selfless joy that I wanted to smile myself.

I grinned and shook my head; would you believe it... The disciples deafened him with a wave of pure emotion; they jumped up one after another and started laughing too. Lena stood there with one leg pushed forward, hiding her smile the way Nemo was hiding his a moment earlier.

The local TV station's film crew arrived the same day. The mournful cameraman who walked round in circles videoing our group was particularly enthusiastic about group shots of the disciples in Apostle City T-shirts. A trim fellow in shorts who looked nothing like a correspondent started asking about our past. His flat voice was really repugnant. He asked questions, but I just wanted to listen: I had goose bumps all the way down my spine. Chilly.

He wanted to know whose idea it was and, after a moment's thought, Nemo pointed at me. That pause hit a raw nerve with me. I wasn't yearning for fame quite that much. On the contrary, I didn't like what was going on. I hadn't felt any blithe fury the night before. But I was the one who invented urban extreme.

The correspondent stepped up to me with his questions.

"Better talk to me," Nemo pulled him up gently.

I didn't object. It was all the same to the correspondent. He started asking when it all started. Nemo told him. He asked about the previous operations, and Nemo produced a tirade bristling with quotes from our own website. The correspondent really loved Nemo's slang, and he listened closely to the spiel about "attacking the heights" and "cables".

"Have you got any video footage?" the correspondent asked.

Delighted, Nemo said we did. Anticipating the question, he said he would make it all available and let them copy it. They got to the previous night. Nemo willingly told him that about "a hundred" people had been present and "the operation went off brilliantly".

"Basically, everything went well. But there were mishaps. After all, you understand, it's urban extreme – that's dangerous." A false note surfaced briefly in his voice, but he easily suppressed it. "Things didn't go as smoothly for the other lads as for me. Our Lena almost fell."

He knitted his brows and ran his open hand over his face. Well done, Nemo! Five points! You're suffering, but you're bearing up.

"Lena?" The correspondent looked at our Lena. "You almost fell off?"

She nodded.

"Okay, why don't you tell me about that. Ah, now that's it! What's the goal of urban extreme?"

Alex looked at him. Then at the camera that was switched off. I looked at Alex. I wanted to know the answer too. He looked at the camera and the lake. The correspondent was about to add something, but Nemo interrupted him.

"Lena can tell you about that. Our Supreme Master."

"Supreme Master?" the correspondent said with genuine surprise.

"Yes... You see, we've got our own philosophy."

The correspondent gave Lena a suspicious look, then he called over the curly-headed cameraman.

"We'll do a couple of sync shots now. Where's best, Sasha?"

The mournful cameraman indifferently waved his hand with a cigarette in it at the lake. The correspondent dragged the limp Nemo over to stand with his back to the lake. They took out a tripod and planted the camera on it. When the cameraman started attaching the buttonhole microphone to Nemo's collar, he suddenly lost his nerve and started asking what he should say.

"Well, the same thing again..." the correspondent said thoughtfully, looking us all over. "When we start recording, you look at me."

Probably the plan for the piece was already maturing in his mind. Lena was nibbling on her fingers and looking at Nemo. He was thinking. Memorizing his words. The correspondent examined Nemo's face carefully, and Nemo took fright. His habitual gloss evaporated. Silence fell. The trees rustled. The ducks on the lake quacked.

"Just a moment now..." the cameraman muttered, twirling

a handle with his face stuck in the viewfinder. And then, with surprising crispness: "We're on."

"Tell me, please, Alex," the correspondent started up without a pause, "what is urban extreme, and when did you start practicing it?"

"Well, urban extreme... it's a kind of sport... extreme and not extreme at the same time." Despair flared up in Nemo's eyes. "We do these stunts and at the same time we... kind of... stroll round the city, at night. When did we start... somewhere about... well, four months ago." Nemo looked at me, adding in my track record.

I could feel how uncomfortable he was.

"And what events have you already held?"

"Operations..." Nemo corrected him, and that perked him up a bit. "We've made a descent from the Colossus, a crossing between two buildings and, sort of, made our way across the tops of buildings. Yesterday we climbed across a bridge. Under the bridge. Across the bridge, only underneath."

"And you don't have any problems with the police?"

"The police?" Nemo asked in surprise. "Why would we? No, no problems with the police. What are we doing? The police don't even know about us, after all, urban extreme's just a sport, we only stroll about at night and climb tall buildings, but we don't steal, and we don't interfere with anyone."

Nemo looked at the correspondent in surprise. He hadn't been expecting the question about the police.

"That's good!"

The correspondent raised his hand and the cameraman switched off the camera.

"All right... The Colossus, is it that?" He gestured towards the Colossus.

Nemo nodded. The correspondent wagged his head.

"Lena!" he called next. "Let's try you."

Lena groaned, laughed, hid her face in her hands and said

from where she was that she couldn't. The cameraman had already unhooked the buttonhole mike from Alex. He stood there, waiting. The correspondent gently tried to persuade Lena to come out. Then, red-faced and incredibly delighted, she uncovered her face and started smoothing out her magnificent dark hair. She smiled, looking from the camera to the correspondent and back.

"We're on," said the cameraman.

There was a click of deja vu in my head; for a second everything seemed unreal, the repetition was so absolutely identical.

"Tell me, please, Lena, you also take part in the operations, do you?"

"Yes, I'm an active member of Apostle City," Lena began jauntily. "I participate directly in the operations." She swung her head, and my heart swung with it.

"But yesterday there was some kind of mishap at the... operation, am I right?"

"Yes, something did happen." She laughed. "It was nothing. My foot just slipped, but then I climbed back. The whole thing only lasted five seconds."

"Oh, really? But wait, Lena, you actually fell off, didn't you?"

"Yes, I fell off. I really did. My foot slipped... and then I climbed back."

"No, no... Tell me about it in more detail, talk about it..."

"Hmm... All right. As I was moving along the girder, my foot suddenly slipped on the rust, then I slid right off and fell. I was perched with just one foot against the girder, literally hanging on the safety rope. If not for the safety rope I'd have fallen straight into the river."

"Now tell me, why does Apostle City exist?"

"Well, you see, we're not just a group, we're a sect. There's Good and Evil..."

Lena started expounding. The correspondent realised she wasn't joking and instantly lost interest. Lena carried on with what she was saying, but he wasn't listening anymore. Without waiting to be told, the cameraman switched off the camera and lit a cigarette. Either he understood for himself the value of the religious ideas of Apostle City, or they were so used to working with each other that they intuitively guessed each other's wishes.

After that they took a few more shots of us from various angles, asked the disciples to do a few push-ups and started cadging the video cassettes with our recordings. Nemo said I'd give them everything, and we went round to my communal apartment. I brought out the cassettes, and the correspondent said the piece about us would be on that evening, and there'd be a repeat the next day. And he would definitely return the cassettes.

We watched the piece separately. I slouched around the room, pretending I wasn't waiting for the news at all; Sergei sat at his computer. But when the clock showed the right time, I ran to the TV and switched it on. Sergei immediately abandoned his mouse and swung round on his chair to face the TV. As if to spite us, the news didn't start for ages, they showed adverts for ten minutes. I'd never noticed that before.

The title sequence started. I was annoyed to realise I was feeling nervous. Then came immediate disappointment – we weren't mentioned in the trailer. Boring subjects followed one after another – the zoo, criminal news, a new fleet of taxis, the police.

"A new youth movement in our city," the anchorwoman began in a quiet voice. "A group calling itself Apostle City practises extreme sports right here in the city, at night."

Then she stopped talking and started straight at me. They started the piece with my own shots from the Colossus. A network of lights.

"What you see on the screen," said a voice-over in the correspondent's familiar flat tones, "are high-level shots of our city. Not from a plane. Simply from a great height. A group of young people calling themselves Apostle City have got together to practise extreme sport."

All this time they were showing our night shots, and especially us in our robes. It looked really cool, and I even felt proud, although it wasn't my idea.

"They spend their free time way up high, at night. And they don't do it for money. Alex, the leader of the Apostle City group, tells us that their main goal is to show that sport is important for people, even in modern urban society."

Alex appeared on the screen, looking unlike himself. The leader of the group.

"Urban extreme is just a sport, we simply stroll about at night and climb up high buildings."

"It really is a sport," the correspondent rattled on, "and, like any sport, it involves training..."

(They showed our disciples doing push-ups.)

"...and also danger. Extreme sport is always extreme, even if it's urban."

Lena, looking unlike herself, in all her glory.

"As I was moving along the girder, my foot suddenly slipped on the rust, then I slid right off and fell. I was perched with just one foot against the girder, literally hanging on the safety rope." At this point they showed the correspondent's expression of concern. "If not for the safety rope I'd have fallen straight into the river."

"More than a hundred members of the movement took part in the latest event held by our young sportsmen. With events developing at this pace, we can hope that these young folk from our town will soon be famous... throughout Russia," the correspondent concluded triumphantly.

"Class!" Sergei declared happily.

He pulled out his mobile and started dialling the others. The lines were all busy. They were probably calling on theirs.

The next day my parents called and said someone had seen me on television. Not them. I was sitting there with the disciples. That was right, I was.

It was one change after another for urban extreme.

* * *

Now we started to get famous. Not thanks to the TV piece, naturally – who watches local TV? But the people who saw us on the bridge and then on TV started telling their friends about us, and they told their friends. Our disciples started singing the praises of Apostle City on every street corner embellishing their personal participation every which way, but Nemo didn't mind. Although Lena wasn't always glad to see new people.

Amusing. We didn't start training more, we didn't start preparing more thoroughly. On the contrary, the crossing of the bridge that I did alone, that first time, came to seem ideal by comparison with the goofs of our joint crossing. But your face and your name "on the box" is like a seal of approval. A "qualified" stamp in your work record book, regardless of the kind of work you do. And now we were different. Not just a group of young people with their own hobby, but "famous" extreme sportsmen. People from the right circles wanted to find out about us. Teenagers visited our site. They abused us up hill and down dale, and then in the next line they wanted to join Apostle City. Sergei started trading in T-shirts and equipment, placing his advertisement right there on our web site, and we didn't have to worry about money any longer.

Nemo changed even more drastically. There was a note of consciously disguised arrogance lurking in his voice now. Sometimes it poked its ugly head out. In entirely innocuous answers to simple questions like, say, "Will we make it?" – about the bus. Nemo would answer "Sure We Will!" with three capital letters, almost choking on them, and behind the words you could read: "We're the famous Apostle City sect, aren't we?"

When they phoned us (him) from the publicity department of one of the night clubs and invited us to take part in a promotional event, he wasn't even surprised. He called Sergei, and they discussed the price. We were informed about it at a general meeting, just like the disciples. The club was planning a dance party sponsored by a manufacturer of sports clothing. They wanted us to come up with something "in our style". But our name was a buzz word now, and we were invited with a couple of break-dance teams. Nemo got us all together again, this time with the disciples and announced a brainstorming session. I refused immediately.

Instead I went to look over the club. After a quick inspection of the actual premises, which were hopelessly low, I cast an eye over the neighbouring buildings. I soon found what I was looking for. The club's small balcony overlooked the street. There were buildings on both sides. After that it's simple, right?

When two hours later I found our group surrounded by an aura of liquefying heat and still without a single sensible idea, I briefly relayed the concept of the forthcoming operation. Rope, street, two buildings. Elementary.

Neither Nemo nor anyone else so much as cheeped about repetition. I wasn't bothered about that any more. It was absurd even to think of the forthcoming operation as genuine urban extreme. Perhaps I was hoping we'd pull something off in a couple of weeks' time, but in the meantime I simply put my trust in Nemo and Sergei, with their commercial instincts. Right now I just strolled along the avenues, leaving urban extreme and silver clouds for later; for better times.

"What, are we just going to climb along that rope? Above the street?" asked Dima.

"Everything's cool, Dima, it's not obligatory," Nemo said

reassuringly, far too reassuringly. "The three of us will go, with someone else."

"No!"Dima protested. "I'll go too, that's not what I mean! Maybe there's something more impressive we can do. Are they just going to stand on that little balcony and watch us crawling along a rope for ten minutes?"

What the lad said was quite right. Watching unfamiliar figures dangling on ropes for half an hour is about as boring as it gets. This was the first time I felt concerned about my spectators in urban extreme. I thought of myself as a clown who has to make the public laugh. This thought proved to be surprisingly unpleasant, and I drove that clown with red hair out of my mind.

"Maybe we could make little wheels?" said Dima. "And ride across on them. And if we incline the rope, we could get across in no time at all."

Nemo looked at Sergei. Sergei shrugged. He was the one who supplied our equipment now. In the end he arranged with the same shop that they would let us have everything we needed for the period of the operation. They liked our idea fine, only they decided to make a contribution of their own to the plan. They decided to make us fasten large ribbons on our backs, like banners. The banners would carry the name of the shop, the trademark and title of this year's collection.

This time Nemo didn't even look at my plan, just told me to give it to the disciples so they could prepare the operation. After consultations with Sergei and the manager, at which neither I, nor Lena, nor the disciples were present, he told us the date and the time we had to work towards.

I approached Sergei with questions about the equipment, but he told me to forget about that, because it would all be waiting for us at the club. We could dress any way we liked. Like during the day.

On the appointed day, at the appointed time, just thirty

short minutes before the performance, Lena and I met outside the appointed club. We went in through the service entrance, as Alex had told us to do. No one recognised us, but they let us in when we introduced ourselves. Then the manageress came running up and greeted us effusively. Nemo turned up. The three of us were taken to the cloakroom, which also served as the dressing room.

Then the manager gave each of us a cellophane bag that crackled repulsively and said:

"Your costumes."

And she didn't mean sports gear. Under the cellophane there was even more cellophane, every item was packed in it. I looked at what was in it, and I felt like laughing.

The threads they'd got for us to wear were red. T-shirts, pants, trainers. Lena had skimpy, figure-hugging shorts. Red ones.

Nemo unpacked everything that was meant for him and started getting changed on the spot. I hesitated, and then started unpacking my gear.

"What about me?" Lena asked, nonplussed.

"All the backup dancers get changed here..." said the manageress, seizing the initiative. "Don't be shy, you only have to go as far as your panties."

As if to confirm what she'd just said, a herd of wet, sweaty girls came running into the cloakroom, dressed in identical short, black, skin-tight pants and mesh tank tops. Standing in formation by the wall, like trained horses, with their faces almost pressed against it, they started pulling their clothes off rapidfire, as if they were stinging their skin.

Nemo was concentrating on getting changed. Lena was still gazing at the girls, nonplussed. I started pulling my jeans off too, trying not to look at her. The naked backs of the group of back-up dancers had the usual effect and I had difficulty getting out of one trouser leg.

Then Lena made her mind up. She didn't turn away towards the wall. With a still, stony, absolutely calm expression she pulled off her blouse. Her breasts turned out to be small, not entirely regular, with dark nipples on blindingly white skin. I realised I shouldn't look, I was burning up with shame, but I looked anyway.

It was the first time in my life I'd ever actually seen a girl's breasts, all right?

Lena met my gaze indifferently. It was like being tossed back. I instantly switched my gaze to the moles on the squirming backs of the girls by the wall. I even forgot I had to get changed.

Nemo finished donning his red uniform. He saw Lena.

"Good girl, that's the spirit!" he said approvingly, with his eyes fixed on her trembling breasts.

Lena smiled feebly, knowing that was what she was supposed to do, and I felt burning humiliation for her and for me. She pulled off her trousers and was left in just her panties. She was freezing. She was ashamed, she didn't like the place, and she was humiliated by what was happening. She twisted and turned those stupid communist shorts with fumbling fingers, unable to look at anything else now; and she couldn't think about anything else but her own humiliation. She was totally transformed into a cold, pitiful, almost weeping bundle of nerves, and I felt madly, achingly sorry for her. I wanted her, madly, furiously. And in my detestable eyes that humiliated us both.

Without looking up, Lena pulled on the shorts. And the T-shirt. She straightened up. Smoothed out her hair and looked up at us with her arms crossed. Nemo, who had been shamelessly admiring her body all this time, laughed; Lena's stance was so expressive. I'd already got changed too.

Without saying a word, we left the room together. We walked out of the club, shunning the glances of the customers jostling outside the entrance. In fact, many of them could have given us a hundred points' start as far as loud dressing was concerned. Round the corner, behind an old building, a cleaned-off ladder leading upwards was waiting for us.

We climbed up. The roof turned out to be sloping. We were met by Misha and Dima, who didn't recognise us at first in our red gear. The other two were waiting to receive us on the far side. Nemo said hello. Succeeding quite well in making it clear that it was none of his business, Dima asked why we weren't in black today. Nemo replied that it was a requirement from the sponsor, and no more questions came up. That reply was clear enough to everyone. I could see Dima wanted to ask something else, but couldn't bring himself to. His movements were either too rapid and fussy, or too sluggish.

"Aren't we going to send anyone across on a test run?" he suddenly asked. "Before the banners."

Everyone, even Misha, understood perfectly well what he was asking about. Everyone remembered the "bridge".

"No," said Nemo, deliberately not looking in his direction; as if it was just a paltry technical detail. "There's no need."

From the window of the club they waved to us with a crumpled poster instead of a flag. Nemo waved back, cautiously walked across to the edge of the sloping roof and looked down. Then he came back. The rope was attached to the chimney stack on this side, to create an angle. It was pulled tauter than I'd ever seen before. Nemo accepted the silvery mechanism from Dima, ran it to and fro along the rope and put his hands through the loops of the handles. Misha was assembling the other two.

There was a crash of deafening music and the bass notes gave me a pain in the belly, I was so unused to it. Nemo was standing by the chimney stack, skidding the wheels up and down the rope.

"Attach the promo material," he ordered.

The disciples bustled about, winding the cord they were holding ready round his chest. They hooked the tail of the banner over the line, so that it wouldn't dangle. The music from the club was turning somersaults. Suddenly a crowd of urbanites started sticking their heads out onto the club's little balcony. The crowd was like a rubber eye oozing out of a toy that's being squeezed slowly. The music lost its independent significance, transformed into the accompaniment for the show.

There was rumble and a flash behind us as the fireworks started up. One after another, in different colours, all over the place. I didn't notice when they waved from the window and Nemo started gliding down the cable; I saw him when he was already halfway across. A long ribbon with English words on it was fluttering behind him. He reached the other side and immediately started pulling in the ribbon, like a parachutist after a successful jump.

"Go on..." Misha whispered to me.

I walked over to the chimney and took hold of the device, thrusting my wrists through the loops. On the far side, they were disentangling Nemo from the banner ribbon. Lena's slim arms embraced my chest and I felt her tying the banner on me. I gave her a questioning look.

"Don't do anything," said Misha. "Wait for the wave from Nemo."

I looked over at the far side. Skidded the little wheels about on the line. Nemo was watching the window of the club, and I was watching Nemo. He raised his arm and started stretching slowly upwards, still not looking at me. Then he jerked his hand sharply. Lena slapped me between the shoulder blades.

I pushed off and started gliding. The cord of the banner pressed tight against my chest, but the ribbon trailed behind me. I hung there calmly, and the opposite building moved towards me. More fireworks blazed up over the club. Then I was received on the far side and dragged the ribbon in after me.

After that we waited for Lena. Then went downstairs and had a word or two with the manager. After the job, we all went home.

* * *

We took part in several more publicity events of that kind. After that, we didn't have to pull any more stunts. It was assumed that everybody already knew who we were. We got changed into the sponsor's outfits backstage, and came out to the audience with musical accompaniment. Or just simply stood there while the curtain rose, making all sorts of "cool" gestures into empty space. They wrote "Apostle City" on the posters advertising the show. Afterwards they gave us money.

Most of the time, the people at our feet hadn't actually seen us in action. And somehow we just didn't get around to setting up a real operation. But they still yelled and screamed as they applauded. Many people in the hall didn't even know who we were, where we'd come from and what we did, but they still screamed anyway. Others actually insulted and teased us, like children teasing monkeys in a zoo, or vice versa. But so what? Half an hour's work – and there's the money.

People started coming to our meetings and staying. The sect had got its modus operandi off pat ages ago. Lectures from the Supreme Master, knots from Nemo, T-shirts from Sergei. Lena successfully propagated her philosophy among the fresh disciples, not worrying about anything else. Then the little problems started.

One day while finalising yet another agreement to support some event, the sponsor started questioning Nemo about the sect's philosophy. Nemo told him about it as best he could. The sponsor scratched his chin and said that wouldn't do for them. They wanted sport. Our strange views had already spread among certain groups of people and they were giving the sect a bad reputation. And giving rise to rumours. And he, the sponsor, didn't like that. And he wasn't the only one.

Nemo said everything could be fixed.

At one of the sect's meetings, when a fair number of people had already gathered (at least twenty people came every time),

Nemo announced that Lena had something to say. Lena stood up and walked out in front of the audience.

The people looked at her curiously. Lena hesitated for a moment, then she threw her head back and her eyes glinted.

She said we shouldn't get too hung up on the ideas of Good and Evil. She said urban extreme was primarily a sport, and we shouldn't forget that. She spoke in words that weren't hers. And she also said that to participate in urban extreme, you didn't have to adhere to the old philosophy. It wasn't compulsory at all. Absolutely not compulsory.

Essentially, she told us to forget about it.

I was upset. She loved her idea, and I remembered the way she could talk about it for a long, long time.

From then on we started calling ourselves the Apostle City "group" or "team". It kept the sponsors happy, and no one else even noticed.

At the same time, rumours started to reach us that we had acquired lots of imitators across the city. Just like us before our "commercial" period began, they carried out operations, and they were also trying to get themselves noticed. But they didn't have Nemo or Sergei, so most of the time no one could even remember what they were called.

It was funny, we hadn't done anything worthwhile for ages, but we were still absolutely bona fide idols for a huge number of teenagers. According to Sergei, sales of T-shirts and equipment were constantly growing. Even though we did practically nothing to make that happen. He said we were his most successful project ever. He wanted to "invest in us" and was planning to set up production of a heap of useless knickknacks and souvenirs with our logo and name on them. Key-rings, for instance.

Basically, once we abandoned philosophy, our final problems disappeared and we were transformed into a good and promising business. It could now be said that at the age of twenty-one, Nemo had his own business. Lots of people listened to what he said; lots of people wanted to idolise him. He was making money. As he strolled round the city, he kept looking around eagerly, hoping to meet a former classmate or acquaintance. In short, he'd won this round.

He ordered a new site from some design company. He bought a normal address in the Internet, on a paid server. He didn't wander round the special interest forums any longer, or the municipal site forum – he had his own forum now, which he ran and where everyone respected him. Apart from the ones who hated us and only visited to vent their spleen on us.

Our site was a popular one, heaps of people visited it. It could bring in money all on its own; just from the advertising, not even counting Sergei's trading. The front page always carried a banner with an advert for some well-known firm.

Sure, it was boring now, because we were in charge of it. I visited it sometimes, to read what they were writing about us, but the picture was always the same. Half of the people lauded us to the heavens, half called us motherfuckers – Nemo made sure that postings like that were promptly removed.

He forgot his martinis with apple juice and switched to whisky with Pepsi. Instead of the job classifieds, he actually started looking though the 'cars for sale' columns. He forgot about Almodovar and studied the faces of cinema managers.

Neutrality completely disappeared from his own postings. The virtual Nemo started taking his own opinion very seriously. He never even came close to a heated discussion, and he didn't end his exchanges with the abstract conclusion that arguing was pointless. He stuck to his guns and pushed through his own opinion, acting with such enormous self-assurance that disciples immediately expressed their absolute agreement with anything he said and trampled his opponent into the ground.

Apart from the promotional events we were always getting invitations via e-mail or on the pages of the forum. We were invited to take a look at a new urban extreme team, to make a showing at a convention of extreme sports fans, to listen to music by a new young group that had unexpectedly been inspired by our modest activities. One day I even got a letter inviting me to go to a school and talk to the pupils. The assumption was that urban extreme is an exceptionally useful activity that keeps kids off the streets. I politely forwarded the letter to Nemo, but I was a hundred per cent certain that he wouldn't reply – there wasn't even a whiff of any money involved.

Dima and Misha had now become acknowledged Apostle City masters in the eyes of the extreme sports community although, in actual fact, they hadn't really taken part in an operation even once.

Basically, we were all up to our ears in urban extreme.

But the other thing was that I'd started feeling sick at heart again. How could that be? Life on every side was crammed to overflowing with urban extreme. New ropes still in their packaging and equipment with fresh manufacturers' logos gathered dust in my room. I signed T-shirts and CDs of our videos. People were always writing to me, looking for advice and support. Girls wanted to get to know me, although the only thing they knew about me was that I was in the team. Every now and then our name was dangled above the city on banners across the streets. There was a pile of key rings with our logo on the table.

But I was still sick at heart.

I remembered the black sky, the streetlamps. I remembered the lightness and the web of lights down below. I started watching my own videos. Not the team's edited video clips, but my own recordings on my old camera, one after another. Half the cassette was nothing but pitch darkness, but I could still make out familiar places and outlines; I felt the pounding of my heart and the dampness of my palms.

Seeing the way I hovered at the window in the evenings, gazing at the black sky and the night-time city, Sergei advised me to take up a hobby. In translation, that meant finding something to do that I could spend money on. I just grinned ironically. The circle was closed. The record had skipped back to the beginning.

But then Nemo would show up and call us together for an event. Sometimes they were like a genuine operation, but they took only a tenth of the usual time and they were meant for the spectators, not us. A simple rule – long means boring. A simple rule – it's the fact that's interesting, not the process. Five minutes sliding down lines, a descent on ropes, and we were eagerly imbibing the undeserved applause of the spectators. Five minutes later, they'd forgotten all about us. But it was a life of sorts. Better than what other people had, I thought.

* * *

The hot sun roasted the city as I walked along the shady afternoon street to the shop. To get a blank cassette for my camera. My mobile phone rang. It was Lena calling.

In all the time we'd known each other, this was the first time she'd called me. I stroked the smooth casing, pressed the answer button and raised the phone to my ear.

Lena paused for a moment, and then...

"Dima's dead," she said.

She told me that last night Dima had gone to the bridge alone. Presumably he wanted to make the crossing. He had climbed up onto the support, then set off, edging his way along. He had barely reached the water before he fell at a very bad spot. He had impaled himself on a piece of metal embedded in the concrete bank of the river. His abdomen was ripped open, and everything spilled out into the black water. He couldn't shout. To judge from the wound, he tried to climb out for another fifteen minutes or so before he lost consciousness. I listened. When she finished the story, Lena switched off the phone.

That day, we all got together. Nemo informed us that he

had already dealt with the mourning. The background on the site had been changed to black and Dima's photo had been posted with the caption "For Urban Extreme".

Nemo said that we would never forget Dima. Everybody was very sad, even those who had come for the first time and had never even heard of Dima. Misha and our other disciples looked totally shattered. Lena was absolutely devastated. She sat on the dirty concrete parapet in her green shorts – she'd forgotten you shouldn't wear bright colours after something like this – with her sandals dropped off her feet. Her black hair completely covered her eyes. She sat there with her bare feet spread wide apart and her folded arms resting on her knees with her face nestling against them.

Nemo said that the death of a City Apostle was an extraordinary event. Mourning was declared. He said he would arrange for black T-shirts to be made, with Dima's photo on them. Everyone who respected his memory and urban extreme should buy these T-shirts and wear them.

Right then they called him from the TV news. He covered the microphone with his hand and told us they wanted to do a piece on Dima's death. Then he muttered confusedly into the phone: "Just a moment..." He thought, and I watched his sad, noble face. The seconds clicked off the cents. I looked for his emotions, but couldn't see any. I couldn't see grief, pain, doubts, or fear. Only the serenity of the blue sky overhead and the transparency of a summer day.

"Yes," he said into the phone. "Come."

They did a piece about us; a very sad piece, and Nemo said what a great young guy Dima was, what a brave, courageous urban extremer, and what a loss he was for Apostle City.

We acquired even more enemies. They started vilifying us. Some even called us murderers outright. Lena mentioned that Dima's parents had phoned Nemo, but Nemo didn't tell her or me anything about it.

One day I approached Nemo. I wanted to put an end to all this. I represented hordes of children and teenagers clambering ever higher, up towards the night sky of the city. Any one of them could fall and end up lying there dead. We invented all this. I invented all this. And I wanted to put a stop to it. The operations... I did those for myself. I didn't think everyone would want to try it. I didn't expect it to become fashionable. I didn't want that.

Nemo shook his head. He replied that none of us were to blame. You might just as well blame the builders of a building or a bridge for the death of someone who fell from it. He said this was extreme, and it was dangerous. "We have to do what we do," Nemo concluded.

When Dima died, many people started to hate us. But even more started to idolise us. The popularity of Apostle City soared higher than ever before.

* * *

I was lying on my back on the parapet beside the lake. With yellow clouds drifting across the yellow sky above me. The hot city didn't want to part with its heat. I could feel the warmth of the stone and the heat of Lena sitting beside me. There was no one else there. I'd arranged this supposed date. Lena hadn't made much of an effort to tidy herself up. Bare feet in flip-flops, T-shirt, shorts. But I liked her the way she was.

The ducks were calling. The sun outside, the world's permanence and the warmth were intoxicating, they made our surroundings unreal. The sounds of the yellow day merged into a single clamour that seemed to be circling round and round.

A phone rang an unknown melody. Lena answered. Nemo asked where she was and said he'd come over.

I was going to tell Nemo I was leaving. There was no blithe fury any more, no city night. Urban extreme was a business.

Apostle City was a mere chimera, a trademark. I readied my arguments for rejecting it, traced the threads of the conversation. I had invented urban extreme and made the city rooftops a place where I could feel alive. I had invited him to join me, so we could scale even greater heights. I had allowed him to make up a story, so that it would seem more interesting.

I would probably never go back up there again, either with Apostle City or alone. The surface of the city had ceased to be the surface, or maybe it had risen higher – I didn't know where to.

When Nemo learned about my decision, he seemed sad. He said nothing for a moment, gazing at the blue sky.

"It's a tough decision for you," he said. "But I understand your choice. I just want to ask you to take part in one more operation, the day after tomorrow, our last one together."

He didn't try to persuade me to stay. I realised he didn't need me. I felt really rotten saying it, but I didn't have any more value for Apostle City. I could easily be replaced by Misha or someone else. The only reason I was needed for the forthcoming operation was because it was hard to find someone else in one day.

Then Nemo told me something that was hard to believe.

A central TV channel had taken an interest in us. They didn't just want to do a piece about us, they wanted to do a whole series devoted to urban extreme and its founders, that is, Apostle City, that is, Nemo. They'd asked us about operations.

They'd promised to arrange the crossing from the TV tower to the Colossus for us.

Three hundred metres above the city. During the day.

I got up and looked at Nemo. There was nowhere higher to go in our city. I didn't want to think about it or imagine it. I didn't want to see it. None of it was the way I'd pictured it. Not at night, in secret, with no urbanites, but in the daytime, openly, under the sun. We'd climb up and fly from the north to the west, and everybody would watch us soaring. And possibly envy us. That was what urban extreme had become now. It had come out into the open, come down off the rooftops, put on weight and even changed colour – bleached white.

I didn't know what to do next, but I knew there was no way I could get out of this crossing. Lena was as happy as a child. She positively skipped around Nemo as she asked about the details.

The TV people wanted to have a preliminary talk with the three of us. To conclude agreements with each of us separately, at least orally. To discuss terms. The only thing they knew about us was that we were "famous" here. They'd gathered all their information from the website and rumours. That was why for them Apostle City was a trio: Nemo, Peter, Lena. The figure of Nemo completely overshadowed us in our native city, in the eyes of the local urbanites, but from a distance we looked like a tight-knit trio.

The TV people were staying in a hotel in the city, but they also had a big bus stuffed with equipment, and all the power of money from the capital.

The discussion didn't take place at a table in a cafe, or in a hotel room, or by the lake. We sat in the leather-clad foyer on the second floor of the hotel, waiting for our appraisers. We could hear the incomprehensible dialogues between the chambermaids and various everyday sounds. In some strange way the tedium and anticipation produced a cosy kind of feeling and the desire to spend eternity here – as if we were sitting in the dentist's waiting room.

All three of them appeared at once, in business suits, walking along in a creeping triangle. The leader was immediately obvious – a huge tall man, rigid, with a broad, arid face: he held himself apart from his colleagues. Greeting Nemo and nodding to us in passing, he sat down in the middle of the big black sofa opposite us.

His first companion, rather stout and disorganised, followed him almost step for step. Bouncing in his hands he had a black briefcase and an open file with protruding sheets of paper covered in typing. First he sat down on the sofa to the right of his boss, and only then said hello. His eyes immediately started gliding over us. He took note of the personalised notepad I was holding, and the gel in Nemo's hair, and Lena's flip-flops. She immediately started feeling embarrassed, and remained embarrassed to the end of the meeting, obviously cursing Alex, who had dragged her here without letting her get changed.

The third one was tall as well, but with a sad, thoughtful face. He walked over to us, shook hands with me and Nemo; he performed a bow in front of Lena, smiling and lowering his head. He also looked us over, but he wasn't looking for signs of his own superiority, he was trying to understand what kind of people we were. He sat down on the left of his leader.

The leader paused in ritual fashion. Then he told us a poetic story about what lay ahead for us and asked us about our past.

"Tell me about what you call 'urban extreme'," he said to Nemo.

Nemo started explaining off the top of his head. He started haltingly, often directing the thread of the story towards me, but they didn't take their eyes off him. Then Nemo calmed down, remembered the texts on the site and grabbed at them. He started spouting the right expressions and the fashionable phrases.

Nemo proceeded with his speech, successfully avoiding the commercial details. No one interrupted his smooth delivery. Nemo put across very coherently the idea that we were a team of extreme sportsmen who had conquered the rooftops of our city with our sport. Admirers. Danger. Respect from our fellows, hatred from the envious.

The plumpish one opened his file. Started leafing through the sheets of paper. I imagined myself in his place on that leather sofa, in a black suit in this heat, and I shuddered. This wasn't at all the way I had imagined these men. And I was astounded at their stern, almost pompous air and bearing. I don't know what Alex had been expecting, but Lena and I sat there with our heads bowed.

Having concluded his brief history of Apostle City and our merits, real and imagined, Nemo stopped. For just a few seconds. Realising they weren't going to make us any offer right then, he continued smoothly. Having stated that we would be interested in going further, Nemo expanded elegantly on this guileless thought, not forgetting to substantiate his ideas along the way. I listened to his melodious voice. Nemo was good at squirming on a hot frying pan.

"I see, I see," the chief interrupted him.

Nemo immediately fell silent and assumed an air of genial attention. He looked at the men sitting on the sofa and all three of them looked at him.

"Have you ever done any sport before?" they asked Nemo.

Nemo replied that he hadn't. But immediately added that he had always been keen on extreme sports, watched the relevant TV programmes, studied the urban culture of extreme.

"And what about the martial arts?" they interrupted him again.

This time Nemo simply shook his head, looking at them thoughtfully.

"But you do have extensive experience of promotional events," the fat one suddenly put in, and his tone of voice suggested that he'd said something absolutely hilarious. They glanced at each other and laughed. We waited. Nemo waited.

"So that's the kind of extreme sportsmen you are," the plumpish one said, laughing. "Took up extreme sport, just like that. Sportsmen. A good thing you didn't take up aqualung diving."

They laughed again. Then the sad one suddenly piped up.

"Yes, interesting... Many well-known extreme sportsmen we've come across have never been based in professional sport. Very often, like these young people, they simply started from scratch."

The tall one, still laughing, nodded smoothly in agreement. His smile faded. The plumpish one looked at him and nodded too.

"Okay," the tall man agreed. "So much for the sport. We have to make a TV show. The rest of it doesn't interest us. I'd like to make sure you feel the same way. We don't want any problems during the shooting, do we, Alex? You realise what you're doing when you call this 'urban extreme'?"

"They did it for some time without any financial return," the sad one reminded him.

Nemo didn't say anything, he didn't understand the question. His aristocratic facial antics stalled. The tall man rephrased the question.

"I want you to say this to me, Alex: 'I know that urban extreme is a commercial business and there's nothing more to it'."

A pause. A creak of leather. Slim rays of sunlight through the blinds.

"I know that urban extreme is a commercial business and there's nothing more to it," said Nemo.

"Good... But what's this philosophy of yours?" the tall man suddenly asked.

The threesome turned more serious. Why had they latched onto Lena's ravings like this? I'd always known there was no sense to these ideas, and the only thing that lent them any significance was the conviction of our Supreme Master, heh-heh. But then, that applies to lots of things.

Lena quietly shifted forward in her armchair and started telling them about it, mentioning that the sect had relinquished its ideology. They didn't let her finish.

"I see..." said the tall one, glancing at a sheet of paper in the plumpish one's file. "Lena. Tell me, please, how seriously do you take all this? Nobody will allow even us to use air time to propagate weird ideas. Do you understand that?"

Lena nodded; Nemo was nodding too.

"That doesn't mean you have to stop thinking the way you do," said the sad one. "Just that you shouldn't make a show of it." The tall man raised his voice. "In that case, say this to me: 'I entirely refute my religion and declare that urban extreme has nothing at all to do with it'."

"I entirely refute my religion," Lena confirmed. Etcetera.

Then they turned their gaze on me.

"Peter, do you have anything to add? Do you want to object or agree?"

Silence. They said nothing, waiting for a reply. Thirty seconds. Who drew up this dossier of theirs, this idiotic nonsense? I made to reach for my notepad.

"He's dumb," Nemo explained.

All three started nodding in sympathy. Then they turned their attention back to their papers. The main thing they were interested in was responsibility for our lives. That is, no one wanted us to be struck by any disaster during an operation. But if something of the sort did happen, none of them wanted to be held responsible, even though they organised the entire thing.

We signed what they told us to sign. They told us not to worry about anything else.

* * *

Before the event, Nemo and Sergei decided to hold a promotional party. They thought we were moving into the world of big business, and an event like that would be good for the cause. They hired a second-rate cafe and invited the right people. For stage-dressing they invited all the well-known extreme sportsmen in the city. With the agreement of the cafe's management, they decorated it in an appropriate style. Faultlessly. No one knew what was coming next, but in our city a party like this was definitely a bid for leadership in extreme sport.

The walls were hung with old skate boards and any posters that could be found on more or less relevant subjects. There were film posters, and posters of bands from every different musical style, and our own promotional creations with Lena in a revealing swimsuit. Colourful, chaotic, oppressive. Impeccable.

When the party started, the room was already packed with people. People with invitations and without tried to force their way into our bright heaven. Fake bouncers with skinny necks stood at the door and took bribes to let people in, attempting in vain to match the style of their Hollywood prototypes.

A local band of the street music variety was invited. They rapidly got drunk, with the result that the process of performing songs was substantially disrupted.

I sat in the corner and tried to join in the party by consuming a small amount of beer. The scene that was developing was phony. It all looked like a game. The urbanites scattered around the tables, put on their bright-coloured protective cloaks and played the parts of non-urbanites.

Everyone in my field of vision was straining like grim death to match the generally accepted stereotypes of his own social (or asocial) role. It looked like one of those canvases stretching right across the museum wall, on which the artist has depicted some epic scene or battle panorama. Every individual was doing his utmost to demonstrate his own character, as observed in the video clips on some music channel. Alas, there weren't enough ready-made characters to go round, and some were repeated.

Take the two skateboarders sitting over there in their loose threads, talking to each other in loud voices, reeling off numbers and incantations in English. They've both ripped off the same image, so they're perceived as "a pair of skateboarders", not as two different people.

In the opposite corner I see drag racers. Only they're

not genuine drag racers; their cars are feeble. Their cool isn't measured by their speed on the road, but by the spring suspension of their slang and knowledge of an automobile's insides and a race car driver's moves. They're extreme theoretical mechanics, not drag racers. I enjoy watching their enthusiasm – they shift through aerial gears as they argue.

All these people were sitting there, making conversation. Music, hubbub, the clinking of glasses with alcohol. There are various ways of fitting yourself into society. Sometimes even by thinking that you're defying it.

Not many girls came to the party. Guys with painted-on smiles kept propositioning them. I observed the unsuccessful attempts with interest and envied the successful ones. I never could emulate that; especially in a fine, jolly setting like this. I was left hopelessly behind.

I felt like the oddest one there. While all our guests were trying much harder to be alike than simply be. Now isn't that a cute irony of fate?

I'd been thinking I'd fitted myself in. That I could play by these rules. But it turns out I can't. Either there's something lacking in me, or the opposite. But what's stopping me? Why not? Apart from these kids posturing for each other, there were people here who really did earn their money in different ways from everyone else. Me, for instance.

I always used to be afraid I wouldn't be able to be like everyone else. Well here's my chance. I have a chance to be even better; to earn money, not from heavy physical labour, but by flaunting myself in front of a video camera in someone else's fashionable gear. There's nothing, absolutely nothing, bad about that. It's just a job, right? Count yourself lucky.

I was too hasty about leaving Apostle City. Naturally, I had absolutely no need to regard myself as the leader. I could even just sit beside Nemo and nod solemnly. Smile when I was told to, and take my share.

My life had definitely improved, after all. I'd seen a lot and felt a lot. How lonely I'd been before! I only realised that now. Savagely lonely, really; behind an impenetrable brick wall. I screened myself off there, didn't touch a single living thing. I didn't believe I could. As I very gradually got used to Lena and Nemo, I realised I could be just as good as the others. Better than the others. The magic of the night transformed me into their king. And they saw my crown!

I learned to watch people. I learned not to turn away. If I could take one more step, just one more! I was stupid to look at Nemo and not understand him. He lived a perfectly normal life – that was an impossible dream for me! But right now... maybe it just might work out, eh?

Nothing extraordinary had happened following Dima's death. Nothing could be changed now. Nemo understood what was what. And I want to be like him, don't I? I'm Pinocchio, my friends. My wooden eyes are tired of being wooden; a rare case – almost every urbanite I come across in the street is my idol. What's stopping me? Well?

I glanced into the dark glass of the cafe. The entire glittering picture was there, complete with all its mirror-reflection characters. I looked perfectly in place among them. There, that's me! The urban extremer, one of the leaders of Apostle City! I want to be normal. I have almost everything. And soon I'll have the rest of it!

I went to look for Nemo, who had disappeared without trace, to tell him about my decision: I was coming back to Apostle City.

It turned out badly. When I'd searched the entire hall, I set off to round the cubicles and came across Nemo *and* Lena. They didn't notice me, those infatuated daredevils in their closet. It turned out very badly. I'd suspected as much for ages; felt jealous. I was jealous of her with everyone. With Nemo the same as everyone else. But, of course, you ought to have guessed sooner, my dear, darling idiot Peter. There's no rage, just helplessness, my hands hang limply at my sides. What was I thinking? Why hasn't life taught me anything – hasn't all my futile kissing research shown me my place on the hard shoulder of life's road? I'm really funny! Ha-ha-a! I'm really funny! Lena, Lena, she probably really likes being with him. There, my imagination immediately presents me with a picture of her naked legs in the most surprising positions. Ha-ha!

And then, for the first time in my life when I wasn't up on the rooftops, I felt blithe fury. I actually froze dead in my tracks.

Life hands us some unusual experiences sometimes.

* * *

We took almost no part in the preparations. I walked round the city in which the heat was subsiding and looked upwards. They'd contrived everything quite wonderfully for us. Closed off the traffic in the centre. I watched the black steel cable being slowly unwound from the immense reel in the truck that I was following without hurrying, as if it was a hearse. Disciples I didn't know helped to settle the cable evenly.

Lots of things had become clear to me now. I looked at the sky. You can lose as soon as you accept someone else's rules. But I wanted to live by the rules. I wanted to stay in Apostle City, become huge and famous. Normal. But when you accept that you're normal, the defeats become painful.

It was me she was ashamed of that time in the club, not Nemo.

Her slim hands.

* * *

At the entrance to the TV tower they recognise me and let me through. The sweet banner of fame. I get changed in a closet, looking at the clothes left by Nemo and Lena. My gaze automatically shifts to the door – to see if it locks on the inside. A crooked stairway leads upwards.

I climb up. The normal building comes to an end. On the roof I see Nemo + Lena.

We all greet each other affectionately. They don't know. I turn away.

I look at the silhouette of the Colossus, standing over the city like a black mountain. The slim thread of the cable disappears into the air on the way towards it. The slightly hazy air sets the outlines of objects quivering, and that helps me not to lose their true scale. The dimensions of it make me catch my breath. I look at the pinnacle of the tower, the spot that the cable runs to.

It's time to climb right up to the top – onto a narrow little platform. It's frightening. The iron rungs drone under my hands. A light wind shakes me. The city is so far down below that there is no height. No cars or people, not even buildings or trees. I start getting furious. Higher, higher! They're real bastards, absolute bastards. They could at least have told me. I wonder if she shouts?

The TV tower is dirty. How can there be dirt up here? Let's climb higher. You wouldn't believe how long a climb like this takes. It's frightening, that's why I want to go higher, higher! Faster!

I grab with my hands and twist the palms slightly. The skin scrapes. I want to cause myself pain. I want to make meaningless sounds with my lips. This is all blithe fury, reliable symptoms. Blithe fury comes from fear, but doesn't it feel great, eh? I clamber upwards, onto iron covered with a pattern to prevent slipping. I intentionally lean my hands against the cold, bleak metal.

The others are panting behind me – the couple that I introduced, ha-ha, and the cameraman. Oh, but it's beautiful here! Like up above the sky. Beautiful. White clouds, little black clouds, the glory of the city's insignificance down below. The thick, black cable clenched in the grip of a massive winch.

And hanging on it is a terrifying device that looks like a large, homemade bicycle. That's just what it's like! There's thunder in the distance. Or in my ears. But why is there only one? Who's going to fly to the moon?

Nemo explains that it's a bicycle built for two. Lena or me? Lena's staying. Lena does what Nemo tells her. The cameraman starts setting himself up. He chats with his boss on the phone. I wish I had your skills, my friend.

Nemo and Lena walk in circles round the black metal object. I walk too, but separately, only they don't see. It shouldn't look like a bicycle. That's all so the camera can be mounted. You grab the handles with your hands anyway. Then they fasten you in – you don't sit on it.

The thunder rumbles. Thunder. The cameraman looks up disapprovingly. Tells us to quickly get ready. Nemo poises himself timidly. So do I, but not timidly. I could crawl across, everything inside me is seething, come on, come on!

The thunder rumbles. There's a smell·of ozone. I don't believe it! It can't be, surely? The hunger for ozone. The damned heat, damned summer. The cameraman stops and starts chatting on the phone with his people again. Nemo caresses the handles, clasping and unclasping his hands. The smell of ozone.

Large drops fall down from the sky. A sign, a sign! The cameraman doesn't think of himself, he throws his waterproof jacket over the camera. Rain, the first rain, how I've been longing for you!

It gets very loud. The ground disappears. There is no ground. A grey abyss. It's really interesting to walk to the edge and glance down. There's nothing there.

"It's all off!" the cameraman yells. "Let's go down!"

Ha-ha! He's joking. He doesn't know us very well!

Nemo nods in agreement and goes down on his knees. He's insane! I run over and grab him by his wet T-shirt. Where are you going? Where to, Nemo? He doesn't understand me, he doesn't understand anything at all. I pull him towards the machine. Let's go! Let's go! He nods his head, indicating the rain, gestures round with his arms. Surely, my dear friend Nemo, the water hasn't stopped you? But it's so beautiful, isn't it? Everything inside me starts quivering, I can feel every drop inside me. I pull Nemo. He tries to break away, he's bewildered.

To hell with him! Lena, come here, come with me. She comes willingly, trying to understand my smile, but suddenly understands and stops. Shakes her head.

"Later, Peter! They can't video it now!" Nemo shouts through the squall of water from the heavens.

"You can't!" shouts the cameraman. "Everything will be ruined! There won't be any shots, and your event will be down the tubes!"

Down the tubes, ha! Calm down! Calm down, cameraman. We're at a point in space outside everything. No ground, no sky, no surroundings. Nothing but grey water, grey, water, bottomless. A thick cable leading to nowhere.

He takes me for an idiot! Try again! I give Nemo my hand. Let's go! But Nemo tells me no. Lena! Come on, let's go! And Lena shakes her head – no.

I'm alone! Alone, here, up on high, on a mast in the middle of grey space! I grab the handles and click the right strap on. I can't fasten the left one now, but that's okay.

"Hey!" the cameraman calls, bawling his lungs out. "What are you doing? It won't work like that!"

Nemo runs over to me and starts saying something. But everything inside me is rampaging. More, more rain!

"Cool it," says smart Nemo. "Think, what's more important to you: urban extreme or her? Why these pointless gestures?"

He saw me when I saw them. Or sensed me. Nemo, my dearest Nemo. How differently we understand urban extreme.

"I won't let you leave the team," Nemo shouts. "You'll be our front man! We'll push your image everywhere. You're the best urban extremer in the city! But to prove that, we have to video this! Later, after the rain!"

Prove it to who, Nemo? I look straight ahead. Into the grey infinity. Take a firmer grip on the handles. The cameraman curses.

Nemo grabs me, holds on. "No!" he yells, "No!" Ah, the blithe fury! Pushing me, pushing me! I should stay here, wait for the rain to end. And then, a proper life. I can be normal. Earn money. Stroll around during the day. See the sun. A proper life and, like everyone else, I'll lose.

Nemo hangs on me.

I squirm like a snake. Lash out backwards with my leg. I hit Nemo, in the stomach I think. Suddenly I'm so light and I push off.

The platform disappears from underneath me, and the same instant everything disappears. Slowly at first, then faster and faster, the rain shifts to blow straight in my face. There's nothing – only the black streak of the cable, only my forward motion. There's nothing. Grey haze everywhere … There's nothing. Water lashes straight at me. I'm flying, flying against the water! I'm alone. There's nothing else in this world. Time has stopped. The water's seething inside me. Effervescing over me. Like that time. Like that time. Dangling over the foam. The sea was seething under me, the waves were seething over me. I hear my mother's sickening shriek. "He's hanging there!" A rough jacket presses down on my throat. The sea foams down below, so sublimely below me. I watch, small and entranced, with my mind totally immersed in it. My mother calls. But I don't want to answer. It seems like I can, but I don't want to. Soaring above this vastness and thinking: Is this death? Is this what the grown-ups talk about? It's so beautiful soaring...

And the water blowing in my face. It's all behind me. I've flown away! Flown away forever! I won't stay there, I won't! And not because I'm afraid to be normal! Ah, what point is there, what point, what tomorrow do I have? What tomorrow do all of us have? Wake up, we're different. There won't be any yacht or white beach. Our dreams are unattainable: they hover in the transparent air of the future, not on the upper storeys of skyscrapers. The way to them doesn't lie along tall staircases and lifts that break down every other minute. There is no way to reach them. No way. Ever.

As you recall your dreams, you won't swallow blood and take another step against your will, because "there's a little bit left". After years of travelling, you won't be a single breath closer, because they hover in the transparent air of the future and their music is inaudible.

This is bad. This is not romantic, not easy, not condescending. This is painful and bad. Powerlessness is a precise word. Having conquered mountains, seas and God knows what else you're powerless to change anything. And you know this: you know it for certain, but you go and gnaw on the mountains and plunge your face into the seas, laughing because you can hear the music of your dreams.

I'm sorry, I'm sorry. I'd like to be different. Not become different – that's impossible – but be different. To smile in the orange air of July; to look through the patterned glass at the hot street: at our street. To echo the laughter, clench the fingers with the silver ring, remember the names and know the prices.

Where's the cure? Where do wounded birds recover so as to be urbanites? To be people? In the grey infinity of August, there is nothing more agonising than this question. Strident and excruciating, flowing like electricity through my shrieking muscles; it pulses within that old wound. Murderous. Inexorable.

Forget it. Forget it. We won't have any expensive cars or luxurious mansions – even if we possess them, they won't be ours. Inside you're the same. Even swathed in cars, in money, in anything you like; inside you're alone, and possessing makes no difference – in the daytime, we're always on the asphalt.

Shattered forever, we look up, into the black, transparent sky, where our dreams are soaring.

Forward, forward! And the Colossus grows out of the grey abyss. I fly towards it, drinking the rain. How fast! There was nothing before; now there's only the Colossus. It's right in front of me, big, bigger than my life. Right in front of me. Under me. My aeroplane smashes into something, jerking me and wrenching my arm painfully. I detach it and fall onto the black aerodrome of the Colossus. My right leg hurts. I stagger, and fall. Slowly and sadly, vanquished. Onto my knees, looking up into the grey abyss. Then onto my back.

Grey infinity above me. Rain falling down from above. It's flying at me. And there's nothing. How good it is. How good it is, thanks for this moment. I've never felt so wonderful. Nothing exists. I'm going to lie here for eternity. I'll stay here forever. With my face turned towards the sky, feeling the wet drops flowing down over my face and knowing that nothing else exists. Only blind infinity. There is nothing else, and I am happy.

I am happy.

The moment comes when everything switches off. Feelings, joys and sorrows, cold and warmth. Everything is transformed into a single continuous flow, slowly hurtling down at me from above. I lie there and watch this water, delighting in the unusual pictures on the strange smooth surface of the endless flow. I feel neither cold nor warmth. It is simply there with me, and I simply watch.

I can't freeze. I can't warm up. Now there are no more problems.

When something stops the pain, that's called anesthesia. And that's the recipe for life.

> *Sometimes I feel like I don't have a partner*
> *Sometimes I feel like my only friend*
> *Is the city I live in, the city of angels*
> *Lonely as I am, together we cry...*

COMPLETE GLAS BACKLIST

Larissa Miller, *Dim and Distant Days*
a Jewish childhood in postwar Moscow recounted
with sober tenderness and insight

Anatoly Mariengof, *A Novel Without Lies*
the turbulent life of a poet in flamboyant
Bohemian Moscow in the 1920s

Irina Muravyova, *The Nomadic Soul*,
a family saga about one more Anna Karenina

The Portable Platonov, a reader
for the centenary of Russia's greatest 20th century writer

Boris Slutsky, *Things That Happened*,
biography of a major mid-20th century poet
interspersed with his poetry

Asar Eppel, *The Grassy Street*
graphic stories from a Moscow suburb in the 1940s

Peter Aleshkovsky, *Skunk: A Life*, a bildungsroman
set in today's Northern Russian countryside

ANTHOLOGIES

Squaring the Circle, winners of the Debut Prize for Fiction

War & Peace, army stories versus women's stories:
a compelling portrait of post-post-perestroika Russia

Captives
victors turn out to be captives on conquered territory

NINE of Russia's Foremost Women Writers
collective portrait of women's writing today

Strange Soviet Practices
short stories and documentaries illustrating
some inimitably Soviet phenomena

Childhood, the child is father to the man

Beyond the Looking-Glas, Russian grotesque revisited

A Will & a Way, women's writing of the 1990s

Booker Winners & Others-II
some samplings from the Booker winners

Love Russian Style, Russia tries decadence

Booker Winners & Others, mostly provincial writers

Jews & Strangers, what it means to be a Jew in Russia

Bulgakov & Mandelstam, earlier autobiographical stories

Love and Fear, the two strongest emotions
dominating Russian life

Women's View, Russian women bloodied but unbowed

Soviet Grotesque,
young people's rebellion against the establishment

Revolution, the 1920s versus the 1980s

NON-FICTION

Michele A. Berdy, *The Russian Word's Worth*
A humorous and informative guide to
the Russian language, culture and translation

Contemporary Russian Fiction: A Short List
11 Russian authors interviewed by Kristina Rotkirch

Nina Lugovskaya, *The Diary of a Soviet Schoolgirl: 1932-1937*,
a real diary of a Russian Anne Frank

Alexander Genis, *Red Bread*, essays
Russian and American civilizations compared
by one of Russia's foremost essayists

A.J. Perry, *Twelve Stories of Russia: A Novel, I guess*

**As of March 1, 2011 Glas books
are distributed in North America by
Consortium Book Sales and Distribution**